Y0-CCJ-493

**Highest Praise for Candice Fox and
Her Archer and Bennett Thrillers**

HADES
WINNER OF THE NED KELLY AWARD
FOR BEST FIRST FICTION

ALSO BY CANDICE FOX

Hades

Fall

Available from Kensington Publishing Corp.

EDEN

AN ARCHER AND BENNETT THRILLER

CANDICE FOX

PINNACLE BOOKS
Kensington Publishing Corp.
www.kensingtonbooks.com

For Tim.

The night of the boy's murder he was working, wandering along Darlinghurst Road in the crowds of workers, picking pockets, begging, doing stunts for coins. Later the boy would think of his life in the city streets as the Winter Days, because even in the summer they seemed cold and damp, the daylight short.

It took years for the boy to forget how to remember, when one day ate into the next and nothing broke the monotony except the stabbing death of a whore or the chance find of a coin on the concrete. The sun shuttered above the buildings, on and off, counting the days. The boy wandered, head down, practiced at sniffing bins outside restaurants to identify treasures hidden within, at slipping through cinema fire exits to search for popcorn and sweets, at scaling tall buildings to raid clotheslines strung across cramped balconies.

Sometimes the boy felt he could have been ancient because all that came before the Night of Fire and Screaming was darkness. Now and then when he slept he returned to the fire, saw the faces of the woman and the man he supposed must have been his parents against the windows, heard their pounding on the glass behind the bars. Whenever he tried to remember how long ago the fire happened, who those people were and why they had died, how he had survived and how he had got to the city, he was confronted by blackness— a door closed, locked, impassable. He didn't know how old he was or the name those screaming people called him. When the police and the kindly women who had spotted him came to take him, they said he looked eight. He was happy with that. They'd also said he was mute and malnourished, but he didn't know what either of those things were. He'd fled the van they put him in and kept his eye out from then on. He didn't like the police. He didn't know why.

He wandered and tried to forget.

On the night he met the French Man, the boy was sitting on a set of steps down from The Goldfish Bowl, which was alive with laughing and shoving, the toppling of glasses, the slapping of beer caps onto the pavement.

The French Man came walking up the hill under the Moreton Bay fig trees, the smoke from his cigarette winding around a row of sailors advancing behind him. The boy moved off the steps and headed down to meet the sailors, stretching his dirty face into his brightest smile. The French Man caught him by the elbow and spun him in a half circle. The sailors parted to let him through.

"What's the hurry, petit monsieur?"

The boy wasn't fussy who his marks were. The French Man didn't look like a cop, so he would make an easy meal. His accent was slurred and heavy. Perhaps he'd been drinking down at the waterfront. He smelled of cigarettes and wine, but his hair was neatly combed so that the ridges stood out across his curved scalp.

"Hello, sir! Got a coin?" the boy asked. "I can dance, I can sing, I can tell jokes. I can balance a penny on my nose."

The boy did a handstand and walked in a circle on his palms on the dirty pavement. His black-soled feet waggled in the air. The French Man folded his arms and laughed, and a couple walking their dog stopped to watch.

"That's very good, Monsieur," the French Man smiled. "What else can you do?"

"I can make a coin disappear," the boy boasted.

The couple laughed. Two other men stopped to watch. The French Man fished a penny from his pocket and handed it to the boy.

"Abracadabra, hocus pocus!" The boy swirled his arms in the air. Everyone smiled. He slipped the copper into his sleeve and dropped to one knee.

"Ta daa!"

"Magnifique!" The French Man clapped his long thin hands. "Now give it back."

"I can't," the boy claimed. "It's disappeared."

More laughter. The boy did another handstand as the crowd clapped and then dispersed. The French Man remained, his thin lip curled slightly at the corner.

"Another coin for the show?" the boy asked.

"I'm afraid I'm fresh out. Plucked me dry. Are you hungry, boy?"

"Starving."

"Come on, then. This way. I've got a fresh batch of sausages waiting for me at home. Two streets back." The French Man flicked his head toward the crest of the hill. "You're welcome to a bite, little friend. Most welcome."

The French Man kept walking as though he didn't mind leaving the boy in the wind-swept street. The boy looked down the hill and saw no more sailors coming. As it swung back and forth, the French Man's wrist glittered with a silver wristwatch. The boy licked his lips, brushed aside his fear, and followed.

Rain was dripping in silver streams from the corrugated iron roof of the terrace house in Ithaca Road. The boy huddled close to the French Man as the wind rippled through the huge figs. He tried to get a feel for a wallet or a coin purse as he brushed and bumped against the man's side. There was none. The boy circled the man, sometimes ahead, sometimes behind. The French Man laughed and ruffled his hair.

"You're a small boy. Got to bend to get ahold of you. Quick as a ferret."

"How many sausages will there be?"

"Enough for a belly as small as yours. You've got an accent to you. Sauerkraut, is it?"

The boy shrugged. He knew he spoke funny but he didn't know why.

They stepped up onto the porch. The French Man jangled his keys. Inside, the house smelled damp, as though something in the walls was rotting and about to drip out of the wallpaper. The boy skittered down the hall to a table under a grimy kitchen window. It was covered with shining, glimmering things. The boy looked over the mess and tried to pick something to lift before the man caught up. He pocketed a shiny lens. There was a paper bag stuffed with small square photographs. The boy glimpsed bare limbs, naked chests. When he put his hand on the bag the French Man brushed it away.

"What is all this stuff?"

"This, my small friend, is the Polaroid 110B, the Pathfinder. Newest thing on the market. It develops pictures instantly. Poof! Right in your hand. Like magic," the French Man said, and winked. He picked the camera out of the clutter and held it in the light. "You don't have to go to a store. You can develop your own pictures, right here, at home."

"Are you a photographer?"

"Sometimes, yes."

The boy let his eyes wander to the French Man's face. There were scars on his cheeks from burns or acne, marbling the surface of his high cheekbones. "Here. You take a picture of me and I'll take one of you."

The boy giggled and took the heavy camera in his small chubby hands, turned it, looked through the viewfinder. The French Man struck a pose. The device hummed and zinged in the boy's hands, seemed to zap like an alien thing. Light exploded off the walls. The camera spewed out a blank picture, which gradually rippled with light. The boy watched it develop with barely contained rapture. Magic. The boy let the camera go with reluctance.

"Your turn."

He smiled and struck a pose. The flash burned against the backs of his eyelids. He wondered if he'd ever had his picture taken before the Night of Fire and Screaming, if there were pictures of him somewhere still, smiling and playing. The thought made the boy a little sad. The French Man snapped another picture of him standing and staring at the floor.

"You ever seen Sugar Ray? The boxer?"

"Course I have!"

The boy clenched his fists and hung them above his head, his puny biceps flexed as small cream-white lumps on his stringy arms. The French Man laughed and snapped a shot. The boy growled and brought his fists together at his belly. Another zap, hum, a spewed picture. The French Man flipped the photos onto the table without looking at them. The boy laughed nervously, shifting from foot to foot. The room seemed a little small, suddenly. The French Man snapped another picture, and the boy forgot to pose. He was simply standing there. Being him.

"Take your shirt off."

The boy frowned a little. He slipped the shirt over his head, smelling it as the cloth passed his nose, three days or so of sweat and scum and rain. The boy cupped his hands and did a pose of his side as he had seen the boxers do. The French Man snapped him.

"I'm hungry."

"Just a few more."

The boy sighed. More pictures. The air in the room was hard to breathe. His cheeks felt hot. He didn't know why.

"It's no fun anymore. Let's eat."

The French Man snapped him again, crouching by the table, eye level with the boy. The light made the boy's eyes water. He reached out and pulled the camera down. The man lifted it again.

"A few more."

"No."

"You want to eat, you do as I say," the French Man grunted, showing teeth. The two front ones were gray as steel. The boy looked down the hall at the front door, so far away the darkness swallowed it, giving only a slice of silver at the bottom where the moonlit street blazed. "We're friends, aren't we, boy? Good friends. Friends don't argue with each other."

The camera flashed again. Now the pictures were falling on the floor. The boy picked his shirt up. His fingers were numb, the blood raging in his ears. Embarrassed, somehow. The French Man's fingers flashed out, ripped the cloth from his fingers, and flung the shirt by the pile of pictures. The boy's face stared up from the photos. Afraid.

"I've got to go."

"You're not going anywhere."

"I said, I want to go!"

The slap came like a burst of heat, soundless, before the boy knew what had happened. His ear pulsed, hammering against his head. The French Man shook his head slowly, *sadly, then reached up and took the boy's face in his cold hand.*

"Don't disappoint me, pretty one."

The boy turned, twisted, tried to scramble away. They collapsed to the floor, the man a dead weight. The air was squeezed out of him. His stomach churned, clenched, tried to suck oxygen into his lungs. His mouth was on the floor, lips collecting dust.

"You do what I say, when I say."

The French Man pinned his neck against the boards, righted the camera in his other hand. The boy kicked out, struck the table leg, pain flooding his bones. The man snapped another shot, then placed the camera beside his face.

The boy reached out, sweeping it into his arm. In the same movement he rolled beneath the weight of the man and used the momentum to swing the camera up and over, into the side of the man's head.

Then the Silence came.

He had felt the Silence only once before—on the Night of Fire and Screaming, when he had stood in the street motionless and watched the people burning. It felt something like being underwater, sounds pinging softly, all else an endless nothingness, slowed by numbness, decaying moments, the dripping of time.

The boy was on top of the French Man, the camera in his hands, beating it down on the man's face over and over without sound, without sensation. The face was breaking, losing shape, becoming wet. The man's hands were fumbling at his face and neck, scratching, wringing, twisting, punching. Time passed. The camera fell away. The boy used his fists.

When the door of the terrace opened the boy was stand-

ing by the table, looking down at a picture of himself standing by the table. When the men's voices broke the Silence the boy lifted his head. There were shadows in the hall, one larger than the other, a great hulk of a man whose shoulders scraped the narrow walls and head ducked beneath the ornate frame of the kitchen door naturally, as though he'd been here before. A smaller man walked in front, cast in shadow by the beast. The boy wiped at a tickle on his upper lip. He looked at his hands. The blood was smeared to his elbows.

"Jean? Jean? You fucking frog prick. I know you're here. Time's up. I want my money, you hear me, cocksucker?"

The first man was wearing a suit the color of gray ocean. Beneath the suit, old muscle languished to fat, making him look like an elderly retired war captain, his once-powerful frame ruined by peacetime. His hair was gray and a deep groove was cut into his chin from a clean knife wound that had split his bottom lip in two. The giant was not as well dressed but gave the same impression of darkened skies and old wars, a bearded bear with a nose that dominated the front of his face, broken and twisted, a fighter's nose.

The boy and the two men looked at each other, before all eyes fell away. The men took in the smashed and broken thing that had been Jean the French Man, lying twisted at the boy's feet. There was a gun in the old captain's hand, hanging by his side, forgotten. No one spoke. The boy lifted his palms and examined the blood on them, the mangled knuckles swollen twice their size, the wet and watery almost-orange blood sliding down his wrists.

"Well, would you look at this, Bear," the Captain said.

The Bear said nothing as the Captain wandered forward and crouched beside the boy. He lifted a photo from the floor and flicked the blood from it. The boy standing. The boy with his biceps bared. He looked at them all, considered each in turn, laid them in a neat pile. Jean wasn't breathing. The Captain stood and looked down at the boy.

Slowly, a smile crept across the Captain's face. Then he began to laugh. The Bear wasn't laughing. He wasn't even smiling.

The Captain laughed and laughed, and then cocked the hammer on the pistol and put two bullets into the French Man's face. Jean's body bucked twice as though electrified. The boy thought of the burning bodies on the Night of Fire and Screaming, the way they spasmed and shook. The Captain laughed again, a gentle snort, and walked into the short hall that led to the other rooms.

"We'll deal with him in a minute," he said to the Bear. "Put him in the car."

Hades woke thinking he'd been shot. The great weight that seemed to fall and then wrap around his chest, the noise, the pain. He'd taken a bullet before and this was how it felt. But the thump on his chest was only the cat. The pain was his old man's bones snapping into action, the noise his perimeter alarm sounding, an old fire alarm screwed to the wall above the door. Someone had entered his property. Hades groaned and rolled onto his side, flopping out of the bed like a swollen fish. The cat weaved around his stubby ankles, suddenly full of affection after the terror of the alarm. It was usually a bitch of a thing. Hades kicked it away and slipped his flip-flops on.

It had been months since he had been visited this late. He'd put the word out that he had retired, that all the problems he had once been happy to fix were to be taken elsewhere. He wanted to spend his declining years free of harassment by cops, forensics specialists, journalists, and true crime writers. During the day, the workers at his dump kept these scavengers away—Hades' dark past was common knowledge among them and was at the heart of a brotherhood of loyalty and silence. At night he was vulnerable. His daughter Eden had insisted on installing the alarm when she had managed to walk all the way up the dark drive, into the house, and right to his bedside without waking him. Eden, always the predator, had made the alarm loud enough to induce a heart attack.

Headlights swept the kitchen. One of the few clocks in his extensive collection that actually kept time chimed an hour past midnight as he reached the screen door. He picked up a Ruger Super Redhawk that was sticking out of a flowerpot and tucked it into the back of his boxer shorts. The double-action Magnum tugged at the hem, felt cold against his ass crack. The gun was far too big to be practical, but if he was going to go out one night in a revenge attack, a shoot-out with the police, or a dance with burglars, all of which were equally likely, he was going to do it with a gun proportionate to his reputation.

The cat followed him out and bolted into the blackness. He hoped it wouldn't be back, but knew it would. A red Barina with plastic eyelashes hanging over its headlights gripped its way uncertainly over the last rise before his shack and stopped with a jolt in the dust. If this was some kind of attack he was pleased by how undignified the approach had been. It didn't speak of organization. When the driver slid out of the seat and came into the murky lights, he let his head hang back and looked at the stars.

"Oh God. Not you."

"Hades!"

She fell on him, rock-hard breasts against his chest, nails in his hair, an assault of smooth limbs and wet kisses, cigarette smoke, perfume. Hades pushed her off. He resisted the urge to smile. It would only encourage her.

"Get off me, Kat."

"I've missed you. God, I've missed you. It's been too long. It's been ages."

"What are you doing here, for chrissake? I don't

have time for you. I'm retired. It's the middle of the night."

"I love you, Hades."

"Go away."

"No, Hades, I love you. I need you."

"Oh, don't tell me."

"Please, Hades." She stood back and clasped her hands like a child. "Please help me."

He looked at her, let the silence hang the way he used to with Eden when she was a teenager, disappointment so deeply felt it could not be squeezed out into words. Kat had come in her usual getup—the six-inch heels and cheap nylon minidress, the half-dyed black hair falling out at the sides in wispy singed spikes. It was more than that though. The track marks on her ankles weren't from smack, as she'd have you believe. Hades had seen these marks faked plenty of times by undercover cops—a little cayenne pepper and ink under the first layer of skin and irritated welts pop up like the angry sores of the addicted. The mascara was intentionally clumpy. The multiple piercings in her ears were magnets. Underneath the manufactured cheapness was a very beautiful woman, a clever woman. A seasoned killer.

Hades had caught Kat out once. She was sitting in a café in Glebe with a girlfriend, fresh-faced and vibrant, the makeup gone, her hair short and neatly bobbed, a gold watch she'd probably stolen hanging a little too loosely on her wrist. Hades had heard somewhere that she was a financial adviser or something. He wasn't sure. He didn't care.

Whenever she turned up, he played along with her little game because Kat was just one of many actors, hustlers, con artists, and tricksters who came to him in the night with bones to bury. Over the years Hades had been awakened by numb-headed drug mules who had waited for their moment to cut down their bosses; by lady killers in expensive linen suits, hit men with cold eyes and false charm. Wasn't he one of them, too? Hades had spent decades crafting his tired old man image. Sure, he was getting on. He ate too much and fell asleep in front of the TV more than he actually watched it. But Hades was deadly. So was Kat. Under the stars that night they played out the roles of a worn-out ex-warlord and a skinny prostitute.

"What have you done now?" he asked.

"It was an accident."

"It's always an accident with you."

"Oh, Hades!"

"Come on." He waved at her impatiently. "Get on with it."

She clopped back to the car, all guilty eyes and pouty lips. Hades watched her struggle with the trunk. Nickel bracelets jingled on her wrists. She thrust the trunk open and the overhead light flickered. Hades looked in and let a sigh ripple out of him.

"How many times I got to tell you, Kat?"

"What?"

"You're not wrapping them right. I've told you this."

"Hay-dees!"

"Look." Hades leaned over and lifted the end of the tarp that contained the body. "You leave the ends open like this and you get DNA in your car. Hair. Eyelashes. Blood. Piss. Dirt and plant fibers from the tread in his shoes that will put him in your street, in your driveway.

They can put a body in your trunk from a single flake of fucking dandruff, Kat. You know this."

"So what am I supposed to do about it?"

"You tuck the ends in before you roll." Hades illustrated with his hands. "Lie the body out flat, arms down. Like a burrito. Tuck, tuck, roll. Tape. Tape, Kat, not fucking bungee cords. You shouldn't be using tarp, either. You should be using plastic drop cloths. I can give you some. Tarps have a weave in them. They're not airtight."

"Hades, I'm not as clever as you, okay?" she whined.

"You never rolled a fucking burrito?"

"I don't even know what a burrito is. What do I look like?"

Hades shook his head, felt exhausted.

"The whole car will have to go. They'll have your DNA in the front and his in the back. You need to start thinking about these things, Kat."

"You talk too much, Hades," Kat said, patting the side of his head, letting her fingers follow the rim of his ear to the nape of his thick neck. "You're always talking. You're always mean to me."

Her breath felt warm on his face. Hades cleared his throat.

"I do it because you're going to get yourself caught one of these days. And I don't want to be the one who has to come after you before you testify."

"Would you hurt me, Hades?"

"Probably not."

"Sometimes I like being hurt."

She was against him, kissing him, before he knew it. She'd got into his arms the way a fox will slip through a gap in a fence. Feral. Dangerous. He sighed again and surrendered. She always did this. He always fell for it. But in a way he kind of liked falling for it, knowing it was coming, wondering how she would make it seem spontaneous and wild each and every time. The concubine. Hades imagined that this was what it was like with the men she robbed and killed, leaving work and smoking on the corner, being approached by a cute, vulnerable, irresistible little whore in a painted-on dress. Cold, tired, gullible. Give me your jacket. Take me home. Play with me. Hades withdrew from her and rolled his eyes.

"Get in there." He cocked his head toward the house. "Make me a goddamn coffee while you're at it."

"Don't be long," she said, victorious. Hades grumbled and shut the trunk. His hard-on was almost painful but he never put play before work, even when the play was just a ruse to get out of his body disposal fee. A twenty-thousand-dollar fuck. It was cheap and nasty, but he didn't mind. It had been years since a woman had wanted to jump Hades' bones. He wasn't fussed. Women made things difficult, and the last thing he needed was more difficulty in his life.

First things first. He would drive the car back to the new fill grounds where the complex layers of rubber, vinyl, industrial biochemicals and trash were not yet finished. He'd slip Kat's nameless victim in there, where the compressed layers, encouraging the development of leachate acid as a natural biodegrader of human waste, would eventually completely dissolve all trace of him as it had with hundreds of others over the years. He would grind the car's identification off, leave the vehicle to be crushed into a cube and finished off in an industrial incinerator in the morning. Then he'd go to bed with Kat. Hades wondered gloomily if the reward would be worth the effort as he wrestled the keys from the lock. She'd take everything she wanted out of him in a matter of minutes and leave while he was asleep. He was making a mental note to put his wallet and keys away when he noticed the dark shape at the bottom of the hill.

Hades took a short wander to the crest of the hill. Stood. Listened. The car was idling, its headlights off. He felt a twinge in his chest, a leftover spasm from the fear that the alarm had generated. Hades began to walk again, a little faster this time. The car's windows were down, blackness in the cabin, impenetrable. He got no farther than ten meters before the car began to move, passed the gates in a blur of dark gray, before disappearing between the trees.

Hades stopped, out of breath.

The television was on, but the knocking broke through the chatter of morning programs, to snap me awake. The first sensation was the wetness under my face. Cold drool. Camel mouth. The place smelled damp and reeked of kitty litter. But still bearable. I could leave it a couple more days. I sat up and felt a nudge in the small of my back. I fished around and retrieved an empty Jameson bottle. The pain—dull, heavy, everywhere.

The knocking came again. It was her. She came every day. I hung my head in my hands and groaned, long and loud, so she could hear me. She knocked again. The day before I hadn't let her in, and she was waiting for me hours later when I went to get a pizza for lunch. Immaculate, in gray jeans and a knitted top that hugged the top of her perfect ass and fell to the backs of her cold, pale killer's hands. Sitting on a bench in the foyer, reading a magazine. Waiting. Watching.

Eden knocked again.

"Go away!"

She knocked. I crossed the apartment in two steps, kicked newspapers out of the way, and flung open the door. Her hand was raised for more knocking. She took me in with those expressionless crow eyes, head to toe, let her hand fall, and waited for me to go on my usual tirade. I did. She listened to my swearing quietly, thinking. I don't know what I looked like but I know what I smelled like. I'd expected the performance to get rid of her. When I tried to slam the door, her boot was in it.

"We've got an appointment."

"I'm not going. Are you listening? Are you fucking stupid? I wasn't going yesterday. I'm not going today. Eden, I need you to leave me alone." I walked away from the door. She closed it behind her, wrinkled her nose just slightly at the smell.

"Have a shower," she said. "We leave in twenty."

I went into the kitchen and popped myself some Panadol, chewed them, angry. Her eyes wandered over the dirty plates balancing on the back of the couch, the dusty curtains blocking the mid-morning light, the gray cat pawing at the balcony door. Martina's cat. Yes. All right. I'd let things slip since Martina died. Since I'd been shot and Eden had saved my life. It had locked me to her, silencing me forever on the true nature of her being, the nights she spent stalking Sydney's killers and rapists and molesters. I'd shot and killed a serial killer, deliberately, and Eden had stood with me through the investigation that followed with her untouchable self-assurance. We were bound, Eden and I, and I hated her for it.

She came into the kitchen and watched me swallow two more Panadol and an Oxycodone. I liked the Oxy, had got onto it after the bullet. My shoulder was mostly healed now, but I kept up the act to get the drug. I was supposed to go to physiotherapy to get rid of a twitch that sometimes developed in the last three fingers of my right hand, the only real leftover from the wound, but I wouldn't go. Anything to get the Oxy.

Lovely, sleepy Oxy. There were three sheets left in the packet. I pocketed them.

"What are you staring at?"

"A problem."

"Am I a problem for you, Eden?" I raised my eyebrows, shook the twitching from my fingers. "You going to do with me what you do with all your other problems?"

She licked her teeth, looked almost bored. Not answering struck a chord with me. Deep down inside I knew she could do it, I suppose that was why. One of these nights I could wake up and find her standing over me. I liked to fool myself sometimes that Eden had a heart, that I'd wrung a laugh or two out of her over our months together, that she would at least have trouble killing me. Most of the time I wasn't so sure.

"You need to have a shower and come to this shrink's appointment with me," she said. "You need to do this two more times so you can get signed back on duty. You need to go back to work and get over this thing with Martina. Until you do all these things you're a problem for me, Frank."

"Don't talk about fucking Martina."

"Martina is dead. She's dead, Frank."

I shook my head at the floor.

"I don't like your unpredictability right now. I want you to get off the drugs and stop drinking."

"Honey, my mother died years ago and she was the last woman who got to tell me what to do."

"Have a shower."

"No."

"Have a shower."

"No."

She stood waiting. I considered my options. The first was picking Eden right up off the floor and carrying her out of my apartment. In my mind that was fairly easy—even with all the weight I'd dropped after the shooting I still had a good thirty kilos on her. But she was slippery. I'd seen her put down men twice my size with minimal effort. I didn't know if she had trained in any martial arts but I wouldn't be surprised. She'd also been known to pull knives and guns from secret places on her body, which was always a shock because she dressed like she knew she had a kickass body—athletic and sprightly with curves only where they were absolutely necessary. I scratched my neck and looked at her, summoning all my Jedi power, and willed her silently to budge. She didn't. I also knew she could hold a Mexican standoff for days. She had no emotions. No needs. I spewed some more venom under my breath and left her.

I took half an hour in the bathroom just to piss her off, to get something back. I finished up and stood in front of the mirror, counting off the minutes on my watch. Then I went out into the living room and grabbed a shirt from the back of the couch.

"Not that one," Eden said, handing me a clean shirt she'd plucked from my wardrobe. "You didn't shave. You need to shave."

"You need to stop beginning sentences with *you need*."

"You will shave."

"Leave me alone, Eden."

She relented a little and held open the apartment door for me. In the car she flipped the radio on and turned up the air-conditioning. I rolled down my window, let the warm autumn air come rolling in.

We turned onto Anzac Parade and headed into the city.

Eden was listening to the radio. Had that intensity about her—a cat about to strike, unnatural stillness.

"We're going to get put on this, you and I," she said.

"On what?"

She turned up the radio.

". . . the third woman to go missing from the area in as many months. Police won't say at this stage whether the cases are related but are asking the public for any information about . . ."

I reached over and flipped the radio to a station blaring celebrity news.

"I'm not on duty."

"You're going to be put on duty if they link this missing prostitute to the others. We're the serial killer team now, Frank. That's us. Jason Beck gave us that title. They're going to sign you on and put us on that case, whether you like it or not."

"Does that mean I don't have to go to the shrink?"

"No."

"I'll refuse the case. My shoulder's no good."

"What is your plan?" A little frazzle seemed to edge into Eden's voice for the first time that day. I felt slightly uplifted. "You're just going to languish away in that hellhole of an apartment eating shit and listening to Chris Isaak until you depress yourself to death?"

"Sounds good to me. If no one bothers me for long enough the cat will probably dispose of my corpse. Ah, the circle of life."

"You're not funny."

"Depressing myself to death would be very artistic of me. I always wanted to be artistic."

"Just stop."

"You stop."

"I asked Hades if he would give you some work," she said. She was driving one-handed, hanging her French-manicured nails over the edge of the center console. Now and then she rubbed them together, the only outward sign of her irritation. "He said he had plenty you could do."

"Why do you call him Hades? He's your dad. You should call him 'Dad. ' It's very weird to do otherwise. You don't want people to think you're weird, Eden. They might catch on to you. To your little game. Is that why you ended up a serial killer, Eden? Was Hades a weird father? Did he train you in the dark arts?"

"You better watch your tongue, boy-o."

We looked at each other. My jaw felt locked.

"You're completely without friends or hobbies right now," she said after a time. "Binge drinking is making you ineffectual."

"Oh dear. I wouldn't want to end up ineffectual. That would be ghastly."

"Hades needs help. He's old. You need something to keep you busy."

"I'm not working for Hades, honey. That's my final word on that."

Eden swung the car out of the traffic. The car behind

us honked. She pulled up behind a taxi and I jolted in my seat as she yanked the emergency brake.

"Listen, Frank, here's how it is," she said, clasping her hands. "I'm going to keep coming to your apartment until you do as I say. I'm going to keep calling you on the phone. I'm going to follow you down to that disgusting pub where you spend your nights and I'm going to get in the way of those sluts you take home with you. If all that doesn't work, I'm going to start hanging around *inside* your apartment, and you won't be able to get me out. I've had a key for weeks. I'm not going away, so you make the decision now to get up and get moving or the consequences are going to get more and more inconvenient for you."

A little color, a light pink, had come into her cheeks while she was speaking. That was the only indication that she meant what she was saying. I had to give her a little smile. For all the terror and heartache and frustration she brought to my life, for all her intrusions, her insults, her propensity for the word "dead," I couldn't deny that Eden cared about me. If she was forced to kill me, she was going to make it her last option.

"You've got a key to my place?"

She sighed.

"Seriously, how'd you get a key to my place?"

Eden pulled the car back into the traffic.

I'd made it clear early on that I wouldn't be having private sessions with the shrink. Eden and I were required to have ten tandem sessions before we could be signed back on to work. The private ones were optional. The shrink had encouraged me to sit alone with her so she could address issues with me that she thought were "too private" to discuss in front of Eden. I told her she had my permission to discuss anything she liked in front of Eden and that she'd have to shoot a tranquilizer dart into my ass and hog-tie me to get me to do any more than was required. The paperwork Captain James handed to us stipulated that we needed to *attend* ten sessions. It said nothing about participation.

For the first session I'd simply sat in the chair and hung my head back over the headrest, examining the water stains on the ceiling. Since then I'd been stonewalling Dr. Stone, using all my years of training as a detective to keep a conversation going while revealing nothing about anything. It was kind of fun. I'm not sure Stone agreed.

Surprisingly, Eden was with me on this one. The last thing Eden wanted was anyone examining her past, or even her present, lest they should start scratching their heads about her, as I had begun to do when we met. Eden had a strange vibe that I'm sure she worked hard to keep under control. She was either very attractive to people or oddly repelling, like a pretty but deadly insect.

I didn't know much about Eden's childhood, but her father, Heinrich "Hades" Archer, had been one of Sydney's most powerful criminal overlords back in the late sixties and early seventies. Eden and her brother Eric both joined the boys in blue, even though the two of them had made records in academia while completing their undergraduate degrees and been offered countless scholarships and fellowships to further their studies in science and forensics.

To my knowledge she'd never entertained a boyfriend, though wherever we went men walked into telephone poles at the sight of her. Her colleagues at the station were deeply afraid of her, and no one would say exactly why. No, any digging by our shrink into Eden's character wouldn't have been pleasant for the moonlighting serial killer. While I was usually fairly brazen about my refusal to participate in our psychologist's appointments, Eden gave up just as little, albeit more politely.

Eden and I sat in the waiting room of Dr. Imogen Stone's office. She pretended to read a magazine, flipping through the pictures, those predator eyes fixed and unseeing and her clockwork mind ticking away. I watched her, bored. She had quite a pointy look to her when I examined her carefully. She appeared in no way friendly, possessed none of the roundness and softness you would associate with approachability. Streamlined and fluid, like a shark.

When Dr. Stone walked out she made me think of a big-eyed kitten. She was blond and golden skinned with a sprinkling of freckles on her small nose. Short and pretty, the girl next door.

I realized she was speaking to me. Eden caught me checking out Dr. Stone and looked embarrassed. It was the Oxy slowing me down.

"Frank?"

"Yeah, yeah, I'm coming."

"Coffee, either of you? Tea?"

"Frank will have a coffee," Eden said. Dr. Stone made the coffee in a little kitchenette behind her desk by the huge windows. When she handed me the cup I got a whiff of some delicate perfume. I wondered if she could smell me. There was still scotch in my veins.

"You've lost weight again, Frank," she said as she took her seat.

"Keep your eyes off my body, Stone. I'm not a piece of meat."

"Are you experiencing a loss of appetite?"

I sipped the coffee. Dr. Stone waited, her legs crossed and hands on her notebook. She really had co-ordinated her shoes well with her outfit. She was all cream today. The cashmere on her shoes was touch-able, like the shimmery stockings.

"You're going to stare at my shoes all session again, are you?"

"You really do have good taste in shoes."

"Thanks," she said. Stone was easier to frazzle then Eden. She shuffled the folders and the notebook. "I've just got the report back from the inquest into the shoot-ings at the Avoca Street church. Looks like your col-leagues are prepared to accept your account, that Eden's brother Eric accidentally discharged his weapon at you, Frank, and that Eden, you mistook Eric for the killer and shot him dead. They're still puzzled as to how six bullets from your weapon ended up in Mr. Beck's head at a trajectory that would suggest he was lying on the floor and you were standing over him. Is this something you think we can talk about today? Either of you? Eden?"

I looked at Eden. She was sitting upright in her chair.

"I'm afraid I don't recall anything further about the

moments before the shooting that I haven't already put in writing to the inquiry board," she said.

"Let's get away from actions," Dr. Stone said. "Let's talk about feelings. How do you feel when you remember that time in the church? Can you remember entering the building?"

Eden said nothing.

"Frank, what about you?"

"I'm sorry, Doctor. You lost me at 'Let's talk about feelings.'"

Dr. Stone licked her bottom lip. I sat sniggering at my own joke. I nudged Eden to see if she'd heard it. She was rigid as pine.

"Tell me how you feel. Seriously. It will have no bearing on your masculinity, Frank, I promise you."

"You women and your lies."

"I want to know if either of you are returning to that day in your minds, either voluntarily or involuntarily, because I think it's important that we put a name to how the event made you feel so that we can deal with it properly. Eden, you need to deal with your brother's loss and any blame you might have assigned yourself for accidentally killing him. Frank, you need to deal with having been injured and with whatever caused you to shoot Mr. Beck. Until we deal with these emotions neither of you are going to be fit to move on with your lives."

Eden pulled a thread out of her jeans and curled it around her finger. She rolled it into a ball and placed it on the arm of the couch. I watched.

"Frank, you're obviously not coping with what's happened," Dr. Stone said.

"What are you picking on me for? Pick on Eden. She loves it."

"I'm picking on you because whether Eden has dealt with the trauma of this event or not she is clearly still functioning. You're not functioning, Frank."

"I'm deeply offended by that. I'm here. I'm not even that late."

"You *reek* of alcohol," Dr. Stone said. She rolled her eyes up in her head on the word "reek" to illustrate her point. "And I heard pill packets crumple in your back pocket when you sat down. You're doing the stand-up comedian act to deflect attention. We've played this game seven times now. I'm over it. I've got two more sessions with you guys after this one, and I really would like to stop beating around the bush if we can, please."

"Jesus. You're pretty ballsy for a shrink," I laughed. Eden gave me a warning look.

"I'm a cop shrink, Frank. I'm used to being fucked around. It gets boring."

I laughed more. I'd never heard her get this fiery. She formed the words with perfect coral pink lips and they zinged in the air like electricity.

"Let's talk," she said.

"All right. I'm talking. I'm doing it. What do you want to talk about?"

"Tell me about Beck's last victim, Martina Ducote. I understand you and her were close, Frank."

I stopped smiling. Eden watched me put the coffee on the small table between us and hang my head back over the edge of my seat again. For the rest of the session, I was silent.

The boy wasn't sure how he got to the car, how long he had been sitting there in the front seat beside the Bear, if the Bear Man had spoken to him or what he had said. He stared at his palms for a long time, at the blood.

The Bear was watching the boy with interest, a cigarette wedged between his fingers and his huge elbow resting on the sill of the open window.

"What's your name?" the big man asked.

"I don't know."

"You don't know?"

"I don't remember."

The man drew on his cigarette, blew smoke out the window. Ahead, the orange light of street lamps danced in the rain. The man and the boy turned as they heard the front door of the terrace house slam. The Captain was a dark shape in the night, adjusting the cuffs of his shirt.

"What's he going to do with me?"

"I don't know," the Bear said.

"Is he going to take me to the police?"

"No," the Bear laughed. The boy watched as the Captain closed and locked the front gate behind him. He carried what looked like a laundry bag over his shoulder.

"Did I kill that man in there?" the boy asked.

"If you didn't, Caesar did."

"I didn't mean to kill him." The boy's teeth were chattering.

"I wouldn't worry about it," Bear said. "No one's going to cry over him."

Caesar thrust open the back door of the car and hurled the laundry bag onto the seat before sliding in. Instantly it was hotter in the car. The boy sunk into his seat. Neither the Bear Man nor Caesar spoke as the car glided into the night. The men smelled foreign to him, of smoke and salt and blood. The boy felt afraid. There seemed to be no possibility of escape, but he was reassured by the Bear Man's calm driving, the cigarette slowly leading to another, the sigh he gave now and then as they pulled up to empty traffic lights burning red.

The boy only realized he was falling asleep when the car came to a stop. Caesar got out and stood smoking by the car with the huge hairy Bear.

"You won't do it even if I ask you to, will you?"

"I don't do children."

"Then we have an interesting little problem here, don't we, Bear? Because I don't dirty my hands like that, either, and I don't want you driving him somewhere and leaving him. If he doesn't remember me, he'll rem mber you."

"This doesn't need to be a problem," the Bear said. "He's a good kid. He's obviously got spunk. Let him hang around a bit and see if we can use him for something . . ."

"You can't watch him all day long."

"Yes, I can."

Caesar stubbed his cigarette out on the ground. The door beside him opened and the Bear Man encircled his arm in his huge hand. He stumbled and grabbed the man's trousers. Caesar was gone. He was being led toward the house. Light, noise. A turntable just inside the door was playing "Georgia on My Mind." He brushed against a woman's bare leg. She looked down as she went past him, her painted lips falling open and eyes frowning.

Bear's hand loosened, slid to his wrist, held his hand. There were people everywhere, most of the men clothed and the women not. The boy looked into a dark room and saw bodies moving and smoke curling. Somewhere he could hear a game of pool, the crack and tumble of balls. He was at the back door of the house when he saw the girl standing in the kitchen holding a glass of water and staring at him.

The first thing he thought was that she was painted gold, a perfect sheen on her cheeks and the tops of her arms, the soft curves in her throat where the skin dipped over bones and ridges. That was the second thing, the shape of her, like a fleshy bug, with bones speaking their poetry from beneath the gold in the armholes of her loose tank top. Her wide nose and huge black eyes told the boy that she was at least partly Aborigine.

He looked back at her as the Bear took him down some stairs into a lush wet garden. There was a greenhouse with a tiny work shed attached. The Bear stopped and reached up and there was light. The boy was lifted onto a bench covered in tiny pots, seedlings, jars and bottles of every conceivable size and shape, tools rusting and half-polished, strips of fabric, and tubes of ointment.

The girl bumped into the Bear's leg and he yelled out.

"Jesus, Mary, and Joseph. Sunday, you scared the shit out of me."

"Bear, who's that?"

"Nevermind who she is. Were you born in a tent?"

The girl named Sunday shut the door of the little shed. The boy tried to guess how old she was. She mustn't have been much older than him, but he couldn't be sure. Bear heaved a heavy sigh and wet a cloth in a sink by the door.

"Follow me around like a fucking puppy, you do. Always underfoot."

"What's your name?" Sunday asked.

The boy tried to control his shaking. Bear wiped the blood from his cheeks and neck roughly with the cloth.

"Oi! I'm talking to you!"

"I don't know," the boy said.

"Whatcha mean, you don't know?"

"He doesn't have one," Bear said, irritation saturating his voice. "Sometimes people just don't have names, okay? His mama got too busy to give him one, just like I'm too busy right now to listen to all your jabbering. You want his name? You sit over there and think of a good one to give him."

Sunday perched on the edge of the sink and looked at the boy with her head cocked. Bear took the boy's nose in his huge fingers and felt where one half of the bone had slid up and over the other.

"This is going to hurt," he said, before sliding the bones back into place with an audible crunch. The boy wailed.

"Francis," Sunday blurted. "We can call him Francis."

"We ain't calling him Francis. He ain't no nancy."

"Thomas."

"I got too many Thomases in my life already."

"What about Henry?"

"He's German. He needs a German name."

"What's German for Henry?"

"Heinrich."

"Good," Sunday said. "Heinrich is an ugly name. An ugly name for an ugly, smelly boy."

"This ugly, smelly boy is going in your bed tonight," Bear said. "There ain't no other place for him."

The girl gasped. "No, he's not."

"He sure is."

"He's not, Bear. He's not." Sunday slid down from the edge

of the sink and slapped the big man hard on the shoulder. He didn't seem to notice. He was examining the boy's right hand in the light of the overhead lamp. The tiny bones behind his knuckles had been crushed, and two fingers bent at strange angles, deeper toward the palm than they should have been.

"You really made a mess of this," Bear said. "Somebody better teach you how to punch, boy."

"Bear, he's not really sleeping with me," Sunday continued. She turned to the boy. "You're not sleeping with me."

"Sunday, you shut your trap or you go straight back where I found you," Bear said. His voice was soft, but the certainty in his words left no room for negotiation. The girl stormed out of the shed, slamming the door behind her. Bear snorted with laughter as he massaged the bones in the boy's hand back into place.

"Women, uh?" he said. "Painful."

I told Eden I'd think about doing some work for Hades. It was about all what would make her let me out of the car, stop her driving me around and lecturing me on my drinking, on what I could catch from the pub skanks, on what Martina would have wanted me to be doing.

I started to ask her how she felt about Eric's death and that shut her up fast. I felt bad. I got the impression not that she missed Eric or that she loved him but that somehow her lack of emotion, her natural inability to feel anything for any other human being, made her afraid. I tried to imagine what it might be like to be unable to love. I had no doubt that I'd loved Martina. I'd only known her a few days but I'd loved her.

When I swung open the apartment door I was shocked by a wall of perfume. I walked in and heard myself grunt in disbelief. Someone had cleaned the entire place—scrubbed it, washed it, bleached it, organized it beyond recognition. There were books in a bookshelf by the bedroom door that I'd forgotten I had, a vase of my mother's that had been wrapped in paper for years was on the polished glass tabletop exploding with flowers. *Actual* flowers. The kitchen was gleaming and empty of all things—the filthy sandwich-maker was gone, the dishwasher empty and airing, the window open. I went into the bedroom and sat on the bed by the cat, who was curled like a circular cushion at the foot of the bed. All my clothes had been washed and ironed and hung in the closet. The sheets were new. This must have taken a team of people. I called Eden.

"I'm driving."

"I want my keys back," I said.

"No," she answered.

"I'll change the locks."

"That would be a waste of time."

"You want to mother someone, Eden, you should go and have a baby."

"Stop acting like a baby and I'll stop mothering you."

She hung up. I threw the phone on the bed and went to order dinner.

Driving into the Utulla dump made me nervous. The dump had been referred to by police as "Utulla Cemetery" since Hades Archer acquired it back in the eighties, but dozens of searches had failed to confirm suspicions that Hades buried people here for a fee. Knowing Eden's secret, how she spent her nights and what she and Eric had done in the past, confirmed for me that Hades had been the one to show the two fledgling killers the ropes. I'd never found a body to fit Eden's killings, although Eric's attempt to kill me was confession enough.

Hades and his children were a superior breed of urban predator. However afraid of Eden I was sometimes when she gave me a crooked look or when I heard noises in my apartment in the night or when I walked home from the pub and felt eyes on me from the dark, Hades made me more afraid. Hades didn't exhibit the same cold, emotionless, obviously detached murderous persona that Eden did.

I'd met him once and he'd been charming. He had a number of friends in the police force, acquired simply through his friendly, giving, likeable character. He was funny, I'd heard. Really funny. I felt somehow that at least with Eden, I'd feel something before she did away with me. That rush of coldness surfers feel when a shadow passes beneath them. With Hades, I wouldn't feel anything. He was that good.

The huge gates, a complex filigree of twisted metal, chains, bottles, car parts, tires, and strips of melted plastic, were open. On the first turn toward the hill I passed a group of kangaroos made from mismatched mosaic tiles. They looked so real in their shape and posture I slowed down, instinctively expecting one to panic and leap in front of the vehicle. On the next bend, two stainless-steel and colored-glass Komodo dragons guarded a lump of sandstone as big as my car, one basking, one clawing at the air as I passed.

As I drove up the hill I got a sinking feeling that I was wandering into a trap, that I was edging closer and closer to the point of no return. People would hear that I was working for Hades if I did it long enough. It would circulate in whispers around the office, slide under doors like smoke, glimmer in eyes as I walked through the offices. A connection made. Linked in. Hooked up. Frank Bennett and Hades Archer—known criminal association. But I shrugged the feeling off. I was being reckless. It was something I'd become comfortable with.

I told no one I was coming in an attempt to make an inconvenience of myself, but a man appeared to be waiting for me as I pulled up under a "No Parking" sign made from bottle caps nailed to a wooden board. He was carrying a mug of coffee and wearing a battered cap. Two small piggy eyes were wedged between the cap and his dark beard. He looked at his watch as I approached.

"Morning, Frank," he said.

"Uh, morning . . . ?"

"Steve. Hades told me to wait here for you. Show you what you're doing."

"I didn't tell Hades I was coming."

Steve had that "Let's get on with it" look that a lot of laborers get in the morning. I reached into the back of my car and took out a water bottle. The heat was already oppressive, made heavier by the previous day's rain. I felt the hangover stir in my stomach as I leaned over. I popped two Panadol and shut the car.

"You had breakfast?"

"Not really a breakfast person," I said.

"You need breakfast. We've got a barbie on."

You need.

"Yeah, maybe later," I said. Steve led me down a dirt path. There was no sign of the old man. He had a strange garden going on around the house, disorganized, like he'd just been throwing random seeds on the ground and letting them survive or die as they wished. A huge pumpkin vine was woven around white roses towering over what looked like chives. A rabbit as big as a golf buggy had been constructed out of a wrought-iron frame and furred with knitting needles. It reared on its hind legs, its huge head turned back toward the gates.

"Look at that thing," I said as we passed.

"Yeah," Steve said.

He led me over the hill and through streets carved between piles of trash as high as two-story houses. Car bodies, bookcases, ladders, toolboxes, washing machines, television sets, compressors, gas bottles, toys. Street signs, rusting and bent where cars had run into them, had been resurrected and placed at the intersections of bare earth pathways. We emerged into a clearing at the bottom of the hill and were confronted by a huge pile of metal, three meters higher than I and at least twice as long.

"Hades wants you to sort this." Steve gestured toward the pile. "It's mostly donation material. He wants three separate piles—copper, aluminum, and steel or iron." He slapped a pair of gardening gloves against my chest. I took them and put them on.

"You got a hat?" he asked.

"No."

"Not real prepared, are you?"

"Preparation is for Boy Scouts."

Steve sniggered. "I'll get you one. If you change your mind about breakfast, the work shed is on Marine Parade. Really recommend it."

"I'll be all right," I said.

I started at the bottom of the pile. Copper pipes, lead pipes, a car axle. A shopping trolley, an engine block, various gears and cogs. Rusty saw blades, washing machine barrels. Steve came back with a hat and I quickly soaked it with sweat. The sun was beating down, almost ringing in the silence with its intensity. My hangover stayed away for the first hour and only my joints and the muscles in my back gave me trouble. I stopped and drank half the water, which was warm as a cup of tea. There was no shade. Sweat itched in the hair on my calves and tickled as it slid down my ribs.

My thoughts wandered. First there was the curiosity brought on by what I was doing—what sort of machine this battery might have come from, how old that set of sink taps was, why someone might have thrown out this perfectly good set of bolt cutters. As the work became monotonous I found myself thinking about Martina. I shook these thoughts away for a while and thought about other girls. She returned to me, this time in the box they'd put her in, the half dozen or so people who had attended her funeral. I wondered how someone so beautiful could have been so alone in life.

When I couldn't get away from Martina in my mind I went to a tiny slice of shade that had developed by a stack of cars nearby and popped two Oxys. I wondered if it had been a mistake to get away from my apartment, my television, the booze. I stood in the shade and felt sickness swell in my stomach. The hangover. I told myself that working harder would get rid of it. Get rid of Martina. I drank the rest of the water and went back to the pile, stripping off my wet shirt.

Hours passed. I tried to control my thoughts. Surely the shrink had given me some strategies for that. All right. My earliest memory. My dad. My dad taking me fishing, sitting under a bridge at Illawarra, yelling as loud as I could when the train went overhead and not being able to hear my voice. Catching toadfish and kicking them back into the water. What did I remember about Mum? Animals. She always had animals around. Baby bats plucked from the fried bodies of their mothers hanging on power lines—stinking squeaking things, furry, leathery balls of bones. Bones. Martina's bones. Martina's bones in the ground. I'd left her. I'd fucking left her.

I went back to the shade, breathing in, breathing out, sweat dripping off the tips of my fingers. It didn't stop the vomit. There was nothing in me but booze. I stood there gripping the bumper of a half-smashed Corolla and spitting.

Hades' laughter reached me through my throbbing ears.

"You didn't eat anything," he said. He was leaning on a cane at the entrance to Tropicana Avenue, a few meters away from me, his eyes dazzling in the shadow of his heavy brow. I spat, couldn't catch my breath. He laughed again.

"Come on," he said, and cocked his head.

"I'm fine. I'm all right. It's just a hangover."

The old man continued walking. I followed reluctantly. He led me back through the piles of trash toward his shack.

The sickness rose again. I didn't want to go in there. I didn't want to be alone with him. It wasn't fear, but a deep trepidation at what he might tell me, what he might want me to know, that heavy mutual understanding that I didn't like what he was, what he had been all his life, what he had raised Eden to be. I'd been built for catching killers. We were supposed to be natural enemies.

He held open the door and I entered. I hoped he couldn't see that all my muscles were twitching, not just the fingers, the way they danced against my thigh. Sunspots clouded my vision, emerald green and swirling. It was cool and dark here. I wondered where my shirt was.

"Sit there," he said and pointed to a chair at a small table by the wall. He took a water bottle from the fridge and set it in front of me. I drank, looking at the things hanging from the ceiling—ornate glass Christmas baubles and hand-painted teacups, a lizard skeleton still fully assembled by cartilage, spray-painted gold.

Hades put a roast beef sandwich together on a plate. I took it, thanked him, and shoved it in my head.

"Bet you feel like an idiot."

"It's nothing new."

I finished the sandwich and worked on the water. It was painfully cold in my throat.

"Lost weight since I saw you last," he said. "Lots of weight. You must have really liked that girl."

"I did," I said.

I was struck by how similar talking to Hades was to talking to my father. There was a battle raging inside me—a desire to hear what he thought I should do to fix all the problems in my life tangled up with an old hostility, a need to make sure he didn't find out anything about me he could use. He turned the handle of a mug on the table toward him and resumed a coffee my presence must have interrupted.

"Funny what hard work will bring out in you," he said.

"I needed it."

"You want some more?"

"I think Eden will nag me to death if I don't come at least a couple more times, and that's not how I plan to die."

"Not that kind of work," Hades said. "Something more in tune with your official employment."

I frowned.

He smiled.

The old man folded the newspaper on the table between us with one hand and set it aside. It was a stalling gesture. A bit of silence, in case I hadn't caught on yet, to help me realize that offering me trash-sorting work had been a ruse all along. That was how Hades did things. Set up games and created shadows. Observed, listened, tested you. Broke you down until you were vomiting from heatstroke. Embarrassed you in front of others, offered you a redemption ticket with something more dignified. Setting aside the newspaper was a metaphorical setting aside of everything we both knew and need not say in polite conversation.

You're on the edge, Frank, and you're making Eden and me nervous. We own you. I need you to do something for me, and you're going to do it whether you like it or not.

"I've got a problem," Hades began. "It's something I'd usually deal with myself, but seeing you're more skilled at this sort of thing I thought I might entrust it to you. I've been thinking of you almost as part of the family for some time, you know. You're my daughter's partner. It comes easily to me."

Part of the family. Sharing in the secrets. Obligated. Till death do us part.

"What's the problem?"

"I'm being watched. I don't like it."

"Who's watching you?"

"I don't know. I've laid a couple of traps and come up empty. Seen the fucker only once with my own eyes. I know he's around though. I can smell him."

I sat back in my chair.

"Just watching? Nothing else?"

"Nothing yet."

"Why would someone want to watch you?"

Hades gave a small laugh in answer.

I felt stupid. "Okay. What have you seen?"

"A car, a couple of weeks ago. A Commodore, gray. Nothing so brazen since but I feel it going on."

"He a cop?"

"I've been assured he's not."

"Are you assuming he's male?"

"Yes. All I've seen is the car."

"You got cameras out there on the road?"

"I do now. Haven't caught anything."

It had been a long time since I'd been on a case. I was hungry for it.

I reminded myself where I was, who I was talking to.

Hades watched me thinking, sipped his coffee, set it down and looked at it.

"Journalist?"

"They're not usually this persistent."

"Is it a threatening kind of watching or a curious kind of watching?"

"How am I supposed to know a thing like that?"

"It's an instinct, I guess."

Hades was silent for a moment.

"I'd say threatening. Like letting me see the car was a kind of hello. Now there's uncertainty. Worry. It's not a very nice thing to do, even by my standards."

I made like I was considering. Weighing my options. We both knew I had very little choice.

"How much?" I asked.

"Ten grand to start you off, ten grand again when you catch him. Plus expenses."

"I won't be catching anyone for you, Heinrich," I said. "And I'll need to think about this a little. But if I do agree to it I'll tell you who he is and why he's watching you. That's it. You want to hire me as a private investigator, I'll privately investigate. You want an accomplice in whatever you plan to do to him, you can go elsewhere."

"Good enough," the old man smiled. "And please, call me Hades. Everyone else does."

I went silent. A deep discomfort had begun to grow in the top of my stomach, under my ribs, hard like a stone. I knew that nothing short of finding Hades' watcher would shift this ball of anxiety. I was in this now. The mere fact Hades had told me he was being threatened meant I was on the case.

I must have sighed, because Hades laughed as he got out of his chair. He sounded like a man who liked trapping things, watching them bash around the cage.

"Coffee?" he asked.

That evening I was feeling good. A combination of sun exposure, a couple of tall ice-cold beers, and a new project to work on had me pretty upbeat. I sat at the bar in my local with a coaster and pen and began planning how I would tackle Hades' problem. I made a couple of calls, just to be certain that there wasn't a pending investigation, state or federal, that might mean that someone was surveilling Hades. My list of things to do was pretty extensive when someone brushed against my shoulder. I looked up into Eden's eyes as she sat down beside me.

"Jesus, Eden, you're like a bloody stalker."

"Lovely to see you, too."

"What have I done now? I've been an absolute angel today. I didn't trash my place. I went and spoke to Hades. I surrendered to his blackmail with a hand-shake and a polite smile. I've had two beers. Two." I held up two fingers.

"If I had a doggy biscuit I'd give it to you," she said. "I'm here to brief you on the missing girls case. We've been signed up, as predicted by yours truly."

"I've got two sessions with the shrink left yet."

"And you're doing them, back to back, tomorrow morning."

"Oh fuck off."

She nodded to the bartender. "Merlot."

"What do you mean I'm doing them tomorrow morning? You're coming with me, aren't you?"

"I did mine this afternoon after Captain James signed me on."

I exhaled. The tiniest smile crept to the corner of her mouth as she took the wine from the bartender and sipped it.

"I can't believe you'd leave me alone with that woman when you've seen how she bullies me," I said. "You obviously have no regard for my spiritual well-being."

"You're right. I don't."

She took a slim shoulder bag from beside her and brought it to her lap, slapped a manila folder on the furry bar runner in front of us.

"Happy birthday to you."

"Urgh. I'm not doing this on an empty stomach. Can I get you dinner?"

"As long as you don't go telling anyone."

"Oh. Should I take it off Facebook then?"

She smiled wider.

"Relationship status: It's complicated."

She laughed. It was a deep and soft musical laugh, something I'd heard only once or twice since I'd known her. Two or three beats and it was gone. It was thrilling, getting Eden to laugh. Something I imagined circus trainers feel when they get a tiger to stand on its hind legs for the first time.

We moved to a booth and ordered steaks. I accompanied mine with a scotch. I was surprised when Eden slid onto the leather seat beside me. She smelled good. I'd been attracted to Eden when I first met her—she was beautiful and dark like an enchanting witch from a fairy tale, and as with all practiced evil beings she could look like a child in the light of one room, a queen in the next, a she-wolf in the dark. But over our time together the attraction had changed. My fear of Eden, of what she had done and what she was capable of, bound me to her like a magnet. In some ways I wanted to know everything she had done but was afraid of letting her get her claws deeper into me. She was irresistible, like the carnage of a road accident. Something inside me wanted to see the blood, hear the screaming. I wanted to know exactly how bad she was.

"These are our missing girls," Eden said, opening the folder and laying out three photographs.

They could have been sisters but for the tiniest of details—one's nose was a little upturned, one had curly hair, one smiled with big square white teeth while the others brooded. They were all in their late teens or early twenties. One was posing with another girl at what looked like a nightclub, one was sitting on a milk crate smoking a cigarette, one was taking a melodramatic half-profile self-portrait. They were all blond.

I didn't feel anything, not then. I didn't know these girls, and nothing so far told me that they were dead. I sipped my scotch and tried to memorize the faces.

"This is Ashley Benfield. This is Keely Manning. This is Erin Kidd." Eden pointed to the photographs in turn.

"Uh huh."

"Missing sixty-four days, missing thirty days, missing four days."

"Any movement on the bank accounts, online accounts, or phones?"

"No."

"Check the bedroom closets of all their boy-friends?"

"They were all single at the time of going missing." Eden shifted Keely's photograph up above the others. "Last seen leaving her mother's house in Narellan to meet a friend in the city. That was the story, anyway. We've confirmed that she was actually going to Bankstown to get drugs and go on a three-day sex binge. She wasn't a full-time prostitute—she'd get her pimp there to rent her a motel room and she'd take as many customers as she could over the three days. Live off the money for a couple of months."

Keely was the curly-haired one, smoking a cigarette on a milk crate, skinny bare arms curved forward against the cold in a stripy gray and orange hoody. She was a pretty girl under all the makeup. Eden set her photograph aside and put up the photo of the profile shot.

"Ashley was a full-time prostitute," Eden said. "She was couch-surfing between girlfriends' apartments when she slipped through the cracks. No one reported her missing for five days because everyone thought she was somewhere else. Last seen leaving Penrith Panthers alone at midnight after playing the poker machines there for four or five hours. A crew of locals was with her and offered her a ride but she said she wanted to walk."

"Silly girl," I said. I looked at her photograph.

"Now this one," Eden said, moving to the last photograph. "Gave us our most promising lead. Erin was a recreational prostitute. She's been in and out of a few different jobs over the years but she was sleeping with a couple of guys in Camden for rent just before she went missing. She was supposed to have been seen hitchhiking on the Pacific Highway out of Camden four days ago, but we can't confirm that."

Erin was in a nightclub in the photograph, smooshing her face against another girl's for the picture. Her eyes were bright and wild, the pupils huge.

"What's the lead?"

"One of the guys she was sleeping with is Jackie Rye," Eden said, flipping through the folder and extracting another photograph. "Jackie's got a permanent girlfriend, another young girl, but they're on and off again all the time and it looks like Erin might have slipped in there to knock boots with Jackie in the off period. She was only at his farm a short time. Over the past year Keely and Ashley have lived there, too—for a couple of months each. It's the one thing all three girls have in common."

I looked at the photograph of Jackie Rye. It was a mug shot, so the pale, washed-out look was very familiar, the shadows under the eyes and in the deep hollows of his cheeks and the slight yellow tinge to his skin. He was almost bald, a tuft of hair on the very top of his head combed back and the hair at the sides of his head slicked into what might have been a curly ponytail or mullet. His lips were pouty, which suggested to me that he might have been missing teeth.

"What do we know about Super Creep?"

"The usual history of small-time aggressions." Eden slipped a stapled pile of police reports in front of me. "Mostly drunken and drug related. Three sexual assaults and no convictions recorded, all withdrawn before trial."

"This is sounding like a good tip." I flipped through the report. "Except for the fact that he's been a fucking angel for five years now. What? He found God?"

"Came into money. Daddy died and left him the farm."

"What did he say when we pulled him in?"

"Nothing. He hasn't been pulled. No one at the farm has been questioned at all. Best hope is that none of them know we're even looking."

"Why?"

"There are approximately eighty people involved in the day-to-day running of Jackie's farm. It doesn't look like much but it's big business. His costs are low and profits are high. He sells specialty organic meat and other produce to major supermarket chains all over the West. He also makes a lot of cash from housing horses. There are two separate camps of workers with caravans where up to five people live at a time. Here and here." Eden slipped an aerial map from the folder and pointed to two clusters of white blocks in a huge brown wasteland. "People come, and people go. Jackie takes anyone and he's notorious for it. Runaways go there either to work on the farm or to hook up with the farmworkers and share their beds. He's given a new start to plenty of violent criminals, people on the run, laborers looking for money on the side. It's a living, breathing community of deadbeats. It's not as simple as just locking Jackie up, no matter how good he looks for it. All these girls seem to have stayed at Jackie's place long enough to give it as a stable address to their parents. But there's nothing to suggest Jackie himself even knew who Ashley and Keely were, that they were on the property. If we string Jackie up and he's not the killer the whole camp'll know before we have time to put up the fences."

"Okay. So we bring them all in. All eighty."

"You ever tried catching eighty cockroaches at once with your bare hands?"

"You sound like you have a better plan."

"Captain James wants to send me in undercover," she said.

The steaks arrived. Eden shifted to the other bench and began hers. It was rare. She noticed me watching her.

"I'll be fine, Frank."

"What if you have to sleep with someone?"

"That's your first concern? Of course it's your first concern. It's all you think about."

"You've never been undercover. I have. You have to do things to keep your identity. Things you don't want to do."

"I'm sure it was traumatic for you."

"Eden."

"I won't be sleeping with anyone."

"What the hell am I doing while you're in there? Standing outside the fence holding my dick?"

"You'll head the surveillance team."

"Oh, okay. Parked in a van outside the fence holding my dick."

"Frank."

"I don't like this," I said. "Why you and not me? I'd be a lot safer in there than you."

"Why?" she asked.

I was about to tell her that it was because I was a man, but she gave me that look, the hunter's glare, and it halted the words in my mouth. Watching her slice her meat in the soft gold light of the bar, I'd succumbed to her camouflage. Her thin silky fingers, the way she tucked a wave of inky hair behind her ear, revealing the sparkle of a modest diamond. It was all bullshit. She held my gaze for a second or so, showing me the emptiness buried deep in her pupils, and I remembered that I was in the company of something very foreign.

I cleared my throat. "You might be right."

"You get your meeting over early tomorrow morning and I'll get working with the team on an alias. We'll meet at, say, ten?"

"When are you thinking of entering?"

"Tomorrow night."

"This is all happening very fast."

"Spoken like a true commitment-phobe."

I ordered another scotch and she finished her steak. I wasn't very hungry. She reached over and stole a french fry from my plate with the swift, seamless actions of a bird. We small-talked for a while and then she checked the time on her phone like she had somewhere to be. Early in our partnership Eden and I had silently established that despite our opposing sexes and the usual social rules we didn't kiss or hug hello or good-bye. In fact, I rarely touched her. When she left tonight, though, she gave my forearm a couple of little pats and smiled.

I sat with my scotch for a long time wondering what that meant.

Eden liked driving at night. Hades had driven her and her brother through the city in the dark with the windows down in their younger years when they refused to sleep. She liked the shudder of wind through the car and the people creeping along the streets, some dancing and falling, drunk, some strolling arm in arm. She liked the way the city throbbed and glowed like an egg sack nestled in a black cave, writhing with ill-formed life.

Tonight she began the ritual by taking a packet of cigarettes from the glove compartment and lighting one, hanging her elbow out the window. She didn't smoke, didn't hang her elbow out the window of the car usually, but this brought a little of Eric back to her. And lately she didn't feel as though she could continue the night games without him.

She turned up the radio and let her speed drift down ten under the limit, preparing her mind for what was to come. *Do you remember?* Eric would ask her. *Do you remember that night?* Eden wondered sometimes if half the reason she and Eric had let the need control them was to preserve the rage, the fear, the fragmented memories of the night their parents were murdered.

Over the years, some memories had died, but now and then something new came to her—she and her brother crying together in the trunk of the car, the tape muffling their helpless sounds, or words on the wind, pleading, as they were dragged from the house. Gunfire. Maybe Eric had been chasing these memories through all those years of killing, trying to get as much out of that night as he could, as if somehow he could return to it. Change it. Do something. Warn them.

Eden knew that was impossible, but she liked to think about it sometimes. Dream about the woman she might have been if Hades had not saved her, if she had not been reborn a killer. She might have been an artist, she thought. But there was art indeed in what she did now.

She pulled up outside Vinh Lim's apartment block and sat looking at the gold squares of light above her. Life—buzzing around in little boxes aligned toward the sky, people laughing and watching television and cooking dinner and going to bed, blue and white light flickering on chipping vermiculite ceilings. Students, most of them, like Vinh.

She let her eyes rise floor by floor to Vinh's balcony, to the lounge chair where he spent his Sunday afternoons oiling his stocky hairless body and sunbathing, calling other drug dealers on the phone. Because, yes, Vinh was a student, and like most students he had figured out a way to do as little work as possible for maximum returns. But unlike his neighbors, this wasn't through a combination of cash work and government benefits, a little petty theft or kinky massage services—Vinh's family serviced much of Kensington, Kingsford, Rosebery, and Alexandria with ecstasy. Eden had been watching him for a couple of months, intrigued by Vinh's deadly reputation and the combination of this power with his strange obsession.

The first time Eden had been inside Vinh's apartment she came across the obsession accidentally. Vinh had been way down her wish list of potential nighttime playmates—she had bigger and badder targets for her cravings than him—but she'd been passing through and decided to do a little inventory, find out if Mr. Lim was worth her time. If he'd be any fun.

The living room, small kitchen, and guest bathroom were all minimalist, clean, stylish. Chrome, black glass, red velvet. She had wandered into the bedroom and found a huge painting of a Japanese dragon hanging over the bed, inset with mirrors, the ferocity in its design impossible to ignore. Eden had pulled her gloves on and toured at leisure, picking up things, examining them, getting a feel for Vinh. She opened his laptop and went through its video and image files. Nothing interesting.

Her instinct had told her, the first time she had laid eyes on Vinh, that he was worthy of a spot higher on her wish list. That there was more to him. She didn't know what. She and Eric had only ever been interested in other hunters as their prey, and Vinh was just a convenience killer who snuffed out lives to feed his business. In order to fulfill the ritual, in order to bring back the memories, in order to play the game as it had to be played and finally satisfy that bloodthirsty urge inside her, Vinh had to be badder than this. He had to be a true prize. Eden went to the door to the spare bedroom and tried it. The door was locked. She smiled.

The door took a couple of minutes. Eric was the one good with mechanical things—locks, bolts, small machines, gadgets, engines. When she got it open, Eden was confronted first by the eyes in the dark. She switched on the light and looked around.

Stuffed animals. Hundreds of them. There were

ponies and monkeys and piglets and bears, the whimsi-
cal characters of Japanese cartoons, horned and speckled and scaled, staring at her from the floor, shelves,
bed, crowded around the little desk. Eden closed the
door and stood in the center of the room, the main attraction in a packed stadium of stares.

Most of the animals were infants of their species.
Most of them had grossly oversized innocent eyes.
Most of them were undeniably female, a distinction
made merely by a pair of pigtails, a set of eyelashes, a
little tutu Velcro-strapped around a fluffy waist. Some
of them had been altered, their mouths or crotches slit
open and narrow fabric tubes inserted, then re-stitched.
Eden let her eyes wander to the computer in the corner
of the room, the toys sitting there. The favorites. She
went to the computer and switched it on, knowing
even before it began to power up what she was about
to find.

Now, two weeks later, Eden sat looking up at Vinh's
window and remembering the army of toys, the things
she had seen on the screen, the way the light played
about the faces of the toys behind her, the way the
small screams through the speakers seemed to come
from among them. She decided she would line some of
them up around her on the shelves and windowsill of
Vinh's bedroom as she worked on him, let their big
buggy eyes watch.

The lights beyond Vinh's balcony doors flickered
on. Eden got out of the car.

It was always loud in the house of Bear and Caesar. It took a couple of days for Heinrich to get used to it. At night the women danced, sang, giggled, played, and the men wrestled with them and drank. Men came to the door and knocked and hollered—they always seemed happy to see Caesar and a little afraid of Bear, who spent most of his time at the front door, talking quietly and smoking.

Heinrich couldn't sleep for the nightmares about the French Man and for Sunday kicking him in her sleep, so he wandered the house and watched and listened. Everyone seemed to want to feed him as soon as they saw him. He'd never eaten so well in his life. The women, some of them naked all night long and some of them clad in tiny under-pants and corsets, patted his head and kissed him and brought him bags of sweets. His first year there, Heinrich hoarded some of what he received under the bed and in his cupboard in case he got no more, in case someday Bear took him by the collar and put him out on the street as quickly as he had welcomed him in. Heinrich knew never to get com-fortable.

During the day while all the women were asleep, the men workers came. They were skinny and dry and dark-eyed crea-tures, sorting cash into bags, organizing it into packages and tying it with string, talking, and swearing. These men ignored Heinrich. He followed Bear around and tried to make sense of the conversations he heard. He could never predict when the

Silence would come over Bear. One minute he would be talking softly, gently, slowly, and then Caesar would give him a look and he would grab someone by the neck and drag them out of the house. Heinrich watched the violence with fascination. Bear's face was calm, his lips parted, his eyes downcast, as his hands crunched bones and spattered blood up onto his cheeks.

Some nights Bear took Heinrich down the garden path and into the greenhouse, where they sat on wooden stools at the huge wooden table and worked. They potted tiny seedlings for hours together, saying nothing, pinching the little white lives into the rich black soil and lining them up in trays. Sometimes Bear talked and Heinrich listened. The big man got out his heavy, glossy books and pointed out plants he was growing. Heinrich learned their Latin names and when he got them wrong Bear made him say them over and over. Sometimes they sat together and read other books—mechanical manuals and sports magazines and books of poetry. They dived into books about Greek mythology in the summer and Heinrich tried to follow their strange, winding tales, to remember names and gods of things.

Their most important work was harvesting the plants. Some of it was marijuana, which was fairly easy to dry, chop, and package and could be done with careless hands. But Bear's special plants, the plants no one but him was allowed to touch, took a lot of training to handle correctly. All of them were deadly. They harvested cassava root for concentrated cyanide, Abrusprecatorius for abrin poison, Ageratinaaltissima for milk poison.

Heinrich didn't know what Bear did with the hundreds of tiny bottles of deadly potions but he loved the exacting art of dissecting the root bulbs, milking the seeds, boiling Cerberaodollam down into a dry powder and mixing it into spices. In the early days, when Heinrich's hand and wrist were still strained from the killing of the French Man, the boy merely watched and marveled at how such huge coarse fingers could reap such meticulous work. As the weeks passed, Bear began to give him assignments. Later he often left his apprentice alone to work while he smoked and chatted in the garden.

The only thing Heinrich didn't like about the house of Caesar and Bear was the girl named Sunday, who was always within arm's reach. She would wander in the garden behind the house, pouting and sighing and yelling abuse at them. But Bear never gave in, never let her so much as watch their business in the greenhouse. He said that a woman with Sunday's kind of temper let loose with the means to kill could bring the very world to its knees.

Heinrich didn't know what that meant, nor did he really consider Sunday a woman, but he followed Bear's rules and didn't tell Sunday anything about their lessons, even the ones that weren't about the plants. At night when he tried to sleep, curled at the very edge of the thin mattress they shared, she was constantly whispering, half teasing him and half pleading for some crumb of information on Bear and what he'd talked about that night. Heinrich didn't like Sunday, but sometimes he felt sorry for her. Most nights she cried in her sleep, called out for her mother, and he did his best to ignore it.

Whenever Bear and Heinrich would go on a "trip," Sunday would want to come along. Today was no different. Bear was there, standing over the bed the two children shared before the sun had risen, as he had done dozens of times before, his enormous frame outlined in the pale silver of the dawn waking outside the windows. Heinrich jolted awake. Sunday sat up beside him and rubbed her eyes.

"Five minutes," Bear said, cocking his head. Heinrich rolled out of bed as the big man disappeared.

"Tell him to take me," Sunday said.

"No."

"I'm coming." She grabbed her dress, a yellow and white floral frock that was far too big for her, and wriggled into it. Heinrich tugged on his shirt. "I'll be ready in just five seconds."

"No," Heinrich repeated. "It's too scary for you. You're only a girl."

"I'm ten times braver than you are."

"Forget about it."

"I'm coming."

"No, you're not."

"Will you guys shut the hell up?" someone yelled from the shadows. Groans and the creaking of bedsprings. Sunday slapped his arm. It stung.

"Yeah, Heinrich. Shut up."

Bear passed the doorway, eclipsing it for an instant. Heinrich ran after him. Sunday weaved her hand with his, squeezed his fingers.

"Come on," she begged.

"Sunday, get back to bed before I clobber you," Bear grunted.

They walked out to the car. The unmown grass at the front of the house was wet with dew. The moon hung, a white eye, over the terrace rooftops of Darlinghurst. The car door opening was like a gunshot in the crisp silence.

The man and the boy drove off, leaving the girl standing on the lawn. Bear lit a cigarette, steering with his knees.

"Women," he said.

They drove to a house in Surry Hills. It was a small brick hovel set back from the street and hidden at the front by *unflowering bottle brushes and weeds as tall as Heinrich's shoulders.*

"Got your whomping stick?" Bear asked. Heinrich lifted the short wooden club Bear had made him from the lower half of a piano leg and waved it in the air. The man took a step back and kicked in the door.

Bear didn't usually carry a gun. He said they made him nervous. When they entered the little house the Bear Man simply stood in the doorway to the living room with his hands by his side and hollered. A woman began screaming, gripping her hair. Her robe had fallen open and her breasts oozed out like deflated balloons. Heinrich felt his heart pumping in his neck.

"Samuel Pritchard!" Bear yelled.

"Oh Jesus, Bear, please. I was coming round today," said a wide-eyed, skinny man in the corner of the room. The man reminded Heinrich of a frilled-neck lizard. His shoulders were all bone and skin, his jaw wide and flat and flapping with desperation.

"Today is here," Bear said. "I want Caesar's money."

"I was going to come today and talk to Caesar, Bear, I swear to God . . ."

"Caesar's done talking. Pay me."

"I swear to God!"

"Pay . . . me . . ."

"Bear, please!"

Bear looked down at Heinrich. The boy had been waiting for the look. He took his whomping stick to the nearest window and lifted it high over his shoulder. The window exploded in a shower of glass. The woman screamed again and another man got to his feet.

"Hey! This is my house!"

"Pay me, Samuel," Bear said.

"I can't pay today. Bear, please listen to me?"

Bear nodded to the boy again. He went to another window and obliterated it. The glorious, glittery, smashy noises awakened something in the boy. He felt his limbs twitching. It was hard to breathe. He giggled a little, felt rage burning behind his eyes.

"Pay me," Bear said.

"Now, wait just a minute. He doesn't own this place. Get him out of here."

"Help!" the woman screamed. "Help!"

"I can't . . . I don't have . . ."

Bear nodded at the boy. He went to a wall hutch that was littered with dirty plates, cups, mugs. Heinrich smashed everything, whomping and whomping, glass and porcelain chips spraying on his shoulders and neck and hair. Fragments of china scattered at his feet. Shelves came down with a crash. He laughed, and the sound was unfamiliar to him. It was a guttural sound, like a cough.

"You're next, Sam," Bear said.

"I don't have anything to give you, Bear. I don't have anything!"

"One last chance."

"Please, just . . ."

Bear nodded at the boy and the Silence came over him. It was a warm and soft enveloping silence, like a hug—although it had been years since anyone had hugged the boy. The boy floated in it, his head lolling and eyes rolling, drifting on a summery wind. He was breathing in and out, and the whomping stick was rising and falling, and that was all he knew. The thing that broke the Silence was Bear's hand gathering up a handful of his shirt back and dragging him into the present.

The air was cold in his lungs, and he was heading toward the door of the house, and dozens of people were staring at him from the couch, the walls, the stairs, the street outside.

"Did I do good, Bear?" the boy gasped. The whomping stick was wet with blood.

"Maybe too good, little soldier," Bear said. "Man can't pay us if he's dead."

They went to the car, got in, and the big man tore away from the curb.

"Boy," he said after a time. Heinrich lay the whomping stick on his thighs and looked up at the big man beside him. "Boy, I want to ask you a question. And it's important, okay? You're not in trouble, I just, I want to know. You know?"

"Sure, Bear."

"Before that night when I found you," Bear said, looking at the windscreen. "That night when the French Man came. Did you . . . ? Have you ever killed anyone before?"

Heinrich settled in his seat, looked at the dashboard.

He could remember some things, but not all. The Night of Fire and Screaming flashed around him, yellow and white, and he saw again the faces of the man and the woman in the windows. He remembered tears on his face—could feel them with the fingers of one hand. In the other hand he felt a small paper box, shook it inside the dream and felt the matchsticks rattle.

Bear watched the boy as he sat dreaming.

"I was only playing," the boy said.

It was sunset before Eden got to the road. Or Eadie, as she would now be known. Only the gold of a forgotten day lit the horizon, but the dirt beneath her feet was still warm. As she trudged along, huge brown lizards slid away warily from the sound of her into the long grass. The pack on her back had been messily stuffed with clothes and felt lopsided, and high into the rib bones in her back a drink bottle or deodorant can protruded, rubbing up and down. She'd walked for five kilometers in the setting sun and a healthy stink was rising from her, which was good. It would all add to the story of the lonely woman feeling lost.

Frank had stopped, stared, and then laughed when he saw her undercover getup that morning. The team had shopped at the local thrift shop, buying flannel shirts and cotton tank tops, faded jeans, and cargo pants, and some of the female staff had gone for a jog in the station gym wearing the collection to produce a bag of unwashed, scrappy clothes. A makeup artist had been hired to bleach her long black hair badly, leaving a good four or five centimeters of regrowth, and she'd dried the ends until they frayed and split. Her eyelashes were taken down a couple of shades to dull down Eden's dark, exotic look, her eyebrows were dyed, her long nails were clipped, and she was encouraged to chew a couple so they wouldn't look so deliberate.

Eden didn't mind this treatment. She was thinking about the kind of person Eadie Lea would be. She stood in her flip-flops and shorts and her moth-eaten tank top and let them admire their work while her mind wandered. Finally, they swapped her BlackBerry for an old scratched-up Nokia, gave her a used wallet with her new identity cards and receipts and coffee vouchers, bought her a packet of Winnie Blues and a lighter. They told her she had been born again.

When she was about to leave, Captain James asked if she was going to give Frank a good-bye hug. It would be a while before she would see him again. The team, nervous and fearful around her at the best of times, paused with measured awkwardness. Frank didn't look overly enthused, either. When she wrapped an arm around his neck he squeezed her close, and laughed a little in her ear.

"We'll be watching," he said.

She supposed Frank was watching now as she walked, but she couldn't know that for certain. Over the coming week, there would be no way of telling when he was watching and when he wasn't—there would be no earpieces, no radio or phone contact, no secret meetings the way there were in the movies. Eden was equipped with five different cameras. She wore one as a short pendant around her neck, a pinhole device disguised in a patterned teardrop made from silver. The other four—hidden in a tin drink bottle, in a deodorant can, a book, a pair of sunglasses—were to be set up somewhere in her new life. On Monday morning she'd get the train back into the city under the pretense of attending to some business and change all the batteries. Until then, she was on her own. She wouldn't know if she was doing well, if she'd uncovered something connected to the missing girls, if she was heading down the wrong road. She'd only know when she met the team on Monday.

Eden walked, her head down. There was a lot of pressure on her.

She reached the gates of Jackie Rye's farm just as the skin on the sides of her feet gave up and white and pink blisters emerged. Eden hadn't owned any flip-flops in her other life. She bent down, took the flip-flops off, and hooked them on her fingers, walking carefully on the rocky clay.

Almost as soon as she breached the rickety wooden boundary three huge mixed-breed dogs bounded toward her, emerging on the horizon as wavering shapes hovering above the land with their speed. They surrounded her, a rabble of howling, growling mongrels, dancing in the dirt. She walked on. At the crest of a soft hill she came into the view of a group of men standing by an open-bed SUV. Big men. They watched, emotionless, as she approached, like hairy mannequins hung with filthy rags. They were near a shed with a leaning bar that was lined with brown beer bottles.

Eadie stopped.

"Jackie here?"

One of the men flicked his head toward a group of caravans clustered at the bottom of the hill. Eadie walked on. The men's eyes followed her.

Lamps were lit and moths and mosquitoes were gathering in the gloomy light. When she reached the first caravan she listened but there was no sound. Eadie heard laughter from the next van. She stood outside it for a minute or so and tried to think about the sort of things normal people said and did, the way they looked at each other and the way they moved. Because that was what frightened her most in the end—constructing Eadie Lea as a believable human first and the kind of person who would fit in around Jackie and his friends. She knew she came off a little strange in real life, because she was different, because her true nature, the killer, the monster, was rarely far from the surface.

Eadie stood in the dark outside Jackie Rye's caravan and listened to *The Simpsons* playing on a television inside, people laughing and talking, and forks scraping on cheap china plates. She breathed, then reached forward, knocked, and pulled open the screen door.

The room was full of smoke. That was the first thing that hit her—lots of people wedged into the half-dark smoking cigarettes, which created a coiling ceiling blanket in hues of royal blue and sunflower yellow lit by the television in the corner. Her eyes wandered over two creatures sharing a tiny foam and crushed-velvet couch by the kitchen counter, one lying in the lap of the other, hairy and thin and pig-eyed in a way that left them sexless to the casual observer. Eadie noticed other sets of eyes in the dark, bodies stretched on the floor in the space between the couch and the wall, crammed in and around a plastic deck chair in a corner, lying on the bunk bed in the tiny annex bedroom. The last pair of eyes she found belonged to Jackie Rye, who was sitting in a green velvet recliner by the sink, looking back at her through the smoke he exhaled.

Jackie gave Eadie the impression of an emaciated king, the way he was lounging with one leg up over the arm of the chair and the other flopped on the floor, leaving his tiny worn shorts draping open, the darkness in the thigh holes blessedly impenetrable. Everything about him suggested dark hair and wet skin, spent bodily needs and unwashed crevices. His saggy upper lip stretched as she made eye contact and he lifted and adjusted a sweat-stained cap on his head.

"What's this? A visitor?"

"Jackie?"

"Who's asking?"

"I'm Eadie." Eadie shifted her weight from one foot to the other, scratched her scalp. "Some guys sent me down here looking for you?"

"You found me," Jackie said. "You must be after a bed."

"Yeah."

"Well, baby, this ain't no fucking hotel."

Everyone in the room laughed. The impression was alarming. Nine or ten sets of almost identical hacking laughter, forced laughter, going off like two-stroke motors all around her. Eadie held her ground. The laughter drained away and Jackie began again, relishing, it seemed, every minute chuckle. Eadie got the impression that people around here laughed at Jackie's jokes a lot.

"All right, everybody get out."

They left, one by one, uncurling themselves, rolling, sliding, extracting limbs that had been wedged between milk crates, out from under shelves, from between the limbs of others. Eadie stood aside and watched them go. On their way out, one of the sexless twins stopped and stared and licked his or her teeth as he or she looked over Eadie's backpack, even reaching out once and grabbing the bag and shaking it to hear if it rattled. They all smelled. Soap and water couldn't combat the endless stink of their lives—sheets that never saw a washing machine, animals that left their smells on couches and pillows, sex that was had haphazardly up against things, the reek ignored, blended in, absorbed. Eadie thought she was alone with Jackie until a tiny voice called from the dark beside his recliner and she saw the shape of a young girl sitting there.

"You're pretty, aye," the girl said. Eadie followed the words with the exact same thought about the girl, so for a moment she felt as though her thoughts had been laid bare. The girl was swimming somewhere in that glorious period between puberty and late teens, everything about her milky and soft, with an impish pointy nose that she probably hated and elf ears that curved forward a little too much, the big round eyes of a newborn rabbit. She was wearing what looked like a cotton shift in royal blue, braless and pantyless, flushed from the heat.

"Thanks." Eadie cleared her throat.

"Siddown," Jackie said. Eadie shifted some sheets and pillows aside and sat on the couch where the twins had been. It was damp. "How'd you hear about this place?"

"I been staying with some girls I know in Wauchope. I was in Cronulla before that with my husband. I'm just trying to get away for a bit, maybe get some money behind me before going up north. I'm kind of . . . laying low, you know?"

"Laying low? From him?"

"Yeah."

"Punched on, were ya?"

"Little bit."

"Got any sprogs?"

"Nup."

"Lucky."

"Yeah."

Jackie sucked in that flappy lip and chewed it, let his eyes wander until they settled on her breasts. Eadie scratched her upper arm, covering them, then let her arm fall.

"Well, look, it's pretty crowded round here right now."

"Aww please, Jackie, let her stay," the girl whined. The small man reached out and shoved her head the way a man might shove away a dog.

"No one fucken asked you."

"I'm a hard worker. I've done some track work in the city. I'm best with horses but I can do other things. I learn fast."

"Most of the girls here don't work that way," Jackie said.

Eadie could feel Frank watching, his presence in the room like a heat hanging about her shoulders and the back of her neck. She reached up and fondled the pendant camera, remembered what it was, and dropped it.

"My girlfriends told me sometimes you make an exception."

"Hey," Jackie laughed, throwing open his hands. "Doesn't bother me how you make your living. But you decide you're gonna work for me and then you start sharing that pussy around, you understand those boys who employ you gotta pay me for the labor I'm losing. You either work for me on whatever I put you to, whether it's horses or whatever I got going, or you work for them boys and they pay me for the privilege. Most likely, you won't get a day into straight work before one of these boys puts you in his bed. But I find out you're freelancing that tight round ass and I'm not getting what's owed and I'll have you out on it before you can spit."

"I'm good for my word."

"Word's as good as shit round here."

The girl leaped from where she was crouched, onto the couch beside Eadie. She was all arms and hands and cold fingers, hugging and molesting Eadie's hair and neck in a flurry of affection. Eadie felt sick.

"Oh, I can't wait for us to be friends," the girl said, gathering Eadie's ponytail and curling it around her fingers. "Jackie, baby, can she live here with us?"

"No. I got enough mess here as it is. Take her to the empty van near Pea's, and tell Pea to take her out in the morning. And don't you fucken come back 'til my show's over. Sick of your noise."

Eadie tried to pick up her bag but the girl had it. *The Biggest Loser*'s opening credits had begun and Jackie turned up the volume until it was painful. It was a relief to be out in the night, despite the heat, which met Eadie's face like a hot breath.

"I'm Skylar," the girl said, letting her hand trail down Eadie's arm and into her hand. "I'll show you everything."

I wasn't really expecting to find anything the next night when I set out for Utulla to catch Hades' watcher. I spent the night before and all that day near Rye's Farm, cooped up in a van parked behind a liquor store in Camden with a tall, gangly ginger bloke named Juno, one of those 100 percent gingers so speckled and spotty and orange all over he was fascinating to look at. Hipster glasses with thick black frames and an unkempt flame-orange beard. Juno fit into the van the way a spider might fit into a straw, all joints and thin limbs tucked in toward his center, fingers clicking and tapping, sensing vibrations in the string and things near to his grasp.

It was clear to me within minutes that Juno was new to our station and had never done much for the force other than tech work. For one thing, he was constantly going on about how "hot" Eden was, even in her feral down-and-out camouflage. He talked about all the gear littered around the van, the cameras and monitors and radios and laptops, like they were his impressive and successful friends. I got sick of his jabbering midway through the night and wandered into the liquor store just for something to do. The Jack Daniel's pre-mixers I bought were from the back of the fridge and painfully, gloriously cold in the summer night. All we were doing was watching Eden sleep anyway, in her unnaturally still and silent and beautiful way. I got out of there before Juno started sketching her in charcoal.

* * *

Juno was useful for the techy little iPad-looking thing he lent me, a flat-panel computer no bigger than my palm that had an infrared display. I planned to use it to catch the watcher. He gave me instructions in about ten thousand words more than were necessary, so I was pretty confident I'd be all right.

It was weird driving the company car on a job without Eden. I wondered if all this restlessness might have been a strange kind of longing now that Eden was nowhere that she could hassle me and intrude in my life. Eden being away meant that I was thinking about her, trying to fill the empty spot in the car with some vision of her and what she'd do and say and think as we drove along. This was awful, because it meant I was thinking about Eden all on my own, without prompting. I didn't want to be the kind of cop who thought about his female partner when she wasn't around, whether it was romantic or not. It's a sure sign of weakness—and weakness leads to addiction.

At the entrance to the wide dirt road that led to the Utulla dump I veered off and hid the car on the edge of an embankment. I stripped down to my black tank top and cargo pants and made sure my boots were laced tight. I tucked some small binoculars, a 9mm, the tracking device, my mobile phone, and a pair of handcuffs into the various pockets of my oversized pants.

Without much of a plan I walked toward the dump. Eden was the one who organized our operations. She would think about things for long quiet hours, sleep on it if she had to, draw maps and calculate approaches and write up contingencies. I like to wing it most of the time. Sometimes just turning up somewhere and hanging around, chatting to local store owners or ordering a coffee and reading the paper in the general vicinity of wrongdoing can throw up some useful clues.

Hades had seen his stalker once, in a car on the road to the dump, but the other times had simply "felt" that someone was hanging around. I wanted to know how easy it was to see Hades in his shack from the road. I wanted to know what it took to sit out here for lonely hours watching, just how dedicated this guy would have to be, what he hoped to see.

I had a sweat going before I got far. I stuck to the mud tracks in the road to muffle the sound of my boots and glanced up at the stars, which were blazing like pinholes of lightning between the dense canopies of the trees that lined the road. There was no moon to speak of and now and then animals rustled and scampered in the blackness around me. Things seem farther in the dark. I reached the end of the road, where Hades had seen the car, in about twenty minutes. My hair was slick with sweat and the tank top clung to my stomach. I crouched by the gates and took out my binoculars, had a look at Hades' shack. I could see the kitchen, but there was no Hades. A slice of curtain or something, bright green. I watched. In time Hades walked into the kitchen, sat where I assumed he always sat at the table facing the door, and read his newspaper. It was the briefest flash of stern face, gray hair, collar. Then he was gone.

I let the binoculars drop. What was the point of all this? The experience of seeing Hades there had been exhilarating, I had to admit that. It was a cheap thrill, though. He didn't know I was there, and that gave me a little zing in a very simple, ironic way. After the thrill wore off, he was just a scary old crim no different to plenty of scary old crims I'd come across in my career.

Whoever was after Hades wasn't feeding his curiosity to endure the sweat, the patience, the physical discomfort required to stalk the old man out here all alone in the bush. It was fury, that fuel. Real fury burns low and strong, sometimes for years, but the explosion potential is always there. I knew this from years of looking down at the mangled bodies of unfaithful lovers, abusive fathers, overly successful sisters, those who had ignored a quiet fury for too long, until it got out of control, turned, and came back to bite them.

I set myself another hour to wander in the bush. In time I came across an old shack and walked up onto the porch to have a look. Inside were two bare desks and empty bookshelves, a couple of couches covered with sheets. I wondered if this had been some kind of teenagers' retreat in Eden and Eric's old days here. I tried the door. It was locked. Above the porch steps hung a hand-carved fairy windchime, its slender body intricately chiseled from beechwood and strung with a collection of mismatched bells that tinkled when I reached up and touched it. I turned the fairy in my hands and noticed a single word, "Eden," carved into one of her dragonfly wings.

I sat on the porch and pulled out the device Juno had given me, set it on my knee, and waited for it to power up. The thing worked like a GPS, gave me a colorful layout of the land constructed by Google Maps and a blue ball telling me where I was. The highway out to the Utulla dump loaded, along with the dirt track and the dump grounds illustrated in a pleasant stone gray. The map adjusted as it found my position and the blue ball began to radiate waves on the screen. I was alone in the shapeless green wonderland of the bush around the dump.

But in the middle of the Utulla dump a red dot was glowing. I tapped the screen and a bubble emerged with some data and a phone number. The device was triangulating Hades' phone. Right. Now, all I had to do was see who else was around.

To the north, just off the highway, was another red dot. It was stationary. I tapped the dot and found the number for the mobile phone my device was detecting. I hit the arrow alongside the number and a web page opened. John's Tire Lot. Of course. I'd seen it on my way in. I wandered and played with the device. Two more businesses up on the road were blinking their presence. I shifted the map around and looked out to the east. Nothing.

I walked along the barbed-wire fence separating the bushland from the dump and fiddled with the device's settings. West, nothing. South, nothing. It was kind of fun, watching my progress on the screen, an insignificant blue bubble rolling along the earth, surrounded by a few other idle blobs and, as I widened the map, dozens and then hundreds of others. I found my car on the map, another red bubble, giving off a signal. My mobile. I stopped walking and chewed my lip. Then I slid my hand into my pocket. My mobile was there.

I walked faster and, as I did, whoever was giving off

the red bubble at my car seemed to sense this new awareness and began to move. I shoved the tracking device into my pocket and ran. I was back at my car within minutes. There was no sign of the watcher.

I pulled out the device and looked for him. The red dot was moving toward the east, winding a diagonal path through the bush to the highway. My car had spooked him. I tapped the bubble and a window emerged, but the number was replaced by a series of dots. I pocketed the device and took off.

The embankment was steep. The thin fingers of bracken clawed at my bare arms. I stopped, held my breath, listened. I couldn't tell if the sounds I heard were footsteps or my own breath. Ahead through the trees glowed the orange lights of the highway. Something passed before them. I stood still. The voices of the insects fell and there was a strange warm silence.

I was aware of the watcher's presence behind me and to my right, half a second before he swung at my head. I ducked and his fist glanced off my ear. In those first frenzied seconds I remember thinking how rude that was, how cowardly to try and clock me without even saying hello. I spun and ducked and threw myself at his legs. He was all taut limbs and rock-hard fingers and pointy elbows in the dark.

We wrestled, teeth glancing off skin, and bones jolting with more accidental luck than real strategy. It was pure chance that my gun slid out of my back pocket and the light from the highway hit it just right so that he saw it and I didn't. The man in the dark lifted the gun above his shoulder and clubbed me in the face with it. I sprawled in the wet earth.

"One guard dog ain't enough, uh, bro?" The man laughed. He dropped the gun beside my head and stepped over me.

It was light by the time I got off my ass. I don't know how long I sat on the embankment in the dark with my face in one hand and my gun in the other, blood running between my fingers and down my wrist, trying to come to full consciousness. Whenever I tried to get up I swayed, and I wasn't game to lie down in case I passed out. So I just sat there breathing and thinking about what I should do next.

I went back to the car and took out a notepad. I wrote down everything I could remember about the watcher in the dark. Tall. Wiry. All bones. What felt like short, hard hair in a shaven Afro. A sort of Aboriginal-sounding inflection to the end of his phrase. *One guard dog ain't enough, uh, bro?* Then I put the notepad away and drove in to work.

I woke up at around five in the afternoon, the grossly clean bedroom full of pink light, my phone vibrating under my shoulder.

I took the call with my notepad on my knee and my pen moving slow, crookedly. I was getting old. Once upon a time I could get in a good punch-up and carry on for days like a kid with scraped knees, never slowing, the pain becoming part of every moment until suddenly it was gone, as though it had never been.

Gina at the station gave me three names living in the Sydney metro area that matched the partial print from my gun. From them, I picked the guy who was identified as Indigenous Australian on his criminal record, short wiry hair, bony, previous assault charge. Gina was good for squeezing things through the lab that should have been placed in the queue, things that didn't need to be written down in the logbook or explained to bosses. Some women, you just have to give them a look. They're the kind of women who had good fathers. I sat for a minute and thought about sleep, staring at the name on the paper, the man who'd hit me.

The Watcher. Adam White.

I'm coming for you, Adam, I thought.

Eadie slept little. She'd lived in places like Jackie's farm before, when she was growing up at the dump and for a couple of months during her specialist training—city-limit places where the air was thinner and colder than it should have been and carried sounds for miles. A cough would reach her as she stood at the window looking out at the yellow lights, even though her caravan was away from the clusters of others. It was up against a fence, nestled in overgrown weeds and grass that for all manner of creatures probably acted as ladders up to the badly sealed window in the filthy kitchenette. The cough could have come from anywhere. There was laughter out there, too, and the lowing of cows in the first light hours.

Inside the caravan things crawled and crept and shuffled about. Eadie lay in the damp sheets as the sun was rising, watching some elongated grasshopper-like insect wander across the chipboard ceiling, feelers out exploring, touching mold spots and lumps of dried toilet paper hurled there. Cigarette-stain clouds spread out before it like burned wastelands. She wondered if it could fly. She didn't want to crush it but would if it pushed its luck.

She heard the girl, Skylar, coming at a sprint across the barren dirt. Sounded like she jumped on the foldout stairs. Eadie was tying up her hair.

"Breakfast is on and you're gonna miss it."

"Yeah yeah," Eadie called.

The girl came bumbling in, child on Christmas morning. Dust-covered pink Uggies and a denim miniskirt. Eadie hadn't realized how oddly shaped she was, short and nimble but somehow layered with pale milk baby fat on her thighs and above her breasts. Cellulite under the skirt. Bad diet begun long ago. Something to grope in the dark. The peachy face and rabbit eyes were beaming with curiosity beneath layers of unnecessary makeup. Eadie imagined Jackie spooning the girl in his gray-stained bed.

"Heard from the ex?"

She was straight to the drama, this one.

"No."

"Rude."

"It's a bit of a rude business." Eadie pulled on a denim jacket and stood looking at her chewed nails. The girl was going through her things, taking the sunglasses from the counter and trying them on like a bored kid in Daddy's big office. Eadie took the glasses.

"Do you want this?" Eadie held up the deodorant can with the camera embedded in its base. "Gives me a rash."

The girl took the canister, smelled its tip.

"Mmm, yum. Thanks." She bounced on the bed. "So what happened with your ex? Tell me everything. Was he sleeping around? My ex was. Some short slut from his work. Fat, too. I mean I'm short but I ain't fat. This bitch was like your reflection in a car door. Fucken wide."

"Cushion for the pushin'," Eadie said.

"Yeah, man. I mean, honey, you gonna trade in? *Upgrade,* for fuck's sake."

Eadie smiled. A girl child talking about exes like a

seasoned housewife from the North Shore. She couldn't know how ridiculous she sounded.

"Men are idiots."

"So?" The girl pulled her leg up, exposing floral undies in the hollow of the skirt, settling in for a deep-'n'meaningful. Truth or dare.

"Oh, you know," Eadie said. "Let's go get this breakfast."

"Oh."

"It's too early for this. Really. Trust me. It's a pathetic story, hardly the sort of intrigue you're imagining."

"The what?"

"Nevermind."

"All right then." Skylar jumped up and pulled down her skirt, seemed to want to do a little dance but, because of the limited space, settled for an enthusiastic stamp of her boots like a soldier marking time. "Sorry, I talk too much. I'm just excited, you know? It's been ages since I've had a mate out here."

"You do talk too much," Eadie said. She held open the door. "But that's all right. You can do the talking for the both of us. You can be the company rep."

"The company rep." Skylar laughed too hard, mouth open, teeth like a sheep, some missing in the back. "Yeah, that's me."

The meal sheds were little more than a pair of flimsy aluminum carports touching unevenly in the middle. They were concreted into the barren earth, surrounded by dry white dog feces. The dogs rushed out to welcome them as they headed across the plain, a three-legged kelpie, some half-dingoes, and a collection of scruffy rat-dogs.

Several heads turned as she approached. The groups were oddly segregated by sex. Some women in ragged Kmart sweaters and Ugg boots were smoking around a wooden picnic table, a two-liter Coke bottle swaying between hands. In the group of men Eadie recognized the androgynous twins from the night before, one staring at her, heavy browed, the other picking its nose. Blue smoke leaked from the men's table. Skylar grabbed a paper plate and passed one to Eadie. She loaded it with a pair of black chalk-like sausages and reached for the bread.

Plenty of eyes on her. None of them Jackie's. She wondered where he was. A plastic kettle stood at the end of the table, a box of coffee sachets, tea bags, sugar packets lumped together in a Tupperware container. All of them McDonald's brand. Someone had done a smash and grab at the local.

Eadie turned to ask Skylar if she wanted a coffee and found a rock-hard male chest where the girl's face had been. Eadie looked up into a leathered face, jewel eyes peeking from beneath a scarecrow fringe of sun-scorched blond. Trucker cap, bright yellow. Eadie took it all in and went back to her coffee.

"You're new," he said.

"I am."

"You're hot." The bigger man hooked a finger around her ponytail, let the blond hair slither through. "Wanna date?"

"I'm here as a laborer."

"You're funny."

"No, really," Eadie said.

"What's your name?"

"Does it matter?"

"Does to me."

"Eadie."

"Eadie. Cute. Greedy Eadie, stealing all my sugar packets. Keeping those fine round titties for the horses and the pigs. What a fucking tease."

Eadie didn't smile. She slapped the sugar packets in her hand to loosen the old grains. The man reached around her to take the Tupperware container. They were wedged between two foldout tables, nowhere to go. Eadie ignored the cock against her hip. The casual brush of her ponytail as he righted himself.

"Pass the milk?"

Eadie slid the jug over. His hand grabbed at it, her fingers, entrapped them in his own. She shook him off. Laughter from behind her at the men's table.

"You didn't ask my name. How rude."

Eadie let out a sigh, staring at the kettle, waiting for it to reboil. She worried a nail with her teeth.

"It's Nick."

"Good on you."

"Let's think of some things that rhyme with Nick."

"Let's not." Eadie poured. Watched the water fall on the old coffee without encouraging the black grounds to mix at all, water on dirt. She thought of her new espresso machine at home, the five grand she paid for it, the manual it'd come with and the chapters explaining how to get the perfect crema, how to make sure the press didn't scorch the powder. The smell of it. Eadie scraped at the coffee with her plastic spoon.

"Let's just have coffee and get to work."

"What a bitch of a thing to say." Nick licked his lips. "I'm only playing games. I give you a compliment and you just brush it off. Who are you?"

"I'm someone who doesn't like games." Eadie smiled, turned around, found herself almost pressed against him. The heat of his body enveloped her. Too much Lynx, not enough soap. He smiled back and reached for the kettle. His hard groin pressed against hers. She bore it without stiffening, without letting her eyes leave his own. She thought of thrusting her hand up, knocking the cup into his face. It was almost as if he was tempting her to. His eyes through the steam. Challenging.

"Well, you come tell me when you want to learn how to play, Greedy Eadie."

Approaching the table where Skylar had settled was very much like the first day of high school. At least she'd had Eric to walk her onto the barren grounds of Utulla High and see that she got to the right classroom, but when recess came around she'd been alone in the jungle for the first time, and the loss was aching. She remembered the groups of children sitting hunch-backed against the wind, making mounds of wrappers and apple cores and orange skins in the center of circles like witches swapping runes, laughing, throwing things, trading and comparing cards.

Eden was aware of being a misfit from the first moment, as she stood beside the door to the classroom, trying to find a slot. She'd watched for a while and then gone back inside where her teacher was sorting piles of assignments on her desk. An adult. Someone like Hades who would look down at her, guide her with a steady hand on her shoulder.

She had crept to the back of the room and sat there a good ten minutes, watching the sorting and the sighing before Mrs. Daniels noticed her and ushered her back outside into the turmoil.

"It's important to fit in, Eden," the teacher had said. "Here, let me find you a buddy."

Eadie supposed that Skylar was her buddy now, even though the girl hardly seemed at ease with the others at the table, sitting at arm's length on the end of the bench, eating a sausage with her fingers. Eadie toyed with the camera pendant. Frank was there, too, she supposed, though she couldn't hear him, the way he broke into any kind of tension with a joke, taking the self-deprecation in exchange for the comfort of others. Eadie sat next to Skylar in the cigarette smoke and sipped her coffee. One of the girls was illustrating an argument, standing with one leg up on the bench on the other side, waving her arms.

"I said you can have him. You fucking take him, ya mongrel."

"Mongrel bitch," someone confirmed.

"You know what she's like. Ain't the first time. Ain't be the last. Fucking lunch-cutter."

"What pacifically did she say'd gone on?"

"Aw, just that she'd been there watching a fucking DVD. Thinks I came down in the last rain. I did so much for that bitch. I gave her everything."

"So what then? Did ya have a go?"

"Did I have a go."

Laughter. The plastic bottle was passed around, but not to Eadie. She watched it, smelling the bourbon. She perked up a little, listened to the retelling of the story about the fight. This, at least, was something she understood. Violence. Brutality. Skylar offered her a cigarette and she took it, lit it in cupped palms. It was years since she'd smoked. The wind was carrying desert heat across the farm, already baking the morning. Soon Uggs would be replaced by flip-flops, sun for shade. A fly, in her hair, waved away, back again on her temple. The dogs at their feet, snapping, growling at each other.

Eadie sat on the edge of the bench with Skylar for a good ten minutes before the conversation ebbed. Eyes on her. She flicked the ash from her cigarette onto the ground, watched it fall.

"Is this Nick's new root?"

"No," Skylar said. "Eadie's working with Pea."

"Jesus, you've got your priorities screwed up, girl," someone laughed. "I'd rather be bent over Nick than a pile of horse shit."

"What's her name?"

"Eadie," Skylar answered.

"I weren't talking to you."

"Eadie," Eadie said, glancing up.

"Girl, you'll change ya mind, or Nick'll change it for ya. Ashley's been gone what, two weeks now? Man's got to be horny as fuck. Two weeks is ten years in a man's world."

"Horny as, mate," someone agreed.

Ashley, the missing girl. Eadie tried to keep her expressions neutral, disinterested.

"Yeah, maybe," Eadie said. She tapped her cigarette out on the edge of the table. A woman approached, short and round all over, shoulders sloping to fat-coated arms and hands, calves that would never fit boots. She was wearing ex-army coveralls, the epaulets and name bar torn off with only the crest remaining. Her black curls were pinned behind her ears and under glasses with taped frames. A face like a bronze moon, down-turned, creased with hard years.

Everyone looked. Fell into silence.

"This her?" The woman flicked her dimpled chin at Eadie.

"Sure is." Skylar leaped up, standing upright like a soldier presenting a prisoner to a commandant. Eadie swung off the bench and rose to her full height, a good forty-five centimeters above the stocky Pea.

"Well, let's go." She gave Eadie a look up and down and spat in the dirt. "Ain't got all fucking morning."

Heinrich looked forward to the dogfights every month, sitting on the back porch and watching the men wrestle the animals and train them on mutts lured in from the city wilds. Somehow he knew that what he was watching was wrong, but there was some thrill in containing the excitement as he watched, suppressing the desire to get up from where he sat, howl with the dogs, growl and cheer and gather up the blood, rub it warm between his fingers. It made his face hot. His secret joy.

He'd get as close as he could to watch the beasts tumble and dance and snap in the chicken-wire ring before someone noticed him and pushed him away. One time they'd let him tie the rope harnesses for the bulls, loop the slobbering, panting beasts and attach the truck tires they dragged around and around the yard, building muscle, each dog like a miniature ox within weeks—massed, veined.

Sunday would stay inside during the training sessions, refusing to look out the windows, squealing and covering her ears at the sounds. She had watched once when John Boy and Uncle Mick had cut a new dog, clipped his ears off neatly with a pair of shears, making an uncatchable monster of it. It's better for the animal, John Boy explained as he heated the shears with a cigarette lighter. They get cut off or they get ripped off in a roll. Uncle Mick stood nearby with a fat white terrier struggling between his legs, filing teeth. Sunday turned gray and threw her guts up in the garden. Everyone laughed.

On fight night Bear was the escort, the encourager, the

showman. The more people they could bring to the event, the happier Caesar would be.

Heinrich's job was to dart into the apartment blocks, houses, buildings, knock on the doors, thrust out his chest and say, "Good evening, sir. Your ride is here." Sometimes the men he talked to peered out their doors, saw Bear in the car and nodded. They'd grab their coats and follow the boy out. Sometimes they came out without their coats, leaned on the passenger side window and squinted into the darkness of the vehicle.

"Who's in?"

"Ricky's got a couple of good rollers. Going to play Sharky's big brute from December."

"What happened to Old Mark?"

"Two broken legs." Bear didn't look at Heinrich. "Rug accident, I heard."

"Treacherous, those rugs. The Persians, I hear."

"Won't have them in my place."

Laughter. The men tossed their coats into Heinrich's arms. Or they'd wave the big man away with promises for next month. Heinrich would clamber back into the front seat as the car rolled away, asphalt moving beneath his feet. By the time the sun set, the pickups were finished and they headed back to Abercrombie Street into the crowd that lined the pavement. Bear didn't need to push his way through. People parted for him. Heinrich struggled forward before the sea of legs and hips and skirts and feet closed on him. Caesar was at the basement door, talking to Uncle Mick about the dogs.

"That it?"

"Yeah."

To Bear, "That prick. Fishburn."

"Had a quick look. Not home. Boy went round the back. Nothing. Stuff's still there."

Caesar glanced down at Heinrich. The boy chipped paint from the doorframe with a fingernail.

"Send your little sidekick round there tomorrow. Pass on my disappointment and get what's outstanding."

Bear nodded and thumped the boy's shoulder. Caesar glanced again at the boy, creased his brow, the faintest twitch of furry gray eyebrow.

The big man led him downstairs. The noise was rushing up from below as Heinrich descended into the dark, it was going past his ears and spiraling upward—stomping feet and cheering and laughter and the smashing of glass. He could hear screaming. The birds. There were mixed fights before the dogs—cocks and sometimes a ferret, a pair of teenagers with a rivalry of some sort. There was no music while the fight was on. It drowned out the cracking of bones and the splatter of blood and the smack of flesh on the concrete. But now and then between bouts someone struck up a guitar, trying to soak up some of the money going around.

Heinrich could barely see anything from the floor of the basement. He was swamped by backsides and elbows. As Bear shifted forward, he grabbed onto his coat, allowing himself to be pulled through. It was getting to be a shameful thing to do—the constant need to scramble between people or have a path cleared for him. A couple of nights earlier he'd been moping around the greenhouse, scrubbing pots with barely any enthusiasm. Bear had had enough.

"The hell's got your goat?"

"How old am I?" the boy asked. Bear looked at him through his glasses, dazzling in the light of a candle over the tiny samplings in his hands.

"I dunno. Twelve? Thirteen? 'Bout eight when you turned up probably."

"How old's Sunday?"

"Bout the same."

"She's taller than me."

"Heaven forbid."

"I'm gonna end up taller than her, right?"

Bear had laughed, turning back to his work.

"There's no telling."

"I can't be short."

"There's worse things to be."

"Bear."

"Look." The big man turned, hung a huge arm over the back of the chair. "Being short's not the end of the fucking world. A woman don't mind if you're short, long as you can fight, you got money, or you're great in the sack. Work hard enough and you can get to all three, even. All right?"

"Yeah. All right."

"Now shut up and get back to work."

By the time Heinrich made his way to the front of the crowd the pit was empty but for two men half-heartedly sweeping feathers and bits of flesh from one end of the concrete ring into a heap at the other where the mess would lie with the shit and blood and piss of losing dogs, parts of other birds, a lump of shirt ripped from one of the teens. The winner's owner climbed out of the pit with his bird under his arm, its feet struggling, wet and black. A couple of dogs were next. Heinrich watched the money pass hands all around him, names and notes scribbled on notepads buried in palms, men shouting across the pit and holding up fingers.

Two cages were lowered into the pit. The dogs were snapping, throwing themselves at the wire. Heinrich saw Sunday on the other side of the ring, talking to two men. One whis-

pered in her ear, bent low, smiling. She was laughing in an odd, heavy way. Lopsided. She was still wearing that yellow dress but now it was higher than it used to be on her long gold legs and was caught up in a black wool sweater. She was barefoot on the beer-soaked floor. She hooted at the dogs, cheered. Bear's hand fell on the boy's shoulder and he jerked at the feel of the man's beard on his cheek.

"Listen here."

"Yeah?"

"I'm gonna say this once, and you don't repeat it. See that man up there with Caesar? Don't look just yet. Guy in the leather jacket. Blond. You don't go anywhere near him, you understand?"

"Huh?"

"Don't go near him. Don't talk to him, don't look at him. Don't go anywhere with him, even if he tells you it's okay with me. Get me, boy?"

"Why?"

"You know not to say 'why' to me."

"All right. All right."

"Good man." The Bear squeezed his shoulder, thumped him too hard, made him wobble. Heinrich felt a strange shift in his stomach, a flush in his cheeks. Bear never spoke like that, like he felt something.

He snuck a look across the pit to where Caesar was standing on the stairs with a thick-headed blond man in a brown leather jacket. The two were talking, holding short glasses, looking at the crowd. Heinrich didn't see anything especially threatening or interesting about the forbidden man. There was white and gray in his temples, smile lines cutting deep into the corners of his eyes. The man put his hand on his hip. A revolver. A cop. Heinrich tugged at Bear's sleeve.

"He a cop?"

Bear gave him a look. Heinrich scratched his neck and turned back to the fight. He knew there were cops in the crowd. There were cops who passed things to Caesar sometimes, met him in the early hours in uniform, rode in the back of the car in plain clothes. Heinrich had never been afraid of cops. He knew to be polite to them, take their coats and hats when they arrived at the house, send the women to them straight away, bring them drinks. You don't talk nothing but the weather, Bear had said. Sunny day, isn't it? Cold out there, isn't it? Warming up, isn't it? That's it. Get me? Heinrich wondered why this cop was different. But he didn't wonder long. The cage doors were lifted and the dogs began to dance.

There was always a clear favorite. It was usually size, but tonight it was attitude—one of the dogs was obviously more afraid, and the fearful one is the one who fights harder, that doesn't want to die. A dog that isn't quiet and trembling before the door goes up, piss running down its back legs, bashing its head on the cage walls in terror at the sound of the other animal, isn't a dog worth betting on. The one that makes the noise, makes the threats, gives a performance— that's the one distracted, the one that doesn't believe he can be taken down.

The raging beast tonight was the smaller one, a caramel mix with a black snout, waxed up all over to make it hard to pin, two perfect pink scars where they'd clipped it long ago, a tail docked from birth. It wasn't a new fighter and didn't move like one. The other, some kind of charcoal thoroughbred, came out of the cage and was immediately driven back against it. Glances snatched from the corners of eyes, puffed chests, exposed gums, bouncing strides and thrusts of legs, and then the lunge, the roll, the frantic scratch of claws with no grip on wet cement as one backed the other into the corner, scrambled out, rushed up against another wall. The crowd was howling. First blood in three seconds.

Heinrich looked across the pit at the man he was forbidden to speak to, shouting in Caesar's bent ear. Sunday was nowhere. The boy glanced back to see the thoroughbred's right front foot stripped of meat to the pink bone, flapping flesh, hopping. It was pretty much half over in a minute. A limping finish. Smart bets were being paid already. The mutt got the big fellow's throat and swung back and forth. Wet, squelching bites, the happy mumbled growling of a mouth washed with blood. Heinrich put his hands in his pockets and looked up at Bear. The big man was smiling, shifting notes from one hand to the other.

"Here you go, short stuff," he said, flapping a note in the boy's face. "Don't lose it all in one pop."

Heinrich grinned and pressed back into the crowd. Elbows and arses. He pushed, pulled, squirmed, shuffled his feet on the wet floor. A penny buried in grime. He reached down and scooped it up. Uncle Mick was there on the corner, arguing, pointing into the pit. He took plenty of tugging to bring around.

"Where's Sunday?" Heinrich asked.

"No idea. Care less."

"Take my punt on the next one?"

"Oh, Jesus. Yes, all right."

The man snatched Heinrich's note and stuffed it into his pocket. Two more dogs were being lowered into the pit. Heinrich had a quick look. Breathed the thick air. He searched for Caesar and the forbidden man. They were gone. Bear was talking to someone in the crowd.

"Hurry up, dickhead."

"Sorry." Heinrich chewed his lip. "All right. The black one."

"All in?"

"Yeah."

Uncle Mick nodded and folded his arms. Heinrich heard a familiar voice behind him. Caesar was drawing on his cigarette, the dogs in the cages forgotten, his eyes on the faces in the crowd. The forbidden man. The cop looked down at Heinrich. The boy turned back to the pit, straightened his jacket, cleared his throat.

"This Bear's sidekick?"

"Yeah."

"Who's he belong to?"

"Search me." Heinrich turned for a second, saw Caesar shrug. "Care less. Bear's always bringing in stray cats. Been doing it for years."

"Stray cats." The cop laughed. Heinrich looked up at him. "Stray cat, are you, boy?"

Heinrich chewed his lip. A smile danced on Caesar's thin scarred lips.

"That where the nigger girl came from?"

"Yeah, and others. I don't know why he does it. Half the time he raises them up and they go wild on him. Break his bones."

"They don't bother you."

"Now and then they bother me," Caesar glanced down at the boy. Heinrich dropped his eyes. "Mostly he keeps them out of my way."

"I don't know how you stand it," the cop said. "I hate cats. You know how to get rid of unwanted cats?" the cop asked the boy. The boy shrugged. "You feed 'm to the dogs."

The push was so unexpected, so light, that Heinrich hardly

felt it. He reached up and touched the cop's hands as they touched his chest and they felt gentle, warm even. He hadn't known how close he was to the edge. There wasn't time to make a sound before he hit the bottom of the pit. And then the air was out of him, his elbow split inside the jacket and leaking, his vision vibrating.

The crowd was screaming. The dog in the cage nearest to him in his ear, the sound making his eardrum pulse, too loud to be anything but a physical sensation, a punching of noise. Heinrich rolled. Blood and feathers on his palms. He wasn't sure what of it was his. All he knew was that he couldn't move as fast as he should have been able to. A weight had fallen over him and his limbs weren't responding in time with his thoughts. Bear was on the edge of the pit, his arm outstretched.

"Here," the Bear said. "Come here. Get up."

Heinrich looked back at Caesar and the cop. Caesar was smiling. The cop was smiling. Caesar nodded to the man holding the rope that released the door of the black dog's cage. The man paused, looked at the boy, looked at Caesar.

"Get up, Heinrich!"

Heinrich got to his feet, only to feel the weight of the dog slam into his legs. The concrete floor rushed up at him. His hands splayed out, rolled him, gripped limply at wet fur. He didn't feel the bite. All he felt was the hot breath and the wetness, the pressure on his forearm, his shoulder, the back of his neck, as he rolled.

"No!"

"Don't you dare," Caesar shouted, pointing his gun finger at Bear, a hundred miles above Heinrich in the tumbling, lamp-lit world. "Don't you fucking dare!"

Howling from the men above him, bottles thrown into the pit, popping and exploding and spraying off the walls. Heinrich glimpsed money changing hands through the blood in his eyes. He struggled into the corner, closed his fists, finally the bones and flesh responding. He struck out wildly, turned, struck out again, a hammer of blows. The second cage door lifted.

And then the Silence came. Everything responding now. His fingers unclenched, gripped, dug, held on. He took the gray dog down with his hands, lay on it, gouged at the eyes, raked, and heard snarls coming out of himself or the beast— or both. The other dog had his calf, tugging, and Heinrich could do nothing about it. The gray dog threw him off, came around, blind, rose up on its hind legs, danced. Heinrich blocked it with a forearm, knocked against teeth as hard as stone. His shoe was off. The boy grabbed it, beat at the beast with it. He punched, felt the rock teeth again against his knuckles, cracking and wedging a rough, warm tongue. He lost the shoe. Reached out. Grabbed glass. Mashed it in the eyes.

The dog rolled, scampered off. He twisted and threw himself at the black one, the big one, the one he had picked as a winner for its depthless eyes and its restless feet and the piss all over him. The boy swung his leg over it, almost went too far, wound an arm around a neck thicker than his own waist. The legs scratched his own. The boy sat up and squeezed. He had a moment to look around. Bear and Caesar and the forbidden man, watching, expressionless, their hands by their sides, pillars of a pier standing strong against an angry ocean of men. The boy realized he was growling but he couldn't hear the sound. The Silence had it. The dog was slipping. He dug his nails in. Twisting, slipping from his grasp.

Heinrich leaned forward, gripped the mouth, gums, teeth. Gripped the open holes where the ears had been. Pushed one way, then jerked the other. Felt the snap, the rush of warm air.

The boy dropped the limp dog and stood. Out of the sea of people, Bear landed and grabbed the shoulder of his jacket. There was nowhere else to hold the boy as his knees went from beneath him. His arms were ribbons.

I found Adam White at the Courthouse Hotel out the back of Newtown, right at sunset, a position his landlady at the end of the street told me was his standard for the hour and the day. The hotel was on a corner two streets back from the hip wonderland of King Street, a catwalk already being strutted by office workers on the way home to their damp Ikea-furnished pads above the bookshops and online daters searching for each other in the light rain, phones out like guns.

The main hall of the hotel was wallpapered with newspapers from twenty years ago and hung with Christmas lights. It was dark, the air thick with expired beer. I glanced around the U-shaped bar. White was hunched on a stool at the outdoor bar under an umbrella, nursing a beer. I walked up and tapped White on the shoulder. I gave him a second to turn, then punched him square in the face.

It's never good form to punch a man from behind. It's not right, either, to insult him with a glancing blow. I smacked him hard and felt the impact ripple up my arm, crack my knuckles for me. The sound was wet, unexpected, accompanied by a little breathy yowl. It was good. I hoped it was as good for him.

White stumbled off the stool but didn't go down like I had. His glass danced off the counter and spread out on the bricks at our feet. The bartender dropped the tray he was holding on the rubber mat.

"Whoa!"

"It's all right." I held up a hand. White recovered, wiping at the bloodless scrape on his left cheekbone with the back of his hand. I brushed his skin off my knuckles. He took me in for a few slow seconds. The cut on my face and the bruising seemed to get his bearings back. Then he began to laugh.

"What took ya so long?"

I kicked the base of his shattered glass against the wall of the bar and signaled the bartender to pour White another.

The young man behind the bar didn't look like the violent type. Tattoos and piercings and oddly shaved hair, something that decades ago might have meant he was dangerous, were diluted by a backpack full of books under the bottles behind the counter. University type. They thought violence was the language of the weak and tattoos were soul writing on skin. I probably agreed about the violence, to a certain degree, but I also knew that when a man gives you a good thump you do him the courtesy of matching his gesture.

I ordered a scotch on ice and the bartender put the glasses up. When I'd paid he just about ran inside to tell his manager. There were a couple of other patrons in the garden, barely interested now that White had failed to swing back. He laughed again as he took his drink and nodded toward a picnic table set in the back corner under another umbrella.

"Damn," he said as he sat down across from me. "Got you good, didn't I?"

"Not classy, using a tool," I said.

"Hey, you brought it with you, bro."

He laughed and held the beer glass against his eye. It was swelling shut. He was as I imagined him from what I'd heard and felt in the dark—tall, lithe, smooth, a weird boyishness to his smile contradicting the graying in his short dark curls. The clothes had the same odd effect of juvenility and age, an oversized denim jacket with intentional fraying on the cuffs over a pair of navy trousers that hung too low in the crotch and were pulled up too high at the waist with a cracked leather belt.

"Adam White. Congratulations. You've been discovered, which is obviously what you intended all along." I made a little half-bow. "My job is to tell Hades Archer who you are and what the hell you want. Now I feel like I'll have earned my money if I can tell him what your fucking problem is. What you do after I leave here is up to you."

"I'm not running off just because the old man knows my name, and I don't have to tell you shit, boy. My fucking problem is with the old man."

"You're playing a dangerous game if you want my opinion, mate. Best you straighten up and spit out your grievances before I lose my patience."

"I really don't want your opinion, and I really don't care about your patience, aye." White laughed.

I sipped my drink.

"Just tell me what you want. You might even get it."

"What I want is a conclusion," White said. Left a lingering poetic silence. I folded my arms. "You know about conclusions, right? Being a cop and all? Things happen, meaningful things, and they have to happen for the world to keep turning. People lie and cheat and steal from each other. People murder each other. But you, you know, you understand, right? These things need to be equalized. The scales need to be balanced. You know what I mean, don't you, bro?"

"I didn't come here for a philosophy lecture."

"I know. You came here for an explanation. I'm providing it, bro."

He put his palms out. He was well spoken for someone so badly dressed, someone who peppered his conversations with "bro" and "aye." I made a "get on with it" gesture.

"Ask Hades what he knows about a girl named Sunday," White said. He rested his forearms on the table and clasped his hands. "Ask him how she died."

"Sunday?" I asked. "Sunday who?"

"Her surname was White. Sharon Elizabeth White. But everybody called her Sunday."

"So you reckon Hades knocked your sister off?"

"My aunt."

"And when was this?"

"Around about 1979."

I laughed. Maybe it was the wrong thing to do, but I couldn't help myself.

"Oh dear. Oh God, that's funny."

"Laugh it up, bro."

"Are you serious?" I squinted through tears.

"I'm deadly serious."

"You're on some vigilante mission to avenge your aunt's death?" I snickered. "Who are you? Batman?"

He sipped his beer.

"Look, mate," I said. "You're kidding yourself. I mean, I get it. Hades Archer is a bad, bad man. I can't imagine some of the things he's done over the years. If he did knock your aunt off, chances are he doesn't even remember doing it. And even if he does, even if I rattle it out of his ancient, decaying mind with a bit of new-age hypno-past-regressive therapy, and the old crocodile happily tells me, *yeah, sure, I remember that bitch, I put her black ass in a oil drum and dumped her in a creek*, I can't imagine what you think you're going to do about it. You threaten Hades hard enough and he'll come after you. And he doesn't look to me like the kind of guy who negotiates."

"I don't care what he does or what he says. I'm going to haunt that man until he tells me what he did to Sunday. I want to know."

"What the hell do you care what he did to your aunt? You couldn't have even known her. How old are you?"

"My mother loved her." The man leaned over the table so that I could smell the beer on him. "You understand that? My mother loved her."

He was out of breath as though he had run around the block. He'd done well to keep the rage down while I laughed at him. It wasn't something I saw often as a cop. A bit of self-control. I was beginning to think Adam White was a good match for Hades.

"My mother spent her whole fucking life looking for Sunday White," Adam said. "It was her purpose. It was her calling. She'd never had a moment of happiness until she found that woman. Imagine a kid raised in the wilderness. In the desert. Imagine what it's like to grow up without love, because that's what it was like, bro, growing up with the reformers. When she's an adult wandering in this kind of crazy loveless wasteland of a city she finds her own sister, her own blood, and suddenly she knows what love is. Hades

Archer took Sunday away from my mother and she never got that trust back again. Not even when she had her own kids. When she had me. It was never the same. Something was taken from her and I had to watch that eat up everything she ever was."

"This is all very deep and I'm sure very moving." I cleared my throat.

"I think you understand better than you know, bro," he smiled. "You're a cop, which means your dad was a fucking prick."

I chewed my lip, shook it off.

"Let's just cut the sermon and be straight with each other, Adam. You're going to get yourself killed for some nothing justice mission." I leaned forward, looked in his eyes. "They're never even going to find your bones."

"Here's the thing, bro." White opened his hands again. "My family might have been happy to accept what happened to Sunday last generation, when they were too timid and sick and powerless to do anything about it. My uncle drank himself to death in the early eighties. My mother was raised in homes. Institutions. She wasn't the kind of person to answer back, to question things, to seek satisfaction. And when she died, she didn't even have the words to write out what she really felt, what she'd really needed all along. She just blew her brains out. Bang. And you know what? I feel good that she's at peace. But she left me here, and I've got to be selfish. I've got to feel right about it all. I'm not happy to let the old dog lie. I demand satisfaction, always. Always, bro."

"You talk a lot." I drained my drink. "I don't have a notepad, so I'll just sum this up as I'll present it to the old man. What you're saying is you blame your mother's shitty life and your own on an aunt getting tangled up with the wrong crowd decades ago. You're going to piss the old man off until he admits what he did and says he's sorry, like some fucking girly school-yard catfight. You know what, bro? Your mother should have sought some fucking counseling. And you know what else? I think you're bored. The motivation behind your vendetta is really thin, mate. If you can't figure out what to do with your life, go get a hobby. Take up dance classes."

"I have a hobby, bro. It's setting things right. Making people accountable."

"You're not Batman. This is not Gotham City. You will not be satisfied by this. You're going to end up a missing person and they're going to put your file at the bottom of the pile like they did with your fucking aunt."

He sniggered over his drink.

"I'm trying to help you, boy. You hang around that dump long enough and you'll become a permanent fixture, I guarantee it."

"Oh, please." White smiled, made begging gestures with his hands. "Please tell him to come after me. I film everything I do out there. Handicam. Wireless feed. I'd love for that old man to get fed up one night and come down the hill and shoot me. I'd just love it."

"You're filming? Oh, this is just priceless."

"Everything. Everything, bro. Who goes in. Who comes out. The old man reading his newspaper hour after hour, night after night. He needs a hobby, you ask me."

"They got a name for what you're doing, Adam."

"So tell him to charge me. Make me hand over the tapes."

I scratched the back of my neck. My face hurt. White's left eye was barely a slit now and it was weeping. He dabbed at it with the back of his slender hand. I thought for a while, turning my glass on the tabletop. There was no telling what was on those tapes. Or who. I didn't think they'd lead to any direct legal danger for Hades—he had connections high up in the police force and the tapes would go from the front desk to the incinerator before anyone even knew they were there. But if they ended up on a journalist's desk . . . or on the Internet.

None of this would reflect badly on me, of course. I had no stake in keeping Hades out of jail. Except that his going to jail would be cataclysmic for Eden, making her dangerously unpredictable about what she would do to punish those responsible. Which would include me. I wondered if White knew what he was seeing out there, knew how very valuable those tapes were. I could only hope he was doing it as an insurance policy in case anything did happen. At the least he had to be aware that Hades was being visited by unsavory characters.

"What would be a satisfying conclusion to you? Huh? What would settle accounts with the Justice League?"

"Knowing what happened. Being able to bury my aunt with respect and dignity."

"That seems simple enough."

"You'd think so, wouldn't you?"

"Why not?"

"Because he says he didn't do it."

I rubbed my eyes. They were heavy. Aching.

"When was this?"

"A month ago. To my mother. Just before she shot herself. She had one last stab at the truth and the old man denied her. Didn't even offer her a place to sit down. She'd driven six hours."

"And what?" I said. "Hades is supposed to believe that if he admits to what he's done and gives up her remains you'll just toddle off, all fair and square?"

"He'd better hope."

I got up, swung my leg over the bench.

"Stop going out there, Adam."

"Why would I, now that I have company?"

I walked away, heard his laughter as I reached the door of the pub.

Eadie began her day in the stables. She began at one end of the building, scraping the wet hay and manure into a wheelbarrow, transporting the muck to a bin at the end of the concrete lot, returning, doing it again. Her shovel moved swiftly and the lifting, twisting, hurling, the pressure on her knees—it all felt good. Eadie liked to work out. Liked to feel her heart beating in her neck. To be breathless.

She cleared one stall down to the bare concrete, her lungs full of the earthy, grassy smell of the beast, now and then the acidic ammonia of the animal's urine at the back of her throat. She swept the stall out until it was only thin mud at the bottom and then put the pressure hose onto it. Her boots were too big and rubbing holes through her socks into her feet, but she didn't mind. She liked being dirty and sore. Knew she would earn sleep.

She led the animal back into the stall and stood while it snuffled in her palm with its warm velvet nose, black eyes wary, blinking wire eyelashes. Animals didn't mind her. She'd always wondered at that, given what she was deep down inside.

She moved to the next stall and led the horse out into the sun, ducked when it tried to nuzzle the side of her head, roughly, a kind of loving head butt. Sweat tickled her temples. She wiped hay dust onto her cheeks and forehead. Being dirty reminded her of home.

She had always been a homebody at the dump. Eric was the adventurer, wandering off into the labyrinth of trash and coming back at night with things he wanted to show her, pieces of broken jewelry and toy guns and little wooden boxes with rusted hinges. She liked to be around Hades when she was little, bringing him coffee in bed and letting the smell of it bring him out of his restless, snoring slumber, sitting with her legs under the blanket while he drank it in silence, watching his face come back to its regular shape.

It was probably a year before she stopped being afraid of him. Even learning what he did for a living endeared him to her. The first time she snuck down to the back lots and watched him heaving the body of some fallen drug lord into the compacted trash, she was awed at his care and delicacy. The way his tired arms lay the shoulders of the man down gently, how he crossed the hands over the chest. It was people that Hades disposed of, not things. Once it had been her destiny to be laid down by him like that, her face passive and sleepful as the nylon sheet came over her, the rubber after that. Her deep, acid-filled grave.

The adult Eadie was spraying out the fifth horse stall when Pea returned. She was covered in filth, too. The squat figure leaned on the rails and watched her work for a while. It was uncomfortable. Where Pea stood there was no way Eadie couldn't hit her with the back spray. She didn't know whether to go on or stop. The gaze was lowered, critical, the lips snarled. Eadie stopped the compressor with her foot.

"Lunch," the woman said. Eadie followed her out to the sink to wash her hands. That earned a frown. She wiped her hands dry on her filthy jeans, supposed that might make up for the insult of hygiene.

She walked through the stable doors to the back area. Other animal workers here, all of them men, were sitting on milk crates or the bare earth, smoking, drinking coffee laced with bourbon. A milk crate piled up with sandwiches, ham and cheese, tomato and cheese, pickles and cheese, Vegemite and cheese.

Eadie glanced around for Nick. He wasn't there. Neither was Skylar. She took a milk crate close to Pea, but not too close, and nabbed the first sandwich she could reach. She flipped her sunglasses down, knowing it was better to have two cameras recording the stubbled faces and scarred hands, profiles that would be checked for violence, kidnapping, drug charges. Eadie looked around but took nothing in. It was Jackie she wanted to spend time with. Skylar would be her ticket into his company.

"You know, I ain't never seen a stable mucked out so slow," Pea said. "You never done this shit before?"

A couple of the workers sniggered. Conversations drained away. Eadie coughed. The sun was belting through the cheap sunglasses.

"Didn't realize we were on a clock."

"We're always on a clock. Life's a fucking clock."

"I'll speed up then."

Pea looked around. The men laughed.

"The hell you doing down here?"

Eadie leaned back, chewed her sandwich before she spoke.

"What, on the farm?"

"No. The stables."

"Working," Eadie said.

"You working or you wasting my time until you decide which dick you gonna sit on up there at the breakfast sheds?"

More laughter. One of the older men swigged a beer, yellow light dancing off it from above.

"Come on. Lay off, Pea," someone said.

"I'm not planning on sitting on any dicks, all due respect," Eadie said.

"What's the matter? You a fucking dyke or something?" Indignant.

"Actually, yeah."

There was a group inhalation, a few groans of excitement. Eadie felt the air change. She'd let the words tumble off her lips thoughtlessly, but as they hit the ears around her she understood it to be the right move. Lying was easy. It had been a little while since she'd played any really entertaining lying games. They'd been Eric's specialty. The first lie was always the best, made her cheeks feel hot, her hair stand on end.

"I heard you were married," Pea snorted.

"I was."

"And now you've decided muff-diving is your game."

"It's not really a decision," Eadie said. "Or a game."

"Imagine that," Pea mused. "Imagine you come home from work one day and your wife is horizontal with another chick."

"It wasn't like that," Eadie said.

"What the hell's wrong with you? You hate men or something? Plenty of men here. You hate them, do you?"

"No. I don't."

"Plenty of girls here," one of the younger men said. "If, you know, you want to do a reenactment of that night."

Laughter, Pea's the hardest.

"All right, leave her alone now, Pea," an older man said, getting up from his milk crate. He pointed to the two women in turn, the beer in his hand, swinging. "You, put ya back into it. And you, find some other feathers to ruffle."

The men left, laughing, chattering about the new gossip. By nightfall it would be all over the farm. Pea looked at Eadie appreciatively, as though she'd won something. Eadie wasn't sure exactly what. She was looking forward to lying again. To seeing what else would come out of her under a little squeeze. She reached forward and took a water bottle from the cooler at the center of the gathering and stood with it.

"They're not gonna like that around here," Pea said. Her tone had changed.

"I ain't got time for what they like," Eadie said as she went back into the stables. "Clock's ticking."

I came up on the van fast, the Jack Daniel's pre-mixer bottles in my fingers, and thumped on the door with my foot. I heard a yelp from within. The ginger spider. Juno rolled open the door and glared out at me from beneath a watch cap pulled too low over flaming blond eyebrows.

"Get your hand off it."

"Asshole," he said, watching me get in.

"Here, take this and shut up."

I handed him the second Jack Daniel's and crawled into the space beside him. The whole van smelled like teenage body odor, mildly sexual, full of unfulfilled dreams. There were fast-food wrappers everywhere, orange plastic cheese and a stack of crime novels knocked over by his feet, some fantasy titles with dragons on the cover, a couple of Anne Rices.

"You know, you're supposed to be watching."

"I watch."

"What are you getting?"

Juno took a notepad from the ledge before him, handed it to me. I don't know why. It was unreadable. There were some good sketches of birds, and some naked ladies with black wings.

"There are a few nasties getting around," he said. "Nicholas Hart, couple of previous charges for assault, assault with a deadly, arson, and a sexual assault that didn't stick."

Juno fiddled with a laptop wedged between the

monitors. Cleared dirt out of the corner of his eyes, yawned, drew up a still from one of Eden's cameras of a lanky blond man in a cap.

"Gave Eden a good rub at breakfast this morning. He's on parole so we could snatch him up any time, but I'd like to see a bit more of him first."

"Okay. Who else?"

"There's Penelope Goodman." He double-clicked on another still. A plump woman in coveralls.

"What's her deal?"

"Just a couple of domestic violences way back, but she's such a bitch I thought she warranted mention."

"That it so far?"

Juno picked his long teeth with a fingernail. The exhaustion was radiating off him now as his eyes wandered over the monitors.

"No Jackie?"

"No. No Jackie yet."

"When?"

"Eden's pretty chummy with his current screw. Might be her ticket in. Gave the girl the deodorant can camera, which was clever, except the girl put it on the bathroom sink backward so we've only got audio from that one." He pointed to a blank monitor, the shadow of a can against a tiled wall.

"Anything interesting?"

"Some mildly interesting telephone conversations by Rye. Mainly drug deals though. Nothing about the missing girls. I emailed the files away for a transcript."

"Well, we're in. I guess we just wait."

"So is Eden gay?"

I didn't even register the question at first. I'd found a sleeping Eden on one of the monitors, her body turned toward the camera, a slender arm hanging over the edge of the bed. I understood what drove Juno to watch, hour after hour. She looked like a Botticelli. Sleep took all the hard edges off her.

"Is she what?"

"Gay."

"What?" I turned back.

"She told a bunch of workers today she's not sleeping with anyone at the farm because she's gay. Is she?"

I laughed. "She's not sleeping with anyone because she's a cop."

"Yeah. I know."

"Does it matter if she's gay or not?" I couldn't keep the humor out of my voice.

"No."

I started laughing and couldn't stop. He looked like he wanted to punch me, but I outranked him by about two decades of grueling cop work. So the best he could do was pout and scratch the back of his bony white neck.

"Shit, give me a break. You live someone's life for two days fucking straight and you get to wonder about them, that's all. I'm just curious. '

"I get it." I wiped my eyes, gave his shoulder a slap. "She's a beautiful woman. Just don't fall in love with her. Don't even think about it. She's not your type. At all. Okay? Not even close."

The young man didn't seem to know what to think of my assessment. We both watched Eden on the screen for a while. Yes, the outside of Eden was very attractive. Like a beautiful poisonous flower. But the truth was that she was no one's type. I hadn't considered what her preference was from the moment I

learned what she and Eric had done. What I was sure
she still did. I had the feeling sexual partners would be
fleeting things for Eden if there were any on her radar
at all. It was dangerous to be close to her. I was way
too close as it was.

The gay card was a good move. I couldn't see the
ferals on the farm being very supportive of such a con-
temporary admission. It would grate on female sensi-
bilities out there in the grassy badlands. The men
might not be so hard on her because she was a beautiful lesbian and would fall into fantasy category and not
be an offense against their masculinity. In any case, the
admission would stir up trouble, bring out a few true
colors, drop a few masks. I wondered if she'd planned
on it. It would certainly make for interesting viewing.

I sucked the Jack Daniel's dry and was about to go
out for another when Juno's voice stopped me.

"What was that?"

I looked back at the screen.

"What?"

Juno was leaning forward, nose up, like he was trying to smell the monitor at the same time as he
watched it. He let his head drop, grabbed the mouse,
did some things. Zoomed in. Zoomed back out again.
Sat back in his chair, unsatisfied.

"What was it?"

"Thought I saw something move in her caravan."
He tapped the screen with a speckled finger. "Here."

I looked. Saw nothing. The image wasn't great but
there was nothing moving on it. I widened my eyes,
slitted them, blinked. Nothing.

"A shadow," I said.

"Maybe."

"Probably a gay pride march."

"There." He stabbed the screen. "Look."

I looked. The door of Eden's caravan was ajar. The camera gave us a view of Eden tilted down from her head, the camera probably on the bedside table, arm, elbow, the end of the bed lost in darkness. Beyond, lit from what was probably the kitchenette window, the caravan door. It was swinging open slowly. I felt my stomach clench.

"Shit."

"We got backup on standby?"

"Yeah," I glanced at him. "Response time's about five minutes. But just wait a second. Let me see who it is."

A figure slid into the van. Stooped below the sagging roof. The figure seemed to sway. Put a long hand out, steadied himself against the slatted bathroom door.

A pylon of a man, all lean, square construction, symmetry, the solidity of something built slowly from the ground up. Deceptively strong. I knew his type. The skinny junkie thief you try to pin whose core body strength flips you over despite your bulk.

"Christ almighty, it's Nick Hart. We need to call this in." Juno grabbed my arm. I could feel his nails through my shirt.

"Hang on."

"He's going to hurt her." He was almost shouting.

"Just wait." I pulled his fingers off me. "I know what I'm doing."

Nick was at the end of the bed, looking down at her. Eden hadn't moved. Her breathing was low and deep. Mouth open. Women hate it when you see them sleeping with their mouths open. Like there's something about that image that could ruin all the hard work they put into the rest of their appearance.

Juno was panting. He grabbed his phone from the counter.

"We need to—"

"You blow this operation without my approval and I'll kill you."

"Your partner is in danger," he wailed.

"I know."

"He's—"

"I know!"

Nick Hart, the shadow in the dark, was touching himself. Trailing his fingers down the bulge in the front of his jeans. He stood there for what seemed like an eternity. My heart was thumping. I silently pleaded for Eden to wake. She didn't. I reached for my phone. Held it. Didn't dial.

Nick kneeled on the bed, eased his weight down. Put a hand down by her waist. Even if she woke now all he had to do was fall on her. A hand reached for her face, hovered over it, didn't touch. I took the lock off my phone. Poised my finger to dial.

Eden rolled. Something in her hand. Something big. It swung up, over, just as Nick dropped on top of her, met the side of his head on the way down like a police baton meeting a kneecap. A half-thump, half-crack, followed by a grunt. He fell sideways instead of down. She was on top of him, the long handle of the frying pan she'd used across the front of his throat. She put a knee in the pan itself and both hands on the end of the handle and leaned down. Her mere weight. Crushing. Juno and I had our mouths open now.

They stayed like that, the two figures, for maybe a

minute. I could tell she was really strangling him. When you strangle someone, shut off the airway all the way, they don't make a sound, not those loud grasping choking noises you see in movies. It's a silent death. Every few seconds the click of grinding teeth. But that's it. Strangely peaceful for the person doing it. Juno stirred first, grabbed at his phone again.

"She's going to—"

Eden's voice came over the monitor. Her nose was touching Nick's. Breathing air by his breathless lips.

"You should be so lucky."

She let him go.

Juno stood up in the van, bent in half, eyes locked on the screen. He dropped his phone and grabbed his watch cap with both hands.

"Jesus Christ!"

I hadn't realized I'd been holding my breath. I exhaled, filled my lungs, panted as I watched Nick Hart crawl out of Eden's caravan. She darted over to the bed, grabbed the camera, wrenched back the curtains and showed us the landscape outside. Gray earth lit from nowhere like the surface of the moon. Nick Hart fell into a circle of men who were laughing, cheering, trying to bring him to his feet.

"Check up on these guys," Eden said. She sounded calm. Unrattled. "I'll find out their names tomorrow."

Juno was looking at me. I licked my lips and nodded at the laptop. He understood. Rolled the film back, took a screenshot of the men in Nick Hart's posse.

"Well, hopefully you get it now," I said, pulling open the van door again. "Not your type, mate. Not at all."

At first Heinrich wasn't sure whether or not he'd done well on the Night of Teeth and Tearing. As he lay in the cold morning hours trying to remember, trying not to sleep, he wasn't exactly sure what had happened at all. He knew he ended up in the dog pit and everyone was staring at him, pointing, howling, throwing things, and he'd killed the two animals, prize beasts. The one thing he was sure of was the soft but swift push from the forbidden man, the police officer standing with Caesar. He'd pushed him in. Why?

He only hoped Bear would tell him.

Heinrich lay unable to move. He guessed the sun was rising beyond the curtains. He didn't know where Sunday was. She hadn't slept in his bed for a month. Sometime during the morning he fell into a hot sort of daze and thought she was there, stroking his hair, which was a very un-Sunday-like thing to do. But whenever he spoke to her she didn't answer, and when he opened his eyes she'd disappeared.

He lay listening to Bear wander about the house in a restless, lumbering way from the moment they got back from Doc's. Heinrich had been to Doc's place plenty of times before but had never been the patient. He awoke in a single lockup garage somewhere in Paddington around midnight, he guessed, stretched out on a Ping-Pong table and covered in blankets and sheets. Plenty of people were there. Some of them held him down as he squirmed, covering themselves in his blood. A girl was crying, holding a towel around his neck, almost choking him.

"It's all off," she'd wailed, looked at the ceiling. "There's bones. God!"

"Shut up. Hold him and shut up."

Someone put a vodka bottle near Heinrich's lips and he drank for a second before Bear appeared out of the bright gold light and knocked it away.

"None of that. He feels it. Every bit of it."

He was saying sorry, over and over, but no one listened. Someone put a rag in his mouth, pulled it down by either ear, locked his head to the table. It tasted of salt. Then there was fire. Slow, poking, stitching, knotting fire.

Bear walking in the dark, back and forth, the kitchen to the front door to the back door, across the veranda. Heinrich dozed to the rhythm of it, jolted at the sound of neater hard-shoed footsteps meeting those of the heavy soft Bear.

"Don't start," Caesar's low milky voice.

"I can't even. I can't even speak."

"You've been like this for a long time, Bear. Your head stuck on the little things. The rat boy. The nigger girl. The angry housewives who buy your potions and lotions to knock off their angry hubbies. You need to get your head out of your ass, my friend. The baby games are over. The boy, Jesus. That was just a bit of fun. Thomas has his mind on bigger things and he is going to lead us to bigger things."

"I cannot have that man around me."

"You put a price on that? Because having him around is going to change things for us. There's only so much you can do with making loans and breaking bones. It's about to start raining gold in this town and you're under an umbrella counting pennies."

"Get away from me."

"Bear, I need you with me on this."

"Get away."

Bear came into the bedroom as the first white light was leaking from beneath the curtains. Heinrich had closed his eyes a couple of times but had felt hot breath on his face, dog's breath, and snapped them open. Bear pushed him into a sitting position and pulled his legs around, gathering his trousers around his feet. Everything hurt.

"Bear."

"You get up, you get dressed, you get moving. No matter what happens, understand? No one ever sees you hurt."

"Bear." *The boy's face was wet.*

"Come on." *The big man pulled him to his feet, wrenched his shirt down over his head, and tugged his bandaged arms through. He pulled an extra cardigan on before his usual denim jacket, wrenched it across in the front, Heinrich's eyes on Bear's huge fingers as they worked the tiny plastic buttons.*

"We make like this never happened, boy. Understand?"

"Why?"

"Because you'll write your reputation today."

"Why did they—"

"Nothing happened. Get it?" *The big man wiped the boy's face, hard—a pawing, took the sweat and the tears and the dried blood. Pushed down his crazy hair. Turned him and thumped him on the back. They walked out into the kitchen. People were waking everywhere. Men standing in the kitchenette, drinking coffee, sharing cigarettes. They looked down at Heinrich. One turned, glanced at Bear.*

"Well, look at that. It's Dogboy."

"He made it, huh? Well, whattaya know?"

One of the girls slipped into the kitchen and touched Heinrich on his hair. The boy felt the world sway. Felt himself trembling beneath the clothes.

"Toast, baby?"

Heinrich felt sick.

No. Please, no.

"Yes, please," he said.

Nothing happened. Get it?

Heinrich sat at the counter while the girl made the toast, sprinkled it with cheese, grilled it. The men watched him. Bear handed him a glass of milk and he swallowed three or four times before putting it to his lips. He thought of cold things, of still things, tried to make like a block of ice. Bear watched him over his shoulder, a look he only had when Heinrich was working with the really dangerous seeds, the oils, the things that could kill him if he breathed too hard. More people came into the dining room, leaned on the big table, murmured. Heinrich ate the toast. It tasted like rocks.

"What's that boy's name?"

"Heinrich."

"Heinrich the Hound Hunter, ay?"

"What a tough little scrap."

"Let's see the wounds."

"What wounds?" Bear said. No humor in his voice, but people chuckled anyway. Heinrich finished the toast and climbed off the stool, steadied himself against the counter. Everyone was looking at him. He went to Bear, brushed the crumbs off his jacket, looked up the great height to the man's hairy face.

"We going out, or what?" Heinrich asked.

Everyone laughed. Bear smiled.

It was a good sleep. I got home and sank a quarter bottle of scotch or so, then popped three Oxy and showered, leaning my head against the wall, thinking. Worrying, a little, about Eden. I knew I didn't have to worry about Eden but I did anyway. Got to convincing myself, as I did sometimes, that she was a woman like other women I'd known, who needed guidance and protection, who was likely to do silly things if left alone too long.

I woke up with the cat on my neck, sprawled across from shoulder to shoulder like a great woollen scarf, heavy enough to make me catch my breath. It yowled when I shoved it off. I knew cats could kill babies lying on them like that. Cot death. Cat death. Could they kill cops in their forties who drank too much? I lay looking at the creature. Pretty little killer. Like Eden. I don't know why I kept it, what piece of Martina I hoped could be preserved by a lazy, angry, smelly thing that whined all the time and had probably forgotten she ever existed.

I wanted to see Hades but I didn't have the time, so I called while I laced my boots, the phone wedged in my ear. "You owe me ten grand."

"That was swift." His voice, gruff, grating on years of whisky and cold air.

"I don't really have the time to be otherwise."

"Eden?"

"Doing what she does."

"You tell her to come out to me when she gets off."

"Yes, Dad."

"So."

"Did you kill a girl named Sharon Elizabeth White?"

Dead silence. I listened to it. Tried to fathom what would come next. I straightened up and held the phone against my ear.

"This again," he said finally.

"Seems so."

"No, I didn't kill Sunday."

"Well, you've got a problem then, haven't you?"

"Who is it? Her sister?"

"Sister necked herself." I patted the cat. "Nephew's on the case. Adam White, badly dressed, hell of a right arm swing."

"It never ends, you know."

"I can imagine."

"You want to solve my problem for me?" The old man set his coffee mug down. I heard it clunk on his kitchen table.

"No, I don't. I really don't."

"You find Sunday's killer and I'll give you a hundred grand."

I stopped patting the cat. It head-butted my arm, walked around the back of me, climbed onto my lap.

"That'll make for interesting conversation with my accountant."

"Get an ABN. Register yourself as a private investigator. I'll pay through my lawyer. Anonymous, unless the case is ever investigated. Which it won't be."

"I can't just—"

"Don't spend it too quickly in your mind. I don't see you getting it. Nobody ever found Sunday."

I felt cold. The way he said it, like there was a Sunday to be found somewhere, cold bones lying in dry earth. No one ever found Sunday. *I don't do this shit for fun, boy-o.*

"I'll come out there this evening," I said. He hung up. I shook myself all over, decided to put thoughts of Hades and his dirty money out of my head. The eager cat got under my feet as I headed out into the kitchen to feed it. Soft toes squished under mine. It hissed and skittered away from me.

I wanted to make sure I wasn't late to a meeting with the families of the missing girls. They'd agreed to get together at Keely's mother's house, but I'd seen footage of them fighting about the girls on the news and knew tensions were frayed. I sat in traffic and beeped and sweated and swore, crunched Oxy, and tried to find a radio station not saturated with advertising. White noise. I phoned headquarters half an hour before the meet time and told them to warn the families to break out the cigarettes.

I parked outside the Manning house and noticed a few men were following my advice, standing on the pebbled concrete steps peppering the garden with orange butts and ignoring each other. If not for the number on the mailbox, there would have been no distinguishing this place from hundreds of other rental town houses lining the street. They all shared the same neutral tones— apricot cream, pastel pink, ivory rose. Hardy plants that would withstand the blazing treeless summer sprayed from garden beds in black and red spikes.

I walked up to the house thinking about the girls. This was the last place her family had seen Keely before she headed to Bankstown to grind out some cash in the sex trade. What she usually did was sink into the body-perfumed sheets of the upstairs bedroom until noon every day, when *Dr. Phil* woke her, then off to the shops for cigarettes and frozen lasagna—a cycle with its own biology. The pretty lazy girl with the curly hair.

One of the men on the doorstep jutted his chin at me. Same curls. A brother? I'd wondered if there would be press hanging around the front of the missing girls' houses, but by the look of these two I could understand why there weren't. These were the kind of guys who'd chase you off the lawn with cricket bats given half the chance.

"Getting hot in there," he said.

"Sounds like it. Sorry. Traffic."

I offered my hand but he didn't take it—held the screen door open instead. Maltese terriers crowded at my feet, three of them, the haggard panting of animals fed too much and locked inside with dope smoke all day.

I led my brigade of dogs into a small living-dining room. Venetian blinds, some missing, blocking off a view of the yard. Yellow clouds on the ceiling. The reek of smoke. Everyone turned and looked at me. The only sound was the consistent peal of budgerigars in a cage hanging from the edge of the window over the oven in the open kitchen. The bottom of the cage was misshapen and covered in spaghetti sauce splatter. As I neared the cage, the birds panicked and flapped around, spraying seed husks and feathers out of the bars.

"Frank Bennett." I offered a hand to the nearest woman, a big hulk of curly-haired suburban mother I assumed to be Keely's mother. Tit tatts. Her whole arm seemed to take the tremor of my contact like a seismic monitor made from cellulite.

"About time you got here."

"Let up, would you, for Christ's sake," another mother said from across the room. The Kidds. About five of them, crowded around one of the overstuffed faux-suede recliners. Mother, father, confused pre-teens, all of them thin-faced and angular. I picked out the Benfields across the chess board from them, holding down the opposite recliner, Mum and Dad only. The thin rodent-like Kidds and the fat speckled, curly Mannings. The Benfields distinguished themselves by being economically superior to the others, given the disdain with which they observed their surroundings. Mrs. Benfield brushed at her forearms like they were picking up toxic dust. The only two people in the room who seemed to be getting on were a pair of toddlers sitting on the shag rug in front of the television, trying to swallow bits of Lego.

"I'm really sorry about the time." I cleared my throat, tried to face them all. "I understand you're all frustrated. And you're right if you're thinking you're probably going to spend the next couple of hours repeating to me everything you already told my case workers over in Parramatta. I'm the principal on your case, however, and I've got to see you all together. So I'm going to try to make this as painless and as meaningful as I can."

I was very careful to get my "ful" and "less" in the right spots. There was a silence in which they all made sure. Then everyone tried to talk at once. No one invited me to sit down. So I went to the couch in front of the toddlers and sat anyway. One of the babies began fooling with my shoelaces.

"Mr. Bennett, was it?" said Mrs. Benfield, still scratching her arms. She was making me feel itchy. Someone thrust a coffee into my hand, spilled it on my fingers, on the throw over the couch.

"Hi, yes."

"We had a principal on our daughter's case. What happened to Detective Ellis?"

"When we conclusively connected your daughter's case with those of the other missing girls, the file shifted out of Missing Persons and over to me and my partner. I'm sitting down with Detective Ellis and Detective Costa this afternoon to get a briefing."

"Who's your partner?" asked someone behind me.

"Eden Archer. You might have seen her on the news. The surgeon case."

"Ellie who?"

"Eden."

"What kinda stupid name is Eden?" The father, Michael Kidd.

"Who gives a fuck what her name is? Where *is* she?" One of the brothers, accusatory.

"She's operating on this case in another capacity right now."

"The fuck does that mean?"

"She's off," I turned my head, gave him my profile, "doing other shit. This is a one-man job."

"A one-man job. You hear that? Three young girls missing and they send us one fucking guy."

"There are plenty of people working on the case right now." I rubbed my eyes. "But sitting here with you for a briefing is a one-man job."

"I'm writing to the papers about this."

"Mr. Kidd, I understand you're upset—"

"So, the cases are connected." The Benfield father seized the floor with an expression like he'd smelled something foul, like something rotting inside him was giving off fumes up the back of his throat. Rage. "They're connected through Jackie Rye, aren't they?"

"Right now Mr. Rye is a person of interest. There are a number of persons of interest at present." I slurped my coffee, wondering what I'd find at the bottom if I ever got there. It tasted of margarine.

"You arrested him?"

"No."

"The fuck not?" One of the Kidds.

"Look," I held up a hand, "I know what you want right now is action. Arrests. You have to understand that sometimes making an arrest straight away can be the worst thing you can do. Your case is being handled with the utmost tactical consideration. I can't tell you how, but people are on this with everything they've got, and some very dangerous shit is going down for members of my team. Trying to pull apart the investigation is a natural reaction, and I totally get it, but it's a waste of time. Everything that can be done is being done."

The crowd considered this for a second or two. The babies at my feet babbled and sang. The one with the shoelace fascination, a Manning by the curls, grabbed my fingers and pulled herself up by them. I sat and let her tug at my hands like the reins of a horse, jostling, investigating the buttons on the cuffs of my shirt. The baby's trust seemed to win me over to the watchers. Their attention left me and turned on each other.

"Someone should be taking these lot aside and talking to them about how long they've known Jackie Rye," the Manning father snapped. He stabbed a finger at the Kidds. "I haven't heard a single thing yet about your relationship with that man. Your daughter introduced our daughter to him. You *knew* he was trouble and you let my daughter—and your own—go out there."

"Erin was the one who knew Jackie. We met him once."

"Didn't you buy a car from out there?"

"Yeah?"

"Wasn't that two years ago? Don't you also buy speed off him? Haven't you bought speed off him in the last six months?"

"This has nothing to do with anything." The Kidd father was burring up, shoulders back, chest out like a gorilla trying to ward off a rival, nipples jutting at his damp T-shirt. "Stop thinking you're some kind of fucking Sherlock Holmes. This fuckwit's been spreading shit around the entire town about us and how we raised our kid."

"Oh fuck off."

"You fuck off."

"I don't have to spread any shit about your mob, mate. You do it just fine yourselves."

"Our daughter is missing, too, you moron."

"Is she? Is she, or is she out there somewhere with

him? She and Jackie are probably selling my daughter's bones. Erin could have talked Keely into anything, she was such a manipulative little slut."

The Kidd father was up, halfway across the room before he found himself tangled in the arms of one of his sons. I sat back and watched, making notes on the pad on my knee. This was what I'd wanted, after all—for them to forget I was there, to talk about speed and stolen cars and who knew who and didn't want to implicate themselves. The women were sneering at each other now, about boyfriends stolen and skirts worn too short and a birthday party ruined by a drunken confession. The babies seemed used to all the turmoil. One stood by my knee, trying to take the pen from my fingers. I reached up and patted down the infant's blond hair, tried to tell if it was a boy or girl in its shabby gray tracksuit.

The Benfields were watching the argument, tears running down the mother's cheeks. She was watching the faces of those around her like she was trying to imagine how they could have appealed to her baby, how she could have felt at home among this type. I'd seen the look before on the mothers of junkie girls whose murders and overdoses and hotel balcony dives I'd investigated back in North Sydney, girls who had been sold, used, discarded like used fast-food wrappers.

Some mothers have bad girls and they know it. But they're always shocked when they see the kind of friends she kept, the bed she died in, the state she'd let her body get into when the clothes were stripped away and she was laid out on a morgue table—meat made of a person you created, a person whose safety you obsessed over once. You ignore these things when you have a bad child. You get blinded by your own love.

I kept listening, sipping my bad coffee. It took a good twenty minutes and about ten pages of notepad for everyone to work up a sweat, a couple of women to storm out, a few death threats to be fired back and forth. I didn't take much notice of the death threats. People like this killed each other in a drunken, angry snap over a barbecue on a Saturday football night, chips spilled everywhere, glasses broken, no time for threats, for thinking, for planning. It was all very boring. The urban-sprawl homicide beat was an easy beat. Dave-o stabbed Johnno. Oh no.

In the lull between arguments, I gathered more information about the girls. Ashley Benfield was the one who didn't fit—hadn't been born, at least, into the kind of life that encouraged recklessness like the other two. Keely Manning had grown up much like my murdered girlfriend Martina—a grimy face in a loud brood, each distinguished only by whether or not her particular crimes for that day would interrupt dinner. Martina told me that she enjoyed the sensation of being bad, liked to be hated because when she was hated she was being noticed, being heard. I wondered if Keely sought the arms of strangers because, besides the money, for once she was the focus of someone's attention even if only for a few minutes. From what her sister told me, something had been missing in Martina almost from the beginning. She never slept. Constantly swirled through violent emotions, even as a child. Would strangle her siblings until they turned blue in the face and then seconds later want their affection.

But Ashley. Ashley was different. I listened to her

parents while the crowd around us sniped at each other. Ashley had been everything her mother ever wanted. An artist. An academic. A perfect little angel. The Benfields had plenty of photographs of the little girl performing in dance classes, receiving awards on the assembly stage, adding bi-carb of soda to a model volcano to make it erupt pink foam for a science fair. She was gentle, they said. Giving. Was I looking for Ashley now because she had tired of that perfect life? Had someone come along and convinced the girl, as so many bad boy figures do, that everything her parents had put into her had been to benefit themselves only?

I didn't have any kids. I'd come close. But I had no idea what kind of trouble teenage girls could be. Runaways were not my department. All I got to see were the girls who had been found too late and the bad boys with their masks off, crying their eyes out in piss-stained jail cells. I looked at the pictures of bright-eyed Ashley and wondered what she'd been thinking.

The meeting taught me little about Rye and what had made the girls head out to his farm. But I said my good-byes at least knowing a little more about who I was looking for. I stepped out onto the porch where the boys were standing and stopped, flipped my notebook shut. Maybe it was instinct, or the angry dog look I'd copped from the Manning boy when I'd arrived, but he offered me a cigarette and I took it.

"Got email?" he asked. He looked inside. I glanced in after him, blew smoke respectfully over my shoulder.

"Yeah."

"Might email you something."

I gave him my card. He examined it as he spoke.

There was a great nasty ulcer just inside his mouth. One of those that makes it hard to eat.

"I'll email you something I don't want going no farther than your inbox."

I was going to tell him I couldn't guarantee that, but he pulled open the screen door, took his cigarette from his mouth, and walked inside. I lifted my eyes and got a cop-hating good-bye stare that burned me all the way to the car.

Jackie Rye was at breakfast when Eadie arrived. She'd slept badly again, the scratchers and crawlers and wandering things that lived inside her caravan somehow sensing the tension in her body and increasing the volume of their night orchestra. She woke sometime in the middle of the night to the feeling of the camera's black eye watching her like an owl and some long-legged thing crawling in her hair. She pulled it out and hurled it toward the darkness at the end of the bed. Made a promise to herself to block the drains, tape the windows. When Skylar thumped on her door at sunrise she felt pain in the act of waking, a dread so real and deep it made her bones ache.

Jackie's presence at the edge of the men's table made it all worthwhile. He was talking to Nick. Everyone turned when she approached. By now her news had passed on every set of lips. Some laughs. Some scowls. Some assessments based on the new information. Suddenly her long, manly gait meant something. The squareness of her shoulders and her rare smiles. How could they have missed it? Eadie put toast on. Skylar went for the eggs lying hard and dry in a dirty corner of the grill.

"People been saying things," the girl said. Eadie hadn't heard her usual scared-cat sprint to the door that morning. The girl's lips were restless, being chewed.

"I imagine they have."

"Is it true?"

"Jesus, Skye," Eadie laughed. The girl looked up, relieved. "It's not terminal cancer They didn't just announce the end of the world."

"Some people think so, though. It's like, city stuff. City people are like that. Not out here."

"People are like that. City people. Country people. People on fucking islands in the middle of the Pacific. People on snowy mountains. Eskimos. Around here, they *move* to the city. But before they move, they walk among you." Eadie wiggled her fingers in the girl's face. She cringed away.

"There ain't no fucking gay Eskimos."

"How many Eskimos you met?"

"Jesus."

"It's not a big deal."

"Spose." Skylar sucked air in the side of her cheek, made a click sound like she was trying to attract a horse. "Don't really care that much myself, to be honest, I'm just telling you how it is. I'm more worried about who's gonna win *Master Chef*. You watch it?" Her elbow in Eadie's ribs, high, bruising.

"No."

"Tonight we're watching it at yours then." She nodded to confirm her decision. "Jackie hates it. I'll bring chips."

She tottered off to the women's tables. Eadie set the kettle to boil. The morning was heating and the dogs that had taken up their places in the shade of the fold-out tables were being harassed by flies gathered on the humps of their backs and behind their ears. Sucking at scratch wounds.

Eadie imagined the police raiding this place, when she had finally pinned down whoever was responsible for the missing girls, black-clad officers knocking over these tables, kicking dirt in these snarling faces, throwing open caravan doors and rifling through possessions, making piles of them in the sun. Because that was what they would do when it was over, secure the killer and make everyone else's lives a misery simply for being here, for being in the company of a monster, whoever it was. Some youth worker would get Skylar off in a corner and listen to her cry and ask when she and Jackie had first had sexual intercourse, assess whether charges needed to be pursued. Someone would probably round up the dogs and send them off to a vet. She watched them squirming as she stood at the table waiting for the kettle, watched the flies walking in the blood. She didn't feel bad.

Eadie didn't notice the men leaving the table until they were all around her, scraping char off the barbecue, opening cupboards, slamming them, emptying the tiny bar fridge of butter, sauce, bowls of onion. Round two. Eadie stiffened as Nick passed behind her. She felt his breath on her neck.

"Look at this. It's Rye Farm's newest hand," Jackie said, leaning on the edge of the barbecue, his thin arms folded. "How's the working life, Eadie?"

"Fine, Jackie, thanks." Eadie poured the sugar. Grabbed for the kettle. It was gone. Nick adding to it, meeting her eyes over the sink, through the fine steam. She'd got his left cheekbone with the frying pan, right where the flesh was at its thinnest on the bottom rim of the eye socket. It would have hurt. The handle hadn't left a mark, but she'd likely crushed something in there, left it rubbing, angry, hard to swallow. There were capillaries burst in the corners of his eyes.

"Bet the hard work's helping you rest easy," Jackie said.

"Sure is. Slept like a lamb."

"Everything nice and . . ." the small man licked his flappy lips, glanced at Nick, "secure over there in your van?"

"More now than it was," Eadie said.

"Good. Good. You never know what creepy crawlies might come wandering in at night."

Jackie squinted at the sun, seemed to want to say something more, selecting the best words, like a man choosing the pig that would be slaughtered that day from the dozens of wide-eyed squealers waiting in the stalls. She watched him and felt Nick at the end of the table, tapping his fingers on the plastic surface, watching the water bubble up around the temperature gauge.

"I'm glad you're feeling happy here," Jackie said. "Glad you feel like you fit in. I'm not sure everyone feels that way. I'm sure some people around here feel like you're a . . . square peg, I guess they call it."

"Nothing wrong with being a bit square, Jackie." Eadie shrugged off her jacket and folded it in her arms, over her breasts. A loving bundle of denim. She felt a muscle tighten in the corner of her left eye, the only thing in her body that reacted to the tension in her mind.

The kettle clicked. Boiling point. Eadie heard a clunk behind her, felt the earth shudder under her feet as the tabletop slid onto its side and she was stalled

like a horse between the table at her hips and the table
at her backside. She met Nick's eyes as he tipped the
kettle, knocked it good and hard from the side, no
room for error, flushing the tabletop with scalding
water. Eadie dropped her denim jacket on the table in
the half a second it took for the burning water to reach
her, pressed it with her hands, made an instant dam.
The water rushed around the jacket and fell at the sides
of her body. She felt it splashing on her ankles, the
burn of tiny droplets that would do hardly any of the
damage the full kettle would have done to her stomach, her hips, her thighs, her crotch. The men around
her sent up a yowl of apparent surprise. The women
nearby turned, stepped away from the benches they
leaned on, curious.

Nick's eyes. The cold black eyes of an insect.

"Ho!" Jackie laughed, clapped his hands. "Look
out. That coulda been really nasty."

"Jesus, Nick," someone said. "Watch what you're
doing."

"Clumsy fucker."

"You'll have to be quicker next time," Jackie
laughed, folding his arms, watching Nick's face. The
tall man said nothing.

Someone slapped Eadie's shoulder in appreciation.
She fought the impulse to grab the hand and crush it in
her fingers. Eadie took the soaked jacket, still hot to
the touch, and slid out from the trap between the two
tables, wrung it onto the dirt. Skylar came bounding
toward her.

"Man! What happened?"

"Just an accident. Someone trying to give me a

bath." Eadie shook the jacket off, walked over to hang it on a string connecting the two carports. People at the barbecue were laughing. Jackie demonstrated what happened to the women, the rush of water with his loose hands, those hands tightening around an imaginary bundle. Jackie grinned and winked at Eadie as she walked away toward the stables.

People called him the Dogboy of Darlinghurst and stopped calling him Heinrich altogether. For a couple of years it was the Bear and his Dog who arrived at the back doors of suburban houses in the early morning hours to whisper in kitchens with women about what this poison would do or that one, how long it would take husbands or bosses or mistresses to start coughing or choking or turning blue, what those moments would be like for the ones who had to watch and explain.

It was the Bear and his Dog on Sunday mornings on the front doors of terraces in Redfern and Chippendale with the whomping stick and the list of names, Bear and Dog on the logs down by the pier in Woolloomooloo watching the navy boats and eating Harry's pies, Bear and Dog picking a path through crowded bars to the back booths to talk to dark-eyed foreign men about the girls at the house.

The Night of Teeth and Tearing always seemed to come up during these meetings. Heinrich would sit, folding coasters into squares, with one ass cheek off the booth because that's all that would fit beside Bear. The eyes would fall on him in the lull of words and someone would say, "Hey, isn't that the dog-killer?" Bear liked to tell the story, to rub Heinrich's head with his oven-mitt hand until his hair was all messed up.

He did this even when Heinrich was fifteen, or what he guessed was about fifteen, when his shoulders spread out and his knuckles developed calluses and his nose had been broken enough times that no one took pity on him when it happened. Heinrich had noticed that—the slow disappearing of pity, and care and affection, particularly from the women, the gradual change in those creatures who once only wanted to put clothes on him and now only seemed to want to take them off. Heinrich was just warming up to the idea of letting these giggling, whispering, lip-licking beings have their way one of these days when Bear pulled him aside in the hall and told him not to shit in his own nest, whatever that meant.

And even though he was the Dogboy of Darlinghurst, the boy was always landed with tasks given to someone who hadn't accomplished anything. Bear would tell him that these were the things he needed to do to make sure he kept his feet on the ground. Heinrich was still the runner on fight nights and he was still kept away from the dog training. He still had to read to Bear in the greenhouse, even though he was pretty good at it by now and even liked reading in his own time. And he was still responsible for all the cleaning work that went on back there, sweeping out the dirt and hosing the floors and watering the seedlings and labeling the bottles. Heinrich was still the carrier of messages, the keeper of keys, the filler of glasses, the protector of coats and hats. But he didn't mind. It meant he never missed anything.

Over the years the boy began to understand just how much of a hold Caesar had on every person he came into contact with, from the girls at the house who couldn't leave because they had no families and no money and couldn't read, to the junkies wandering Darlinghurst Road who couldn't go too far because Caesar was the only one who could get them what they needed even when they couldn't pay for it up front. You couldn't even get out of his grasp by killing yourself because Caesar got to know everyone you'd ever loved before he gave you a penny, so that he could hold them all in his hands like mice when you couldn't pay as they tried to claw and squirm their way out of his big fingers.

When you came to Caesar you left with a stain, even if you didn't know it yet, a tiny ink spot on your cuff or your palm or your shoe, something that would grow and spread overnight, a cancer dancing over skin. And his reach went everywhere, no matter how low down you tried to crawl into the dark, no matter how high you climbed or who you dragged in front of you. Caesar sent the Dog and the Bear to clamber through the hatches of navy ships to pick up bags of guns, to talk to men in bunks and engine rooms, to stand on the bridge and look at the city and talk to angry men in white. He sent them into warehouses to walk through streets and alleys of machinery parts, cameras, televisions, blenders, costumes, leather jackets, fur coats, shoes. Bear would sit in the car with the boy and his list, rubbing his hands to keep them warm.

"Know where these came from?" Bear would ask, holding up one of the cameras, turning the thing in his hands. Heinrich always felt a little sick around cameras but couldn't remember why.

"Where, Bear?"

"Vietnam. Bet you can't tell me where that is."

"Sticking out the side of Cambodia."

"Sure is. Crazy shit going on over there right now. Boys killing boys your age. Younger. Going mad and hacking them up like fish."

"Doesn't sound any good, Bear."

"No good at all, boy. We got eight thousand boxes here, six cameras a box. How many is that, young scholar?"

"Bout forty-eight thousand, I reckon."

"I reckon, too. Never miss a thing, Heinrich. Never let anyone give you a job unless you know what it is, what they're going to make from it, and whether or not you're getting yours, fair and square. Someone tells you they've got a hundred gold necklaces, you count them. Someone tells you they've paid the dealer, you call up and check. Someone tells you a guy's dead, you call his mother and ask when the funeral was. Always watching, always listening, always checking. You get it?"

"Got it."

There were rare times when Heinrich missed things and it was only ever when the forbidden man was involved. Heinrich had learned that his name was Savet and that he was a detective sergeant, but nothing more. When Detective Sergeant Savet arrived at the house Caesar would look at the boy the way that a man looks at a collarless dog wandering in his yard, trying to decide if it deserved brutality or could afford to be ignored. Heinrich would wander away, find girls to tease.

Bear always got angry when Savet was around. When Heinrich would ask what was going on, Bear wouldn't answer. It wasn't often that Bear didn't answer something. He had answered so many questions when Heinrich was little, even tried to tackle things he couldn't know—like where had Heinrich come from, what had happened to the people in the burning house.

"They were probably good people," Bear would say. "One of them was probably short."

From what Heinrich could tell, all Savet wanted to talk to Bear and Caesar about were boats and planes and maps of Vietnam. Heinrich didn't know if the man had been in the war or what. He walked with a limp and had the same hard-edged look that Heinrich had seen in boys coming back from the Nam, the sideways glance and quick turn of someone who had been crept up on a few times too many and couldn't sleep properly because of it.

The thing that worried Heinrich most about Detective Sergeant Thomas Savet was that he was sure the cop had the Silence in him. Once he watched Savet being run off by Bear when Caesar wasn't at the house. Savet had stood on the path at the bottom of the steps and looked up as the big man yelled and threatened and his face had been placid, calm, unhearing.

"You really hate that guy," Heinrich said afterward as Bear stood panting on the porch looking at the empty street.

"Warmonger. Filthy . . . greedy troublemaker."

"Why's he keep hanging round here?"

Bear grunted, kicked a cat off the porch that had been whining and wandering around his feet.

"You know that Kingsley kid that went missing? In the papers?"

"No."

"Neutral Bay kid. Rich. Volleyball."

"Oh yeah, yeah."

"He solved that." Bear pointed to where Savet had been standing. "They're telling us this lazy ignorant fool solved that."

Bear looked at the boy as though the very fact that Detective Sergeant Savet had solved a murder made something very clear but, as often happened in his life, Heinrich found himself on the very edge of understanding without really knowing what was going on. He didn't like the feeling. He was more comfortable following directions, staying out of the way, keeping his head down.

Heinrich opened his mouth to offer something, some half-committed line that would assure Bear that he wasn't an idiot but not reveal the crushing emptiness in his knowledge. But before he could do it Bear walked inside the house and slammed the door.

I got home about three in the afternoon and was walking up the stairs to my apartment when I got a whiff of some perfume ahead of me, something light and expensive and European. When I looked up the shrink was standing there with her arms folded, leaning against my door. I stopped walking and dropped my hand, let the keys jangle against my hip.

"What have I done now?" I said. "Go away."

"You're such a charmer, Detective Bennett."

She was all baby blue today, a T-shirt that crumpled up toward her hips and curved nicely around her taut biceps, tiny blue studs shaped like flowers in her ears. Gray skinny jeans that she could pull off without looking sag-bottomed. Cashmere boots with round toes. I got up close to unlock the door and was struck by how small and freckly she was, like a little hairless leopard.

"I don't have to play doctors with you anymore, Stone."

"I'm not here to play doctors with you," she said, slapping a bunch of files against my chest. "I've been trying to call you so that you can take these back. They're originals. I'd have paid to have them sent but it's not my responsibility."

"Oh and you were just in the neighborhood, so you thought, you know," I shrugged, gave a flourish.

"I really was just in the neighborhood. My mother lives two streets back."

"I'm a cop. I can tell when people are lying. Especially women."

"Oh yeah?"

"Yeah. Confess, Stone. You've been up all night outside my windows watching me shower. Taking photos. Sticking them in a scrapbook."

"You're so weird."

I took the papers, held open the door for her. The cat trotted toward us, meowing like a needy wife interrogating me about where I'd been and who I'd been with.

"I didn't know you were a cat man, Frank."

"I'm not a cat man." I gestured at the animal. "It's a man cat. Coffee? Tea?"

"Coffee." She dumped her handbag beside the door like she lived here. I frowned and began herding beer bottles off the sink. Wondered if I had any milk. If it was any good. I opened the fridge and exhaled.

"How are you?"

"I'm fine," I told the fridge.

"Busy?"

"Yep."

"I've been following the missing girls in the papers," she said, perching on the arm of my gray Ikea couch. "Not much movement there."

"Oh, there's movement," I said. "You just can't see it."

We talked about the case for a little bit. Kept it vague. How the families must feel. Similar cases. I forgot to switch the kettle on, remembered. She laughed at me. I glanced around and felt a little less embarrassed about my single-man hovel now that Eden had taken care of it for me.

The cat was whining, looking at me, pawing at my trousers.

"So, all this work, Frank," Stone said.

"Yeah?"

"I was hoping it'd keep you all squared away. But it's not, though, is it? If we're really honest with ourselves."

I looked over. She was examining an empty packet of Oxy she seemed to have plucked from between the couch cushions. I went and took it from her and slipped it into the bin.

"Did you manage to take a look at this place before you started psychoanalyzing my color scheme?" I asked. I motioned to the room. "Noticed how fucking immaculate it is? It's like a showroom in here. It must be exhausting to be so critical all the time."

"Your cat's starving."

"It's not starving." I snatched the box of cat food from the top of the fridge, tried not to trip over the animal as it wove between my feet. "I fed it yesterday."

Dr. Stone was watching me as I fed the cat, rinsed its water out, patted it a little as it crunched the kibble. My face felt hot.

"Do you feel like I'm attacking you?"

"I feel like you're trying to decide what social disorder I have from how I tie my shoelaces," I said. "What is it? Bipolar?"

"Are you trying to undercut my credibility in order to defend yourself?" she smiled.

"I'm not defending myself in my own house." I scratched the cat's rump. Its back leg twitched in pleasure.

"What's the cat's name, Frank?" she asked. I looked at her.

"Gray cat."

"Is it a boy or a girl?"

I straightened. Tried to glance down.

"Don't look at it. Tell me. Is it a boy or a girl?"

I licked my teeth. Dr. Stone cocked her head.

"What's your point?" I asked.

"That's not your cat, is it?"

"It's mine now."

"Is that Martina's cat?"

"No. It's mine."

"Why have you got Martina's cat, Frank?" I could tell she wanted to squint or frown, to let some of the raw confusion flooding through her mind show in her face. But I was sure they told you not to do that in shrink school. So her face remained still and open and understanding, and in a way that was worse, made me feel like an even bigger loser or psycho or addict or whatever her diagnosis would turn up. So I turned back to the coffee I'd failed to make and tossed the grounds out into the sink, rinsed a mug, and set it on the counter.

"Got any other plans, Stone, or was ruining my afternoon it?"

"No, this was it," she said.

I looked out the window until she was gone.

Hades was standing on the steps to his shack as I arrived, leaning on his cane. I'd hoped to be in and out of his place before nightfall but the sun was setting as I clambered up the drive. Some new creature was in the process of being assembled on the knoll in front of the house, a long-snouted thing made from hundreds of birdcages.

We said nothing to each other. When we got inside he handed me a beer from the fridge while I lay my papers out on the table.

"I've had one afternoon on this, so don't expect wonders."

"I rarely expect wonders," he said.

I sat down and shifted a black-and-white photograph over to Hades. A dark-skinned child of one or two sitting on a wooden chair in nothing but a pair of cotton pants, pulling at her feet and looking away. Someone had labeled the photograph in blue ink, identifying it with a serial number.

"Sharon Elizabeth White," I said, unfolding the file that the photograph belonged to. Printouts of scans from the National Archives. "Removed from the care of Donna Anna White by the Victorian Children's Protection Society in August 1956. Report cites vagrancy and alcoholism on the part of the mother. Only child at the time but two others would follow. Both would also be removed—Lynda in care until adulthood and Scott deceased at seven, traffic accident. Sharon's father unknown, father of the other two a steelworker. Mother illiterate, unemployed. Removal wasn't easy, it seems. Lots of trouble caused in the community. Lots of similar removals. A small riot." I pushed a folder toward Hades. It was thin. Handwritten, full of medical notes. Hades was looking at the photograph, frowning. His glasses were on the sink.

"Someone pissed off the local constabulary," I said.

"They would do that," Hades said. "Go in and clear out whole towns. Night raids. Keep everyone in check with the idea that they might get them back if they kept their noses clean. Sunday never talked about it, but I knew it would have been something like that."

"Well, she's in foster homes until five," I said, flipping the edges of the other folders. "A good kid, but a very slow learner. Basically nonverbal. Then she takes off one morning from school. Gone walkabout. For a while police thought she might have been abducted, but she's filed officially as 'Absconded from care' and that seems to be the end of it. Probably presumed a relative took her and closed the case."

"A beach." Hades smirked a little, sipped his beer. I waited. He didn't continue. He seemed to be dreaming, looking at the photograph.

"What?"

"Bear found her on a beach. On a Sunday morning."

I lifted more photographs from the files, shuffled through them. Laid one out before him. A group of people standing on the porch of a large house, lots of women smiling and laughing, some shadowy-eyed lowlifes with big dogs on chains. The girl who was found on a Sunday was there at the edge, looking at her fingernails when the photograph was taken. I pointed to the big man at the back, in the shadows by the door, a hairy colossus.

"Michael 'Bear' Harwitz?"

"That's the one."

I held the photograph up to my nose, squinted. I'd heard things about Bear Harwitz and Alec "Caesar" Steel from the sixties, old academy stories that were probably so removed from truth as to be completely useless to my investigation. Gunfights and towns terrorized and cocaine parties and prostitutes slain in their beds. Hades took the photograph from my hand, having waited long enough. I watched his face. He didn't seem upset about any of it. I imagined he'd never seen any of these photographs before. He finished his beer and caught my eye, set the photograph down.

"What else?"

"Nothing else at this point. A few drug arrests. Twelve. Fifteen. Seventeen. Eighteen. That's it. That's the mark she made on the world."

"That's the mark she made on the public record."

"Who was she to you?"

"She was the love of my life," the old man said. I waited. He folded up the papers before him and put them out of his way. He clasped his hands and looked at my eyes. Concrete and steel and storm clouds in his eyes, the gray of hard times weathered in silence. He reminded me of my father—when that thought came to me I shook it physically out of my head, looked away.

"You kill her, Hades?"

"No."

"I've heard plenty of smack talk about you, old man."

"Like what?"

"Like you bit some guy's thumb off in a bar fight."

He laughed, hung his head back.

"I've been in some good scraps, but not that good. The thumb is connected to the hand by about a million complex, intertwining muscles. Its tendons go as far back as the wrist. You can't just bite it off. It's not a fucking breadstick."

"I heard you know a lot about bodies. How they work. How to dispose of them."

"There's a shovel out on the porch there, boy, and a

flashlight in the cupboard. Go ahead. Go treasure hunting, if that's your idea of a good evening. Plenty have before. I ought to start charging for it."

"You're pretty good with the denials. But you know that I know about Eden."

"Careful now."

"I'm a police officer. I look at the facts. I look at the rumors, even if you say they're not true. You can't be surprised that you're my first suspect."

"I'm not surprised. I'm just waiting for you to get your ass into gear and move on from me. I didn't kill Sunday. I told you that. I loved her. I'm as keen to know what happened to her as that stupid boy out there on the road."

"Then why am I sitting here? Why is Adam White so sure he's got you?"

"Because she was on her way to see me when she disappeared. It looks bad."

I waited while he cracked another stubby.

"She was supposed to meet me," Hades said, shifting back on his chair. "At Central Station. Platform Two. Right outside the ticket booths. Nine o'clock, I said, because she never got up early. She spent the night before at a hotel called Jeremy's. I sent a note, and she got the note. I waited and she didn't come. Something happened to her. She'd packed her things. She was ready to go. And then she was gone, all the stuff still sitting there."

"What happened to her?"

"I don't know."

"Any guesses?"

"Anything could've happened to Sunday. Trouble

loved her. She'd always been like that. She was working on and off for a cathouse in Crest Avenue when she disappeared but she hadn't been there long. Bounced around a lot. Pissed people off."

"So you don't know who nabbed her." I sat back too and hung my elbow over the back of the chair. "No idea?"

"Plenty of people didn't like me. I'd just shaken everything up. Scorned some people pretty bad. But then, plenty of people didn't like her."

"What would be your guess then? Your people or hers?"

"I told you. I don't know."

"No clue."

"If I had a fucking clue I wouldn't have some idiot on my road watching me take a piss and some smart-ass cop boy sitting interrogating me in my own kitchen." He flung an arm toward the door, toward me. "I'd have brought White up here the moment he showed interest, sat him down, and described how good it had felt to slowly and carefully carve the wet, beating heart out of the chest of the man who touched her. If I had any fucking clue who killed Sunday you'd have known about it, because it would've been in the papers, what I did to the killer."

I finished my beer. A bunch of clocks were ticking in the other room, part of some collection, going off like the twittering of tiny mechanical birds.

"Caesar?" I asked.

"I looked into it. Over and over. He and his people were accounted for."

"I thought you were his people."

"Not always."

"Who did you account for and how did you account for them?"

"Caesar was . . . incapacitated the night Sunday went missing," the old man said, raising his eyebrows. "That's all I'm prepared to say about that."

It didn't surprise me how easily Hades slipped from client into defendant mode.

"Who else?"

"His major lieutenants were with him, so I knew where they all were. Tom Savet was at a policeman's ball at the city all night receiving awards."

"Tom Savet?"

"He was very close to Caesar at the time."

"So if you had to guess, you wouldn't say whatever happened to Sunday was something personal?"

"Look, in my time, you wanted to do something personal, you let everyone know what it was. No point in knocking off someone's bird without sending them something. A finger. An eye. Leaving her somewhere. Telling the papers and splashing it about town. That was how you did things in those days. None of this drive-by punk shit. None of this, this shoot-'em-up hooligan crap. You set examples back then. You spoke to people's faces."

I sighed. The old man folded his arms on the table, looked at the windows, the night.

"Caesar and I . . . We had trouble at the time. Big trouble. If it had been anyone meaningful it would have been him. Him or one of his men. But I told you. I looked into it. I looked into it for years. It wasn't them."

"It's going to be difficult to find out what happened if it was just some angry john or a deal gone bad or something."

"You'd remember killing Sunday," he said. "She wasn't any ordinary girl. People still remember her. She was . . . different. Wild."

"Whoever killed her might be dead."

"They'd wanna hope."

"All right. Well. You keep your head down until we chat again. I'll work on this as much as I can but I've got to watch out for Eden as well. Don't cause any trouble. Don't go inviting any guests. And don't, whatever you do, go down there thinking you're going to talk to the guy. You slip up once and it's on tape."

"Tape?" Hades sat upright in his chair.

"He's filming you."

The old man's face hardened. I hadn't thought it could get any more menacing, but it did.

"This is harassment. This is stalking."

"I know it is."

Hades' eyes drifted away from me. I could almost see his clockwork mind ticking away, devising painful scenarios.

"Don't do anything. Not yet."

"You better move fast, copper," the old man said.

I packed the papers back into the folders. I was going to take the last photograph, the group one with Sunday in the corner looking at her fingernails, but Hades' elbow was on it so I left him there with it in the shack. The sun was red over the trash mountains as I walked to my car.

*   *   *

Waiting outside Eden's apartment, Juno was like a teen in the queue for a rock concert. It'd been awhile since I had been to one, but I recognized the shuffling feet, restless eyes, anguished sigh toward the heavens every now and then. Taking his backpack off, unzipping and staring into it, putting it back on. When Eden emerged from the elevator he stopped in his tracks and folded his hands into his pockets, dropped his head. She looked tired. Her eyes flicked to me and there was some of that raw animal rage you see in people who've had their civility worn down to glass.

"What is he doing here?"

"He's the tech. We gotta have him."

"I thought we were just talking tactics."

"We are. There are things he might have noticed that you didn't, though. He's been on the surveillance a lot longer than I have. I've been slack."

Eden narrowed her eyes at the boy, seemed to measure him with a glance. She unlocked her door with exaggerated movements. I stood looking at the black hair creeping into the bad dye job, the way it turned from midnight to brown to burned orange to sunflower yellow over a matter of centimeters. I could see the tendons moving in her white neck.

She flicked the gold halogens on. The apartment was as I remembered it, like some weird kind of gallery hotel, somewhere you could pay to sleep among the art. No signs of humanness about it—no T-shirt lying on the couch or pair of knickers on the floor or empty coffee mug forgotten, stains on the bottom. Everything was sterile, tucked away, folded up, shelved. Furniture-store neat. It was probably a good thing. I didn't know what Juno would do if he caught sight of a pair of Eden's knickers. He stood looking around with his mouth open until I bopped him in the chest and he came to himself.

Eden hung her bag on a hook by the door, punched a code into the alarm system, tossed her keys into a bowl on the kitchen counter. Coming home. She relaxed into her normal posture, discarding Eadie's defensive, hunched stance. She turned to us, pulling off her jacket.

"You, watch him." She nodded at me, and then Juno. "You, order dinner."

Juno snapped to attention.

"What, uh, what should I get?"

"I don't care." Eden walked toward the hall under the loft stairs. Juno looked at me helplessly.

"Not Japanese," I said.

"What, so, anything? Anything, just not Japanese?"

"Anything," I said.

"*Anything?*"

"Just order the fucking food." I put my stuff on the floor by the coffee table. "And don't touch. She'll kill you."

Juno went out onto the balcony, panting, curling the orange ringlets behind his ears around his fingers. I set up the laptop and wandered into the kitchen. I selected a bottle of wine from the rack and grabbed some glasses from the immaculately arranged cupboards. Out of curiosity I opened a few for a peek. She had the stainless-steel knife set of a professional chef and all her cutlery was polished to within an inch of its life. All the mug handles were facing the same way and her foodstuffs were from weird organic stores I'd never heard of. Sicko.

I poured the wine, took a sip, listened to the shower running down the hall. I heard it finish, a door open and close, and headed down there. The hall was warm from steam. There were two doors, both closed.

"Eden, I need to use your loo."

"Go ahead," she shouted.

I was sure her voice came from the door on the right. But when I opened the one on the left, I caught a glimpse of a big room, red curtains, a stiffly made bed. And Eden standing with her side to me, a towel around her hair.

"Frank!"

"Oh God. Oh God! I'm sorry." I slammed the door and started laughing, still holding onto the handle. "I'm sorry. I thought this was the bathroom."

The doorknob twisted in my fingers and she wrenched it open. She was wearing a black satin robe.

"What the hell is wrong with you?"

"I'm really sorry." I stood there laughing, unable to stop. She was looking at my eyes like a wet, angry tiger. "Honest mistake, really. I couldn't hear which room you . . . and . . ."

"Stop laughing, use the bathroom, and then fuck off out of my hallway."

"I just have to stand here a minute." I closed my eyes and drew a deep breath, expanded my chest. "I just have to recover from the single greatest joy of my young life."

She slammed the door in my face. I was still chuckling in the bathroom. I'd seen Eden in her underwear once before and the effect had been just as thrilling, like catching a glimpse of a rare butterfly, so swift and glorious it's gone before your eyes can really settle on it. We'd been upgrading our riot training together down in Jervis Bay at a fire grounds, and she was behind a curtain stripping off clothes saturated in tear gas. Back then I hadn't seen the bright pink birthmark that looked like a prancing horse on her ribs, so perfectly shaped it was almost like a tattoo. The only blemish on an otherwise marble-sculpted frame.

I spent most of my time trying to be a mature, restrained, well-rounded almost-middle-aged man but the sight had set off something juvenile in me—not helped by her obvious annoyance. I went back to the living room, where Juno was sitting rigidly on the couch, setting up his laptop.

"I just saw Eden in the nick," I said.

"You *what?*"

"The nick. The nuddie. Nekkid. Starkers. Bare-assed like the day she was born."

Juno's mouth was hanging open.

"No way."

"Way."

"I bet she's hard, man."

"Like a stone."

"She's gonna kill you."

"She's gonna kill me," I agreed.

Eden came out of the hall drying her hair in a towel, wearing pale jeans and a long gray shirt.

"You guys quite finished?" she asked, hanging the towel on the back of one of the kitchen stools. "You want to call the papers?"

"No, we're good," I smiled. "That's a really pretty birthmark in a really pretty place though."

"One more word about it and I'll slap your face off."

"I know you will." I shook my head like I was clearing water from my ears. "All right, let's work."

Eden took the wine I'd poured her and sipped it long and slow. She gave me a filthy look. She wedged herself into the corner of the couch and put her feet up next to my leg. Her toenails were perfect pink squares, but she had a scar on her left foot about eight centimeters long and white as porcelain. I'd glimpsed other scars on her ribs. I wondered where she'd got them, then came to the natural conclusion and stopped myself. It was easy to forget what Eden was. Now and then I liked to pretend she was just a strange and beautiful woman and that her social awkwardness was nothing to worry about. That she wasn't, in fact, something that I spent most of my day hunting and most of my night dreaming about hunting. The fox to my hound.

"There are a couple of people out there who worry me," she began, cupping the wine with her hands. "Nick's and Jackie's natural tendency toward violence make them stick out among the pack. There is genuine malice everywhere though. No one has a problem joining in. I don't know how we're going to separate suspects if everyone's willing to egg each other on."

"That was a clever move by the way," Juno piped up. He grabbed his wineglass and tried to hide behind it. "The gay thing. Everybody's a little more aggressive now."

"Thanks," Eden said. Her voice was flat.

"And, and this morning," Juno swallowed. "Man, that was swift."

"What happened this morning?"

"Forget about it, Frank. Jesus. Move on." Eden waved at my computer.

"Well, I have something that might put a nail in it." I leaned forward and drew up my email. "Got this from Keely's brother. Says he found it on his sister's phone and moved it to his before Missing Persons took it."

"Why'd he do that?" Juno asked.

"People do weird things when someone's missing," I said. I started the video, turned up the sound. It was scratchy.

A mattress in a small dark caravan, barely visible against the green mesh of bad lighting, the pillows stripped and a sheet heaped at the side. A body curled, arms bound behind her at the wrists and elbows, making her shoulder blades meet painfully in the middle. A mop of curly hair, dark, maybe black. She turned, moaned, looked at the ceiling. A slice of white breast, pointy as an elbow. A body moved before the camera, threw something into the corner of the room. Jackie. Another figure in the mirror beside the bed, leaning against the doorframe, arms folded. Jackie climbed onto the bed. Boxers only. White legs from a distinct line high up on his thighs. One of those men who always wore short shorts so he was ready to go at any second.

"Oh God," Juno put his wineglass down, covered his mouth with his hands. "Oh. Oh no."

Eden was watching passively. She sipped her wine. Juno got up after a few seconds and faced the balcony doors.

"That's Nick?" Eden pointed to the man in the doorway as the figures moved on the bed.

"Yeah."

"Who's this, then? Keely? She's got the curls."

"I thought so at first, but there's no tramp stamp." I pointed to the back of the girl on the screen, milk white in the dark. "Keely's got a big tribal across the top of her ass."

"This some girl we don't know about, then?"

"Could be."

Juno was covering his ears and shaking his head. I stopped the video a couple of times, looked at the shapes in the dark, tried to see if there was anyone else in the mirror, in the hall behind him. The footage was terrible. It had probably been shot and downloaded in a couple of formats, moved from computer to phone to computer, downsized and then upsized.

"This singles Nick and Jackie out from the others," I said.

"Is this enough for an arrest?" Juno said, taking his fingers down from his ears carefully, in case the video started up again.

"No."

"Why not? That's . . . that's rape."

"It's a nonconsensual-looking sex scenario. There's nothing to say it's not role play."

"I'll bet the girl will say it's not role play. That's . . . that's sick, man."

"Well," I said, "you find her for me, Juno, and we'll ask her, huh?"

"Who is this guy?" Eden asked me, jutted her chin at Juno. "Are you out of the academy or what?"

"He's a civilian."

"How do you get to do what you do?" Eden was squinting. "You're not even signed on."

"I've got a pretty unique skill set." Juno sat down, gulped his wine, coughed. "They had me break into some mob computers on a contract basis last year, Captain Renalds in Drug Squad. I told them I could do surveillance. They offered me a job, but . . . I want to go to the academy in November. Do it properly."

"You're going to the academy? You're softer than Camembert cheese."

"Some things I just don't like." Juno's face flushed a painful pink. He gulped more wine. "Jesus. It's not every day you see something like . . . like that."

"Would you not drink that wine like that," Eden snapped. "It's a fucking Armagh."

"Sometimes you do see shit like this every day, Juno. Sometimes you see worse. You learn to switch off."

"I don't want to switch off."

"Then look for another job," Eden said.

"Give him a break." I grabbed Juno's neck, shook his head for him. Something about him made me want to grit my tooth. "He's only a boy. He's got a big heart. A big, orange heart."

"Why don't you get your boy to prove his worth on this video then? I want to know who that girl is and whether or not she's still alive."

I shifted the laptop over to Juno and he began clicking away.

"I gave Skylar the deodorant can camera," Eden said, leaning over me to frown at the boy. "What did you pick up on that?"

"Nothing much," Juno said. "Nick doesn't visit Jackie in the cabin a lot. It's mainly a TV room for everyone else in the park, and Jackie and Skylar's love nest."

"Have you been watching a bit of Discovery Channel action, Juno?" I snorted.

"I can't watch them. The camera's still turned around. She hasn't used the deodorant."

"What do they talk about?"

"They fight a lot. They're either fighting or talking about how in love they are."

"The mean sweet cycle," Eden said.

"What?"

"They abuse you 90 percent of the time, shower you with affection 10 percent of the time. Classic abuser behavior. You hang in for the 10 percent because it's kind of a reward for all your hard work."

"Boring," I yawned. "Sounds easier to be single."

"Not for these girls. They're afraid of being alone. No self-confidence."

We sat watching Juno work on the video. He felt our gaze, writhed.

"I just don't get why the brother would hide this video," Juno said. "It's sick."

"There's no telling," I said. "Might have thought it was Keely and didn't want a bunch of cops watching her. I've seen it before. Family hides the victim's past, even to the detriment of the case."

Juno clicked away, minimizing things, drawing up other programs.

I put an arm over the back of the couch and Eden glanced at it beside her, irritated.

"Your dad wants to see you," I murmured.

"How's all that going?"

"Fine. A little trip down memory lane required."

"Is that what this is all about?" She reached over and poked the scrape on my face, the yellow bruise fading now, almost gone. It was rare to be touched by her.

"Ow. Yes."

"How is he?"

"He's all right."

"How're you?"

"Don't start on me. How're you?"

"Oh, you know. It's a hard place." She sipped her wine, rolled it in her mouth. "Lots of pricks out there. They get bored. Pick on each other. Nothing I haven't seen before. It's high school dynamics. Cliques. Alliances. Fringe dwellers."

"And you're on the fringe?"

"Me and the girl. She might be next. I worry about her. She's not bright. She's like a happy rabbit, bouncing around, looking very much like prey."

"Someone's idea of tasty. You managed to get a proper look around yet?"

"Not yet. A couple of restless souls about at night."

"Oh yes, I saw that. We both saw that. You've got a good swing there."

"Shoulda been a cricketer."

"So where from here?"

"I want to get into the kill sheds. Out the back, into the grasslands. Tomorrow night maybe. They have a bonfire on Saturdays. I'd have stayed if I didn't need the batteries changed. No one seems to be bothered that I'm coming and going—they think I'm sorting out my divorce and looking for a better job, and they're happy at the idea that I might leave. The girl, though. She thinks I'm off having some big adventure. I don't want her to tag along. Next time there's a bonfire I'd like to stay," she said.

"You thought about checking the pigpens for samples? Sending some bloods back? I saw a documentary on this guy in the States, this pig farmer."

"These pigs are pretty domestic," she said. "He sells them to Coles. It's not the way I'd operate. A stupid move if you ask me, feeding your victims to pigs. The thing sits there with your evidence inside it waiting for someone to come along, trip on a finger bone in the mud. Stupid."

I sat watching her face. She was casting a critical eye over Juno as he worked. I wondered what she did with her bodies. I wondered where the six men I knew she and Eric had killed had ended up, if they might be found someday, if I might live to see Eden arrested for what she truly was. A beautiful taker of lives. I only half-wanted to know why she did it. At what point had she and Eric decided that they would follow through on their dark fantasies of personally issued justice? Did she carry on the dark life now that Eric was gone? Had her underworld father taught her how to do it?

The doorbell rang and Eden buzzed the delivery girl up. She brought bags of steaming curry-smelling boxes to the table.

"What is this?" I said as Eden unpacked the bags, lifted lids on dishes laden with vegetables I didn't recognize. Nothing smelled familiar.

"Ethiopian." Juno ducked his head.

"Ethiopian?"

"You said I should order anything."

"You get told you can order anything and *Ethiopian* is the first thing that comes to mind?"

"It's all right." Eden gathered some hot flat bread out of a paper bag. "You'll like it. Here. Have some of that. Mix it with that."

Juno let a long breath out of his body as Eden dished out the food. I saw his chest deflate and his tiny stomach bulge. There was sweat in the ringlet curls in his temples. I sat staring at him.

"Ethiopian?"

"Give him a break," Eden laughed. "He's only a boy."

On the night that his world ended, Heinrich was on watch. Watch was Heinrich's most hated of all jobs because he learned nothing from it, and Bear told him he must always be learning if he wanted to have a good life. When he attended Bear's meetings or barged into the houses of men who owed Caesar or rounded up gamblers for the fights, even when he chased whores into the back alleys of the Cross and cornered them and wrung a little information about their johns out of them, he always learned something. How to make a girl cry. How to duck a good swing. What a broken bone sounded like. How to make someone agree to something that was entirely bad for them, and do so in a way that made them happy, made them laugh and slap your back and order you drinks.

But once a week on watch nights, Heinrich was alone on the porch of the house in Darlinghurst and he was not allowed to read by the light of a candle, so he learned nothing. He would sit on the old leather couch there with one hand on a cat or a dog, and he would stare at the street, the abandoned lot across the road, the wire fencing, the town houses beyond that, the pub on the corner—watch it all descend into the late hours. Watch nights were long nights. The moon shrunk against the burned orange sky, saying good-bye, leaving him to rot.

When he spotted the figure walking toward the house from the pub, Heinrich got up from the couch and stood on the steps. When the light of a street lamp fell on her, Heinrich felt a mixture of anger and relief surge through him. He turned, walked back up onto the porch, and pretended to be distracted by the cotton strings hanging from the splits in the couch. Sunday wasn't dressed for the weather, but she hardly ever was. She never seemed to be cold. She came up onto the porch and hoisted herself onto the wooden rail.

"Long time no see, Dogboy."

"Where the hell have you been?" Heinrich gave her a look-over, from her head right down to her feet, the way Bear had taught him to do when he wanted someone to feel small. "It's been weeks. Don't you live here anymore?"

"I don't live anywhere, man. You know that."

"You sure seem to live here when it suits you. Bet you're here to raid the cupboards. Take my blankets. Take whatever cash you can scrape outta the bottom of my pockets."

"I never scrape no cash off you. It's all you can do to give it to me."

"What a lie."

"You know you love me," she laughed, came and sat beside him. She smelled like wine and flowers tonight. Like a party. Like rooms full of people, sour breath, laughter, sweat. Her eyes glittered in the dark, too big for her head. Her hair was everywhere. Heinrich decided to stop looking at her. She scratched around in her little cloth bag and lit a joint.

"Gimme that." He took it from her, dragged half of it up in pure spite.

"How's Bear?"

"Busy."

"The big Shark?"

Sunday had always called Caesar the Shark. His teeth frightened her, the way he laughed his phony angry laugh with his head snapped back and they all showed, right to the rear of the deep pink hole, rows of them, white and pointed, bone crunchers. She'd whispered to Heinrich at night about it *in those early days. He'd shushed her and told her to get off him and go to sleep.*

"Won't be back tonight. Where you been?"

"Fine."

"I said where, not how." Heinrich gave her back the joint, watched the way her lips gathered around it, wet like rose petals. "I look for you everywhere I go."

"That's kind of nice."

"I don't know what you're doing. When you'll be back. If you'll ever be back. Why you ain't here with me."

"What am I gonna do here waiting for you, Dogboy?" she snorted, smoke rushing from her nose. "Drink tea in the kitchen? Sweep the greenhouse? Read penny mysteries? I ain't your wife. I'm your sister, mister."

"You're supposed to be waiting for when we get enough cash to get outta here. Go up north where it's warm. Buy a bookshop, like we talked about."

She laughed. The sound echoed in the street, a tinkle of glass carving the cold air. Heinrich felt his face grow hot.

"I'm always surprised when I come see you. It's always a shock."

"What is, for chrissake?"

"How you can still be such a child when there's so much darkness around you."

"I ain't no child."

"Maybe what happened to you stopped you from growing," she murmured, the joint glowing red against her long fingers. "Maybe you froze in the fire. Someone's lost baby forever. Sometimes I wish I could go back to that time on the beach. Be the baby again. A wet and cold thing Bear gathered up. That was the last time he touched me, you know. There's something nice about being abandoned and then being saved. I do it whenever I can, but it's never the same."

Her eyes scanned the street, caught a little of the moon as it bounced off the newly fallen rain. When they found his own they lingered there before falling to his lips.

She was the one who moved. He couldn't make his limbs work. Her hands wound up into his hair and gripped it, and when he felt the pain it seemed to awaken him and he gave it back, pulled her to him, crushed her. He had to stop her once or twice. Her shaking, hard restless hands in his shirt, her breath in his mouth. She needed him, climbed onto him, pulled his neck. Forced herself against his chest, her lips on his ear. A noose of arms.

After a while, when they were both warm, he held her, rocked her, let her hide her face against his neck. Not being able to see her in the dark didn't matter, though some part of him ached to put shapes and colors to the skin under his hands—where it stopped being soft and went hard, where it was tight and where it was dry and smooth like sun-warmed stone. He squeezed her ribs and felt the bones bend. The sounds she made were helpless things, whispers, pleads, a sudden cry of want, of fear when he tried to shift. He didn't want to sleep until she did, but she pulled the rug from the end of the couch up over them and curled her feet around his, and her kisses on the side of his face, on his neck, pulled him away from himself.

"Will you save me?" she whispered.

He opened his mouth to answer her and his face was flooded with light so hard and white it crushed the sound out of him. The porch lights above, the hall lights, all flicked on at once. There were men above him. Sunday was gone.

Heinrich's first instinct was to roll. He didn't know what was happening or who was above him in the black, the hoods. But he rolled, and the action saved him. The panels in the porch seemed to explode upward in chips and fragments, *getting in his eyes. He covered his head, the sound so loud he missed it, just a thundering in his ears and all around him. They passed over him and into the house.*

More gunfire. Heinrich gripped the ground, breathed wood, coughed, and tasted blood in his mouth. All his bones had locked at once. Unlocking them took frantic seconds. He crawled, one leg dragging and useless, threw himself through the front door.

Screaming. One of the girls running out into the kitchen and being cut down. Men rushing out, naked, falling. One of the men in black went to the open bedroom door and Heinrich watched his shoulders shudder as he pumped the room. People wailing, short, sharp. Silent. The next room, a spray. Heinrich pulled himself behind the armchair, heard shouting, Bear's bellow from across the house.

He tried to get up and bullets pocked the wall behind him, pulled the window down around him in a rain of glass. He cowered in it, pulled his head down against his chest. The blood on his chin, in his nose. Was this dying? The world was turning hard and clicking back into place like a moving picture on a wheel, his body at the center. The gunfire stopped and there was running, and the kitchen windows shook in their frames and glasses fell from the counters.

Heinrich dragged himself across the glass, got up, fell into the doorframe of the back room. There was blood spray and holes all over the walls like black stars. The boy fell into the dark back room, crawled, climbed up the floor as it tilted up before him, a ramp, a ladder without rungs.

Bear was there, under his hands. Shuddering. Wet. Impossibly hot. Heinrich wrapped his arms around the thick heavy head, squeezed it, tried to lift it from the ground.

"Bear! Bear! Bear! Bear!"

He could see two white points glittering in the blackness. Heinrich pushed his face against the big man's face, felt the hair hard like wires. His fingers found the hole in the fat neck, tried to stem the gushing.

"Anigozanthos," the old man coughed the words. "Rufus. Ani . . . Ani . . . Ru . . ."

Heinrich howled. The sound came out of him without words, without sobs, just a noise like a siren that started in the pit of his guts and crept up louder and louder until it met the air, made his ears ache. A scream. The big man held him, limp fingers, weak arms around his middle.

"Oh, boy," Bear said. "Boy."

Heinrich felt him die like a great mountain crumbling to the earth.

Every now and then Harry Ratchet took a moment to close his eyes and enjoy his space. He had been alone a long time now, and yet still, once a day at least, he would stand in the silence of his tiny caravan in Cronulla among the things that were his and solely his—his Ned Kelly memorabilia collection and the damp towels on the floor and the empty pizza boxes on the sink and the Jimmy Barnes records—and feel blissfully alone.

There was barely floor space in this place, a few footholes in the dark between the door and the end of the bed and the television stand, a square of bathroom mat before the bathroom annex. But these were his for treading and no one else's. The shower cubicle he stood in, mere centimeters on all sides of his round and taut and hairy body where weak but blistering hot water fell, it was his. His space. It was all about space for Harry. A handspan of Harry Only Territory was something hard won, and he was determined to enjoy it.

Scarlett had no idea about space, which made Harry laugh now, because the woman had been obsessed with being close. In the early days after Harry had found her, she an uptight career rabbit and he a lazy but presentable week-to-week hound, Scarlett had been able to make a two-hundred-square-meter penthouse in Mosman feel crowded, following him around the huge balcony while he watched the yachts being tossed around, rubbing up against him.

Her couch had been the length of his current lodgings and had cost more, but he'd fought for a centimeter of room on it. She'd have a room full of television personalities and socialites and politicians spread out around her at one of her charity gigs, lights on her perfectly sculpted biceps, everyone's favorite weather girl, male models adjusting their trousers at the sight of her, and she'd cling to Harry's arm like she hadn't found him in the dark one afternoon on set, fumbling with wires, swigging Coke and itching in his uniform polo. He was her star. Her home. The rock she anchored to. Harry could hardly breathe but he liked the money, so he learned how to distract her and slip away, look at the sky, have a smoke without her jabbering at him.

After a year or so Harry got sick of ducking and diving away from Scarlett whenever he got the chance and tried to train her, because the big Four-Oh had made him realize he was onto a good deal and starting again would be a hassle. She'd made the national news, too, so he could give up the audio-rigging game. If it was going to be the long haul with Scarlett, Harry needed to straighten her out and show her who was boss.

The first thing he did was take the money. The second thing was push her mother and her loudmouthed friends out of the picture with a few carefully placed ultimatums. Step three in his plan was positive reinforcement, the way you train little wide-eyed terriers with liver treats—be a good girl, a quiet girl, and I'll come home on time. I'll come home sober. I'll come home and cuddle you. Everything had been snap, snap, snap, the way he wanted it. Sit! And she slammed that ass on the floor before he'd finished making the sound. Then one day she presented him with a white plastic strip with two blue lines and tears in her eyes and talk of names for it. And all his hard work had come down to nothing.

Trump card.

Plan B. His pup had gone wild. Nothing to do with a wild animal but put it down. He'd nudged her down a flight of stairs one afternoon before Christmas, when the thing inside her had started to take hold and ruin her body and her logic. Hadn't worked. A couple more knocks, a couple more quiet nudges, and she'd presented him with the perfect solution to his problem. A 9mm bullet, right in his guts. He lay in the hospital bed and watched her trial, chatted up the rehabilitation girl about it as he clambered along steel bars and walked himself up and down the wide halls with a walking frame—poor Harry, abused and misused husband just trying to learn how to love again. When they carried Scarlett off kicking and hollering on the evening news she'd once sparkled on, her regrowth showing and her eye makeup smudged in a way he knew she'd hate, he thought he was free.

He begun claiming his space again in a little apartment in Eastlakes, steadily chewing through her cash on pretty horses and Blue Label and little Asian women with perky tits. Then a couple of drably dressed social workers had knocked on his door and put a baby in his hands.

Another trump card.

Even from behind the razor wire she was still in his space, filling up the place like a bucket of water in a paper cup.

He took it inside, forgot it for days, lay in the bed in the other room and cried about it, cried louder than it did. He sat on the carpet in its room in those dark first days and watched it wriggling and screaming, the stink of its piss taking up the air. People brought him clothes and toys and bedding for it, so much stuff he had to pile it in corners like he was preparing for a winter, the kitchen cluttered with sour milk and colored plastic and empty jars of muck.

He stood in the shower with it, slept on the floor with it, sat in the car with it, beating the steering wheel, beating his head, beating the windows. He sat outside his ruined apartment with it at the top of the concrete stairs and watched it shuffling and inching around on the damp at his feet like a swollen, snotty grub, watched it edge toward the empty space before the five-flight fall, bulging backside waggling, worm toes squirming up and down.

Harry stood, looked at the fall, the screen doors, dozens of them, most hiding angry Indians in leather jackets who would hardly know how to answer a phone let alone testify to his possible negligence as a father. Harry stood. Harry watched. Then Harry put his foot out, pressed against the soft, papered rump with his toes, gently-gently, softly-softly, until it tipped.

Harry stood now in his shower remembering his own screaming. He kept screaming and screaming when the ambulances arrived, screaming and screaming when the cops arrived, screaming and screaming when the two homicide detectives showed up. A lanky guy with dead eyes named Doyle and some black-haired vixen he couldn't remember the name of, distracted as he was by the way her jeans cupped her apple-shaped rump.

He sat on the edge of the ambulance and watched that perfect posterior through tear-soaked hands as she wandered, calm and curious, through the tarpaulin barrier to where the thing lay dead, around the thing and the people chalking and photographing it, up the stairs, down the stairs, all around. The guy with the dead eyes came over to him and talked and made notes and gave condolences and numbers to call, but the dark apple-bottomed beauty just stood there, off and away from the crowd, looking up at the top of the stairs, looking down at where the thing lay.

Harry was getting a cold feeling about the way the woman was standing and looking and frowning and thinking when she disappeared and he felt safe again. Days turned into weeks. Grief counselors came and went. The sun set and the evening news came on. Harry swelled, slowly opening like a wary flower, and filled up his space.

He toweled off now in his little caravan bathroom annex, stretched his limbs, ruffled his hair in the mirror, laughed. Almost a year had passed, and still the thrill of a room empty but for him. He was smiling at the feel of it as he entered the caravan, but the smile disappeared when he found a woman sitting on the end of his bed with her hands between her knees, restful. He didn't recognize her as the apple-assed stunner from the day the thing died until she stood, turned toward him, looked at him, set her feet apart on his crowded floor. She rolled her shoulders. He noticed the knife in her hand when she adjusted her grip, flicked the thing open so that it shone in the light from the bathroom.

"What the fuck is this?" He threw the towel around himself.

She glanced at his naked chest, belly, wrinkled her nose, sniffed the air. She flicked her chin toward the bathroom as she came toward him.

"You used soap in there, right?" she asked.

I made no appointment at Galaxy Fitness, Randwick. There's a certain joy in being able to walk into anywhere and stop things in their tracks in the name of the law. A couple of middle-aged women at the counter were chattering and filling out forms, their towels hanging over their shoulders, and a young man behind the counter who I'd have said was on roids from the sheer unnatural shape of him. All wads of muscle on probably tired bones and snaky veins, the sculpted eyebrows of someone who waxed weekly.

I went straight to the young woman beside him, a tanned and toned Jack Russell of a creature, caramel colored, short, and stringy. She smiled as I entered and I smiled back and it was on—train departed from Flirt Central. Sometimes it can be like that.

"Morning." I put my badge and a bunch of papers on the counter in front of the girl. "Detective Frank Bennett, CID. I'm going to have to be really annoying and serve a warrant here today."

Everyone looked. The girl's smile dropped. Captain Eyebrows shouldered in beside Jack Russell.

"Morning. I'm the floor manager, Steven Kent. How can I help?"

"Good to meet you." I shook his hand. He squeezed too hard. "Hoping to make this short and sweet. I'm on the tail of a missing person and need some questions answered."

The girl was looking at my badge. The plastic one

pinned to her sculpted chest read "Clarinda: Customer Service."

"Well, I hope I can be of some help." Eyebrows puffed his chest out. "Shall we go back to the staff office?"

"It's all right, mate, go ahead see to these ladies." I waved at the women at the counter, who bristled like birds disturbed. "I'm sure Clarinda here can help me."

If Jack Russell girl had a tail she would have wagged it. Steve scowled, then laughed, hard.

"That's nice but Clarinda's hardly the person to talk to. I'm in charge here. I'd be the most qualified to help you get what you need."

"Uh huh," I said. "That's also nice. But you're busy. I try not to interrupt busy people."

"I can assure you—"

"Unfortunately, regardless of your being in charge, or the best person to get me what I need, a warrant of this type requires me to be overseen in the entirety of my operations here today by the person I serve it to." I shrugged helplessly. "Clarinda, honey, looks like you bit the bullet here."

"But," Steven the Floor Manager opened his mouth, shut it, opened it again, "she hasn't signed anything."

"She sighted my paper first." I curled my lip at Clarinda. "Sorry, Bub."

"What's . . . what's this all about?" Steve squinted.

"Clarinda, have you got an office we can use with computer access?"

"I don't think—"

"She's got it, Steve," I winked at him. "Haven't you, Clarinda?"

Clarinda almost stumbled over her own feet.

"Yep, got it, Steve."

Jack Russell girl came out from behind the counter with a set of keys. Steve swallowed, did some funny jerking thing with his neck.

"Yes, uh. Yeah, Okay. Clarinda, if you could help the detective with anything he needs."

I slapped Steve on his iron-hard back as I passed. Clarinda led me to a room off the side of the free-weights section where laborers and retirees were squatting and staring themselves down in the wall of mirrors. Nearby I could hear an aerobics instructor shouting over some thumping bass music. The little room held a table and a laptop and a couple of desk chairs, some anatomy pictures. There was a set of scales in the corner and a measuring tape pinned to the wall.

"Jesus." She sunk into the desk chair and crossed her legs, adjusted the bottom of her gym tights. "You're going to get me sacked if you're not careful."

"I can't help what the warrant says, young lady. That's the law."

"That was all bullshit about the warrant. Wasn't it?"

"What an accusation."

"Uh huh," she smirked. Swung sideways back and forth in the desk chair like a bored kid in the computer room at school. "So, what's the deal here? Are you looking for one of our members?"

"Well, I might be," I said, sitting down in the other chair, pulling it close so she could smell me. "I'm here on a real long shot and, yes, it'll involve looking at your member files. What we're looking for might take a while. So I hope Steve will forgive me for not wanting to spend the next couple of hours in here with him."

"Oh, he's a pretty forgiving guy." She smiled, played with the mouse on the desk beside her.

"Lucky."

"I didn't catch your name out there in all the macho games."

"Frank."

"Well, Frank, thanks for getting me out of membership emails for a few hours."

"My pleasure. You think our forgiving friend Steve would make us a couple of coffees?"

"He'll burst in here in a minute or so to see what we're up to. So, I guess you could ask him. You'd be pushing it."

"A bit protective of what goes on around his floor, is he?"

"Certainly is."

"Floor manager. The pressure."

"It's tough," she sniggered.

"All right, well, we haven't got all day to exchange pleasantries." I set the folder on the table beside the laptop and extracted a series of photographs. "This is the girl I'm looking for."

Juno had done a great job on the footage the Manning boy had sent me. All the green grain was gone, and the sound had been clarified down to individual breaths and wheezes, muttered words. He'd even transcribed the few words said on the twelve-minute clip and sent a file of ten stills that best showed the girl's face.

"Oh my God." Clarinda the customer service girl frowned at the photos. "What is this?"

"It's no one's idea of a good time."

I'd cropped the photos dramatically, but what was left wasn't exactly family picnic album.

"You're looking for this girl?" She touched the girl's face, the duct tape. "This is . . . Is she . . . ?"

"It's from a video. We're not sure yet if it's fake, so don't freak out," I told her. "We see a few of these every now and then. People find them online, report them, identify people making them and passing them around. It's common. Don't worry yourself too much about what might be going on—that's my job. You just focus on the girl."

"How do you expect to find her? Do you know her name? Is she a member?"

"Well, see. I'm here because I've been looking at these pictures all night long and there are a few things I'd like to test my brain against." I folded my arms, looked at the shots in turn.

"Okay."

"We don't know this girl's name. We don't know anything about her. But she's pretty damn toned, don't you think?"

Clarinda looked at the photographs. There was no denying the girl in the photograph had amazing biceps and the kind of abs a man could comfortably stand on while waiting for a train. In one shot, where the girl in the photograph was down on her hands and knees, her right calf muscle was strained tight, showing the taut slope and ball of muscle you only get from hours of riding bikes. Clarinda took a while to look, before she began to nod.

"Okay. So she works out. That's a clever thing to notice, I guess."

"I thought you might agree. Then there's this. See this here?" I lifted one of the pictures. The black shadow leaning against the wall was so small and fine I could only indicate it with the edge of my little finger. "Is that one of your gym bags?"

Clarinda took the photograph from me. Held it close to her nose. Stretched her arms and frowned in the light.

"Jesus. This *is* a long shot. It kind of looks like a jacket to me."

"Yeah, maybe. But at the start of the video one of the guys has it in his hand. One hand. And he sort of swings it. It hits the wall and falls in a heap. When you throw a jacket or a piece of clothing on the floor you sort of drop it, don't you? It's got no weight. This is like a . . . like a swing and then a thump and then a slide. What would you carry into a room and drop like that? A bag. A bag you'd been carrying for a while."

"Um. Okay." She didn't sound convinced.

"Maybe I'm being overly hopeful."

"Maybe."

"It does look to me, after staring at it for a few hours, like one of those blue and black bags you've got hanging above the counter out there, though. I see them everywhere. College kids carry them. You give one out to every new member, don't you?"

"I can't see the blue." She looked at my eyes. "Couldn't it just be any old backpack?"

"A very clever colleague I'm working with tells me that in pixelated form, whatever the hell that means, there's half a grade median tone difference between the top half of the bag, assuming it's a bag, and the bottom half of the bag—which might suggest that the top and bottom halves of the bag are different colors." I took the picture back. Showed her. "Your bags are blue on the top and black on the bottom. So it's possible, right?"

"It's possible." She shrugged at the pictures. "But shit, man, I don't know how the hell you get anything from this. It's all shadows to me."

"Well, it's worth a try."

"Yeah, I suppose it is."

"So if we get that far, and we're right, we need a name. At one point in the tape that these images are from, one of the men in the room calls the girl 'Shelly.' So what I'm working on here are the extraordinarily unpromising ideas that maybe the girl in the pictures is so amazingly toned because she spends a lot of time in gyms. Maybe that's her bag that the guy carried in and threw in the corner. Maybe it's a Galaxy Fitness bag, and maybe we can find a girl on your system whose name is Shelly or Michelle who has crazy curly black hair like this girl does."

"What if it's Rochelle?"

"Don't rain on my parade, Clarinda."

"God," she laughed, rubbed her eyes, turned to the computer. "I don't like your chances here, mate. Do you know how many tens of thousands of members we have, just in the Sydney region? Do you have any idea how many of those are going to be Michelles? There'll be hundreds."

"Let's stay positive. Think big. Over the mountain. Go hard or go home. All that shit."

"Right." She clicked. Checked me out from the corner of her eye to see if I was still smiling. I shifted closer and watched. She smelled like sweat. Not body odor, but sweat, woman sweat, the kind that gets into your sheets and leaves you thinking about her days after she's left your life.

"Is all your work like this?"

"Sometimes it's worse."

"Is she in trouble, this girl?" she asked, took a chance and looked right at me. "Is it, like . . . Is it bad?"

"We'll see," I said. "If it's that bad you'll see it on the news. You might even see me there. Here. You can tell your friends you know that ugly copper on Channel Seven. Friends in high places. Celebrity connections. You could call me to prove it." I took a card from my back pocket and tucked it into hers. I wasn't usually this obnoxious, but the look on her face told me she didn't mind. She shook her head. Steven Kent the Floor Manager swung open the door without knocking. Clarinda was tapping away at the keys.

"How's the floor?" I asked.

"Fine, uh, good. Clarinda able to help you with what you need?"

"She's invaluable, just like the coffee you're about to make me, which is going to rescue my entire morning. Hot, white, and strong, just like me. And Clarinda . . . ?" I pointed to the girl.

"Oh. Uh, black, Steve. Sorry."

"Sorry, Steve," I agreed.

Steve grumbled and disappeared.

"You're such a dick," Clarinda the Jack Russell girl said. She gave me a cute scowl like she meant it. But I knew she didn't. She'd call.

Heinrich remembered small sections of what had happened after they dragged him away from Bear, but there were long dark stretches between them that were filled with blackness and wailing, the frantic whispering of those left behind after the Fall. He remembered lying in the back of a car, squashed between the bodies of two people, someone fumbling with rags at his stomach, listening to them and the two people in the front as their words rose up and down against his ears, like the ocean through a window.

"We can't go in. We'll leave him out front."

"We can't take him there at all. We need to get him out of the car. He makes it and Caesar hears we took him to Doc's we're all dead."

"He's not going to make it."

"Calm down, Sam. He's gonna bite it. I'm covered in his fucking blood. I'm soaked in it."

"What if he does make it?"

"He won't."

"Christ Jesus. I'm scared. Why are we doing this?"

"Shut up."

"Sam, his eyes are all rolled up."

"Why are we doing this?"

"Because it's the right thing to do. Shut up! All of you shut up."

The asphalt, hard against the side of his head and his shoulder, wet with rain or blood, he didn't know. Rolling onto his stomach, clawing to look, the lights of the car in the dis-

tance. Heinrich the Dogboy of Darlinghurst scraping his head against the tiny black stones because it was too heavy to lift, looking at the door as the light fell on him. Doc looking at him, breathing, grabbing his bag, running away into the street, down to the corner, toward the pub where other men would see him, say he was there, say he never helped the Dogboy when Caesar came knocking.

Heinrich hugging the ground. Gripping it with his nails against the pain. Bending his knees and trying to hold onto it as the earth thundered and shuddered and turned. All of him wet. His socks, wet. Thinking he would be all right if he just kept hold of the moment that Bear had left him, because if he could somehow know just how long it had been, just how far he had gone, maybe he could get back to that moment and change it, wake up faster, run into the bedroom before the shooters went there, call out, scream, fight, do something more than hide behind a chair, anything more, one thing to save them all, to save the man who had saved him. So he lay on the earth and kept his eyes open wide and breathed and tried to remember.

It's an hour or so since Bear died.

I'm three miles from the spot.

Heinrich held the bullet in his stomach and watched the moon creep across the sky. As the light grew, he dragged himself up until he was on his knees, began to crawl.

It's five hours or so since Bear died.

I'm three miles and a few yards from the spot.

He pushed the door to Doc's house open, blundered about, knocked things over, grabbed things he wasn't sure would help him, left blood dark brown and smeared like shit all over the jars and tables and cloths and walls. He packed it all in a bag, holding his guts in with one arm, dragging the lead weight of the supplies with the other, out into the street *again, through the laneways, down the hill, to the ware-houses lining the canal.*

It's ten hours or so since Bear died.

I'm five, six, seven miles from the spot.

He rested in the dark and cold and grit of a warehouse floor, the coiled metal shavings and flat hard carcasses of dead rats and wood chips and screws that made a bed for him. No idea what was around him, five or six feet from the door that led to the seven miles that led to the spot where Bear had died, that spot he would return to, he promised to return to, to fix things, fix it all.

He slept and lost count of the hours, cried at that, cried and howled at that. He hadn't cried, though, when he began to strip off his trousers to see to the hole there, because Bear wouldn't have liked a thing like that, tears shed over stupid things like blood and torn flesh. He twisted the cloth, bit it, fished around inside himself. When he pulled the bullet free and threaded the needle and pulled himself together and washed it all down it was like nothing had ever happened, and he felt good, because that was how Bear would have liked it. He pulled the bullet from his shoulder, but left the one in his guts, because it was lost in all the softness and slippery folds, a little tick buried deep inside him, refusing to let go.

He slept more. Lost more hours.

It's ten days since Bear died.

I'm seven, six, five, four miles from the spot.

Heinrich approached the house from the back alley, stood leaning against the wooden fence and avoiding the shape of it with his eyes. The tape that was around it fluttered in the wind at the edge of his vision, crisscrossed against the doors and windows. He focused instead on the ropes and chains lying in piles in the unmown grass outside the greenhouse until he found himself wondering what would happen to the dogs now that Uncle Mick was dead, because he would be dead, everyone who had been in that front room where the shooting began would be dead. He half-expected to see Sunday here, and then realized that Sunday was a dark hole in his mind that he couldn't bear to step into right now, to wonder how she got away before the shooting began, how she'd known, if she'd known at all.

Heinrich shook himself, let the solid walls of the greenhouse support him as he shuffled through the grass to the door, his heart breaking as he looked through the glass at the pots overturned and cracked and scattered, the dirt turned to mud, the tiny plants shriveled and curling brown in the craters of footprints, tiny lives snuffed in their hundreds, a massacre on the edge of a massacre.

He dragged himself into the back room. The bigger pots here were knocked from their shelves too, trees overhanging, leaves curled and rolled and folded. The one he was looking for was still in its place among three or four others, too heavy, it seemed, to be easily shifted in the chaos. In it, the gnarled fingers of many red flowers, spiked kangaroo paws gripping at nothing in death.

Anigozanthos rufus.

Ani . . . Ani . . . Ru . . .

Oh, boy.

Boy.

Heinrich reached over, grabbed the kangaroo paw by its sticky trunk, and pulled the pot toward him with all his strength. It tumbled, rolled, crashed. He lifted the board from beneath it with shaking fingers and then stopped, breathing, trying to maintain his balance. Heinrich reached into the cavity dug into the dirt beneath the panel and pulled up the bag.

It was heavy. Bear had been close to what he needed to leave for good.

It took all day and some of the night to find Michelle Wisdon. I got home from the gym around midday, slapped a couple of packets of Oxy on the kitchen table, opened a bottle of red, and started at the top of the list. It was lonely work. The cat made a circle of himself on the end of the couch, blinking at me resentfully across the hours. At three or four I got up, fried a couple of sausages and microwaved some instant mash, plugged my phone in when it started getting low, put on some Chris Isaak, thought about Eden and how she knew everything all the time.

"Hello?"

"Hi. Is that Michelle?"

"Yes, it is."

"Michelle, do you know a guy named Jackie Rye?"

"Who?"

"Nevermind. Thanks."

When Clarinda: Customer Service came over at about seven that evening I was barely able to move my shoulders. She straddled my back as I lay on the bed with the papers still calling, calling, calling—kneading my spine and neck and arms, making me groan. Her kisses behind my ears, folding the hard flesh forward, finding the warmth, exploring me. I went back to the kitchen table as she dressed, watched her walking around, bending over, making herself coffee, snapping off a row from a Cadbury's Snack block. I kissed her as she left, on the mouth, like I knew her. When she left she didn't look back. I felt used.

Just after the clock struck nine I hit pay dirt.

"Hello?"

"Hi. Is that Michelle?"

"Yes. Who's this?"

"Michelle, do you know a guy named Jackie Rye?"

Silence, a long one. And then a click.

Gotcha.

It was about eleven by the time I arrived at the excruciatingly lit supermarket in Paddington. I stood in the fruit and veg section for a few minutes molesting the avocados before I recognized her at the checkout, beeping items through for an expressionless Asian couple, the approach of midnight wearing on her shoulders, making them curve forward around her like the wings of an injured bird. The curly hair hadn't shown in her membership photo at Galaxy Fitness. It was only by chance that I happened to be looking at the screen as we trawled through the 174 Michelles in her age range and seen a single raven ringlet poking from behind her ear.

She had it out in all its glory now but seemed to be regretting it. She kept pushing it back as she gave change, looked for barcodes, turned things around in her strong hands. I left the avocados alone and walked to the cigarette counter. She came around to meet me with barely an upward glance. When she hit the counter and plastered on her pitiful checkout-chick smile I put my badge on the counter and left my hands there so she would feel less threatened. I conjured up a pathetic smile of my own.

"Hi, Michelle," I said. "I'm Detective Frank Bennett."

She touched her lips first and then seemed to swallow something hard in her throat.

"Oh, no."

"I'm sorry."

"Christ." She slid a hand up her forehead and into her curly crown, gripped hard.

"I'm really very sorry."

"I knew someone was coming and I still went out." She looked around. Her eyes were wet, ready for tears. "I knew it."

"I was going to speak to the manager first but I wanted to see what you wanted to do." I followed her eyes to the manager, a squat Greek guy standing texting in the tampon aisle. "What do you want to do? Do you want to come with me now?"

"I finish at midnight." She looked at the register in front of her.

"Okay."

"Don't tell the manager."

"I won't."

"I'll . . . I'll meet you out there. At the bus station."

She pointed. I looked. Put my badge back in my pocket.

"Don't run off on me, Michelle. I'm not here to make trouble."

"I won't."

I walked out the glass doors to the bus shelter. Sat there with my hands in my coat.

Michelle came out in a pink hoodie covered in monkey cartoons that didn't suit her but was probably warm. She sat on the other end of the bus bench, waiting for me to talk while she traced the engravings in the painted wood with her fingernail.

"Want to go someplace?"

"I'd rather not get in a car with you."

"I don't . . . I know it probably means nothing to you," I leaned toward her over the bench, "but you can trust me. I'm not interested in anything in the world right now beyond nailing Jackie Rye and his shit-faced sidekick for what they did to you and probably dozens of other girls."

"Words are cheap."

"They are, but they're all I've got right now. Well, not all I've got. I've got a work charge card. We could get something to eat. You hungry?"

"Why are you alone?" She looked at my eyes with her full hurt and I felt my throat constrict. "Don't you guys work in pairs?"

"We do," I said. "My partner's in the field right now. She's a tough nut, like you. But I still worry about her. I'd like to bring her home from where she is as soon as I can. She's relying on me to get this thing moving."

Michelle considered my words, her hands in her pockets and her back hunched under a great invisible weight. In time she got up and walked to my car. Must have seen me looking at it. I got in and shifted all the takeout packets out of her side before I unlocked the door.

*   *   *

I knocked on Eden's door at three a.m. There was light under it, and when she pulled it open she was dressed and her hair was perfect—apart from the horrendous dye job. I opened my mouth to ask why she was up at this ungodly hour and then closed it, slammed those thoughts away into drawers, and bolted the drawers closed.

"What an inappropriate time to visit." She gave me the once-over.

"I try to be inappropriate as often as possible."

"Is it pressing?"

"It's more throbbing than pressing."

She pushed open the door. I scooted in before it could close on me. There was soft piano music playing and that bottle of Armagh was on the coffee table, a quarter full, an empty glass beside it. I helped myself. She sunk onto the couch beside me and hung her arm over the back again the way women do when they're flirting in bars. But Eden wasn't flirting with me. I wasn't sure she'd ever flirted with anyone. Women like Eden don't need to flirt. She could make filling out her tax return look erotic.

"I've just been to see Michelle Wisdon, the girl from the video."

"Don't you ever sleep anymore?" she squinted.

"Eden, the correct response was 'Holy shit, Frank, you found her already? How did you do that? You're a wonder. Look at your biceps.'"

Eden looked at the ceiling.

"Yes, I sleep. But not right now. I found Michelle Wisdon and she's the girl from the video and I turned up at her workplace and got it out of her. All of it."

"And how much was there?"

"Not much."

"Uh huh."

"She tried to play like it was a fakey at first." I stretched my legs out. Put them on the coffee table. Eden bit her tongue. "I brought her round. We got a couple of bags of Maccas and some Jimmy cans and went up to the top of Watsons Bay. Looked at the city. You can get a woman to tell you anything over Maccas and a beautiful view."

"*Your* kind of woman."

"She won't testify, but she was willing to tell me the video was nonconsensual. She thinks Jackie got her with Xylazine. It's meant for cattle. Helps them endure castration. Says she was at one of those Saturday night bonfires they have there and everyone was laughing at how she couldn't put her words in a row. And she didn't know why, because she'd only had two drinks. Literally, two. Then Jackie and Nick grabbed her bag and took her off, told everyone they'd put her to bed. Everyone seemed to know."

"That doesn't surprise me."

"Everyone seemed to know and did nothing."

"It's pretty brutal out there." Eden took the wine back, put it to her lips. Didn't drink.

"Are you all right?"

"Yes, Dad."

"I don't like you being in the middle of something even you admit is brutal."

"You don't like women being in precarious situations in general. It's one of your many Old World masculine hang-ups."

"Maybe."

"You can't protect me, Frank," she said.

"I guess we agreed you don't really need it, do you?"

"No."

"Do you feel sort of . . ." I struggled. Got half the words out and then lost the rest, squirmed under her eyes. "Do you feel like you know Jackie and Nick? Do you feel like they . . . Is there like a kind of . . . an instinct . . . ?"

"Don't wander into dangerous waters, Frank."

"Sorry." I looked away.

"We agreed we weren't going to talk like this."

"We're not. We're not going to. I just. Sometimes I want to know. And sometimes I don't want to know. Most of the time, I don't want to know. But sometimes. I came here tonight and you're up." The words were dropping off my lips. "You're dressed and your hair is done and if I went downstairs and felt the hood of your car . . ."

"Don't."

"It'd be warm. Wouldn't it?"

"Frank."

"Sorry." I drew a deep breath, let it fill me, get to my brain, blow out all the stupidity. What was I doing? What was this going to do other than push Eden away from me, push her back into that shadowy place where she hid like a snake in a cave and considered what exactly it was that made her decide to keep me alive—a liability, a fool who couldn't stop words coming out of his mouth. And yet she kept me alive. Day after day she greeted me like a friend, as much as a woman like that can have friends in her life.

"So we find the bodies," she said. "We find Xylazine in their systems, we nail Jackie and Nick. Boom."

"Sounds pretty simple."

"It's never simple."

"Tell me about it."

"What was the Manning boy doing with this video? Did he get it from Jackie?"

"No. He got it from his sister. Seems my girl Michelle managed to break into Jackie's van and get it on DVD, texted it to the Manning girl as a kind of warning. I think the aim was to circulate it among the girls. Get them out of there. But it never went any further. Keely Manning passed it on to her brother and then promptly went missing."

"Could be that Jackie was trying to stop the leak."

"Could be."

"Huh." Eden sipped her wine. "So the girls got into the boys' greatest hits collection and started jibber-jabbering among themselves, and the boys decided to clean up their mess."

"Maybe."

"So why isn't Jackie after Michelle?"

"He might be."

"Maybe we could give him some help."

"No."

"She wouldn't have to know," Eden said.

"I'd know."

"Did the girl say there are other tapes?" Eden asked.

"A couple of others, but she didn't see who they were."

"And these tapes are in his caravan?"

"Probably not now that he's got the little bunny rabbit living with him."

"Did she say they were for personal use? Or is he selling them?"

"She didn't know, but Juno wasn't able to find any copies of the tape on the Internet. Would have been a dumb move, now that the girls are missing. I'd say they're just for personal use. Trophies of conquests."

"Could be that the other tapes are in Nick's van. Could be that the two of them started out with rape scenarios and then stepped it up with Erin, Ashley, and Keely. We might have tapes of what happened sitting there on the lot."

"You better get snooping then, Super Sleuth."

Eden sighed, cracked her neck.

"When you going back?" I asked.

"Today." She looked at the clock on the wall in the kitchen. "Soon."

"Ahh, Juno should be pleased at the series return of the Adventures of Eden Archer."

"Give me a break. You staying here?"

"No," I rubbed my eyes. "I need to get back to the cat."

"Stay here." She smirked, got up and grabbed a cashmere throw from the back of the couch. Tossed it at me as she walked away. "Jesus. The fucking cat, of all things."

Hades stood up and extended his arms out wide, groaning as the muscles between his shoulder blades stretched. It had been years since he felt stressed. For most of his life he'd had an inward calm and calculation so well-developed that he often appeared nonchalant

Until lately. He was anything but calm.

And that was because Adam White was out there watching him night after night. It was exhausting. It was belittling. It caused the old man to hear voices in his head.

I see you, old man.

Hades breathed through his teeth. Imagining what he would do to Adam White once the young copper had exhausted his search brought a bit of light into his ancient heart. Hades would have to make an example of Adam White. It would have to be something drawn out and humiliating, the way this was—something he would sit and watch with relentless, pressing eyes, something that would make the boy feel naked. He would probably see to it that the boy was, in fact, naked. That always made things interesting.

Hades went to the kitchen counter, topped up his scotch glass, drained it. He glanced down the hall to check the front door was closed before he went into the bathroom to wash his hands—they felt sticky and he didn't know why. That was something that he'd begun to do. Checking the alarms. Checking the windows.

Checking the phone. Checking his watch. He'd started keeping a gun on his thigh as he sat at the kitchen table, a heavy and annoying thing that wanted to slide off his jeans and onto the floor. Hades decided to make a note of it, the way it made him feel. Paranoid. He'd make Adam White feel paranoid for a while before he squished him.

Hades came back from the bathroom and found a man sitting in the chair by the door. He stopped, picked his scotch glass up from where it sat, turned and began pouring a drink.

"You don't knock?"

"You know me, Hades," the man said. "Generally my manners are meticulous. Princely. My mother did an exceptional job of them. Generally I take pride in displaying them, these princely manners."

"But you don't display them where they're not warranted, Mr. Grey."

"I do not."

Hades didn't know what Mr. Grey's real name was. He didn't even know when he started calling him Mr. Grey, if it had been the man's idea or his own. It had probably been about the third or fourth time the man had come driving up the hill toward Hades' shack in his sleek gray Beemer, the third or fourth time he'd extracted himself gracefully from the heated leather seats, the third or fourth time he'd offered the steel-hard hand that betrayed the softness and luxury and excess the rest of him seemed to want to make clear.

Like most of Hades' clients, Mr. Grey was not what he appeared. The princely mannered, perfectly sculpted, hand-woven male beauty he was pretending to be was really a very messy man. Mr. Grey liked to peel skin. He liked to rip at organs with his fingernails. He liked to eat raw and red and throbbing parts. The first time he'd had a peek at Mr. Grey's handiwork as he pried apart the expertly wrapped package the man had brought him, Hades had been shocked at just how messy Mr. Grey could be. Hades had thought as he waved the Beemer off that Mr. Grey was probably someone he should try not to annoy.

Though the dark-eyed stallion in the expensive gray suit was looking pleasantly at him right now, the pistol in his lap loose in his fingers and pointed at the floor, there was no doubt in Hades' mind that Mr. Grey was annoyed. Hades sat down and sipped the scotch. Mr. Grey's eyes followed him, took in the gun on the table where Hades had set it, now useless.

"You gonna let me explain?"

"I'd love for you to explain, Hades."

"You tell me what you saw, and I'll know where to begin."

"I saw a man standing in the bush out there by the side of the road," Mr. Grey said.

"Uh huh," Hades said.

"On closer inspection I saw a man standing in the bush out there by the side of the road *filming*. Filming *you*. And when he'd finished filming *you*, he filmed *me* driving up here to your lodgings."

"It's not a good look, is it?"

"It certainly isn't, old buddy."

Hades sighed. Mr. Grey tapped his index finger on the side of the gun, counting seconds. It was a nice gun. A handsome thing covered in filigree and unnecessary little polished screws. Fitting for a man like Mr. Grey with his flawless skin and glossy nails. Not something Hades could have pulled off. He knew he looked good with a bat.

"This has been going on for some time?" Mr. Grey asked.

"Couple of weeks."

"And what is the purpose of this jaunty little occupation?"

"To piss me off."

Mr. Grey cocked his head. The clean lines of him, the jaw cut with glass and the bones in his neck made Hades think of a Doberman.

"Seems to be working," Mr. Grey said.

"It is."

"This is going to be bad for business, Hades. Very bad."

"No shit."

"It's going to be bad for your business and mine."

"No, it's not." Hades drank the scotch. "He's not interested in you. He's interested in me."

"And you can guarantee that?"

"Lifetime."

Mr. Grey kept tapping the gun like he was sending Morse code. He looked at the kitchen windows. It was the first time since he emerged from the bathroom that Hades got out from under the cannibal's gaze. He rolled his shoulders again, tried to stretch out that twisted muscle.

"Why don't I just do my favorite waste disposal technician a favor and settle this score right now?" Mr. Grey jutted his perfect chin toward the window.

"I'd rather you didn't."

"Why?"

"Because."

"Because?"

"Look, because the boy might be on to something. Okay?"

"You're allowing someone to threaten you, threaten me, because he might be on to something?"

"He wants an answer." Hades sipped, swallowed. "It happens to be a thing I've wanted to know myself for a long time, since back in the old days when a pompous little fuck like you would have gotten your neck snapped for walking into the kitchen of a man like me without knocking first. And I'm getting to thinking that if I play the game just long enough I might get that answer I've been waiting for. I might return things to normal, so that I can go back to drinking my scotch in peace and you can go back to refining your princely manners."

Mr. Grey laughed. Sat back in the chair he hadn't been invited to sit in and laughed and laughed.

"Okay," Mr. Grey sniffed. He wiped his eye with a pale blue handkerchief he tugged from his pocket like a stage magician. "All right."

"All right."

"Well, you let me know when you get your answer, old buddy. You let me know when I can come a-knocking again."

"It'll be soon. Don't you worry about that."

The man called Mr. Grey gave Hades a last look, a kind look, rocking the pretty gun off his index finger so that the aim swung up and down over the old man's walls. Then he left through the front door, pulling it closed behind him.

When the cannibal was gone Hades stood and shattered his glass in the sink.

Victoria Krane had been running Icky's brothel since her father died, and nothing had changed. She'd made sure of it. She had begun her life at Icky's in the back room, heralded into the world by her mother's swift and gurgling exit. Since then Icky's had been her universe, the kitchen her solar system of rotating pots and pans and cans and bottles, the tears and cracks and holes in the papered windows her stars.

She was just about ready to lock the iron door and turn the red lamp out for the night when the boy lurched up the path and into the rose circle of light. He had the look of a creature who should be kept out, all bent over and broken, an arm locked across his stomach and the other gripping the handle of a leather bag. Vicky looked into the hollows under his brow and stepped back from the gate, knocked into the door with her hip. A devil has come to your door, Vicky.

"We're closing, Mister."

"No, you're not."

He stood in the red light of the porch. The glow was hitting a million raindrops in his hair and on his cheeks and on the shoulders of his coat, making him look like he was dusted in fire. He was wearing a man's coat, far too big for him, and he had the squared shoulders and taut neck of a fugitive ready to pull a weapon—more of a spring pulled too tight than a man at all. Vicky glanced into the hall at the girls standing there. One of them caught her eye, knew what was needed.

"Should I get Mr. Parsons?"

The boy seemed to know there was no Mr. Parsons. But Vicky nodded anyway, shivered in her coat, pulled it around her to hide the things crawling under her skin.

"Perhaps you should, Amy," she shouted.

"Open the door."

"Maybe you're deaf. We're closed."

The boy lifted his head and the light fell into his eyes, made them blaze pink like a rich girl's diamonds. Vicky felt something move in her stomach. Her hand was on her throat.

"I'm Heinrich. Bear's boy."

"You," Vicky was really shaking now. "You ain't no Dogboy. The Dogboy's dead and so is the Bear."

The boy stood there.

In time, Vicky's shaking hand raised with a will of its own and pulled the brass handle down.

"Vick—" someone cried.

Vicky yanked open the iron door. She didn't know why she did it. It was like some kind of force had rushed up and over her—an anger, maybe, a horror, the same kind she'd felt when the men came running down the street two weeks earlier shouting that Caesar had cleaned house. Before she knew it the door was open and the boy was inside with her.

In the white light Vicky could see his skin had gone a kind of navy-boat gray and the eyes were just as pink as they had been in the light of the door.

"Now you listen to me," Vicky said, low, so the girls wouldn't hear. "You ain't Bear's Dogboy. Not today, not tomorrow. I don't care what you say."

"Right now I'm just someone's been too long on his feet," the boy said. "There someplace we can go?"

She led him to the back room, where a life had been given and a life had been taken away. He sat on the edge of the bed and she stood by the closed door and watched him. He smelled wretched. Like the loser of a fight. Didn't seem to be wearing much but trousers underneath the coat. His bare feet were black like he'd painted on shoes and the bones she could see were purple.

The boy brought the bag to the bed beside him and unzipped it. He started placing piles of cash bound with paper on the faded floral bedspread. He laid out one stack of cash as high and as wide as a shoebox. He started another, half the size. Then he made a pile of notes twice as big as the two first piles put together. Vicky Krane stood by the door and felt sick. Finally he picked out a stack about as thick as a workman's sandwich and put it on his knee.

The boy pointed to the first pile, and Vicky noticed that he was shaking but he didn't look afraid.

"For the Les Girls, the Harpsicord, and Jenny's on Taylor Street, split three ways," the boy said. "I want them delivered in newspaper. Fresh newspaper. From the morning your girls deliver it. Tied with string."

Vicky heard the girls whispering in the hall behind her. She shifted on her feet. The boy pointed at the second pile.

"For Chief Inspector Ronnie Redford, at the Watch House over near the Argyle. He'll be there on Sunday. Sunday night." The boy coughed hard, wiped his palm on a handkerchief he took from his pocket. "Senator Ted Lockett . . . He lives on Niall Street."

Vicky could stand no more. She went to the bed and sat beside him and wrung her hands.

"And this one?"

The boy coughed.

"And this one?"

"For half of Icky's," the Dogboy of Darlinghurst said, looking at her eyes for the first time. He breathed, turned away from her. Though he was turned she could see the gray skin of his temple bunch as he fought out the pain.

"Not half. Forty-nine percent."

"Forty-nine percent."

The Dogboy panted. Vicky licked her lips.

"We keep the name."

"Of course," he coughed, "we do."

Vicky stood and looked down at him. Watched him fumbling at the buttons of his coat, exposing cloth, reams of cloth underneath. She helped him get down to the last button, and the coughing stopped. He licked blood off the corner of his storm-colored lip. She went to the door and he watched her go, fanning his damp face with the sandwich pile of notes.

"This here is for the girls," he said as he tossed the stack to her. "Tell them to be gentle with me."

Eadie arrived back at the farm before the sun had risen. It was Sunday. The night before had been a big one for the few left behind. She could tell this from the burned things. A black washing machine drum filled with charred sticks in the breakfast area, a Coke bottle melted over the innards thrown in as the flames were dying. There were cigarette butts everywhere. Out near where the pigs were kept the real bonfire was still smoking, sending a weak trail up just before the sprawling dry grasslands, as close to danger and death as a fire could be.

There was one other human moving on the farm and that was Pea. The movement was only to lift a cigarette to her lips as she watched Eadie walking through the gates. Her shoulders were hunched, bunching fat at her belly, her heavy breasts sitting like melons sagging on a shelf. There was no choice but to walk right by her, within six or seven meters. Eadie hitched her bag on her shoulder and nodded as she walked by.

"Morning," she said.

Pea said nothing.

She saw what had been done to the van only as she rounded the corner of the long wooden fences. The spray-painted letters were red and as high as the tiny rounded windows rippling over the corrugated sides of the cabin.

DYKE PIG.

Eadie took in the handiwork and then went over to the van and pulled open the door. The doorstep was wet and reeked of urine. They had pissed at the bottom of the door and flooded the carpet in the hall. The whole caravan reeked of it. She opened all the windows, stripped down to her underwear, and climbed into the bed. She was thinking of getting up again and drawing the curtains when she heard it, the pattering of Ugg boots across the dirt. The door burst open down the narrow hall.

A weight slammed into the bed. Eadie hid her face in the pillows.

"Pull the curtains before you get comfy."

Skylar leaped from the bed again. It rocked and bounced.

"Someone prettied up your van."

"They perfumed it as well. How nice."

"You can come sleep with me and Jackie."

"It's all right. The smell will go," Eadie said.

"Where did you go? What did you do? Tell me everything."

"Nowhere. Nothing. No."

"Oh come on, Eadie, please!"

"I went to a friend's place. Ordered a pizza. Had a few joints. Watched a movie. It was all very tame."

"You're lying."

"I'm really not." Eadie rolled over, faced the girl. The girl spasmed, kicked her legs.

"Stop lying to me. You're turning this caravan into a house of lies."

"What do you reckon I did, if you know so bad?"

"You drove into the city, stayed in a flash hotel.

Drank champagne. Dressed up. Went to a club. Danced on the stage. Raised the roof, baby, raised the fucking roof."

"That's a good list. Is that what you'd do if you were me?" Eadie asked.

"Maybe."

"You never stayed in a flash hotel? Danced on a stage? Raised the roof?"

"Maybe a couple of times." Skylar rolled over, jutted her butt into Eadie's hips, forced a spoon.

"What's stopping you?"

"Oh, Jackie'd lose his shit if I went into the city."

"Lose his shit, would he?"

"Yeah, man. He spent a lot of years doing that himself so he knows how bad it is." She sniffed, wiped her nose on her hand. "Lotsa bad people in the city. Rob you and mug you, kick your head in for no good fucking reason."

"Why don't we go to the city?"

"I couldn't go with you," Skylar snorted. "You'd take me to some dyke club. Everyone'd think I'd been turned. They'd spray my van next. Piss on my nice carpet. I just vacuumed."

"And you just do what people tell you, do you? I'd just make you kiss a girl. Make you cut all your hair off. Wear a flannel shirt and wraparound sunglasses. You'd be hypnotized."

"Maybe." Skylar rolled back over, nose to nose. Eadie could smell the girl's breath. Raspberry toothpaste. Kid's toothpaste. "You think you can turn a person like that? Make them go over to the other side?"

"I don't think so, babe."

"I heard about churches in America taking boys outta the clubs, putting them in vans, smacking the fag right outta them. It was on the news. Sometimes their parents take them to these places to get them fixed. Have, like, a full invention on them."

"An intervention."

"Yeah, man, one of those."

"That's a shame."

"What would you do if someone tried to beat it outta you?"

"Is that a threat?" Eadie rose up on her elbow, pulled the blankets back. "Is that a fucking threat?"

It only took a push, hard and steady with the ball of her foot in Skylar's stomach. The girl grabbed, screamed, rolled, flopped into the space between the bed and the dressers. Breathless laughing, turning to snorts. Eadie pulled her legs back under the blankets and curled up again.

I got breakfast at an outdoor café in the Cross, keeping my eyes low over the bacon and egg roll, a little worried I might see someone I knew. I'd spent some of my younger years as a cop here on transfer nights, Mardi Gras and New Year's and Christmas Eve when the evening air would awaken under the setting sun, become electrified with impending trouble. Busting heads and throwing transvestites off their heels, pulling drunk girls apart and sending them sprawling in the wet with hands full of other girls' hair. It had been a fun time.

I used to have a good little side business in those days of ripping off the right kind of nobody dealers for a little smack every now and then. I'd sell it out in the suburbs to my neighbors, good people who only wanted something to make the backyard barbecue with the in-laws a little more bearable. This was when I lived with my first wife, when I didn't know she was pregnant yet, when I was sort of happy. As happy as I had been up until that point, I suppose, but when you're young you can fool yourself pretty easily into thinking you're happy. First time you have money, you're rich. First time you live alone, you're cool. First time you sell a neighbor a gram, their awe at what you do. You're a double agent, a fucking gangster.

I wondered about it for a while, how stupid I'd been. I ordered another coffee, waited for someone to come along. In a little notebook on my knee, hidden from the eye of passing junkies, I doodled and made notes and underlined things I'd found out about Sunday White. Pulled little photocopied pictures of her out from where I'd stuck them between the pages, mug shots I'd managed to dig out of the Jane Doe files and more blurry group shots a librarian had found in the public records. About ten photographs of Sharon Elizabeth White existed in total. I looked at her face. She looked like a fun girl. A fun and dangerous girl. Little smirk, like she knew I was looking for her and thought it was a game.

I put Sunday away after a while and thought about other woman-shaped bags of trouble I knew. I settled on Eden as the sun rose over me, cast its gaze on the empty public library, the clouded front windows of the injecting room. I worried about her, then didn't. That seemed to be how it was going to go from now on.

Around ten a guy came and sat near me. His belly was hanging over his crotch in two distinct bulges side by side, as though he'd been stitched in the navel to keep the fat bundle from collapsing at his feet. Purple feet, ankles flaking, yellow toes. He fished in his pockets for a cigarette lighter, legs spread wide to accommodate the bulge, and after watching him for a minute or so I reached into my pocket and took out my own, tossed it onto the table in front of him. I don't smoke anymore but I meet a lot of people who do. He grunted thanks, held the flame dangerously close to his gray beard. A junkie girl shuffled into the little outdoor area with us, greasy black hair raked up into a bun above her pinched face. She held out a curled hand for change and whined like a cat, lip snarled in discomfort.

"Yeah, yeah." I cut the speech short and filled her

hand with silver. The old man watched, looked after her as she dragged herself on.

"Wastin' your time," he growled after a while.

"Ah well."

"Anyone feeds those lot gets scammed. Would have thought you'd know better than that, being a fucking heeler."

I smirked. Half at his picking me for a cop, half at my own good fortune at finding someone in my first couple of hours of waiting who was street-smart and ancient enough to have been around when they still called cops blue heelers. Maybe this was the guy I had been waiting for.

"I gotta keep myself in business, haven't I?" I said. "Spend money to make money."

"She'll make you money. Maybe she'll make the council money when they use her for landfill." The old man nodded after the junkie girl as she lurched too fast down the other side of the street, completing the circuit. "Gonna put that straight in her arm like she's playing the slots."

"What else is new?"

"Nothing." He eyed me for a while. I sat back and sipped the coffee.

"What is it then?" he asked. "Those Lebs again? Those drive-by Lebs?"

"Nah." I shifted my chair a little closer, not too close, because I didn't want to smell him and he didn't want to be seen with me. "Cold case, actually. An old thing. From way back."

"You're a bit fresh to be lookin' at old things from way back."

"Maybe."

The old guy snorted. Spat. The Asians running the café all frowned in unison.

"You might call this a private venture," I said. "A freelance job."

"Freelance . . . private . . . bullshit. You jackos talk a lot of bullshit, y'know that?" he coughed.

"Maybe you can help me out."

"Maybe you can go fuck a dog."

"I'm trying to find someone who would've been around when Hades Archer was king of the castle."

The old guy laughed, let his fat head loll to the side, raining skin flakes.

"You really are a fucking idiot. I thought you looked like one, but now I know for sure."

"You could be right."

The old man leaned close, hung a crusty arm over the stainless-steel table.

"No one on this street gonna talk to you about the Good Lord. You might be lucky if someone don't disappear you through a back door just for asking. Bet you didn't know they do magic shows here, too. One minute you're poking the wrong eyes. The next minute . . ." He made a half-slurping, half-sucking noise. Plucked the air.

"What if I told them the Good Lord sent me?"

"You'd be telling a lie."

I leaned on the table, causing it to rock back toward me on its uneven legs. "I'm trying to find Sharon White."

The old man looked at me.

"Sunday."

"Sunday?" He laughed, hacked, coughed, swallowed. Laughed again. "Oh son, you'll kill me. You'll kill me dead."

"I'm serious."

"You must'a been sent by Hades. Because ain't no one else ever believed that black bitch went anywhere worth looking, 'cept for Hades."

"So you knew her, then?"

"Everybody knew her. She was the town cat."

"Well, where'd she go, then?"

"Oh Jesus, that's funny."

I took the lighter from between us. Put it in my pocket. The old man's yellow eyes were leaking into the creases at the corners.

"Thanks for your help." I stood.

"Look, boy-o, Sunday fucked off someplace up north. Years ago. Years and years and years ago." He looked at me with pity. "I hate to tell you, but you're on the tail of a wild goose you wouldn't want to catch. If she hasn't done away with herself simply by being a miserable little shit, she'll be up in Darwin with her jigaboo people surrounded by sprogs and dogs. I just hope Mr. Archer ain't paid you much to learn he loved a no-good mutt, because anyone coulda told him that. No one told him, though. Because you didn't tell Hades Archer nothing, not back then."

The old man considered his own words, rapped the tabletop with his knuckles. His smile sunk, slowly.

"Matter of fact, you don't tell Hades Archer that sort of thing nowadays neither," he continued rapping, looked at the street, looked at me. "You might try Pussy Cats. I don't know. I gotta go. I got people to see."

He got up and walked away on old bones. Before the Asians could chase him I waved to them, pulled out my wallet.

Pussy Cats smelled like pussy cats, which was kind of poetic, I thought. It had that sort of wet, milky smell a cat gives a house, tainted sharply with the acid that comes out of them, something loved turned vile. The crowd there, three men at the edge of the stage and a troupe of groggy Greek teens waiting to go into the private viewing rooms, were undoubtedly leftovers from the night before, leaning on the black walls, sagging in the plastic chairs.

The meathead at the door picked me for a copper and shut the gate between the reception and the rest of the bar before I could get in. He hit a buzzer to call his boss, stared me down, didn't say hello. I wandered on the checkerboard tiles, slapped my notebook in my palm, and stared back. It took a long while for the boss to come down. There was no telling what he was trying to hide up there on the second floor. Guns. Drugs. Underage girls. Underage boys. Exotic animals. Bad cash. Boosted jewelry. Counterfeit sneakers. I was just about to bang on the desk when he popped out of a hidden panel behind it like a squat, hairy cuckoo bird.

"How can I help, Detective . . . ?"

"Bennett."

"How can I help, Detective Benice?"

"I'm after a private word."

"Got a warrant?"

"A warrant isn't warranted. It's just a private word."

"Well, we're all about privates here, aren't we, Chase?" He looked at the meathead. The meathead didn't look back. "Why don't you come upstairs?"

I followed him through the invisible panel. I bent. He didn't. I thought about Jackie Rye and just how many of the world's degenerates were undersize, narrow-shouldered, bobble-headed. He was well-dressed at least. The square shoulders of a very expensive suit brushed the walls of the tunnel ahead of me.

We emerged into another foyer. The backpacker hotel next door. Ingenious. There were probably more tunnels for shuffling girls to and fro, shoving them into rooms rented by apparently legitimate guests from out of the country, rooms that couldn't be busted into using the same warrant issued to search the strip club. The system was common knowledge to cops, but judges never issued warrants for private premises no matter what rumors there were of secret tunnels or magic doors. The trick had always been catching the rats before they fled.

"I should introduce myself," the wiry old man said when we arrived in an upstairs bedroom. "I'm Bobby Springs."

"I'm well aware," I said. I hadn't been. I sat in the wooden chair by the aluminum-foiled window. "A friend of mine tells me you might be able to help me with some ancient history."

Bobby adjusted the sleeves of his coat.

"I can't imagine what friend of mine might also be a friend of yours."

"Well, friends are funny things." I folded my arms. "I'm trying to chase down a missing girl."

"I thought this was only a private word. I'm very

friendly with Metro Missing Persons. And they always bring a warrant to see my girls."

"The girl I'm looking for isn't one of yours. She might have been one of yours, years ago, maybe. I don't know. All I know is you seem to be the guy to talk to about girls who go missing in the Cross."

A woman came into the room without knocking. White-skinned and bruised on her thighs, a redhead who'd tried to make herself more appealing with a bad black dye job and only succeeded in making her red eyebrows stand out like thin strips of fire. She had a cold sore the size of a baked bean on her lip. She put a glass on the table next to me and one in Bobby's hand. Bobby didn't look at her.

"When are we talking about?"

"Late seventies."

"So around the time your mama and your dada knocked boots and made their own little man of the law? Why on earth would that interest you?"

"Let's not bring anyone's mother into this."

"A bit of a blast from the past. Now I'm curious."

"Good. Were you running girls back then?"

"I was running girls in the womb."

"Remember one named Sunday White?"

Bobby thought for a long while, then laughed, slapped both his thighs.

"Who the hell is looking for Sunday?"

"Jesus," I said. "Everybody seems to know this bird."

"Oh, she was a bit of a fixture I suppose. Iconic. A real sharp hustler. She was just everywhere, all the time—parties, bust ups, big news on the street. Not that anyone particularly wanted her around, you know?" He thought fondly for a while, looking at the floor. "If there was a spare lap she was in it, and it pissed people off, I guess. You always remember the ones who annoy you. Who wants her? Not the cops?"

"No."

"Can't be Hades."

"It's the finding that's important, not the looking."

"Lord have mercy, that's a strange request. You know I never heard that girl called Sunday White. Didn't even know she had a last name."

"Well I'm glad you remember her." I sighed, released steam. "Can we talk about where she went? I don't have all day to shoot the breeze, believe it or not."

"I wouldn't have the faintest. Sunday wasn't one of mine."

"Who did she belong to?"

"No one." Bobby waved a dismissive hand at the street. "You might as well ask who the fucking moon belongs to. That's how Sunday was, like a moon. You look around. There she is. Where is she now? Oh, over there. Always somewhere. Drifting, drifting. Can't catch her. Close, but miles away."

"Bit of a wild card."

"You couldn't take her on. I always thought it'd be nice. There was a good market for darkies who had a bit of pretty to them but you can't keep 'em, they're not the sort. Can't read a fucking watch. Go off for a fifteen-minute break and come back three weeks later expecting to be put right back on. Where were you? Oh, you know, walkabout. Walkabout my ass. It's the same now as it was then. You want a girl you know's going to be there when you wake up? Get yourself a

Russian. Old World Russian girls. They forget to make the bed when they're four years old and their daddies kick the shit out of them. That's why."

"Good to know," I said.

"It's all experience," he sniffed and leaned back in his chair, sipped the drink. "You make mistakes."

"What happened to Sunday?"

"I had to guess, I'd say she took a hot shot and someone bagged her."

"You wouldn't have heard about a thing like that?"

"It wouldn't have been breaking news."

"What did you do with your rubbish back then?"

"Oh, Christ, Detective, how long's a piece of string?"

"Take a guess," I said.

"You . . ." He looked distant, eyes flickering over the wallpaper peeling beside me. "You sent it out west with the truckies. You paid a cleaner. You fed the fish. You dug a hole. They were putting flash apartments up on the North Shore like they were walling off the coast against the fucking Japs. She'd be someone's concrete mix."

I slapped my notebook on my thigh. There was no way I was convincing North Shore Metro to start digging under the houses of millionaires.

"Girl like Sunday. Man, it'd be a stretch to bother. You'd have tossed her out into the street."

"Hmm," I said. "No one did, though. I've got no Jane Does that even come close."

Bobby looked at the girl sitting on the bed, examining her split ends. "Bridget here's gonna settle your bill."

I got up. Bobby saluted me as he headed toward the

door. He went through it, then leaned back, squinted at me.

"Think she had a little sidekick named Kimmy or Jimmy or something. Some little short ass with a big mouth always talking. Might be able to point you somewhere."

I was going to tell him thanks, but he disappeared. I headed after him to leave and Bridget the girl with the impressive cold sore put a hand on my chest.

"Oh, right, yeah." I dug out my wallet.

"He said five."

"Right."

She smiled at me, tucked the notes into her back pocket. I knew she'd hold back a few notes but Bobby had probably factored that in. She put a finger into the gap between my shirt buttons and tickled the eagle on my chest. "You in a rush to go?"

"Desperate rush." I took her hand down, gave it a little squeeze, and slipped around her. "But you be good, baby."

"Never," she laughed. I jogged down the dark stairs.

They took lots of breaks on Rye's Farm. Eadie liked it. There was something comforting in the monotony of her tasks—the shoveling, shoveling, shoveling, carrying, carrying, carrying—the way her breathing would synchronize to the task, come fast or slow as her limbs worked like the cogs in a clock. Pea gave Eadie instructions and she followed them. There were no decisions. She could see the appeal of this kind of work for someone who disliked pressure, deadlines, the weighing of options and outcomes.

The breaks fueled those tired hours, gave her mind coal to burn. Eadie kept her eye on the men and women who walked by her stalls, stopped to check the animals, led cows through for checkups or borrowed bits of rope. A look. A sigh. The fiddling of fingers. Eadie began to make a catalog of twitches. She was in no way attached to the idea that Jackie and Nick were going to hand her the key one of these idle afternoons when they'd had enough of being her prey, so she kept the pendant camera trained on anyone who passed, made excuses to go out into the bays to record conversations, snippets, jargon, nicknames. She knew any of the girls or boys in Jackie's happy family could be the game-changer, the loose-lips, the Big One.

Eadie knew that being a successful killer was mostly due to sophisticated acting skills. The same organization, discipline and order required to make it in Hollywood. Most of the killers she'd found difficult to

hunt—either for her nighttime games or her day job—
were such convincing actors that even the last seconds
of their lives had made her question who the real person was behind the mask.

Eadie knew the game was hard to play and that it
couldn't be played forever. She needed her weekend to
slip away, to let her mask fall, to release a little of her
bloodlust on a worthy foe, Harry Ratchett. But whoever had killed the girls was here, on the farm, and
they couldn't keep up the game forever. She was determined to catch the slip when it happened. A laugh
hacked up too late. A tear faked or a crooked smile.

So for that reason Eadie followed whenever Pea
came and banged on the side of the shed she was working in, walked over the dirt toward the sunbaked picnic
tables in the wake of the old woman's squat frame. The
first three or four breaks of the day were smokos only.
She would bum a couple of tokes from Skylar if she
was around or sit peeling labels off the beer bottles
while the others talked, picked at each other, laughed.
Ramble on. Eadie would see and record it all.

There was an awful lot of reminiscing going on
among the people on Rye's Farm, Eadie noticed, as
though they were in the wake of some great party and
all the guests of honor had packed up and left. There
was a lot of talk about high school, the last great event
in their lives, when no one had developed a habit and
power was something seized through weight and
strength alone—and not by money. Eadie would listen,
cleaning under her fingernails with a corner of a plastic
label, letting the pendant do the looking. Someone
would get an iPhone going with music. Pearl Jam. Always Pearl Jam.

Today the topic seemed to be people who had come and who were gladly gone. Eadie edged onto the very end of the bench, one ass-cheek all that was needed, and started digging a hole in the dust with her boot, grinding the lumps of green manure falling from the grooves in her tread.

". . . with a fucking beard," someone was saying, words forced through dry laughter. "A fucking blond beard, real light, from here to here. Boys were calling her the Pirate."

Everyone sniggering. Eadie wondered whether she should snigger along, then decided it was best to attempt to remain invisible. Pea sat down across from her and struggled with a lighter, fat hands quivering, the shakes.

"That foam hair removal shit is ten bucks a bottle. Fuck. There's no excuse. No fucking excuse."

"Keely was blond like that. Furry blond arms."

Eadie perked up, managed a glance at the speaker. A woman of many layers. Metallica T-shirt over tank top over neon-colored Kmart sports bra. Checkered boxer shorts beneath denim shorts beneath layers of chain and leather and cotton holding things up, pulling things down. Eadie thought her name was Maz. A name cutup and beat down and given to an undersized infant who grew into an oversized woman. Most of them had one-syllable names. Except, of course, for her. The outsider. The rug-muncher.

"Keely. Ooh. Ooh," Maz gave a shudder. Everyone laughed.

"Not your all-time fav, Maz."

"I so regret not getting that girl's teeth," Maz smiled. "All I wanted was her fucking teeth. I just wanted to be able to say she never got away from me. At least not in one piece."

"God, you're bad."

"You're a bad, bad girl."

"What did she do?" Eadie asked. Everyone turned. Eadie squinted in the light, tried to feign humility.

"She was an uppity little slut who never knew when to keep her mouth shut." Maz leaned as she spoke, showing gray teeth. "Not unlike some little blow-ins I've met of late."

"Keely borrowed a few of Maz's things," someone sniggered. "Borrowed them, fucking, forever."

"Slippery fingers. Nobody likes a slippery finger."

"Well, maybe some people do."

Everyone laughed. Eadie felt a nudge and only just managed to keep herself from falling off the edge of the bench.

"I should'a borrowed a piece of that girl's brain while I had the chance. Borrowed it permanently."

"I saw something on the news about her," someone frowned. "Like they're after her. The cops. They want to talk to her."

Eadie cracked her knuckles, one at a time. The speaker was a waif named Sal, one of the cleverer of the bunch. Eadie wasn't surprised Sal had watched the news. She had the intelligence to be interested in it. But if Eadie were lucky, Sal wouldn't be the type to watch regularly, wouldn't have put together the pieces and calculated that three of Jackie Rye's past residents were missing, ask why the police hadn't been sniffing around. Eadie had been banking on the residents of Rye's Farm being so transient that few of them would have been there at the same time as all three missing girls. It was better if no one knew the police were looking for the missing girls. Whoever was responsible might decide to burrow or bail before Eadie had managed to get hold of them.

"Keely was on the news?" Maz frowned.

"Yeah."

"Why?"

"I think they said, like, she's missin' or somefink."

Eadie wiped at a bead of sweat on her temple.

"Missing? Since when? Since she took off from here with my fucking DVDs?"

"I don't know. Didn't watch that close."

"I hope she's dead."

A moan of appreciation went up from the table, broke into laughs.

"Aw, come on. No, you don't."

"Yes, I do."

"Not really though."

"Don't tell me what I fucking mean."

Eadie chewed her knuckles. There was no denying Sal had a few more biscuits in her packet than the other girls at the table, but that didn't count for much if her basic danger warning system was faulty. Sal was wandering into dangerous territory, and only Eadie, it seemed, could see the water rippling. Warning Sal was impossible. She glanced at the breakfast sheds and saw Jackie and Nick there, hunched and smoking.

"I wonder if she's in trouble or someone's reported her gone." Sal picked at the splintered tabletop, oblivious.

Maz had a bone and wasn't letting it go. "I'm really fucking interested in how you think I'm some kind of dog no good for her word. Because I've never done nothing to make people think that. I always follow through."

"Yeah, you know, but people talk sometimes."

"You saying I'm all talk?"

"Jesus, you need to calm down a bit." Sal squinted in the light.

"I mean what I say I mean." Maz boasted. "They say they know where she is?"

"No. They just said they're looking. There was a mug shot. A description. A reward, maybe. I dun remember."

"Dead. Dead in the ground."

"Oh, Maz!"

"What?"

"Well, what if she is dead? And you said you wished it?" Sal pleaded.

"Then I hope that. I hope that and worse. I hope some fucking piece of shit from out the back of fucking Bankstown put her in a van and gave her what she needed and then put her in the ground and gave the world what it needed." Maz looked around for encouragement. The women laughed. Pea gave up on the lighter, threw it over her shoulder into the dirt, and held her hand out to the girl beside her.

"No, you don't."

"Oh my God. Somebody put a leash on this bitch, please." Maz's face was taut as nylon.

"Plenty of people steal shit," Sal said. "You don't know what made her do it, maybe she, like, she had some kind of reason, you know, that nobody knew about . . ."

"You're stealing my good air right now, Sal," Pea

said, exhaling blue into the thin white air. "You need to give it up before someone knocks your block off."

An interesting move by Pea, Eadie thought. She'd got the impression so far that Pea enjoyed a good bullying session. No one was as they appeared. Sal herself had perked right up to her full height, the bones in her throat shifting up and down as she swallowed, apparently excited by the challenge of exerting her morality onto the group.

"You know sometimes you have to, like, give people the benefit of the doubt. People, you know. People can . . ." Sal was on the edge of something, Eadie could see. Something prophetic. Opinion changing. Something informed. But she didn't have the words. Hadn't been raised with the words. All she had in her mind were pictures of fairness and hard work and reward. Moving pictures, mental films she had made of a better world. "Maybe, like, she. Maybe if you'd forgiven her, you . . ."

Eadie watched Maz attack Sal, and to prevent herself from getting up, going for Maz, stopping the brutality and blowing her cover, she took pains to catalog just how very many tiny gestures and surrenders and facilitations were needed in the other women at the table for Maz to be able to do what she did to Sal. Eadie counted, one, two, three, nothing moving but her eyes, as the woman between Maz and Sal swiftly got up and stepped back, clearing the path. She watched as Pea leaned to her left, nudging Sal forward when she tried to lean back away from Maz's hands, watched as the three women on her own side of the table got up and moved around behind the fray, blocking Sal's exit.

Eadie let her eyes drift away as the beating progressed, to the horizon, to the stalking silhouettes in the heat haze, who stopped at the noise of the screaming, turned, looked, folded their arms, the way men will stop to appreciate a sunset, witnessing nature at its finest. Eadie remained seated. Bent a little to watch Maz's boot going up and coming down. Thought about the science of blood coated in dust, how it formed little balls, why it didn't soak into the earth right away, how long it took for blood to do that. Eadie witnessed, and Eadie said nothing. She put her hands on the table as they dragged Sal away toward the hose by the stables and only looked down at them when she felt the heat of Pea's cigarette near her fingers. The old woman was watching, too.

"All right." Pea flicked ash onto the blood-wet earth. "Back to it."

Heinrich went into a hole. That was what you did when you were dead. He took the room that had once been Vicky's in the attic of the house filled with giggling and whispering girls and lay under the sloped ceiling in the dark. He hurt. He slept.

In the time that passed after Bear's death, he began to learn how his new body would work, how much strength he would have. He lay and thought about what was happening inside him, bones fusing back together from where they'd splintered apart, tissue strands reaching out and reuniting with torn brothers, blocked blood vessels shrinking and becoming clear and raging with redness again, with warmth. When once the girls came and lay on him, lifted him, held him, put their tongues and fingers into him, now he flipped and pinned them and showed them his strength, made them squeal and cry out.

Sometimes in the dark he thought about Sunday. Tried not to follow those dark paths down into the bottom of his soul where the Silence lived. It would endanger the people around him, those thoughts. The sleeping girls. Vicky with her quiet steps. The men who laughed and blundered about downstairs. No. He would save that for Sunday. He knew somehow she would come to him.

When the girls left him Heinrich used a stick to make the distance between the bed and the table by the tiny window that looked out into the crowded lanes of Surry Hills. He pushed aside the papers and letters and notes Vicky had stacked there and waited for his coffee to come. He leaned his head on his knuckles and planned. At nine each night Vicky arrived with her little brown glazed coffee set and her hair falling out of her tortoiseshell clip. Braless, waify, a whisper in the way she walked and a whisper in the way she greeted him—no lips, just brushes of fingers and nails. Heinrich didn't think Vicky gave her lips to anyone. He would look out the tiny window and talk. Vicky would take up a pen and write.

"Who's overseeing importations down there at the Point right now?"

"Ian Hereward. Brett's son."

"Brett still alive?"

"No."

"Junior got any naughty pleasures?"

"No," Vicky would sigh, tap the name on her list. "Straight as an arrow. Doesn't even sip. They tell me you can't buy that one. Not with the Queen's gold."

"Sometimes money's not the price."

"Well, I don't know what to tell you, Boy. Money's all you got this early in the piece."

Vicky always called him Boy, even though Heinrich guessed he was eighteen or nineteen now.

"Didn't his pretty sister marry some fucking loudmouthed wog?"

"Yeah. An art dealer."

"Junior go to the wedding?"

"No."

Heinrich sipped his coffee. It was thin and black. All his body could take. Luckily Vicky was one of those women who had been around enough of the right kind of men to need few if any explicit directions. She looked at Heinrich as he sipped his coffee, and after a second or two made a note in her book to send someone after the loudmouthed wog.

And that's how it went in those first couple of years, noth-

ing but the gold light of the tiny windows. Heinrich sitting, talking, Vicky making lists, pushing money and people around down there on the earth.

"Who's the Father down there at St. Margaret Mary's?"

"Where?"

"Randwick. Catholic."

"I don't know."

"Get to know."

"Seen the light, have you?"

"I'd like to hear, not so much see," Heinrich would say. "Hear some confessions. Some secret sins."

Out there, on the surface, Heinrich's money walked, passed, tumbled from hand to hand, bumped into other piles of money and multiplied, the way that rats will triple and triple again in narrow passageways filled with torn paper. It was gathered and presented in stacks on tables in backrooms and cardrooms and changing rooms. It arrived unexpectedly into groups of men in the shadows of crowded clubs, was passed in envelopes into bloodstained hands, was tucked into coat pockets as lips brushed against the rims of strained ears.

"That thing. From last week. You're good to go."

"Says who?"

"Nevermind."

The "Nevermind" emerged into the language of prostitutes, junkies, warlords, bikers, chemists selling unlabeled boxes from their back steps and truck drivers taking back routes through the bush. The "Nevermind" trembled on the lips of theater owners on George Street, just before the lights went down, just after the lights went up again by someone's suddenly empty back-row chair, program card on the carpet, spectacles fallen in the aisle. The "Nevermind" was whispered in dreams. In cells. On ships rounding the headlands of Wat-

sons Bay, plunging into the gathering arms of the harbor. Men in hats knocked on the doors of the homes of prison wardens, prosecutors, journalists, men who made their livings holding keys, slamming hammers, wielding pens like swords. An envelope passed. A wink in the light of the hall.

"Who's this from?"

"Nevermind."

In the middle of bank robberies, a group of five became four and one comrade was tripped in the back lot before the gaping van, a foot on a heaving chest, the butt of a rifle lifted in the air.

"Sorry, bub. You need to go away for a while."

"What? Why? Why?"

"Nevermind."

Caesar was at dinner at Dominique's in Potts Point the last time anyone said Nevermind to him. He retreated to Dominique's because they kept the lights and the music low, the place was always clean, and his table always ready, tucked behind a wall of lit cabinets filled with cocktail glasses in the shapes of women and animals. It didn't really matter to Caesar who came along, who snuck into the seats, who wrestled with whom to put something to him while he ate—some grand plan worked out to within an inch of its life, some new avenue for his bloody river to wind down into the hands of the junkies. And though he despised them, resented them, was sickened by their simple travels between self-pity and self-gain, their itchy scratchy twitchy patchy existences chasing after the blessed release he'd been importing with Savet from Nam for years, it was these creatures, the junkies, who had made him what he was.

If there had been some way to get what he wanted out of them without the exchange, Caesar was certain he'd be able to feel joy again. If he could just figure out a way of getting their lifeblood without having to touch or speak to them. He rested his chin on his knuckles. Fucking junkies. He'd be locked to them forever.

"Caesar?" Someone broke him out of his musings. Caesar blinked. Savet had been sitting beside him only moments ago, shifting his prawns around his plate with his fork, and now some sallow-eyed fool was in his place, some soldier Caesar didn't know. Savet was the only man Caesar had ever known who would eat crisp cold prawns out of the tail with a fork. And even then he seemed to eat five or six and then give them up, like they weren't for him. He didn't understand it. The cop had moved down the table, was staring at his glass of whisky, plate full. Caesar felt annoyed. He gathered up another prawn from his pile and dabbed it in the sauce.

"What is it?"

"Tuesday's, um . . ." the soldier said. "Tuesday's shipment, the one meant for the Punchbowl guys. The one that, um, was supposed to come in with, and, um—"

"Would you learn to put some fucking words together."

"Well there's been a sort of, um, problem, and . . ."

"Say 'um' once more and see what happens to you."

"Sorry." The young soldier scratched his neck, hard, left red marks. A few months off being one of Caesar's new clients. Caesar filled his mouth with prawns.

"Tuesday's shipment has been seized."

"No it hasn't." Caesar filled the gaps in his mouth with wine, swished, swallowed, sucked juice from between his teeth.

"It . . ." The soldier sat there gaping, mouth puckering like

a fish. "We got word from Billy down on the wharf that the whole fucking thing's been, uh, uh, it's being held."

Caesar looked around the table. There were six men and Savet, all of them talking except the copper with the restless fork. A young waitress brought a basket of bread to the table, set it within Caesar's reach. He grabbed a roll. The man to his right, some bulbous-nosed stock-shifter-cum-hitman, grabbed one, too.

"I'm not understanding you," Caesar told the soldier. "You're talking gibberish. Nothing has been seized. It's impossible."

The soldier scratched his arms.

"Go back to Billy and tell him to stop feeding you lies."

"Billy's in the clink," the soldier trembled. "Ronnie Redford came down there himself and just started gathering everybody up like sheep into a divvy van."

The fat-nosed man to Caesar's right coughed. Caesar looked over, frowned. Fatty looked apologetic. Spread a hand in the air.

"You've shocked my friend here into choking on his dinner with this despicable news," Caesar told the soldier. He broke his bread and dabbed it in the sauce, munched it between his back teeth. "I sincerely hope what you're telling me isn't true. But if it is, I want you to find out exactly how ten sets of eyes that were supposed to be turned away from my shipment all suddenly turned around at the same time."

"Billy says he heard some guys talking about the seizure over in remand. Said somebody told somebody who told somebody else it'd been cooking for a while and there was more to come."

"And where are all these excited little whisperings leading back to?"

"They didn't say. They just said nevermind."

"Nevermind?" Caesar licked his lips. Glanced down the table at Savet. He wasn't looking.

The fat man was coughing again. Short, hard coughs, like he was trying to dislodge the bread from his windpipe. "I'm hearing this more and more. This 'nevermind.' Someone knocks over my hockshop. Nevermind. Someone stirs up a couple of my girls. Nevermind. Someone seizes my fucking shipment. Nevermind.

"Nevermind. I mind, you little fuck. I don't know what's going on, but I'm really beginning to mind. And you better pay attention to things that I mind. All of you. All of you little shits. What I mind should be all that's on your minds all the time, you understand me?"

Caesar grabbed hold of whatever he could get of the soldier, managed a collar and with it a bunch of warm, loose neck skin. Squeezed, felt the soldier tense and go limp, to lessen the pain by letting Caesar pull him within biting distance.

"Someone says 'nevermind' near me one more time and I'm going to snap. You understand? I'm going to snap, and they're going to be bagging whoever's near me when it's said."

The fat man fell off his chair. Caesar let the soldier go.

The men around him stood up, but Caesar didn't need to. He could see the nameless man on the carpet beside him, see the pink foam that poured up and began cascading down his blackening cheeks. He shifted upward in his chair, threw a glance around the table. People were screaming. Caesar hadn't seen a man's face color like that before. It was like his cheeks were being flooded with something just below the first layer of skin—black ink injected into the fluid there and creeping across the quivering mounds. The man kicked, hard, kicked again, and then went still. Caesar looked at the men *around him, the other diners uncertain whether to get up from their tables or not, hovering inches above their chairs.*

Caesar pushed his chair back, got up, and reached down. He plucked the lump of crusty white bread from the fat man's gnarled hand and raised it to his nose. Smelled something. He didn't know what.

Something that wasn't bread.

I don't spend a lot of time in Glebe, but when I do I go to the AB Hotel. The food is served in obnoxiously large portions and the place is a big mess of levels and private function rooms and lounge areas.

I was in Glebe to pick up some papers from my contact in the archives—some maybes and probably nots from the unnamed mug shot categories, Jane Doe files, and informant catalogs in my search for a Jimmy or a Kimmy connected to Sharon Elizabeth White. Sonya, a short woman who never wore makeup and was always in green, handed me three tattered, badly arranged manila folders and wished me luck. I lost my hold on all the papers as soon as she was out of sight and had to gather them up from the asphalt before they were taken by the wind.

I sat at the bar sipping a glass of rum on ice and looked through the files. I'd already dug up everything there seemed to be in the official records on Sunday, but I'd learned from some old Department of Community Services records that Sunday's sister, Adam White's mother, was in the records, too.

Lynda White had been removed from the care of her mother in a similarly chaotic roundup of Aboriginal children as the one that had claimed Sunday. But the two sisters weren't united in the system—foster family shortages meant there wasn't a home available for two little black girls. Sunday was sent to Sydney and Lynda remained in the southern state. According to a psychologist's report on Lynda accompanying some financial support she'd applied for in the eighties, she'd tracked down Sunday in the Cross when both girls were working in the sex industry in their late teens. What a reunion.

I fiddled with the stack of coasters nearby and stretched my neck, taking a break from the faded transcript to look around the bar. Maybe I could find Kimmy or Jimmy through Lynda. Maybe they knew each other. Were arrested together. Anything. I sighed. My hunting quarry had tripled. I was now trying to follow the movements of three ghost girls vanished into the halls of time. I dropped the archive files and pulled out my phone.

Juno answered after one ring.

"How's the Naked Detective?"

"She's all right."

"Working hard?"

"She does. Works really hard for someone who's not actually a farmworker. It's like she actually cares."

"Well, I'm working hard, she's working hard. Don't you go exhausting yourself watching my partner's perfectly sculpted ass morning and night. Take a break now and then. Rest your eyes."

"I guess I'll try."

"Anything juicy?"

"A couple of things, I guess. Someone vandalized Eden's van. Pissed in it. Fairly classy. I don't have any cameras on who it was, exactly, and nothing was said about it in Jackie's van." I could hear Juno moving things around, clicking. "I ran a check on those guys who were hanging around the night Nick climbed into Eden's bed. Nothing spectacular. Just lowlifes. I get the feeling Eden's going to use the girl to cozy up to Rye. Not basing that on anything really other than the fact that she's making besties with the kid for no other apparent reason."

"I'd love you to keep me updated on that."

"This place is so full of fucking degenerates, I don't know how you're going to pin it on Jackie, man," Juno said. "This morning these bitches laid into one of the younger girls just for giving some lip. Some pretty conversational, nonaggressive lip, if you ask me. Nothing that deserved being bashed half to death and then hosed down for."

"Trash."

"Yeah."

"There's a big difference between mob justice and first degree, though," I yawned. "What you witnessed was likely very routine, a passing thrill for those involved. Something to talk about. You do away with three whole human beings on the other hand. Well, that takes some planning. Commitment."

"So in a way I guess we're not looking for the most outwardly violent."

"Most likely we're looking for the exact opposite. I've got my money on the most organized. The most measured."

A woman came to the bar and stood beside me. She picked up the coasters I'd been playing with and arranged them in a fan shape on the woolly bar runner. I looked up as she tucked a curl of long black hair behind her ear and hailed the bartender from way down the room.

In her earlobes were tiny red earrings.

Ladybugs with gold feet. Painted thickly with gloss.

". . . I mean how long you gotta be doing this shit before you begin to think like that?" Juno was saying.

"It's not the length of time." I coughed, thumped my chest. "It's what happens to you."

I hung up on Juno and put my phone away. Far away. Put it by the canister of straws. I gripped the bar and waited for the woman with the ladybug earrings to go away. The woman with the black hair. The tall, lanky woman with the dimpled smile and the bony wrists who wasn't Martina. No, because Martina was dead. In the ground. Under the dirt because I hadn't been there when she needed me.

I took a packet of Oxy from my back pocket and popped three. Crunched. Made it four.

"Right, mate?" The bartender flicked his beard at me.

"Yeah. Another."

It was only about eight when Max Fara tapped on my shoulder. But I was drunk. Badly drunk. Three drinks past cutoff point drunk, but I've got a pretty good drunk's poker face, and I know how to keep my mouth shut and shuffle the bartenders, so I didn't think I was that close to being turfed.

I'd arrested Max Fara for a series of break-and-enters in my early days on the beat. So often had we encountered each other that we'd formed a sort of understanding that what happened between us wasn't personal, and that I didn't in fact go out of my way to come across him climbing in or out of windows all over Blacktown in his college years. By the time I was getting ready to sit the detective's exam Max, or Mustafa as he was on his birth certificate, had begun treating our little interactions as a cat-and-mouse game. His father was some big government official over in Lebanon, so the thefts had been a game, one with little consequences besides the regular promises that Dad's bail contributions were well spent. Now he had someone to share the game with, and I didn't mind that much. He'd always been nice enough.

"Not you."

"Sergeant Francis Bennett. Oh. My. God." Max flashed a set of huge white expensive teeth at me.

"It's Detective Inspector now, dickhead." I swallowed my rum.

"What are you doing here? You don't live here. Don't tell me all that pavement-pounding and crim-collaring has driven you to the drink?"

It was slightly alarming for Max to know where I didn't live. I pushed the alarm aside.

"There'd be something wrong with me if it hadn't. I'm just having a quiet drink and trying not to associate with any criminals. You know. The usual."

"God, it's so weird to see you. Such a fucking blast from the past. You still a Westie?"

"No."

"North Sydney?"

"Parramatta."

"That's where the big HQ is, isn't it?"

"Been there once or twice, have you?"

"What you doing at HQ?"

"Homicide."

Max submitted to laughter again. His bottom row of teeth were all gold, the center four studded with small white diamonds. I wondered what Daddy thought about that. If he knew. The young man also seemed to be wearing some kind of razor tailored suit with a cummerbund. It had been years since I'd even seen a cummerbund in a shop window.

"This explains why you look so shit. Hanging around stiffs all day. You're beginning to look like one. Look at your eyes."

"Thanks."

"You look tired, old mate."

"You look like a penguin. What is all this?" I flipped his buttons.

"Just styling and profiling, Francis, like I always do." He popped out his chest.

"Christ."

"Let me get you something to perk you up."

I scoffed. Began gathering up my papers.

"Nah, come on, please. Serious. Serious. You've always been good to me, Sergeant Bennett. I've always been such a stupid boy. An idiot. Those days are gone now, all right? Maybe I learned something. Maybe I changed. I remember where I came from though. What I've been through."

"Oh yes, it's a hard life being the idle son of an absent millionaire. You should write a rap ballad about it."

"You always softened it up for my father, even though I never asked you to. I never asked, did I?"

"I don't remember."

I remembered something about him being sixteen and crying in the back of a divvy van, telling me he was going to get thrown out onto the street. Something like that.

"Come on." He swung an arm around my neck, dragged me into his Lynx cloud. "There's a party going on and you're missing it."

"What party?" I was letting myself be led now. Surrendering. Answering the call into the wild. It was so easy. "Where?"

I'd never been to a Lebanese wedding. The experience was something like walking onto the stage of a great opera at the moment of a battle or dramatic death. People were shoving against me, rushing forward, dancing or embracing with cries so deep and guttural or high and piercing they could have been anywhere on the spectrum of human emotions.

The men reeked of cigar smoke and the women of expensive perfume. The food was laid out around the room like the walls of a great fortress—roasted, oiled, fried, bricks of cake, bread, meat. I must have been brushed by every texture of fabric in existence just getting into the room—scratchy gold-embroidered silks and rough leather and wool suits that cost more than my monthly rent. People were unafraid to touch each other, to touch me, dark-eyed beauties with skin drenched in glitter grabbing my fingers, wrenching me sideways, pulling my neck, insisting on a swing around.

Max put a drink into my hand. I must have been introduced to fifty people, ten of them in the dark courtyard area of the pub. A man I didn't know, some cousin or brother or uncle, dabbed a little expensive something, a good and hard-hitting something, into the webbing of my hand. Turning away, respectful gestures for disrespectful doings. My eyes watered. Men yelled in my ears. I indulged a little in cop storytelling, once I'd deemed it safe. A few young Lebanese boys hiding from their mothers so they could stay out late perched on the bricks around the cigarette garden, trying to make like their older brothers, disguising their awe with quizzical frowns. Questions were fired at me.

A wind started in the palm trees above the courtyard, a whipping sound, and the boys looked up, howled with delight as a plastic bucket tumbled off the roof, spilling paintbrushes and rollers into the garden. A light rain. Everyone leaked back inside into the noise. I felt warm. My hair was getting wet. Max put a hand on my shoulder, tried to get me inside, but I wanted to look at the stars, watch the black clouds eat them one by one.

It was some wonky-eyed teenage bartender who finally brought me in, fed up with all the noise and mess the Lebanese function was making of the upper floor. I stood inside the door and brushed rain off the hair on my arms, felt great.

When I looked up and spotted her sitting there at the tables on the mezzanine area I felt even better. A surge of electricity between my shoulder blades like I'd been prodded forward by a cheeky angel, a cupid. She was sitting with some strange half-monkey with a heavy sloping brow that wasn't helped by a quiff turning into a mullet behind his ears, a denim jacket lined with orange faux fur. Dr. Stone looked angry and he looked pleased with himself. Laughing at some joke he had just made. She turned her glass on the tabletop.

I strode forward and grabbed a chair from the empty set beside them, dragged it over, grinned down at her horrified face.

"Dr. Stone, if this isn't the luckiest night of my life."

"Oh Jesus," she said, looked away.

"Mate, I'm Frank Bennett." I offered my hand to the Neanderthal. He considered, pumped it halfheartedly. Wrinkled his big features.

"Curtis."

"I'm sorry to interrupt. I just saw you from up there and I thought, *No, way. It isn't.* And then it was! It was you. How hilarious. You look beautiful, Stone. My God. I mean, what are you trying to do to us, ay?" I nudged Curtis. He swayed.

She was beautiful, though. She was wearing something red. I couldn't tell if it was a dress or a long shirt but it was the color of something freshly bleeding, full of life, and it made her freckles stand out like gold stars. The dress was textured with little upraised squares. I wanted to touch it. She was frowning at her wineglass.

"Frank, you're drunk."

"No, I'm not."

"We're sort of having a bit of a private moment here," Curtis said. "Seems like the best time to catch up would be some other time."

"Is this a date?"

"No. It's not." Stone gave me some eyes that might have killed me had I not been so drunk.

"Well, actually it is," Curtis said.

"Is it?"

"No."

"He says it is." I jerked a thumb at the ape.

"It isn't, Frank."

"Is there some problem with him knowing that it is?" Curtis laughed once, like a cough.

"You'll just encourage him."

"I'm easy to encourage," I admitted.

"Mate, you're really playing with fire right now."

"Hey, I'm just being friendly. Excuse me. We're old friends, Dr. Stone and I."

"This really . . ." Stone licked her lips, looked at me. "You need to just . . ."

"Just tell him to fuck off." Curtis flicked his chin at her. Looked at me. "Mate, fuck off."

"Whoa!" I faked being thrown back in my chair. "Lordy! The new beau's got a temper."

"Just settle down, the both of you. Frank, you're drunk. Now's not a good time."

"You're right. I'll leave now so Captain Caveman here can apologize for using such foul language in your presence. On a first date and everything. What would your mother say, Imogen?"

"Is this guy one of your clients or something?"

"He's . . ." Imogen's explanation trailed off.

"All right, I'm going. I'm sorry. You look beautiful. Enjoy your date."

"It's not a fucking date."

"It *is* a date." Curtis puffed his chest out. "What the fuck, Imogen?"

"Maybe the problem with me knowing this is a date," I paused on the edge of my chair, on the edge of my own hilarity, held my breath to stifle the laugh, "is that she's dressed like a fucking fox and you're wearing a denim jacket with a fur trim."

Curtis stared at me.

"I mean you should have looked in the front windows at her and binned that thing before she ever saw it, mate."

"Wow." The ape glared at Imogen. She licked her

lips. Looked at me. At the ceiling. Then laughed, just once. Then she swallowed it. Pushed at me so that I got out of the chair.

"Go away."

"That jacket looks like someone killed a ginger cat." I wobbled on the edge of my chair. "And then stapled it to the eighties."

Imogen lost control of her laughter. The Neanderthal got up. I got up. Let him push me. There were ten or fifteen young Lebanese men watching from the balcony of the third floor. Ready. So ready.

"Calm down, sunshine. I'm only having a laugh."

"Fuck. Off."

"All right. I'm fucking off," I saluted. "Here I go. Fucking off now. Fucking off sequence initiated."

"He one of your psycho clients or something?"

I didn't stick around to hear her answer. Went to the bar and ordered a scotch. Stood drinking it, laughing to myself about the cat joke. Most jokes involving cats are pretty hilarious. I felt a wave of sadness pass over me, of longing for my cat, Martina's cat, annoying, food-obsessed, self-obsessed little jerk. The Neanderthal brushed me roughly as he passed, heading out the doors. Imogen was close behind him, draining the end of her glass of wine, pulling on her long red coat.

"Hey," I grabbed her when she got within reach, "I'm sorry."

"You should be."

"What can I say?" I asked. "What can I do?"

"Nothing. It's over. He's gone."

"Jesus."

"Look, actually, without meaning to, you managed to rescue me from something really awful. I'd been trying to end it for an hour and a half but the guy likes the sound of his own voice."

"Oh. Right."

"Doesn't make you any less of an annoying fuck."

"Yes, no, you're right, of course, annoying fuck."

"Frank."

"So that *was* a date."

"It was."

"Where do you even find a half-monkey, half-man? I thought they had to grow those types in laboratories."

"It was an online thing." She smoothed down her hair. "I'm not really in the mood for an exhaustive breakdown of it."

"You? You date from the Internet? *You*?"

"Yes. I date men I find on the Internet."

"*Why?*"

"It's almost like you're trying to make me angry."

"All right, I'll stop. I'm sorry, I'm drunk. Let me get you a cab."

"I'm walking."

"No, you're not, it's pissing with rain."

"I live three blocks from here, and I have an umbrella. I won't die."

"I'm walking you. Just to make sure. If you died I wouldn't have anyone to bully and judge me. Invade my life. Stalk me to my apartment."

"You're not walking me anywhere."

"Yes, I am."

"No, you're not," she laughed.

"I'll put you under arrest."

"Wouldn't you just love that?"

I grabbed her bicep and held it, gave it a squeeze. She rolled her eyes at me.

She was like a weather system, inexplicably predictable, something that changed the air and brought electricity to the earth before she arrived, made things tremble. Eadie was starting to believe she knew that Skye was coming for her even before the girl herself had made the decision, and by the time she heard the patter of Ugg boots across the dirt she'd already be feeling that half-smile creep across her face. It was right at sunset and the girl's silhouette cut into the orange light, her boots as pink as the horizon. Eadie said nothing, continued tightening the shoelaces of her runners.

"What are you doing?" the girl said.

"Going for a bit of a run."

"A run? Are you nuts? Haven't you worked all day?"

"Best time for a run." Eadie squinted in the painted day, held a hand up against the glowing red ball caught in the girl's dry blond hair. "Loosen me up."

"It's about to be dark. *Neighbors* is on in, like, twenty minutes."

"It'll keep. It's only Thursday. The good stuff'll be tomorrow night."

"I'll come with you."

"I'm not walking. I'm running."

"I can run." A child's indignation. Hands on hips.

"Better hurry up then. I'm leaving today."

The girl sprinted off, and Eadie pulled her heels into

her backside, feeling the warmth of a day's labor pulse in her quads, groan in her back. Skye returned with nothing about her outfit changed but a pair of worn sneakers—her denim skirt stained with motor grease on the right-hand hem, the pink tank top over the ill-fitting bra. Eadie guessed the girl would learn. Eadie watched her gathering her hair into a bun, not quite able to catch it all, leaving strands at the nape of her neck that if touched would make her shiver. "Go slow," the child frowned.

"Go quick."

"I'll die, Eadie. Go slow, will you?"

"All right, Nanna."

They set off toward the stables, between them, and passed the pigs, the croaking and groaning beasts lying down to sleep. Eadie tasted them in the air. Skylar's face was rigid, the temples pulsating, blood shocked at how fast it was moving and chemicals pouring through veins, trying to calm things down.

"Slow down."

"We're crawling."

"Just. Slow. Down."

"All right," Eadie laughed.

They bounced through the back gates and found themselves in the bush. It was treacherous here. Recent rains had slicked the walking tracks with clay, left rocks disturbed, ready to shift under wayward feet. If the girl turned an ankle, who would care for her, Eadie wondered. Would Jackie cook dinner if she couldn't get around their tiny kitchen? Would he change the DVD? Would he help her hop over to take a piss in the annex next to the bed? Eadie huffed, found a rhythm finally, a slow one but a good one, her fists loose in front of her, gripping air handles, pulling herself forward, dancing. Who did Skye think was going to care for her when she got old? Did the girl see herself and Jackie growing old together? Did she love the man? Did she know what love was?

"Hey! Slow down."

Eadie laughed, slowed again. The girl came up beside her, gripping a stitch.

"I'm gonna. Die. Out here."

"Chat to me. It'll take your mind off it."

"I can't."

"Yes you can. Open your mouth. Lift your head up. You run like an elephant."

"I am. An elephant."

"Do the boys come out here?"

"Yeah. Sometimes. They hunt. Roos."

"Roo meat's good for you."

"It's gross. Too tough."

"They probably overcook it." Eadie took a long breath, sucked in the moist air before it began to give way to the desert again. The trees thinned before them, revealing lantana, sand. "They should watch more *Master Chef*."

"Mostly they don't. Cook them. No one. Likes them much. And there's so much. Pig. Anyway."

"So what do they do with them then? If they don't cook them?" Eadie frowned.

"They just."

Eadie looked over. The girl was uncomfortable. Shrugged. Her breasts lifting, catching the red light with their film of sweat.

"They just kill them."

"So it's just sport?"

"I guess. I don't know. I'm not allowed to go. Only the boys go."

Eadie licked her lips, savored the salt she tasted. She wasn't a betting woman, but she would wager money that Jackie and his team were doing more to the kangaroos out here than simply snuffing their lives out. A bunch of drunk men, a shed full of cutting, grinding, mashing, slicing implements, the dark barren land, and a bunch of helpless animals. It was a recipe for pain. "I'm gonna. I can't. Let's go back."

"Keep going." Eadie was shocked by the callousness in her voice. Softened it. "You can do it. Keep talking. What's down there?"

"Cliffs."

"Come on. Let's look."

"I've seen them. They're boring."

"Come on, I want to see."

The trees thinned to brush, and then without warning a gaping crack in the earth, running in a curve out of eyesight. A dry riverbed. Eadie turned and led Skye along its edge, ducking forward now and then to look into the dark below without slowing the pace.

"Let's stop."

"No. Let's keep going. It's nice though."

"Yeah sometimes. There's water. Down there."

Eadie let the girl go ahead, jogged at barely a pace above walking, more bouncing than moving forward. She spied a lump of blackness on a rock ledge and doubled back, circled before the girl could see, and squinted. Clothes. Burned and blackened. A pair of jeans maybe. Eadie felt her mouth grow dry, looked for some landmark that would remind her where she'd seen the discarded clothes. Just a line of bush. A sweep of desert. A fence etched into the mauve sky like the fine pencil lines of an artist. It was growing dark. Eadie chewed her lip, remembered the camera hanging in the pendant around her neck. So easy to forget.

"Burned clothes," she said aloud, grabbed the pendant and held it near her lips. "I'm seeing burned clothes on the riverbed east of the property. I don't see any landmarks to tell you where. I want these checked out."

"I'm gonna stop if you don't catch up."

Eadie caught the girl in a few strides and sprinted back through the wire fence onto Jackie's property. The kill sheds were ahead of her, absorbing the dying light in their gaping doors. She ran to the front double doors, stopped, and stretched her limbs. The girl came bobbing toward her, stopped, and hobbled when she got within speaking distance.

"Let's never do that again."

"Do it every day. It gets easier. I'll go with you," Eadie smiled.

"Maybe. I want to lose weight. Jackie says I've got flabby arms."

"You don't have flabby arms."

"Yes, I do."

They walked into the sheds together. Stood in the fading light. Eadie could make out a long steel trough, a conveyer belt of hooks parallel to it, within a tall man's reach. Four large stalls, enough to hold twenty pigs each, were swept and hosed bare. These would be hard surfaces to keep clean. The first thing animals do when they see or hear their kind being slaughtered is shit themselves, attack the beasts around them. There'd be blood in the grout too deep to remove.

"They hang them here," Skye pointed. "Upside down. Gut them. This whole thing gets filled with guts. All the way to the end there. Guys stand here with their blades out. Sharp as a razor. Slash, slash, slash. From there, the bolt in the head, to there, the tagging line, it's about ten minutes. Jackie says sometimes they're still twitching."

The girl gave a little wiggle, limp hands flapping.

"Gross," Eadie said.

"Yeah, real gross."

"You ever been in here when it's on?"

"Nuh." Skye wrinkled her nose, stood with her hands on her hips. "I couldn't do it. I like pigs. They're cute."

"I'll bet you like bacon, too, though."

"Everybody likes bacon."

Skye stood looking up at the hundreds of hooks, each pointing the same way and aligned like an infinite row of question marks. Then she shivered, and Eadie felt the same shiver run through her, though she couldn't understand why.

"Let's get outta here, man," the girl said and grabbed Eadie's hand.

"Yeah." Eadie felt the girl squeeze her fingers. "Time for *Neighbors*."

When Vicky knocked on the door to the attic room, she received no response. This didn't surprise her. Often Heinrich lost himself in his thoughts so completely that no amount of noise could bring him out of the complex network of plans being webbed together by tiny spiders in his mind. She entered the darkened room and saw him sitting by the window, a figure shaped like a crone with the same sad, labored movements, lost in his thick brown overcoat, fiddling with things on the table. Sometimes the boy didn't let any light into the attic room, but today a slice of sunset had snuck in and struck the side of his head pink, gold in his unwashed hair.

"There's a girl here for you," Vicky said. She took a couple of steps forward and tried to see what the boy was doing. Another of his creations. After the first year in the room Heinrich had started building things, first from whatever he found lying around, paper folded dozens of different ways into the shapes of reindeer and dragons, fitted together to make intricate boxes that sprung open at the touch. Then he had started meddling with things the girls brought him, coils of copper that he weaved into the intricate scales of a life-sized cobra. He strung beads together and pulled them impossibly tight, made colorful fish that from across the room looked like they would flitter through the air, dart beneath the desk. The girls marveled at his work but it seemed to bring him no joy.

"Heinrich?"

"What girl?"

"She's calling herself Sunday."

The boy said nothing. Vicky tried to see what he was working on. It seemed to involve strips of wire being twisted around fragments of colored glass. She leaned back into the hall and nodded to the girl, who came walking forward and took the door from Vicky's hand as though she feared it would slam shut on her. She was a beautiful thing. All square and taut, robotic almost, like the whirring, mixing, dancing things rich women were putting in their kitchens, shiny and full of joints. She went to the middle of the room, stood looking at the boy. Heinrich's eyes never left his work.

Sunday filled her lungs with air. Let it go as the older woman clicked the door closed behind her.

"I thought you were dead."

"That was the plan."

The boy looked old. His hands looked old as they pulled the wire, clipped the ends, and placed the offcuts in a little bowl like shiny noodles. Sunday wanted to see his gray eyes but they were hidden, so she took a few steps closer and stopped when she saw the muscles in the boy's neck twitch. It hurt to be apart from him. She had been so used to touching him whenever they were together, from those years they slept together as children, his back rising and falling against her cheek, his ankle brushing hers.

"People been talking. This morning Caesar held a meeting with some of his top guys at Mickey Cousins's place down on the water." Sunday picked at her nails. *"That Burgmann guy was there. The customs guy. Some others. They were all talking on the balcony and when they got up to leave Mickey's kid, the one they arrested last year, he goes and gets Caesar's coat from the back of the couch in the living room and hands it to him."*

Heinrich was examining a piece of glass in the light of the window, an almost perfect triangle of royal blue that threw a sky-blue beam onto the wall behind him. "So as he's handing over the coat the kid makes a noise, like a yelp, and he swears out loud, and he takes the coat back and pulls a thorn from the inside of the collar. Like a rose thorn. It's pricked his finger, made a little black dot, and it kills, he says, but no one cares. Caesar puts the coat on and goes to leave. He doesn't get halfway out the door before the Cousins kid's dead on the floor like a stone."

Heinrich lifted his eyes from the thing in his hands for an instant, looked at Sunday's face, just long enough to give her a flash of his cold, hard eyes.

"It wasn't a rose."

"Caesar's going to figure out it's you." Sunday felt a shiver run through her. Rubbed her arms. "I figured out it was you pretty damn fast. Soon as people started saying they'd seen your ghost I knew you'd made it somehow. You better stop with the near misses and do what you're planning to do, or he's gonna send someone round here."

"I'm doing what I'm planning to do," Heinrich said. "And no one's coming round here."

He finished what he was putting together, and when his hands let the sculpture stand on its own she saw a small bird fashioned from glass in a hundred different shades of blue and green, the dark green of beer bottles and the pale sickly blue of church windows, the lime green of cottage doors and the royal blue of medicine jars. The tail feathers were daggers of a deep purple, the glass from where she couldn't guess. The thing's wings were spread and feathered with the sharpest splinters, so to look at it was to feel the ache of beauty but to touch it might have torn a careless hand to shreds.

"Why didn't you tell me you were alive?" She swallowed.

Squeezed her fists to draw the hurt down from her throat so that she could speak. "I've been alone."

He was out of his chair before her eyes could follow him, but his hand on her throat was familiar, the way it crushed her windpipe made her remember that night on the couch, the way he'd wanted to squeeze her, to possess her, to bend her bones. She felt his breath on her face and the wall against the back of her head but she knew better to raise her hands to his.

"You have no idea what alone is like," he said. "I was alone in that house when they found me. Surrounded by dead men and women and girls."

"Caesar and Savet, they——"

"One minute you were there," Heinrich snarled. She felt his spit on her face. "In my arms. And then I wake up and you're gone and they're coming down on me."

"I didn't know."

"Into the night like fucking smoke."

"I didn't know!" she screamed, felt her throat flex against his stone hand. "I loved that man. You know I loved Bear like my very own father. Don't you tell me that you don't."

She was crying in his hands. He loosened his fingers from around her neck.

"I ran from you because of what we did, I couldn't . . . I couldn't understand it. I wanted it but I was afraid. I hurt everything that comes near me, Heinrich, and I needed to keep you from that." She put her hands on his shoulders and was relieved to feel the warmth of them beneath the old coat, the smooth flesh of his neck, the curls at the back of his ears. He stood rigid and she hung herself from him, pulled his face down into her hair. She could feel his heart beating against her cheek.

"You're going to start a fucking war," she trembled.

"It was started a long time ago."

"You can't get him back. Bear is gone. You don't know what they can do to you. This is what they do, Heinrich. They were born to do this."

He laughed. "You can learn with the right teacher."

"Come away with me. Let's go up north. Like we said when we were kids."

"No. We're not kids anymore. Look at you. Look at what you've done to yourself." He had her wrists in his hands, her impossibly thin wrists. He took her face and shoved her, tried to back away, but she yanked him to her. He pushed her into the wood, pulled her hair, exposed her jaw to his mouth. She didn't fight.

I woke to the sensation of a tapping in the center of my chest, the kind of insistent tapping and rubbing you get when a paramedic is trying to bring you back to consciousness. Dr. Stone took my hand from my nuts and put a coffee mug into it. The heat brought me back. I was bent in a banana curve across her stiff square couch, my boots hanging close to what looked like a vase stuffed with dead twigs and my head baking in the heat of a curvy glass lamp. She flipped the lamp off and I tried to move, felt everything creak like it was going to fall apart.

"Oh God," I said. Breathed low and deep. "Why? Why?"

"Yes," I could hear her smile in the new dark. "It's a good question."

Her robed silhouette thrust open the curtains in front of the balcony. I covered my eyes.

"Stop. Go back to where you came from. Leave me here to die."

"It's ten. The day's half over."

I bent my head into my hand and felt dead inside. I twisted, groped for my pills, found my pockets empty. The place was spotless and small, like she'd only half moved into it or like she recognized such a tiny space could easily get cluttered and crowded by the things she owned, so she chose not to own things—to just look at them instead. She walked in bare feet to the kitchenette and retrieved her own coffee. I wondered if she was naked under the red satin.

"Did we sleep together?"

She coughed and swallowed her coffee.

"No, Frank."

"Why not?"

"Because that's the worst idea I've ever heard of in my life." She looked at me, tried to stifle a smile. "You're a train wreck."

"I suppose." I adjusted my shirt. It was misbuttoned and stank of cigar smoke. I tried to rebutton it and only made things worse.

"Your phone's been going off. Could be important."

I picked my phone up from the coffee table. Juno had called me seven times. Imogen came to the couch next to me and pulled her bare legs up beside her. She didn't seem to mind that her feet were touching my butt. I was never going to get her, I decided. She was too together. And she was also right about me.

Seeing the girl with the ladybug earrings the night before had derailed me. I had a feeling that now that it had been so easy to surrender, the next derailment would be even easier. A woman's laugh. Her smell. And wasn't Martina just my latest excuse in a lifetime of excuses to stop and throw away Frank Bennett, police officer, and get wild? Hurt people. Break hearts. Damage myself. Was there something in me that liked to be this way?

Imogen Stone would be able to see things like that in your eyes. Smell it on your skin. I didn't know a way back from the knife edge. I didn't want her to show me, either. See the failure in her eyes when I fell backward after she'd spent so much time standing me soldier straight.

"There's a way back, Frank," Imogen said, as though she'd been sitting there sipping her coffee and reading my mind.

I got up and moved away from her, repelled by her easy morning beauty. Went to the desk by the balcony doors and shifted things around there like a nosy jerk. Empty coffee mugs, the glossy expensive type you see in specialty tea shops. Dozens of manila folders stacked in a corner against the wall, spread out over the tabletop. Client files? I flipped one open.

"Oh ho! Look at this. The juicy commentary of Sydney's best nutcases."

"Not exactly," she said, curling her feet up underneath her. "I don't bring my work home with me. Well, not usually. But you sort of followed me home."

I looked at the papers in the folder under my fingers. Crime scene photographs. Photocopied notes. An autopsy report. I lifted the file and flipped through the pages.

"What's this?"

"Looks like the Beaumont children case from here."

"You writing a book?"

"No," she laughed, sipped her coffee. "It's an embarrassing little hobby I have."

"Evans," I read through the spines of the files against the wall. "Lillee. These are unsolved cases."

"My name is Imogen Stone." She put a hand on her heart. "And I am an armchair detective."

"I can't believe this."

"I don't know what's so hard to believe about it,"

she said. "I'm a cop psychologist. It's one of the lowest paid and least respected appointments in the field. Something must have drawn me here. I like crime."

"Look at you. Jesus. I don't know if this makes you more or less attractive."

She came across the room and took the file from my hands, folded it shut, and dropped it among the clutter.

"I'm not some aging true crime groupie. I provided a lead on the Emily Dooville case. Took me a year and a half. Earned me fifteen grand in reward money."

"Ah ha. I thought those were dollar signs I saw gleaming in your eyes."

"Jesse Deaver, here—that's up to a hundred grand. Imagine if I cracked that. Hello investment property."

"What a little capitalist you are." I smiled. She might have seen a weariness in it because she took up her coffee again and stood near me, not touching me, but warming me somehow with her very presence.

"You just have to do one job, Frank. That'll get you back to where you need to be. A bit of focus."

"Focus."

"Be a cop. A good cop. Morning, afternoon, night. Stop being a man for a while and do your job. Your partner needs you. The families of those girls need you. The next girl in line, the one who's waiting to be the next body you dig up, she needs you. If you can manage to stop thinking about Martina for a while and start thinking about what's happening right now, I think you might be able to put yourself back on the tracks."

I felt something stir in my chest. Some tightness, some desire, like the pull of magnets against my heart, making it beat in my throat, under my tongue. Stone rubbed my hand, and I drank the coffee, felt it making connections in my brain.

"You might be right."

"That's my job."

"We should celebrate by sleeping with each other."

"No, we shouldn't."

"You're probably right."

"Have a shower," she said, taking my empty cup back to the kitchen. "Then get the fuck out of my house."

There was something about Eden. Some natural, beautiful thing. Watching her, Juno imagined, was like being privy to the movements of a majestic and vicious creature in the wild lumbering around the world with all its deadly capacity proudly contained, a thing that everyone knew was dangerous. Panthers, for example. Sleek. Soft. Curved, not needing to advertise their lethality with spikes or ridges or scales or splashes of color.

Eden was very much like a panther. She slept like a panther. With natural exhaustion. Still as a rock. The unbothered ease of the queen of the jungle. He liked to watch it. It made him feel excited and at peace all at once.

Eden going to sleep was one of his favorite things. She had a long wind-down procedure. Unlacing her boots seemed to take minutes. She'd unclip a pocketknife from her belt, an old and much-used thing it looked like, fold it open, examine it. She would arrange things by the bedside, the knife, her phone, a pencil and paper. She sometimes used the pencil and paper, but he couldn't figure out what she scribbled when she sat bolt upright in the early morning hours. Sometimes he thought it looked like names. Now and then she'd made a list and crossed them off one by one, her frantic breathing easing as she did, becoming the calm intake and exhale of sleep once more. In the mornings she always threw the lists away.

Sometimes Juno wondered whether Eden forgot about the cameras at night. But she never forgot in the morning when she disappeared into the bathroom, lifting the pendant over her head and setting it on the counter beside the sink. Beige ceiling squares inlaid in plastic, flowers of black mold. Juno had almost memorized their patterns.

Juno wondered if he was getting too close to Eden. He supposed that was a natural effect of surveillance work. Frank had warned him about it, said he'd spent two weeks watching a beautiful female drug dealer in his early days and had got himself all worked up about her. Small hot car. Hours alone. It had made the final arrest difficult. Impossible to follow the case in the paper after it left his hands. Afraid to know the sentence. Like she'd been a girlfriend. An ex-lover. In his mind they'd been together for years. In truth they'd spent a wordless car ride together to the station and that had been it.

"Nothing but your dick, the girl, and as much junk food as you can cram in the passenger seat," the cop had said, watching Eden on the screen with minimal interest. "You think you know what they're thinking after a while. Put your thoughts into their head. Truth is you don't know a thing about them. You could watch her for the rest of your life. You don't know shit."

The matter-of-fact way he'd said it, leaning back on the milk crate in the corner of the van, his legs spread and his eyes lazy on the Jack Daniel's. *You don't know shit.* Said with the conviction of a man protecting his wife from the glare of a rival male, said with all the arrogance of a beast with a beauty on his arm. Frank was one of those hard cops who had spent too many years throwing his weight around to understand authentic interactions with other males anymore. He had spent too long knowing that his role in the force automatically put him above every man in every room he ever entered, no matter their size, their intelligence, their capability, their history. He used his badge to snag women. Juno could tell. Take the badge away and all you have left is a man with an ego problem. He wondered if Frank and Eden had ever gotten together in their time as partners. Small hot car. Hours alone. He doubted it. Eden was clever enough to see through shit like that.

She stood and Juno got one of his rare daily full-face shots of her as she tied her hair in the mirror, swept it into a bun at the nape of her neck, brushed her blinding white teeth for three and a half minutes as though it was something she timed. Cleanliness was her thing. Organization. Discipline. She'd be suffering out there beyond her natural environment.

Juno sympathized. His cramped little van had become like a stinking cave, never long enough or wide enough to accommodate him, never sunny enough to dispel a strange dampness that covered everything.

The blinking of the monitors and the humming of the machines was like the stirring of organs inside a creature that had swallowed him. It was good to feel that he shared something with Eden, even if it was only discomfort, a longing for home. Juno slapped his cheeks, cleared the burger cartons off the makeshift desk into a garbage bag, and tried to get ahold of himself.

Eden walked out into the daylight and turned toward the back fields. It was too early for work, for breakfast. Juno frowned. Maybe she was heading to the kill sheds to take samples while everyone was asleep. Eden's hands appeared on the screen. Three tiny evidence bottles, no bigger than toothpicks, that she examined before putting them back in her pocket. Frank had been wrong. Juno was inside her head. The evidence of it was everywhere. She was like his avatar, following his commands on the screen. Juno got Eden. Men like Frank didn't get women like Eden.

Eden in the kill sheds. Gloves snapped on fast as lightning, a quick glance toward the doors, and then she began. She knew just where to go. The sorting tables. The slaughter line. The tools. If there was human blood here it would stand out among the pig blood like a fox on a bunny farm. One cell, one single cell, would add to the story. It would be near impossible for Rye and Hart to explain the girls' blood here. This was a man's space. Maybe blood from the missing girls found here wouldn't be enough to convict, but Eden was a hunter and she would hunt down whatever she could—a whisper here and a blood droplet there, clothes charred and burned and left on a cliff edge. She would find hairs and fibers and text messages left behind, sniff out the missing girls, gaining momentum like a hound running after a scent, closer and closer until she made her catch. That's how Eden lived and breathed. For the hunt. Juno knew it.

Eden capped the bottles and pocketed them. She left the kill sheds through the back doors and headed into the bush. Juno watched. He crossed his legs, tried to tap into Eden's mind. She was probably going out to see if the burned clothes had been taken overnight.

Eden turned. Looked. Turned back around. Kept walking at an even pace.

"I'm being followed," she said.

Juno sat up on his milk crate. Felt his muscles tense, his whole body shivering with energy. There was no indication of his own terror in Eden's voice. Her feet kept the same rhythm, the camera on her chest looking forward into the wall of green before her.

"Nick Hart's following me," Eden said, touching the pendant as though to make sure it was still there, making the microphone crackle in Juno's van. "He's at about a hundred meters, following slow. Making no effort to conceal himself."

"Oh God," Juno said aloud. He grabbed for his phone, dialed Frank's number. It rang out. "God."

Eden kept walking. Her boots sometimes crunching on gravel and leaves, sometimes soundless on dirt. She turned and Juno caught a glimpse of the tall lanky figure of Hart between the trees, following the same path through the undergrowth. He seemed no closer. A hundred meters or so. Within shouting distance. In eye-contact distance. And he was making eye contact. Juno could see that. Cold, expressionless, the eyes hollow across the morning shadows.

"He's not gaining," Eden whispered. "I'm not slow-ing."

"Get out of there . . ." Juno cringed. "Get out of there!"

She was heading deeper into the woods. Juno couldn't understand it. Paths forked in front of her and each time she headed into the dark. Juno cranked up the contrast on his laptop. She turned again and Juno caught the edge of Hart's shoulder between the trees, rounding a bend.

"Let's play, baby," Eden whispered.

Juno felt his breath seize in his chest. His stomach was clenched. Eden stopped walking and turned around. He could hear her breath. It was slow and deep. A sleeper's breathing. This didn't rattle her. This was a game. Juno scrambled for his phone, dialed Frank again, and listened to the phone ring out.

Nick Hart locked eyes with Eden before he heard the snap of her pocketknife as it slid open in her fin-gers. Hart smirked and Juno saw his whole body jolt with the laugh. The tall man followed the fork in front of him down the embankment and back toward the farm. Juno panted as Eden returned to her walk.

By the time I left Imogen's apartment that morning, managed to wrestle the image of her out of my mind, listened to Juno's frantic dribbling updates, and hit the station, I was already ruined—and it was only midday. I briefed the captain, assembled a team, located where Juno thought Eden had spotted the evidence on an aerial map, and then grabbed a quick nap in the downstairs changing rooms to avoid collapsing at my desk in front of everyone. I probably looked like a drunk, and I knew I smelled like one, but there was no call for acting like one in front of the young and impressionable beat recruits. It would be a decade and a half before any of them had any excuse to get this run down.

Night had fallen by the time I got to Rye Farm. As the convoy of lights began heading up the highway toward me, I was sitting with my arms on my knees in front of my own car, trying to will myself to stand before any of my cronies saw any weakness. Eventually I moaned at the stars, held my breath, and dragged myself up by my bumper as the convoy switched off their lights and rumbled into a rough half circle in front of me. I had a couple of beat cops for muscle work, a couple of forensics specialists, and a cadaver expert with a dog. Both of the forensics ghouls were women I'd seen around the office but never met—matching ponytails and serious faces, the type who read a lot and smiled a little. I introduced myself as we waited for the cadaver guy to unload his dog. One of them was Nicky, but I didn't catch the other's name. She mumbled it into her chest as she checked her gear. The hound was a shimmery caramel-colored thing with a pink nose and against all expectations it dropped out of the cabin of the handler's truck, bounded over, and hurled itself at me.

"Dog, I've got enough trouble standing upright without you."

The beast shook itself, barked, and tried to dance with me. I looked off toward the ridge over which the main body of Rye's Farm lay.

"Bones, get down."

"You need to get this dog to shut up or you're going to blow this whole thing," I told the dog's handler. He was a worried-looking guy, a brow creased from much disappointed frowning at unruly pups, I imagined. The thing was wearing a blue and white checkered police pattern collar.

"Sorry. Sorry. She's just excited. She's one of my best, really."

"What the hell do you call this? Your dog's wearing a cop costume?"

"I got it at my kid's school fair. Thought it was cute. Jesus. She is a cop. Sorry."

"Dog's name is Bones?" Nicky the forensics ghoul asked.

"Yuh."

"Bit morbid, isn't it?" she snorted, glanced at me. "Like calling him . . . Detective Stab. Detective Strangle."

"Detective Bludgeon," her friend laughed. One jostled the other with her elbow. These girls were more fun than I thought.

"What is this? National Pick on the Dog Handler Day?"

"All right, all right." I took the map from my hip pocket. "Take a look at this, everyone, and we'll get going."

I flattened the map out on my knee and spread it on someone's hood. I'd made a bunch of notes on it during Juno's call and now they were barely distinguishable from the mess of lines and ridges. I thanked my past self for having the foresight to highlight in pink. I pointed to the body of the farm.

"We're not even a kilometer out from this boundary fence, ladies and gentlemen, so the first thing I want to say is that everyone needs to keep their lights and voices down from now until we're back on the road. Minimal radio use. I want you two up there on the ridge looking out, both with a vantage point for our work out here in case we lose comms on the ground."

The two beefcakes standing in as my lookouts nodded, hands in their pockets.

"What we're after is a pile of burned clothes or other cloth. But I want to run the dog the length of the riverbed and see if anything turns up. If it hits on anything subsurface we're to mark it on the GPS and leave it. We're on the edge of an undercover operation so we don't have the time or space for a proper dig. It's in and out."

The dog was licking its ass at my feet. I was losing faith in its natural genius.

"Are you guys close to an arrest here? Shouldn't grabbing any bodies be the priority?"

I tried to think of a less appropriate time for this discussion and failed. I looked at my watch.

"It'll keep. Situation's rather complex."

"It'll keep?" Nicky scoffed. Narrowed her eyes. "This is what you guys do. You make our job harder so you don't have to file paperwork. What about the families?"

The dog handler stroked the dog, avoiding human eye contact.

"It's not paperwork, honey." I pointed to the ridge. "My partner's up there and she needs me not to fuck up all her hard work by digging up a corpse right under the nose of her targets. Whoever this piece of shit's after next needs me to put him away before he can do any more damage. The girl in the ground can wait, if there is one. Risking lives to avoid paperwork is not what I do, so I'm certain you weren't suggesting it."

The forensics girl sighed and took out her flashlight. I straightened and sent the beat cops up the embankment. I was hoping we wouldn't find anything that could be a body. For the girls themselves, their families—and for Eden. Because what I was interested in was justice, not turning back time.

If we found something, the countdown would be on to begin an excavation within the legal time frame. We couldn't hold off if we had any reason to suspect someone might be buried on Rye's Farm. Eden would have to be extracted, and her work would be dismantled. Likely, at the stage we were at, Hart and Rye would get off. We'd be stuck with what we had forensically, which even then would be useless, because it could be argued by any half-witted defense lawyer that sexual or even violent relationships between the dead girls and Jackie and Nick were common knowledge, and they'd expected the forensics to show that.

Rape, violence—it didn't prove murder. Very little proved murder. You could put people in the same room as the victim, on the same night, and not prove murder. Hollywood films teach people that finding the body is the end. Most of the time, it's just the beginning. If we dug now, the best we'd get would be rape if we could find other tapes of Hart and Rye's nighttime games.

Once the beat cops had left, the forensics girls walked ahead, heads down and flashlights sweeping. Only the handler stuck by my side.

"So your partner's undercover up there?"

"She is."

"How come you didn't go?"

"She wanted to."

"Huh!"

"Yeah. Women and their ideas."

The handler let the dog off the leash. He seemed to have established some sweeping motion with it across the riverbed and it followed, scooping the sides, nose down and snuffling, kicking up dust in the flashlight beam.

"Is it just me or did you work on that crazy doctor case?" the handler asked.

I bent my head and kept walking, kicking over stones.

"It's just you."

"The one chopping up kids and selling their organs."

"I know the one you mean. Wasn't me."

"Dude looked just like you. Saw him on the news. I think I read somewhere one of the victims was his girlfriend. Shit like that you only see in movies."

"Could we focus on what we're doing here? This isn't a date."

"Right." The handler took it hard. Nodded ruefully. I felt bad. Missed Eden. I knew how to talk to her. Mostly I talked and she shot whatever I said out of the air like a slow pheasant. It was a system that worked.

I cleared my throat. "It's a good-looking dog."

"She's actually mine."

"Use her to hunt cadavers in your spare time?"

"Yeah," he laughed. "Found me a roo skeleton in my backyard. Must be a hundred years old. Area's been built up since federation."

Bones the Wonder Dog left the sweeping trail and sprinted ahead past the forensics girls in a blur of fur. Within seconds it was barking in the dark.

"All right, shut it up."

"Bones! Sccht! Sccht!"

The beat cops were following us overhead along the ridgeline, hands on guns. The hand on the gun made me think they were new graduates. The late-night assignment certainly suggested it. They were probably hoping for us to find some bones so they could brag to their little brothers.

The dog had hit on what Eden had seen from the ridgeline, a colorful patch of cloth half-submerged in sandy earth shifted in recent rains. The two forensics girls fell onto the evidence like scavengers, marking out a couple of square meters around the area, spraying luminol. We switched off our flashlights and they swept the area with little purple penlights. With the

lights back on, they began excavating into evidence
bags, dirt and all.

"Burned elsewhere and dumped," one said.

"Yeah. Accelerant. Nylon here."

"Probably lost any of the good stuff. Too much exposure."

"We'll get a soil composite."

The talk was almost cheerful. It was probably like
digging up treasure. They went about ten centimeters
down. The clay was cut like dense cake and scooped in
neat triangles. The dog had turned back to its ass again,
now and then letting up to examine the air, almost
frowning.

"Keep along the riverbed," I said when the girls
were finished. "I want to go right to the end. There
might be more."

"Come on, Bones." The handler clapped. "Let's go,
buddy."

The dog looked at the handler, looked at me,
seemed to assess her chances. Then she took off. She
turned and bolted for the ridgeline.

"Oh crap," I managed before the handler was off
after her. The dog loped up the ridgeline and through
the hands of the beat cop standing nearest to her before
turning toward the trees. She was heading for the farm.
I started running, struggling to unclip my flak jacket. I
let it fall and hurled myself up the ridge.

Eden liked being around other killers. If she hadn't been a cop she might have liked to be a prison guard. She thought she might enjoy feeding them daily, watching them, keeping count of them as they slept like so many dangerous pets. It wasn't anything that they did or said, but simply their potential that excited her.

Some of the times that she and Eric had played their games she'd encouraged him to slow down, to simply *be* in the presence of their killer prize—killers almost always being their quarry. Sometimes she'd have liked to draw the deeds of their prey out of them, interrogation style, know what their hands had done and to how many. Sometimes she wondered if this attraction to other killers might simply be a desire to be understood by another. Eric certainly understood where she had come from. What she was. But he'd never been big on sharing, enjoying, relishing their play. It was all frenzy to him. Sometimes she had wondered if it really mattered to him who they killed, whether they deserved it or not.

Now she sat in a ring of people with killer potential. The sexless twins sat in the dirt nearby, one drawing pictures with a stick in the fine grains, now and then glaring, heavy-browed, at Eadie. Nick and Jackie were across from her on milk crates on the other side of the bonfire, like assessors, talking between themselves.

Pea sat among a group of women across the fire, glancing now and then at Eadie. The women were laughing. Pea was telling a story and her voice rose as she threw Eadie a sideways glance.

"I wonder if I shouldn't maybe start locking up the female horses," she sneered. The women laughed. Eadie smirked and looked at her beer in what she hoped appeared submission.

Skylar approached from the direction of her and Jackie's van. Eadie hadn't seen her all afternoon. She thought she saw the shadow of a bruise on the girl's left cheekbone as she rounded the fire, but she couldn't be sure it wasn't the dance of unwashed hair. The girl took a West Coast Cooler from the ice slush in a cooler near Eadie and then stood by.

"Hop down." She flapped her hand. "I want to braid your hair."

"Your majesty." Eadie slid off the milk crate and onto the dirt. The girl loosened her hair and began combing it with her chubby fingers. Eadie thought she heard a dog barking in the distance and turned. Skye pushed her head back into place.

"What's up your ass?"

"Jackie," Skylar grunted.

"Care to elaborate?"

"He thinks he can fuck me like a fucking prostitute."

"Oh dear," Eadie laughed. "No violins and satin sheets?"

"No."

"Men, ay?"

"It's not like that. You know he used to be romantic, when we first met." Skylar pulled at a knot in Eadie's hair.

"I believe you."

"We first met in the town. I was doing an apprenticeship in a salon there. I'd been saving for this for ages and I was two hundred bucks off."

Skylar lifted her foot in her rubber flip-flop and showed Eadie an intricate butterfly tattoo as big as a fist, surrounded by stars. The older woman nodded her appreciation.

"He put the money down straight off. We'd been talking maybe ten minutes. Just pulled it out of his pocket and said, 'Here you go.' We hadn't even been on a date."

"Smooth operator."

"Now everything's just . . . I'm just some pet. Some dog he's trained to do the washing up. He fucks me like he docsn't know me. Well, shit, man, I like a hug every now and then, you know? I like someone to say I love you."

"I love you, Skye."

"You're just saying that because I've got a fist full of your hair."

"I got some dishes back at the van if it'll get you in the mood."

"Shut up," the girl laughed. "Rug muncher."

The braid was too tight, but Eadie didn't say anything. She didn't mind the feel of the girl's fingers in her hair.

"What are you going to do, then?"

"About what?"

"About Jackie."

"I'm gonna turn into a dyke and get a job in the city. Wear expensive clothes and drink wine."

"You can drink wine now. I think I saw a goon bag hanging from the clothesline."

"Good wine." The girl nudged Eadie in the back with her knee. "In restaurants."

"You don't have to be gay to do that."

"Probably a woman would treat me better," the girl said.

Eadie opened her mouth, tried to think how to tell the girl that her life didn't have to be the way that it was, that maybe she didn't have the brains but she certainly had the soul to do what she wanted to do. But her words were cut off when she heard the dog barking in the bush again. Skylar heard it, too. The two looked toward the dark horizon. When they turned back there was an extra man in the reach of the fire's glow, advancing from the direction of the gates. Eadie felt the people rising from their seats around her as the man's pace quickened, all but Jackie, who had his back to the danger. The stranger reached down and plucked Jackie Rye from his milk crate.

Eadie felt herself being drawn forward. She knew the man, though they'd never met. She'd met eyes with him once through the glass of the station waiting room. It was Michael Kidd, the missing girl's father.

"Hey," Skylar screamed. "Hey!"

"I want to talk to you," Michael growled. "I want to have some fucking words with you, you little piece of shit."

It surprised Eadie how small a man could look in the arms of another. Jackie might have command of the farm and everyone in it, but when he lost command of his own feet, as Michael Kidd yanked him into the air, all memories of that power were forgotten in an instant. Nick threw himself between the two men. People were joining them, trying to drag the pair apart.

"Where's my fucking daughter?"

"Mick, Mick, you're not thinking straight," Jackie was saying, the words lost beneath Nick's furious snarls.

"I'm gonna kill you, you fat fuck."

Nick threw himself forward, was hooked and pulled back.

"I want my kid. Where's my kid? What have you done with my fucking kid, Jackie?"

"What kid?" Jackie snarled. "Mick—"

"What have you done with her?"

The big man was heaving as though on the edge of sickness, or tears. He lunged for Jackie again and arms got in his way.

"Just settle the fuck down and come talk with me. Come talk with me away from everyone else."

"I'm not going anywhere with you, you piece of human trash. You've killed my fucking kid."

At the edges of the gathering, men and women stood and stared, hands by their sides, looking to each other for explanation. None of these people, Eadie guessed, even knew Erin Kidd was missing. Who she was. That she had been here once, a grubby face among grubby faces, a hand that passed the bourbon bottle. She looked at Pea's group and saw Sal, her mouth still swollen, blinking confusedly at the others.

"Is that Keely's dad?"

"No," someone said. "Erin's."

"Is Erin missing, too?"

I ran. As I pounded through the bush after the shadow of the cadaver dog I found I couldn't dodge anything—tree branches whipped at my face and arms, caught at my shins. The ground was uneven at best, uphill, and sometimes sheer bracken that thundered and crashed under my weight. My best bet was to catch the dog before it got out into the flat bare earth by the farm, because I knew if it got sight of other animals out there it would really go. Right now it was at a medium pace, stopping to snuffle just within shouting distance, galloping away when it saw me coming. I saw a glimmer of fire between the trees and grunted, shoving myself forward down an animal trail. I felt a splinter of pain in my left knee.

I'd gained on the beast by less than ten meters.

Without warning it stopped on the path ahead and looked back at me. I skidded to a halt, barely able to huff words.

"Stop. Bad. Dog. Bad dog. Come here."

The dog stared. I caught its eyes at the right angle and they glowed green. I could hear my team crashing through the bush somewhere behind me. I stepped forward, arms out in what I hoped was a friendly gesture. What came out of my mouth was not as friendly.

"Come here!" I snapped.

The farm's dogs barked and Bones's eyes widened. I threw myself forward and grabbed at the beast's legs, got hold of a back paw, a hard toe, and yanked it. The thing yelped, was out of my hands and staggering for a second. I fell forward and wrapped my arms around it. We were meters from the edge of the bush.

Skye was trembling when Eadie put her hand on the girl's arm, wrenching her attention away from the men as they turned and trudged toward the caravans. Her eyes were wild. For someone so accustomed to violence, that directed toward Jackie seemed to reach her tender core. Eadie wondered if the girl really loved the creep, if tearing herself away from this life would be more complicated than she first imagined.

"You all right?"

"That was scary," the girl said. "Where did he even come from?"

"No idea. I wish I knew what they were going to talk about, though."

"Same. Let's go spy."

Spy. Always the curious child.

"You'll get us in trouble," Eadie said, leading the girl toward the vans.

"It'll be all right if we don't get caught."

They left the crowd at the fire and skirted around the back of the vans. Eadie almost tripped over Skylar as the girl hurled herself into the long grass beside the caravan and crawled forward on her forearms. Eadie, snuggling in beside her, put her hand in something damp and soft. A cloud of fruit flies swelled around her and she smelled organic rot. A peach.

The men's legs were within arm's reach. A cigarette fell and sparkled like a star.

"There are two other girls missing," Michael Kidd

was saying, "And they've both been out here, and if you think—"

"Missing how? Are the cops onto it?"

"You bet they're fucking onto it. No one's heard from these kids. No calls, no bank account movements, no sightings, fucking nothing."

"Who are the other two girls?"

"You know who the other two fucking girls are, you little—"

"Hey, back the fuck up, dickhead. I'll go ya before you know what your fucking name is," Nick said through his teeth, his big feet shifting in the dirt.

"Who are the other two girls?" Jackie's voice was low, calm. Skylar was wiping her nose on the back of her wrist beside Eadie.

"There's a sex tape," Michael said.

Silence. Eadie felt her pulse hammering in her neck.

"There's a sex tape of you two and some girl from Chatswood or some shit."

"Mate, you don't know what the fuck you're talking about."

"If you've done anything with my kid—"

"You better tell me who the other girls are or you'll be the one the cops are looking for."

"Ashley Benfield. Keely Manning."

"Ashley Benfield's in Freo."

"What?"

What? Eadie thought. Skylar was brushing her hair back from her face.

"The flies!" the girl whispered.

"Ashley Benfield's boyfriend ripped off the Liquorland on Green Point Road," Jackie snorted. "Jordon

Brown. She'd been working there last year for a little while before she came here and she gave him the back door codes. The two of them ran off to Fremantle."

"You're lying."

"They snagged about thirty grand, from what I heard. Melbourne Cup day. She was just kicking off a nice sugar habit so they've probably blown it all by now. Mate, you can believe whatever you fucking like. Ashley Benfield's in Freo and has been for months."

Skye huffed hard through her nose to clear a fruit fly that had landed in her nostril. Eadie froze, and Nick's feet rounded the side of the caravan.

"Tha fuck is this?"

"Sorry! We're sorry. We just wanted to know what's going on." Skylar put on her best whiny face, looked at Eadie for help. She said nothing.

Jackie and Nick emerged from the side of the van. Jackie spat at his feet, flicked his cigarette away.

"Having a good old sticky beak, are we, Eadie?"

Michael Kidd's brow dipped at the sound of Eadie's undercover name. The big man's eyes examined her silhouette in the soft light of the distant fire. Eadie shielded her eyes, scratched her brow.

"We're sorry, Jackie," Skylar howled.

"What did you say your name was?" Michael Kidd squinted at Eadie, and she fought the urge to bite the inside of her lip.

"Eadie."

"Eadie," the big man repeated. He licked his back teeth in thought. Nick frowned at the big man, then at Eadie.

"You two need to mind your own fucking business,"

Jackie snapped at the girls. "I didn't let you in here so you could eavesdrop on my fucking conversations, either of you."

"I'm gonna go," Michael said, backing away. "I'm going." The big man turned on his wide foot and walked away into the darkness. Nick Hart watched him go, then let his eyes drift back to Eadie, cold as an empty house.

"What was that all about?" Nick's eyes were locked on Eadie's. "Do you know him?"

"No."

"You sure?

"Both of you get the fuck outta here." Jackie waved his arm before Eadie could answer, fixing Skylar with a glare and a pointed finger as she tried to hide behind Eadie's arm. "And don't you come back to the van tonight, you nosy little slag. I don't want to see your sneaky, deceiving fucking head."

The two women turned and fled. Skye's hand drifted into Eadie's and squeezed her fingers, wet with terror.

"We're in big trouble," she said.

"You said it," Eadie agreed.

There was something about art that took Hades' mind away, put him in a place of swirling paints and flying sparks and woodchips, where there was no thought, only sensation. He would begin a project, become a machine himself, fixing and bolting and sawing and welding, oblivious to the labor he was putting his body through until he was left exhausted and filthy. He'd lock his workshop and shuffle up the hill toward the shack like an invalid. It would take a burn or a carelessly wielded hammer to bring him out of the warm, lofty place his work took him.

Right now he was grateful for such an escape. It was four in the morning, and since midnight he had been tossing and turning in bed listening to the sounds of the dump, wondering which of them were animals, things rotting and falling over, the wind shuffling things around, and which was his stalker.

His current project was a four-meter-high Australian swan preparing to take flight, wings spread and long neck bent, made from polished copper pipes intricately interwoven and coiled and braided. It was a finicky job, a noisy job, and it shut him into a world away from Adam White. The endless delicate puzzle made his hands ache, gave him pain to focus on. Hades stood by the frame of the thing with his eyes glazed and his hands fusing pieces together to construct the head on his thick wooden workbench. He was happy.

The first lump of brick came through the glass

panel of the workshop door. The sound of it split the thin bush air like an explosion. Hades fell off his stool and hit the ground. Glass all around him.

Hades crawled to the nail cabinet and grabbed the Colt he kept there and pulled himself up by the edge of the workbench. The second brick came through the east window and showered the tabletop there in glass, sprayed fragments all over his tools, his papers, his books. Shards of pain prickled his chest and arms.

Even with the first two blown out, Hades wasn't prepared for the last window to explode inward, glass raining on his shoulders as he hunched against the impact. He ran to the workshop door and charged through it, expecting to find one of two things—an unhappy client with a gun trained on him or a bunch of kids fleeing into the dark. What he found was Adam White standing at the base of the hill, a video camera in his hands.

Hades knew who he was looking at. The boy had Sunday's feral cat eyes, the same sly slouch to his shoulders. The boy smiled and lifted the camera as Hades tried to catch his breath.

"You have no idea what you're doing, kid."

"Oh, I don't know. I think I'm making a good go of it, bro."

Hades lifted the pistol and pointed it at the boy's head. It had been years since he had felt such hard, heavy fury, the kind that sat between his temples like smoldering coals and made his eyes pulse. The gun trembled in his calloused hand. "Do it," the boy said.

Hades didn't do it. Not right away. His trigger-happy days were gone. He knew what kind of a mess could be created with just a gentle, satisfying pull, an exhale of breath, a letting go of thoughts. It would be so easy. He reached into his pocket, the gun still wavering on the boy, and dialed one of only two numbers in the device with his thumb.

"Hades?"

"I'm holding a gun on your creepy little spider," the old man trembled. "You better tell me quick why I shouldn't just exterminate him right this second."

"Jesus Christ, Heinrich," Frank said.

"I said quick." The old man clicked the hammer back into place. Adam White laughed, though Heinrich could see his body was shaking. This was a thrill. A terrifying, satisfying thrill. Something long planned, long worked for. Heinrich felt for the first time the dangerous nature of the boy before him.

"Just wait a second. Wait. He's got you on tape. Right now, he's taping you," Frank said.

"I'll bury the tape with him."

"Hades, listen to me," Frank's words tumbled into each other, "that camera he's holding is wireless."

"I don't know what the fuck that means."

"It means he's filming it there and it's recording somewhere else."

Heinrich grunted with rage.

"Heinrich," Frank's voice was calm, but trembling. "If you shoot Adam White right now I can't help you get out of the mess you'll be in. And it'll be a big mess. You can take my word for it."

"Is he putting a leash on you, Hades?" Adam White laughed, the zoom on the camera extending like an accusatory finger. "Is he getting his muzzle out?"

"Heinrich? Don't do anything stupid."

"I'm being terrorized here. I have a right to defend myself."

"Sure. Sure. You can tell them that in court."

Hades dropped his aim.

"You better solve this thing the right way before I do it my own way, copper," the old man snarled into the phone. "There's only so long I'll play this stupid game."

"I'm on it, Heinrich. I'm doing the best I can with the time I've got."

Hades was watching Adam White walk off into the black forest.

I knocked on Dr. Imogen Stone's apartment door with my heart still hammering from Heinrich's phone call. Since two a.m. I'd been sitting in my car in the street outside Camden trying to get my thoughts in order. The terror of almost losing a police dog into the middle of Eden's undercover operation had left me jittery and uncertain. Juno had texted me some business about one missing girl's father barging into the farm and almost ruining everything. Then Heinrich had called and I'd driven straight to Stone's place.

Maybe I was trying to use her to replace the Eden I needed right now, the grounded and practical and unshakeable Eden I'd come to rely on, the kind of woman who would kill her own brother just to make sure all her plans remained on an even keel. But that was a fallacy, wasn't it? I had no idea how Eden operated. Maybe I would get a bullet in the brain when I became inconvenient, when I threatened her plans. *I'm sorry, Frank. You were warned.* Frank? Frank? I looked up and realized Imogen was standing in the doorway staring at me. I had to shake my head to clear my thoughts before I could answer her.

"Frank?" That robe again.

"Hi."

"What the hell are you doing here?"

"You tell me and we'll both know, honey."

"It's the middle of the night."

"It's the middle of the morning, really."

Imogen shook her head, tried to get ahold of what I was saying.

"Have you slept?"

"No."

"Get in here," she scolded and held the door open. "Jesus, this is the very definition of inappropriate."

She pushed her hair behind her ears and went into the kitchen, took a bottle of milk from the fridge, and drank from it, thinking I couldn't see her. I heard the flip of a kettle switch and the kind of sigh you only give when someone you know is so beyond help they're beginning to undermine your faith in humankind. She came and sat next to me and rubbed her eyes, and I took one of her hands and held it in both of mine.

"I like you," I said.

"I get the feeling I'd like you, too, if you weren't such a complete catastrophe," she yawned. Squinted. Yawned again. "I'll make the coffee. We need coffee."

She went into the kitchen and moved things around. Packet of some wanky espresso coffee from the freezer, the elastic band twanging. I fell asleep on the couch before she got back.

I got home around midday and went straight to the fridge, grabbed a beer, and popped it on the counter. Didn't even look at the cat—no, because the cat was Martina, was an acknowledgment that she wasn't really gone from my life and that it was far too early to be hanging around other women that even half meant anything to me. I stood by the fridge and looked out the window at the apartment block behind mine and told myself that I wasn't "cheating" on Martina because Martina was gone now. Long gone, in the ground, deep and restful, the same place I had put the man who killed her, died with no thoughts of me on either of their minds.

That train of thought didn't help. Wasn't Martina still alive for me, not only in her cat but in Imogen? Wasn't the major thing that had drawn me to Imogen all of that old-world survivalist intelligence wrapped up in beautiful milky white skin, hidden behind dark knowing eyes? Was that going to be the criteria from now on? How much like Martina my partner could be?

Graycat was giving me a good shouting down. The thing that brought me out of my reverie was a claw penetrating my jeans high up on my right thigh, pretty close to some of my crucial bodily equipment. I shook the cat off and got out its kibble, took the food to the balcony with the beast in hot pursuit and poured it with a clatter into the food bowl. The thing nudged its head into the stream of kibble as I poured, scattered it onto the concrete. I really needed to spend more time with the cat.

"Just. Hey! Slow down, fatty."

I sat in the old armchair I keep out there and looked at the traffic, thought about Hades' problem. My problem. Adam White wasn't going to leave Hades alone until I could find out who killed Sunday. Cold cases this tricky needed a team—they were the type picked over by armchair detectives like Imogen for decades, the type written about in true crime books, used in the early papers of budding historians working on their PhDs.

Usually it was child murders that made it out of the

decades of darkness and toward some sort of resolution. They earned armchair detectives the most reward money. Next after children came well-to-do women. Then politicians and actors. People were still staying up all night over who really shot JFK. You could watch the event re-created digitally from ten thousand different angles. The problem was, no one cared about a black girl from the seventies who was no good to nobody, a girl with no real standing in the world, a girl only ever loved by a couple of people, one of them being Sydney's worst gangster. It was no surprise to me, thinking about it, that Adam White got his mind set on Hades being Sunday's killer. He'd probably been the only person on the earth who really minded if she lived or died.

Jimmy. Kimmy. Whoever this friend or co-worker of Sunday's dead sister was, she was probably my best bet at getting into Sunday's world. My brief search into Lynda's known associates hadn't turned up any Jimmy, Kimmy, Jenny, Kenny or anything close to the mark. Her best friend was a woman named Rachael Cricket, a dumpy character with a big grin who was in the mug shots with Lynda brandishing a long green tattoo of a cartoon bug in a top hat. The two had been arrested for shoplifting. That was all I knew. Finding Jimmy or Kimmy was the only way forward I could see, my only means of understanding what the White girls were up to back then, because I'm sure Hades, much as he loved Sunday, was hardly privy to half of it.

Women and their secret lives. I got the feeling Imogen Stone had plenty of secrets, that I could spend years uncovering pieces of her, vulnerable pieces, which she'd been trained all her life to protect. Martina, too. But I didn't want to think about Martina again. I shook my head and cracked my neck. Drained the last of my second beer.

The cat was pouncing and flopping onto its side in the corner of the balcony, scrabbling with something, getting dust and hair clumps stuck in its thick fur. I got up and went over to rescue the creature caught in its clutches and pulled a fairly extensively chewed cricket from its teeth.

"You're disgusting," I told the cat. I reached out and flicked the wretched insect off my palm into the air above the parking lot. I watched it sail into the garden below among the cigarette butts. It lay there, black in a sea of orange fellows. A cricket out of place.

I stared off my balcony and the realization hit me like a punch.

I stood outside the house in Ashfield and took phone calls, one after the other, hoping at some point to be able to stem the stream of information coming from Juno and the forensics team and get to the door hidden behind dozens of bags of rubbish and cardboard boxes, beyond the waist-high grass of the tiny lawn. Four underling detectives were heading to Perth to liaise with the department over there to see if there was anything to Jackie Rye's tale about Ashley Benfield taking off with her boyfriend.

Captain James was threatening to take Eden out of the field if there was, because it seemed to him that a possible double homicide, with the potential for more, wasn't as critical as a triple. Eden's field play was worth three bodies, apparently, not two. Of course, the captain hadn't said as much in as many words. But it was clear. Everything Eden had done would be scrapped if Jackie turned out to be just another double killer and not the kind of glorious sicko serial job that made the department headlines.

I warned the captain that Eden was in a very delicate place and any disturbances to her work would put her life in danger. She'd already been threatened by one victim's father turning up and almost making her in front of the very suspects we were interested in. I hadn't mentioned that Michael Kidd's recognition of Eden had been my fault, that I'd mentioned her name in front of the families out at Narellan, that he'd worked out that "Eadie" had been ingeniously concocted out of "Eden."

When the forensics girl came on the line I moved into the shade of a tree to listen to her report. I knew it would be long. The sun was blazing on my shoulders, making my shirt stick to my ribs.

"There are two sets of female DNA present on a total of forty-two different items of clothing," she began.

"Forty-two?" I scoffed. "The stuff you picked up on the riverbed barely filled an evidence bag."

"Fire is generally pretty good at reducing the size of items, Detective Bennett. Big pile of clothes, plus fire, equals small pile of clothes."

"All right. I'm the idiot. You're the scientist."

"Uh huh."

"I was just surprised."

"Some of these items, like the bras for example, have been reduced to nothing but a portion of a strap. A hook, in one case. That's all we've got, but if we need to we can reconstruct from fiber analysis, find the brand, the size . . ."

"You're true wonders."

"Luckily, some of the items are almost fully intact," she continued. "The pile was burned carelessly. One of the items interests us very much. There's back spray of blood on the rear of a cotton tank top. We don't have a report yet, because we're rushing this through at an extraordinary pace—"

"I realize you are."

"But on sight, a consultant said it's consistent with some blunt-force patterns he's seen. Someone gets hit hard enough and the skull casing is split in the first blow. Flecks of blood travel upward as the object comes back over the attacker's shoulder and then downward as the attacker goes in for a second blow. The victim is usually down by the second blow so you just get this upward-downward pattern and nothing else. We've also got scissor marks on some of the items. Jeans."

"Scissors? Not just some sort of blade?"

"No, the deliberate cuts of scissors, uneven and frequently changing direction. Upward along stretched seams. The jeans were on someone when they were cut off."

"Christ. Well. Good evidence of violence. Sexual element to it, too. Might get us some more time in the field."

"Uh huh," the woman said again.

"Any idea who's been hit?"

"No. We don't have any names on our files. We're scientists. We're impartial. You'll have to wait for the report."

"Yeah." I'd known that and asked the question anyway. Looking like an idiot in front of this woman seemed to be a compulsion. "Thanks for all your help, Nicky."

It's a strange sensation to be glad that evidence has arisen suggesting someone has been hurt, that they're probably dead. Obviously it wasn't what I wanted. I had no malice toward those girls. I felt awful for their families. But from the moment Eden had sat me down and explained the situation, I'd known somehow that they were dead. It had happened, completely out of my hands, and I was more passionate about uncovering what had occurred than feeling unhappy that it had. As hungry as the new evidence had made me, I had to put that aside and think about Hades' case. Each night he was getting closer to killing Adam White. I wasn't sure if White had a death wish, but he was sure playing the game like he did. He couldn't know that the fall of his dice would affect so many people—not only Hades but his daughter, and through her, me.

I'm not a religious man, but I walked toward Rachael Cricket's house with some kind of plea running through my mind, to whatever universal power was listening, that she could tell me something about what had happened to Sunday—that out of fear maybe, or love, she'd kept that secret all these years and was somehow willing to give it to me, a stranger.

I'd managed to track Rachael "Jiminy" Cricket down fairly easily from her extensive dealings with Center link. Not Jimmy, or Kimmy, but Jiminy, named after the wise little green sidekick of Pinocchio I'd watched as a kid on VHS. The green bug in the top hat tattooed on her arm. Maybe she'd been there when Sunday went missing. Maybe she'd helped. Maybe she'd share her endless wisdom with me.

I was on the porch when I caught the first smell of what was inside the house. I couldn't get to the front door through the bags and boxes and rusting items piled up there. From the rust stains on the tiles beneath the windows, I could see this clutter had been there for some time. A troupe of dogs struck up a cacophony as I glanced in the window. I could see nothing but darkness beyond the heavy drapes. Flies tinked and bumped against the window, trying to find a way out.

"Don't be dead in there," I murmured. I knocked on the window and one of the dogs squealed with excitement.

"Rachael? Rachael Cricket?" I breathed deeply through my mouth to cope with the stench. "I'm with the police."

Nothing. I rapped on the window again. The smell wasn't necessarily something dead, I reassured myself. I didn't get that telltale biological perfume the body gives off in the days after it expires, the gasses that build up and swell in the stomach, the fluids that are released. This was rotting vegetables, dog feces—human feces maybe. I walked around the house and was hit with the reek of empty gas cans stacked in a pile as big as a car under the bathroom window, decorated here and there with a variety of hubcaps. Two sheds along the side of the house were stuffed full of hubcaps, in teetering stacks under the spider-webbed ceilings, thousands of space-age pizzas dripping rust and grease.

I pulled some boxes and bags away from the back door. Drenched my socks in what I hoped was rainwater but knew wasn't.

"Rachael? Police. I'm coming in."

I don't like things that crawl. I'm happy to admit that. Plenty of men don't like spiders, cockroaches, any half-squishy legged things you might encounter in a lush backyard garden. Things that come wriggling out of the soil. I'm a homicide detective. I've seen more maggots than most people have had handshakes. Men of my type just puff out our chests and clench our teeth and carry on when faced with creepy crawlies, because that's what you do when you're scared and

you know you shouldn't be. But when I forced open
the door of Rachael Cricket's kitchen I was faced with
more crawlies in one room than I'd ever encountered
together. And I was alone, so I indulged myself in letting my shoulders rise up near my ears, my hands
come out from my sides, my lips draw back from my
teeth, and my eyes bulge from their sockets. Generally,
to freak the fuck out as much as a man can standing in
one place.

What stole my attention was a large glass salad
bowl atop a pile of pots and plates and cups on the
counter, a quarter full of orange grease and three-quar-
ters full of large, black dead cockroaches. Here and
there shiny survivors of the salad bowl massacre wobbled and shuffled over the piles on the floor, waist-
high mounds of everything imaginable. Packets of
plastic cutlery. Labelless cans. Papers. Bric-a-brac of
every variety, assembled according to no scheme—not
what room it might belong in, or how old it was,
whether it was organic, plastic, chrome. A baby's
rocker. A jar of thumbtacks. An empty fish tank full of
moss-covered pebbles and a wooden cross as long as
my arm. More hubcaps, a box of waffle ice-cream
cones chewed through by mice and sprinkled with
their feces. The flies were in their hundreds, most of
them gathered around the windows and the mi-
crowave, some rushing over to examine me, my neck
and forearms and ears, as I came in the door.

Be dead, I thought. *Don't be alive and living like
this.* I drew a breath to call Rachael again, coughed,
swept flies out of my eyes. I waded through the rubbish, pushing bigger items out of my way, crunching
others beneath my boots. There had been a path

through it all at some point but the piles had collapsed. The hall was filled with books and newspapers to waist height, and then things lost their way with stuffed toys and plastic plants, a collection of umbrellas in their cloth cases that went for as far as I could see, rows of them like wrapped bodies lying in the dark waiting to be buried. A two-meter-high papier-mâché flamingo that looked like it had come off an old Mardi Gras float fell as I passed and slid down my back, blocking the exit through the kitchen, if you could call it that. A wave of claustrophobia rushed over me. The dogs in the front room were going mad.

Rachael Cricket was sitting propped against a mass of yellowed pillows without cases in the far corner of the front room, barely illuminated by the glow from behind the drapes. She was a meter off the floor on a mound of items—cushions and boxes and plastic tubs, books and stuffed toys. I stood in the doorway and wondered if she was dead. She looked it. Her skin was jaundiced, the way people get in the first couple of days, and her head lolled to one side. She was all layers—layers of skin folding over each other around her arms and neck, two bony legs poking from beneath a gray blanket. The smell here was worse. I knew from the treacherous path to the kitchen that she was incapable of making a journey down there, and I'd only seen one bathroom off to the right on my way. I tried not to imagine what was in the green plastic bags tied and littered all around the room. There were packets of two-minute noodles here dumped in piles as high as the windowsill. No bowls.

The dogs broke free of the second front room and came crashing over the mounds of newspaper toward me. I picked one up as a gesture of goodwill and held it wriggling in my arms. Its fur was matted with dried hardened shit.

"Rachael, um," I felt strangely teary. I cleared my throat. "I'm Detective Frank Bennett. I'm a police officer."

Rachael said nothing. I jogged the dog up and down in my arms like a babe.

"I'm here about a girl named Sunday White. You used to be good friends with her sister, a long time ago. I got your name from a . . . a shoplifting case back in seventy-seven."

Some reaction occurred, though it was difficult to measure. It was mainly in her eyes, fixed pupils that reduced and then flared with what looked like terror.

"You knew Lynda. She was your friend. Until recently, she's been trying to find out what happened to her sister. You probably don't know what happened to Sunday, or you would have told your friend. But maybe you remember something now. Something that could help me. Lynda thought it was Hades. But maybe there was someone else who was dangerous. Someone else you girls were afraid of."

"Plishman," Rachael said. Her mouth moved, and nothing else. The words came through black teeth and sagging lips. "Plishman."

"Yes, I'm a policeman."

"Plishman."

"You're not in trouble," I said, patting the dog while the others snuffled and licked my boots. I needed to go back. Start at square one. "Do you remember Lynda? Do you remember Sunday?"

"The plishman. The plish." Rachael's eyes moved to me, locked on my face. "The plishman."

I squeezed the dog and felt sad, watching as she frowned back at the window, said the word over and over, seemed to ponder what it meant. I said that I would go, but that I would call someone to come back and help her, help the dogs. The hardest part was putting the dog back among the others, identical fluffy things that had once been white but were now different shades of brown and black and the rusting red of over-chewed limbs. I straightened and headed for the kitchen.

"Sabbet," Rachael said. I stopped in the hall to listen. "The plishman, Sabbet."

Eden had spent a long time finding the perfect apartment to call her sanctuary, and she was obsessively protective of it. Admitting people was always an ordeal. Although she wasn't stupid enough to keep trophies of her playtime in the night, she was well aware that she had unconsciously written the secret of what she was in her paintings, her sculptures, her notebooks full of sketches. They contained violence. Sadness.

Much of what she explored in her art was how to capture those precious moments with her victims that she could treasure: here agony, here hopelessness, here rage. She enjoyed toying with raw emotions. Never were they so raw as when a victim knew death was coming, had accepted it, had nothing left to lose from submitting to it. It amused Eden that so many storybook victims were fierce and heroic at the end, defiant in the face of their reaper. No one was, in her extensive experience. But perhaps she had been playing too long with cowards.

With only eight hours to relish in her sanctuary, Eden wasn't going to waste it sleeping. She needed a battery change and to report in to the station. Rye had called a stop-work so the irrigation system could be fixed and it would be tight getting out and in again without being noticed. While she waited for Juno, she would burn off some of her frustration. She hungered for making art the same way she hungered for the kill.

She worked at the huge trunk of an ancient red eucalyptus she'd rescued from the clutches of someone she was sure had desired the wood for overpriced outdoor furniture. She'd been dying to try out a delicate little miniature chainsaw, suitable for wood artists and ice sculptors, but all she could think about as she curved out a figure from the wood was how nicely the device would go through bones.

She didn't hear her doorbell over the growl of the little thing but the flashing red bulb she'd installed above her door caught her eye, and she lifted up her goggles. She was sweating. She left the chainsaw running as she approached the door and pulled it open, hoping the rumble of the machine might diminish the need for any unnecessary conversation.

Juno. The computer nerd. Eden glanced behind him into the hall and didn't see Frank. She let her confusion show on her face. The guy looked intimidated by her dust-covered apron, the oversized gloves, the chainsaw humming away in her fist. She revved it a little to get him talking. He cleared his throat and readjusted the leather satchel hanging from his shoulder.

"Got your batteries," he said. Handed her a tiny package. She slipped it into the pocket of her apron and tried to close the door. His voice stopped her.

"Everything working correctly?"

"Seems to be."

"Can you, um . . ." He glanced at the chainsaw. Eden followed his gaze. "Do you mind?"

Eden switched the chainsaw off. Left it hanging from her arm, a menacing prosthesis.

"Did you, uh . . . I told Frank about Michael Kidd."

"Frank and I have spoken."

"Right, of course you have." The boy nodded, an exaggerated bobbing, and scratched at the back of his neck. He really was very orange, Eden thought. Furred with it lightly, like a newborn pup. He was a marker for the difference in human genetic breeds, carrying with them colors and tinges and lengths and widths. She found herself squinting, trying to get a better look at him.

"Is there anything else?" she said.

"Look . . . I've been . . . spending a lot of time with you lately. You know. Like, um. Frank said that when you, uh, you do a lot of surveillance you can sometimes get closer to people than you really are . . ." He was struggling now, looking everywhere but her face. Eden enjoyed it. "So yeah, you know, I get it. I get that over the last couple of weeks I've been spending more time with you than you have been with me, really. But, like, I've got to put it out there. I'd like to spend more time with you. Outside work. You know? And have you spend time with me."

Eden squinted. Licked her lip. Tasted the microscopic layer of wood dust there, an ancient dead tree, something she understood better than most people. She shut the door in Juno's face and walked back across the apartment to the stairs. Let the chainsaw roar.

Dr. Stone had come to know my knock. I could tell from the smile she had playing about her lips when she opened the door. I slipped inside, into the dark, and let her lead me down the hall with her slender fingers. We fell into whispers in the kitchen, up against the bench, memorizing the nooks and crannies of each other's necks and ears and shoulders with our mouths, our noses. She smelled like sleep, like the safety of freshly washed sheets. She lit a candle by a windowsill cluttered with tiny, overflowing houseplants and took two wineglasses from the back of the fridge.

"How's the case?"

"Not good."

"This could go on for years. These late-night visits."

"What a tragedy for you."

She laughed. Bit my bottom lip lightly.

"What time is it?" I asked.

"No idea."

"They want to take it off us. Hand it over to regional. They're saying one of the girls is hiding out in Perth. We've tried to confirm it. It's all nods so far. When they get hold of her it'll be swept off my desk. You'll never hear of it again."

"Something tells me you won't let that happen."

"No."

"Eden?"

"No. No one wastes her time."

"It'll come good."

"It will. Something will happen. Some mistake. You never know how close you are until it's over. A phone call might do it. An overheard whisper. It's like those guys you see in movies trying to dig through the bottom of prison cells with a spoon. They don't know how deep they have to go. One day they make one last scrape. There it is. Precious earth." I leaned back against the counter, drank the wine too fast.

"You're not trying to dig out of prison, Frank. At least you shouldn't be."

"I'm digging up something."

"But what are you burying at the same time?"

"I'll ask the questions and I'll construct the metaphors, thank you very much," I pointed to my chest.

She smiled, ran her fingers up under my shirt, over my ribs. I let her pull it over my head. Run her nails up through my hair. I felt taken care of in her presence. Maybe it was the whole doctor thing. The certificates on her walls. The expensive waiting-room chic of the apartment. Maybe this was good. Maybe this was what I needed. Someone to take care of me, someone who I didn't need to feel responsible for. Imogen was pulling my belt off. I scooped her off her naked feet and listened to her laugh against my neck.

It had been a day so long and so hot and so useless to the investigation that Eadie felt flattened, as though a great weight was lying on top of her in the bed and refused to give her more than the necessary inches to breathe. A day of being ridden like the horses she cared for—mostly by Pea, who somehow had an eye on every shortcut she tried to take, every stall she didn't clear fast enough, every beast under her care who looked unhappy.

In truth, all of the animals were unhappy, and it had nothing to do with Eadie's care for them. They were waiting, all of them, for the weather to break, for the humidity to ease. Paint was running. Cows were moaning. Wood was seeping mold. The flies attacked everything, clung to eyelashes and clustered around sweating bellies, walked over food and the rims of beer bottles.

Eadie lay in the dark and looked at the ceiling and thought about the missing girls' bones. She was at that reckless point now, that exhausted point, where she fantasized about going out in the dark and simply digging, anywhere, just so that she was doing something meaningful toward catching the men, giving closure to the families, stopping the same from happening again. It had been ten solid hours of horse shit and the old woman's watchful eyes. She hadn't laid eyes on Jackie. She'd seen plenty of Nick.

At sunset, when she returned to the cabin, he came from wherever he'd been working and took up a milk crate in the shade of the van at the edge of the nearest cluster, fifty meters or so from her door. He stared at her windows. She stared back at him through the lace, standing well back in the dark of the kitchen. Hours passed. She had dinner in the caravan, showered with her ears pricked and her knife on the counter by the camera pendant. She dressed and come back to the stalemate. Someone had given Nick a beer. He sat with his elbows on his knees, just watching.

All right, asshole, she thought. *Watch this.*

Eadie went into the tiny kitchenette, switched on her television, and raised the volume. She drew the blind over the window, shut the doors to the bedroom and the hall, and then brought out the rusted toolbox under the kitchen sink. Rolling up the van's carpet, she pried up the edge of the internal door to the storage hatch beneath. Eadie squeezed into the empty compartment, feeling spiderwebs collapse all around her in the corners of the rusting base as she descended into the dark. She took a dusty breath, pulled the hatch closed, and felt for the latch holding the outside door at the back of the van.

Ten minutes, Eadie guessed, she was in the dark. The nuts on the inside of the hatch door were rusted and required plenty of spit and swearing. She got the top two undone and bent the door forward, then slid out into the long grass. She left the hatch hanging and crawled under the fence and into the field. Skirted the field back toward the farm.

There was no one near Nick's van. Everyone was over at Jackie's. It was *Master Chef* night. They would be gathered there in the darkness like they were the night she'd arrived, wretched laughing mouths and glowing eyes lit by the screen. Eadie glanced about, then slipped into Nick's van.

There was no possibility of switching on the lights. Her hands fell on dirty dishes and mugs and cups in the kitchen sink, fluttered to the curtains and then the blinds. Tiny cracks of orange light flooded the tiny space as she twisted the knob, opening the blinds. Her fingers were wet with sweat. Eadie squinted and came face-to-face with a spread-legged poster of a large blond woman. Hundreds of other porn pictures ripped and clipped from magazines were stuck messily and overlapping on the kitchen cupboards. They seemed to consume the man's interest, those at the back turning hard and browning from sun exposure. Eadie opened the bedroom doors and glanced at the gray, sweat-stained sheets.

The DVD cupboard was by the bathroom annex—a tiny tower of shelves, neatly arranged cases. Cheaply made kids' cartoons, animated series starring foxes and birds and badgers and bears in classic fairy tales. *Sleeping Beauty. Cinderella. Little Red Riding Hood.* Eadie selected *Sleeping Beauty* and popped open the case. A disk labeled with marker: MICHELLE.

Eadie panted, remembered herself, and checked the windows again. She popped open *Cinderella* and read the name. DANICA. Shoving the cases back into the shelves, she ripped out others, popped them open and slammed them closed. JOANNA. NONIE. STEPH. PENNY.

No Keely. No Erin. No Ashley. Eadie clenched her fists, shoved the cupboard door closed.

Eadie lay now in the early morning light and felt too tired to sleep.

When the soft knocking came she was on her feet before she knew what the noise was. The snuffling and whimpering behind the frosted glass told her there was no danger. She pulled open the door and Skylar came rushing in like a sweaty damp beast released from a trap.

"What's the matter with you?"

She switched on the rangehood light. The girl was drooling blood.

"I can't do this anymore," she slobbered. "I can't do this."

Eadie's hands were prickling as she went to the freezer. She popped the ice cubes from the frame and poured them into a dish towel.

"What was the blue about?" she asked.

"Ev-ery-thing," Skylar sobbed. "Everything. Is. Going. Wrong."

"Calm down and hold this on it."

"I. Can't."

"Stop talking. You're safe now. Just lie here and be quiet."

The girl lay down on the left side of the bed, by the cameras.

Eadie curled beside her. Didn't touch her. Thought probably she should. Human beings touched each other when one of them was sad, she knew, but something about it seemed dangerous to her. She couldn't care about the girl. Wouldn't.

The girl was snuffling, letting tears and melted ice run down her neck. The bruise was deep in her cheek, probably rattling loose molars. A good sideswipe. She'd been knocked about before, Eadie could see in the dim light from the kitchen. Something had split her brow long ago on the same side.

"What did you fight about?"

"Money. His ex. You."

"Me?"

"He doesn't like you."

"Most people don't."

"I want to get out of here," the girl said, her eyes on the door.

"We can make it happen." Eadie folded her hands on her chest. "Let's make a plan."

"I don't want a plan."

"Have you got any family out there?"

"I don't want to be with my family." The girl looked at Eadie. Wet fierce eyes. "I don't want to plan. I don't want to pack. I just want to go. I want to just . . . run. With you."

The girl sat up. Eadie sat up with her.

"I can't take care of you," Eadie said.

"We can take care of each other."

"Girl, you've got the wrong idea."

Skylar grabbed Eadie's cheeks, forced the kiss upon her. Salty with tears and shuddering with panicked breath. Eadie sat frozen and felt her mind closing, felt the shutters of her sanctuary coming up one at a time. This is how it was with her, the slow shutting down of a machine with a hidden glitch, a thing destined to attempt again and again to get moving, to function as everything else functioned—but unable to, always unable to, because of that missing part. The closer something inched to her, the harder she faltered. She reached up and took the girl's hands down from her face.

"Girl," she said again, "you've got the wrong idea."

Skylar looked at her eyes, fat tears rolling down her round cheeks. They lay down together in the gloom, back to back, and let the thunder roll them into an exhausted slumber.

It was storming outside, but the sound of it didn't reach Heinrich through the hollering of the crowd in the cellar, the stomping of feet, and the whine of the violin. He had placed Vicky's powder mirror on top of two wine barrels, and he stood there adjusting the Windsor knot at his throat, the crisp white collar of the shirt she had brought him tight around his thick throat.

He finished with the tie, pulled down his waistcoat, and took the dark gray wool suit jacket from the chair by the door and slipped it on. He turned. Vicky was watching him from the corner of the room, her arms folded. She had helped him shave off the thick beard he'd grown in the attic. He went to her and she kissed both his cheeks, as much to feel his new skin as to tell him good-bye.

"You know where you're going?"

"Jeremy's, room six," Vicky said.

"Tell her Central Station, platform two. Nine. Make her write it down. She forgets things. She's not to go out tonight. It'll be wild out there. It won't stay in the room for long."

"Where will you be?"

"Nevermind." Heinrich buttoned his coat.

"I suppose it might be dangerous to know a thing like that."

"You'll have money enough for your own protection. I've left compensation with my belongings in the attic. Joe Harper's coming to see you on Monday."

Vicky dropped her eyes, smoothed out her skirt.

"Why don't you stay?" she pleaded. *"This town will be yours. You'll have everything you ever dreamed of. Everything Bear ever wanted."*

"Bear didn't want this," Heinrich said. He nodded toward the city through the grimy window. *"No one good could want this."*

Vicky watched him go.

There are varying accounts of what happened in the cellar of the Royal Hotel in Darlinghurst that night. Although it had become a rare sight in a crowded place, Caesar himself was present. By the winding staircase, a slice of what had once been the upright, broad military hulk of Caesar stood shadowed by a group of equally disheveled, thin-framed men staring into the pit, storm-cloud eyes following the blood as it was pooled in the corner by the attendant's mop. Later all would agree that Caesar looked lost, pressed by the great weight of some tremendous decision, watching all that he had built begin to lean, to slide, to falter, without accepting the inevitable crash.

Three dogs had been lowered into the pit in cages when the young man walked out of the keg room at the back of the cellar. At first, all eyes were on the beasts. Odds were even, and money changed hands furiously, shuffling from fist to white-knuckled fist. The animals were huge broad-shouldered things shaped more like bush pigs than canines, all of them riddled in their jet black fur with the pink scars of beatings, cuttings, sharpenings. For two of them, tonight would be a welcome death. They snarled and thrust themselves against the doors of their separate cages, shaking their heads and howling above the rumble of the crowd.

The young man in the dark gray suit pushed through the crowd. As their eyes fell upon him, a ripple of horror went through the bodies pressed around the pit. It wasn't only that most knew the face. The Dogboy of Darlinghurst. A dead boy, long forgotten, now a man. It wasn't the black pistol clutched loosely in his fingers. It was his eyes, the way they wandered across the crowd and then settled on Caesar on the opposite side of the pit. They were hard, the eyes of a reaper.

The crowd fell quiet in one swift wave, as though a curtain had opened on a stage. Caesar seemed to be the last man in the room to see the boy. When he did, he showed no recognition. There was no terror, no rage. He watched the pistol rise in Heinrich's hand, swinging upward at the end of a fully extended, powerful arm, and when the aim was leveled no words were said. It was as though he didn't believe it was going to happen this way. No one did. There was silence, then the blast and the flash.

Caesar fell into the pit, seemed to bounce sideways off the dog cage just below him, and crumpled in a pile of clothes and limp hands. The Dogboy stepped down onto a cage and then down onto the bare earth in his shining leather shoes. It seemed someone had given permission for the crowd to react, because everyone at once drew a breath, sucked the oxygen from the room, made it burn. Caesar's handlers were gone, dissolved into the crowd.

The Dogboy's bullet had hit Caesar square in the front of his throat, blowing a hole in his windpipe the size of an eye, sprayed ruby red blood up over his jaw and face, a spotted mask. Heinrich crouched over the older man, the pistol still in his hand, and gathered the wet folds of shirt at Caesar's throat, lifted him, and set him down to wake him from the pain.

"You don't think I was going to make it soft," the Dogboy said when he had the old man's attention. "It wasn't soft for Bear."

Everyone heard the words, strained their minds at the same time as they flew with excitement to remember what was said, exactly, so they could recall it through history. The silence in the room was church-like. Even the dogs had stopped their racket. Caesar opened his bloody mouth and began to speak.

"He . . . Ee," the old man said. He coughed, tried to control his huge rolling eyes, to focus them on the boy. "Heh . . . Ee."

It sounded very much like Caesar was trying to ask for help. The blood in the ancient warlord's throat consumed it. The Dogboy stood and looked down at the fallen man at his feet as he writhed and grasped at the wound. Then he turned, just like that, and stepped back up onto the dog cage, onto the concrete ledge where he'd appeared, back from the dead. Syd Saville, the pub owner, spoke to the boy as he paused there. The man handed Heinrich a handkerchief.

"What'd he say?" Saville asked.

Heinrich wiped his hands and returned the cloth. He let his eyes wander back to the man in the pit.

"He said 'Hades,'" the boy lied. "He thinks he's already in hell."

The boy disappeared into the crowd, and as he went, Syd Saville tucked the bloody handkerchief into his coat pocket. Tom Besset, one of the dog owners, yanked the chain connected to the front of his animal's cage and released the creature on Caesar. The dog finished Caesar in seconds. No one watched

Someone shot Besset dead in the street later that night as he was trying to sell the now infamous beast. They never found out who.

I like to eat when I'm researching. The selection spread before me at the Police Evidence Archives Department in Chatswood was nightmarish stuff for most health nuts. An empty McDonald's sitting right across the street from the huge double doors was a trap I fell willingly into.

There was one other investigator in the records room when I arrived, and my fatty feast drew a scowl I cheerfully ignored. An attendant in the box watching a television set on top of a filing cabinet was enjoying the company of a large desk fan. The rules at PEAD are that you're supposed to wear white gloves to flip through the records, but I forwent the rule and just napkined my fingers extra before flipping pages.

I knew a bit about Tom Savet. Stuff I'd heard over the years in bored-cop small talk. He and another guy had been called to a house in Epping in the early sixties to look at a bloody bathroom and help the old war vet who owned the place find his missing wife. Savet glanced around the scene for about five minutes, they said, and found a boot print on the kitchen floor. It was too big for the vet and had a heavy leftward lean.

From this Savet deduced that a guy named Richard Kea, a known junkie and petty thief, had been responsible. Kea limped on his left leg from a kneecap he'd had knocked in for bad debts. Twenty-five minutes later, at Kea's basement apartment three blocks away, Savet had squeezed a confession out of the guy with a pair of pointy-nose pliers. Eighteen minutes after that they had confirmation of a body in a pipe near Yarra Bay and Kea in the back of a paddy wagon. Wham, bam, initial report to bagged body in under an hour. Now that was some Sherlock Holmes shit right there.

Savet started his record streak by nailing Kea and then went on to mark himself as the top missing persons man in Sydney. The case that got him all the press was that of eight-year-old Elizabeth Kingsley from Neutral Bay. Lizzie had been walking home from netball practice in the fading light of a winter evening, through the quiet suburban streets behind the beach, when she'd vanished. Reports of a red van in the area came up as a dodgy lead but distracted the public in the initial weeks of the investigation. Within twenty-four hours of being handed the case, Savet had turned Lizzie's bones up in a barrel of acid on the ground floor of a warehouse in Dubbo, of all places. The girl was a long way from home. They nailed a truck driver for the murder. After that, everything Savet touched turned to gold.

People ignored Savet's friendships with some of Sydney's nastiest personalities, including Alec "Caesar" Steel when he was at the height of his reign of terror. Most people assumed Savet kept underworld connections to aid his uncanny instincts in digging up bones. They might have been right. I was determined to find out.

I looked over Savet's major case files. There were twenty-six in total. Lizzie Kingsley was his youngest. She looked up at me from the yellowed pages with her frizzy-doll haircut and chubby white cheeks, a netball clutched under her arm. Savet's work on the case was meticulous. I admired his organization, his strict chronology and easy prose through interviews, underlining key phrases, posing questions to himself. The autopsy reports, scene diagrams, and suspect lists were all there, numbered, cataloged. You're supposed to keep your records like this, so that someone can easily pick up where you left off if you're reassigned.

His work made me think of my own, which at the best of times was spread throughout my car and littered around my kitchen countertop, barely legible, half of it on the back of envelopes and crowded around the edges of electricity bills. Savet left no path unexplored, took nothing for granted, and documented everything. He spoke to people who looked unrelated to the case, and from there he drew the most minute but often critical clues.

Tom Savet was a textbook kind of guy. Maybe he'd been leaning on Caesar for some pocket money in the drug trade for a little while there, but there was no evidence of anything but a casual liaison. When Caesar was gunned down by persons unknown in a cellar in Darlinghurst in the late seventies Savet didn't comment to the media, and he didn't attend the funeral. The man had never appeared in any internal investigations, even when the eighties brought a firestorm to every New South Wales policeman or woman who'd ever brushed up against a biker in the street. I doubted Savet had anything to do with Sunday White, whether the two had ever even met. But I wanted to look into every possible avenue before I started speculating about what was most likely Sunday's demise—her lifestyle.

I searched through the autopsy reports of each of

Savet's victims. I read his notes on each closing interview, before the perpetrator was handed over to the court system. I read Savet's personnel record twice and spent the afternoon in the newspaper room reading up on the press coverage of his work.

I was losing interest in Savet. My motivation plummeted when I looked over at the television in the attendant's box and saw a frazzled and track-marked Ashley Benfield falling into the arms of her blubbering parents at Sydney airport. I checked my phone. The captain had called me four times and many of the numbers under his I recognized as press.

I got up to leave and began lumping photographs of victims into their respective files. My legs felt heavy from hours of sitting. I picked up a photograph from the floor and sat looking at it as I worked my legs under the table, trying to get rid of the pins and needles in my feet. The girl in the photograph was Bonnie Melich. Her boyfriend had bludgeoned her to death when he discovered she was cheating with her boss. Her body was discovered in a torched car in the bush near Botany, not far from the airport.

I looked at the girl in the photograph. She was a gorgeous olive-skinned creature, unusually tall, standing in the doorway of the Lord Nelson in the Rocks with a basket of roses in her slender arms. I knew the place well, had begun plenty of pub crawls there in my cadet years. It was a good place for stag nights, too. You could make a lot of noise. The sandstone walls contained a good deal of ruckus.

I'd passed through that doorway where she stood hundreds of times. Could almost feel it around me as I

looked at the girl. Smell the house-made beer. Bonnie
Melich's head was almost touching the top of the doorframe, though. Legs like stilts. I wondered how tall she
was. I looked over at the autopsy report. Five nine. I
looked at the girl in the photograph, then back at the
autopsy report.

They'd moved the bonfire site out into the back fields to dispose of some of the bracken and branches brought down in the storm. It was going to be big. Something about a big fire was magnetic to people, exciting, dangerous, even though the men had lumped stones in a huge circle around the pit to contain it, to stop it wandering into the bush.

As the sun sunk low behind the caravans Eadie sat watching the men build the woodpile up until it towered above them, a strange sense of foreboding in her chest. She hadn't seen Skylar all day, had looked for her at Jackie's van and in the breakfast area, even down at the public phone on the corner which she frequented, constantly out of credit. She knew the girl would come to the fire. Everyone had at some point that afternoon, to load coolers or spread out rugs, to admire the woodpile. Girls sunbaked in the warm fading light, their white bellies lolling on towels, passing oversized Coke bottles around a circle.

Skye came in the calm blue of twilight, Jackie at her side. The busted mouth gave her a worn and aged look. She hadn't bothered with her hair, and it hung greasy and long about her shoulders. She went over to Eadie, and Jackie gave her a warning glance.

The two women stood side by side watching the men squeezing newspaper into the base of the pyre.

"I feel like we need to talk," Eadie said. Skylar didn't answer. Her eyes were on her feet. The girl wiped at her swollen eye and Eadie turned away, pretended not to notice.

"I can get you out of here. But you need to tell me how."

"Let's go to your place," Skylar said. Eadie chewed her lip. She wanted to keep an eye on Jackie and Nick in case they pulled anything at the bonfire. It would be crowded. Dark. Everyone would be distracted by the flames. Nick sat watching her from a milk crate. But the girl looked on the edge. Eadie didn't want her running off into the bush to be alone, or hitching a ride into town. Whatever she was going to witness tonight, she would need to do it with Skylar by her side.

The bush was pitch black, silhouetted against a red sky. Eadie put her arm around the girl and held her close.

"Come on," she said. "I think I've got some Coolers back there."

Juno stung. It was an all-body ache beginning in his brain and reaching right down into the pit of his bowels, flaring out at his fingertips like the licking of flames. He would grit his teeth and wince against the ache, but it was right there on time, always, whenever he remembered Eden Archer's door. Rejection, without so much as a word to soften the blow.

It wasn't like Juno had never been rejected before. He had, plenty of times. High school had been a half-decade-long rejection of his body and his soul, a slow and meticulous inventory of all the ways in which he didn't fit with anyone who mattered, even the weird kids, the Goths, the computer nerds, and the drama geeks. He was far too ginger to ever fit in with the Goths, but he'd always liked their dark side, their hatred. Juno called up that old familiar hatred now as he watched Eden on the screen sitting in the caravan with the girl, Skylar.

You don't fit in the police force, Juno.

You will never be the undercover, rigged up and risking your life for the good of man.

Nobody wants your help, Reject.

Sit in the van away from all the normies, Juno, and let us know if you spot anything.

Juno had begun to think that Eden might be able to see that he didn't belong in the throwaway box. That, like her, he was different. He was valuable. Then the door had swung shut, taking only seconds in real life but in Juno's mind hours. A slow rejection of his soul.

The girl was braiding Eden's hair as the older woman sat on the floor by the bed. Juno leaned back against the wall of the van, shook his head, tried to pry loose the emotion from his gaze. *She means nothing to you. She's just a cold and beautiful animal.*

Juno wrenched open the van and drank in the cold night air. He needed to look at the sky.

Eadie picked at the carpet, her legs bent in the narrow space between the end of the bed and the wall of the bathroom annex. The girl's braid wasn't so tight this time. Her touch was almost gentle. Now and then the girl sipped from the West Coast Cooler at her side, her mouth making a seal on the glass rim and then popping when she drew a breath. The girl gathered strands from behind her ear, made her shiver.

"No man should ever lay his hand on you," she said. No answer came. The girl took her hands from her hair. Eadie licked her lips and carried on.

"No man, no person, should ever tell you what you're worth. I've been alone a long time, and you need to know that being alone is not . . . It'll never . . ."

Eadie reached for the back of her neck, under her ear, where she felt a small but intense sting. She felt a lump, and then the carpet hard and scratchy under her nose as she slumped to the floor. She tried to right herself, exhaled in the dust. There was darkness.

The lights blasted into Hades' bedroom, through his eyes, into his skull. The old man rolled out of bed, steadied himself on the floor, blinked against the stark white light that filled the room. Then the horn began. He heard a guttural groan leave his mouth. The horn came in one long deafening blast, then fell into a series of uneven hoots. Hades pulled open the drawer of his bedside table and reached into the darkness there.

Outside, the gray Commodore was pulled up to within inches of the knitting-needle rabbit, rigged with deer lights over its rusted frame. Adam White was leaning out the window, an elbow on the sill. Hades walked up to the driver's door, reached in, and wrenched the man from his seat.

His fists were frail, arthritic, and full of badly healed fractures. But Hades still knew how to use them. The pain felt good. He lifted White by the collar of his shirt and punched him down again. *Try to put him into the ground*, Bear had always said. *Imagine you can bury him with your throw. Clench just before impact. Good. And again.* Bear had kept his promise, had taught him how to punch, stood over him while he gave it to a pimp with sticky fingers. But the big man had never been able to teach him when to stop.

Hades felt the old tingles of the Silence at the edges of his being, like a warm body threatening to envelop him in its embrace. He stood and breathed, looked down at the camera strapped to the man's chest, a black eye watching him. He put a boot in the camera and felt it crunch under him, felt White's breath leave him as his rib cage deflated.

"Put that on your fucking wireless," Hades snarled.

White was laughing. Hades took the pistol from his pocket and put it into the man's cheek so hard he felt the teeth beneath the blood-splattered flesh. He held him by the neck, pinned to the ground like a snake.

"I appreciate well-orchestrated mind games," the old man said, breathing hard, trying to push back the Silence as it crept forward like a flood. "Oh, I do. But after a time you show some respect and finish a man."

"I know what you did, Hades."

"You don't know shit."

"I'm gonna haunt you," White laughed, a loose tooth bending with his lip as he spoke. "I'm gonna haunt you like her ghost. Like my mother's ghost."

Hades saw that his hands were shaking, but he could not stop them. His right gripped the gun tighter and tighter, pulling down like a vise, and while his mind protested his fingers moved as though driven by some invisible force. He held White against the ground and looked at his eyes and saw Sunday there for the first time—her cheeky grin, the wildness there that had no explanation, that had no cure. Hades squeezed and squeezed, and at the same time his mind screamed out for his fingers to stop their pressure. There was sweat on the gun trigger. His skin slid.

Hades didn't hear the car. Or the cop's footsteps. He heard hurried breath first, then the crunch of gravel as the man slid to a stop, and when he looked up he saw the eye of Frank's Browning pistol in the blinding light off the side of the car. The cop held up a hand, palm out, fingers splayed.

"Heinrich," Frank said. "Come on now, old mate."

"Just in the nick of time, detective," Adam laughed.

"Put the gun down nice and slow."

"You had enough time to do your job, boy," Hades said, his eyes burning in the deer lights. "Now we do things my way."

The trigger springs groaned.

"I found her," Frank said, rushing forward. "Listen to me, Hades. I found her."

The old man struggled to breathe. The trigger spring groaned again as he released his grip.

The first few moments were simply learning which way was up and which was down, learning the nature of the restraints that bound her wrists and ankles, learning how to think again. She was calling back the voice in her head that told her what to do, and when it returned from out of the redness and the pain it told her not to panic. That was always good advice.

Eadie opened her eyes, blinked while the blood and sweat that had run into them stung, cleared, subsided. She was upside down. Her head had fallen back and was looking downward at her hands. She recognized the concrete steel-rimmed trough that carried the pig entrails from the slaughter row down to the end of the kill house to be processed. Hard wet twine secured her wrists to a hook embedded in the trough. Above her, more twine secured her ankles to an iron rod, splaying her feet. Her whole body could be rotated, rolled along the line as different parts of her were cut away, lopped off, and tossed into plastic crates. Eadie swallowed. She was missing one of her back teeth.

"This is what you call the ultimate hangover," Pea said.

Eadie turned and took in the woman across her arm. She reminded her of a squat, round soldier. There was a double-barreled shotgun pointed upward and leaning on her shoulder. Skylar stood by, unreadable, her body dwarfed by the oversized plastic apron hanging from her neck and the sty-cleaning gloves on her hands. She was wearing denim workman's pants taken from the racks in the corner. She looked like the child she was. Eadie breathed in and out, blinking in the pain. She had drugs in her system. Xylazine. Her head and face had been battered. She'd been dragged, she guessed, by the raw feeling of her lower back.

"Have you got any idea who this is?" Pea asked, jerking a thumb at Skylar. Eadie licked her swollen lips, tasted blood and dirt.

"Skye . . ." Eadie tried to find the girl's eyes. They were locked on the floor. "Skye."

"This is my fucking kid."

"Look at me," Eadie said. She coughed. "Look. Skye."

"People without kids don't understand. You try to

do the best for them. Always. From the moment they're born. Skylar's got everything she needs here," Pea said, casting her eyes around the enormous room. "Everything she could ever want. She has food, and shelter, and a man who loves her. When he gets old and dies he'll leave her this place. She's set up here."

Eadie panted as the woman approached her. Wondered if her ribs were broken. Her shirt was bunched against her armpits. It itched. How much pulling power did she have in her core right now? How much equilibrium would she have if she righted herself? She calculated the number of paces to the door. The distance her shout would reach. Where was the pendant camera? Probably caught and lifted off her head as she was dragged. Did that mean Juno had called Frank? Was Frank on his way? Eadie let her head hang back and looked at her wrists. They were bound tight, the skin bunched behind the twine. Bunched was good. She could shift the folds of skin under the twine one by one. With enough lubricant. With enough force.

"Pieces of shit like you come in and think you're offering her a better life," Pea said. The fat woman crouched by her side, flipped the weapon in her arms. "Try to play Mummy Bear where you're not wanted— or needed. Your own mother should have told you that sticking your nose in the wrong place will get it broken."

Eadie had taken a few good knocks to the face, but being upside down magnified the experience. She reeled from the butt of the gun and heard herself wail. It was the first time she'd wanted to cry in years. It wasn't emotion, no. Chemicals had flooded her brain, pounded into her face, made her want to draw up her lips and sob. A command was given, and Skylar stepped into the trough. Eadie looked up at the girl's feet. Blood gushed up her cheek, into her hair, along her arm. She strained at the twine at her wrists.

"You don't have to, Skye. You don't. Have to."

"You need to learn that your fantasies about the outside world are all bullshit, Skylar," Pea said, tying the ribbon at the girl's waist, pulling the apron tight against her body. "Your place is here. And the way you keep trying to follow these stray cats out the door is just getting them all killed. It's time to grow up. You'd be dead out there without your man, without me, without a cent to your fucking name, no matter what you think you know about the world."

Skye's legs were trembling. Eadie could see them beyond her own white fingers.

"What did you think you were going to do? Huh?" Pea snorted. "Start again in the big bad city? Put on a suit and be an office girl? Drink martinis at lunch? You didn't even make it through high school, baby. You'd have failed before you opened your fucking mouth. People would know what you are, Skye."

Skylar was trembling harder. Eadie struggled to breathe.

"You're not a friend to these girls, Skye. Look what you've done to them," Pea murmured. "We're not friendly people. We're bad people. And we belong here, with our own kind."

"Skylar, listen!" Eadie screamed.

"Cut her pants off."

Skye took a pair of scissors from the front pocket of the apron. She slid the blade into the waist of Eadie's jeans. The blade was warm. Eadie strained against the ties, shook her arm so that the blood ran down her wrist. Her skin was on fire.

"Cut her shirt off."

"Skylar, I'm telling you to listen to me. You're not bad. You can stop this now if you just listen to my voice."

"Look at that body." Pea's cold hand ran over her belly, her abdomen, her crumpled ribs. "You probably like women looking at you, don't you, you dyke bitch? You probably worked hard on this body. Skye, start cutting here. We'll open her up first and get a good look inside."

Skylar took a blade from the apron's pouch. A long filleting knife. Eadie knew it well. It was one of her favorites. Lean. Sharp. Good for going deep. She felt the pressure, then the tip pierced the skin, and then there was only heat. The blood ran down her neck into her hair. Dark as ink.

"I'm giving you a chance," Eadie shuddered, looked down at Skylar's dead eyes. The girl's cheeks were wet with tears. "Skylar, I'm giving you a chance to stop."

Eadie inhaled as the knife went deeper, too deep. She pulled her wet hands loose from the twine. Eadie grabbed Skylar's ankles, yanked herself forward, twisted her head, and bit down as hard as she could through denim, through skin, through flesh. Skylar gasped, screamed, and the sound of it swelled up around Eadie. The knife clattered at her head. Eadie let go of Skylar's legs, reached, and fumbled at the blade as the barrel of the shotgun came around to her face.

*   *   *

Juno looked at the monitors on the shelf in front of him, sipped the Heineken he'd bought from the liquor store. All week he'd been parked in the lot behind the shop and had not bought one item, had not taken one sip, hell—he hadn't even gone in for the free wine tastings they did on Friday afternoons. He'd sat there in the heat and the silence and the monotony completely sober except for a single fucking Jack Daniel's that hadn't even given him a buzz.

The beer was painfully cold, hit the back of his throat like a ball of nitrogen. He exhaled, bared his teeth. Eden's pendant camera was aimed at the ceiling again. She was taking a shower. The sunglasses camera was showing an empty bedroom, a blanket on the floor. Juno wondered if she was showering with the girl. If the frigid bitch had finally turned her. Probably. He stretched and settled back against the side of the van and looked at the speakers on the counter. Maybe he would put some tunes on.

Eadie arched her back and twisted, felt the heat of the blast against the side of her face and the spray of shrapnel to the front as the shells plowed through the trough inches from her head. She didn't open her eyes. She heard the telltale singing in her left ear of frequencies she would never hear again. The knife was in her fingers. She swung forward, reeled back, and then swung forward with all her might, crunching broken ribs, crushing torn flesh and punctured organs. She swiped at her ankle. One shot was all she could endure, all she had the strength for. One moment to take in the twine through the blood, to aim, careless of bone or skin or the iron brace, and slash for her life. The blade hit the twine. Cut. She fell, twisted, felt the twine rip.

Pea was reloading the weapon, fingers fumbling. Eadie managed to sit up, to draw a breath before Skylar's arms wound around her throat.

"Hurry, hurry! Jesus, Mum, hurry!" the girl screamed. Skylar's grip was weak.

Eadie twisted, rose up, and drove the knife down into the tender flesh between the girl's neck and shoulder. Pea screamed. Skylar made no sound. Eadie scrambled over the top of the trough and fell in the dirt, her lungs squeezing out hoarse breaths.

"No, Skye, no, no, no. Please! Please!"

Pea pulled out the blade, grabbed at the girl's throat, tried to contain the blood. The girl kicked.

Eadie dragged herself toward the shotgun lying like a broomstick on the ground. She lay on her side and tried to fit the shells into the weapon with numb, sticky fingers. One would do. She held the gun and breathed. The older woman came to herself as the girl's legs stopped twitching. She turned on her heels, still crouching, and looked at Eadie where she lay.

"I gave her a chance," Eadie said, and fired.

Hades sat in his chair at the kitchen table, silent, looking at the file I had put in his hands. My scrawled notes from a phone conversation with Nicky the forensics girl, after she'd finished abusing me for calling her so late at night. His breathing was still elevated from the brawl outside his house. Adam stood in the corner by the hall, his arms folded, staring at the sink. His face was a bloody mask, but he ignored it. The blood dripped from his jaw onto his shirt, a long series of red teardrops.

"Bonnie Melich went missing two days before Sunday disappeared. She was big. Six foot four. You can tell that from where she's standing there, in the photograph," I said. I pointed at the photograph of the tall lean girl in the doorway of the Lord Nelson, the basket of roses on her arm. "You count those sandstone bricks beside her, get out your measuring tape, and there you go. Problem is, the body Detective Tom Savet turned up in the car in Botany a week later, the body which was supposed to be Bonnie Melich, was distinctly shorter. Five foot nine, or thereabouts. The autopsy report puts it down to shrinkage due to the extreme heat, the hardening of the bone fibers, the loss of cartilage. We can tell these things now—I mean, forensic scientists can. They can get it pretty exact, given her age, her approximate weight, the maximum temperature a body can get to in a motor vehicle."

"Detective," Hades said. One word. I cleared my throat, gave it a minute, felt my face grow hot.

"There's no way, scientifically, that Bonnie Melich was the body that Tom Savet found in that car." I reached into my pocket and pulled out a small envelope the size of the palm of my hand. The label on the envelope had yellowed with the years. The handwriting on it was neat blue cursive. A forensics file number, and a name.

"Tom Savet was at a police function the night Sunday went missing," Hades said. "I checked. I checked a hundred times. He can't have been involved . . . He wasn't . . ." Hades murmured.

"They found this in a woman's coat. It was near the vehicle."

I placed the envelope in Heinrich Archer's hand. He pulled a small slip of torn, yellowed notepad paper from it, unfolded it, smoothed out the creases over the stamped stationery header marked "Jeremy's."

One line of text in clumsy lettering, pencil.

Central Station, Platform 2, 9PM.

"Nine . . . nine *p.m.*," the old man said.

"Sunday thought you wanted her to stay in the hotel room until the following night, nine p.m. So she was waiting there that morning, at the same time you were waiting for her at Central Station. Tom Savet, meanwhile, had a new case. He was looking for Bonnie Melich. He needed a body. He needed to keep up the charade of being Sydney Metro Homicide's fastest man."

Adam White's breathing was hoarse. I could hear it from where I stood. I wiped sweat from my brow.

"You . . ." I cleared my throat. "You thought Savet's big game was the drug scene. Caesar's connection in the cops. But it wasn't. His game was murder. He'd wait for a case, provide a body, and fill in the gaps. Twenty-six cases in all. They were all . . . Uh, Jesus. They were all unidentifiable. At least, with the technology you guys had back then. Burned. Buried. Boiled in acid. He was lazy and deadly and he wanted the power. The incredible power that would come to him in the following years. He needed someone that morning, and Sunday was . . . She was there. She was always underfoot. You said it yourself."

Hades and White looked at each other. The old man ran a hand over his short hard hair.

"Why did you spend so long checking Savet's story?" I said. "He wasn't a friend to you. Why didn't you just—"

"Because I was sad, all right?" Hades' teeth showed just for a second as he turned his profile to me, his eyes on the table. "I was sure she'd run out on me. The more I checked the facts, the surer I was that Savet hadn't been there, the surer I was that . . ."

"That she'd left you."

Hades put the note on the table in front of him, smoothed it out, a relic to be treasured. His big hand covered it, as though hiding its awful truth across the years.

"After she was gone, I didn't care," he said. "I'd been so concerned with my own fucking . . . my pig-headed rage. Vengeance. Meaningless vengeance. I turned my back on her for a second, just a second, to do something for myself. For the man who'd saved me. And in that second . . . she was gone."

Adam White was shaking his head. I barely heard my phone ringing beyond the pounding in my ears. I pulled it out of my pocket and looked at it. Juno. I lifted it to my ear, anything to break the tension in the room.

"I'm busy."

"Yeah, um, look. I'm just a bit worried about Eden."

"Huh?"

"I just noticed . . . I just noticed she's off camera. Has been for maybe, like, an hour."

"An hour?" My stomach plummeted. "Which camera?"

I heard Juno inhale.

"All of them," he said.

I shoved past Heinrich's chair and ran out the door.

Pea ran. Memories of the last few minutes tripped over each other as her brain tried to catch up with the events in the kill shed, seemed to want to linger with sickening clarity over Skylar as she lay in the dirt, writhing, desperate eyes searching the encroaching darkness for her mother. The woman who was supposed to protect her.

The visions rushed, slid, exploded, and there was Eadie under her hands, struggling for the knife with red wet fingers, the shotgun now useless, the blast batted away at the last second by something raw and animal and instinctual in Pea that still wanted her own survival even though she knew deep down inside that Skye was gone.

Skye was gone.

She stumbled to a stop beside the water tanks,

kneeled, and vomited in the dust. It seemed her body wanted to purge the visions from her, and when it was done she felt ruined, trembling as she looked at the huge bonfire blinking in the dark across the horse paddock, the bodies that passed before it, making it twinkle like a star. She heard music on the wind. Laughter. Pea gripped the earth and grass beneath her, tried to control the sobs that racked up from low in her heavy body.

She needed a plan. Couldn't make one here.

Pea found the wire fence that lined the horse paddock and inched her way along it, fists clenched on the wire and fumbling at the posts toward the gates. There, she knew, was one of Jackie's trucks. She picked out the truck from the darkness and ran to it, wrenching open the driver's door and closing it behind her. Warm. Quiet. There was a canister of kerosene on the passenger seat, stinking, intended to fill the lamps in the stalls in the west corner of the farm. Pea rolled down the window, breathed in the night air, and tried to calm her breathing. She gripped the wheel and bowed her head and shuddered with sobs, giving herself mere seconds before she straightened in the seat.

At first she thought she had pulled a muscle in her back shifting upward and back behind the wheel. Then she heard the voice of the one named Eadie and felt the girl extract the filleting knife from where it had plunged through the soft foam of the driver's seat and into her spine.

"I'm sure it's not all that bad," the girl said.

Pea gasped, could draw no more than a quarter of a breath. Her legs were numb. She watched as the girl, now a ghoul with a bloody mask, climbed from the cabin and shut the door behind her. She was wearing only workman's pants, the bra, a vest of her own red, red blood. The hole in her belly gaped, inches deep, inches long, a vertical eye-shaped slit she ignored. Pea tried to lift her arms from where they had fallen in her lap. Somehow, the limbs refused the message, simply lay there on her thighs as though detached. Eadie walked to the driver's side door, pulled it open, reached across Pea's body, and poked the canister of kerosene with the tip of the knife until it pierced the plastic and sent the clear liquid gushing down the seats.

"I told Skye I know bad people." Eadie straightened, slamming the driver's door shut. "I know them, because I'm one of them. You made that girl what she was. In the end, even though her heart was telling her to stop, all she knew how to do was follow you. When you give birth to something, you should be held responsible for what it becomes."

Eadie reached in the car window and turned on the engine. Pea thought she should probably have been able to smell the kerosene, but for some reason, she couldn't. She could feel the fumes in her eyes, feel the tears they produced rolling down her cheeks. Eadie turned the wheel of the vehicle toward the bonfire in the distance, put it into drive, and let off the emergency brake. The car began to roll. Eadie shuffled beside it, limping, one arm clutching at the hole in her abdomen, the other extracting a packet of cigarettes from the pocket of her workman's pants. She put a smoke in her crooked jaw and struggled to light it against the wind.

The ghoul she had become shuffled, seemed to drag her leg behind her. Pea thought of the undead. She tried to scream, but no sound would come.

When the cigarette was half-smoked, the ghoul reached into the car and jammed it between Pea's slack lips, where it burned, red, at the edge of her vision.

"Bye, Pea," Eadie said, her voice haggard in the wind. "Nice workin' with you."

Pea closed her eyes and felt the cigarette falling, tried to force her lips to shut around it. They wouldn't. The car kept rolling on, and the ghoul stopped following.

❧

There was already a team assembled at the gates of Rye's Farm when I slid my car to a stop on the gravel drive. Ten men in flak jackets, with another truck on its way from the south. I'd spent the frantic drive from Hades' dump on the phone, so it seemed these men had arrived in only seconds. In the distance I heard a chopper whomping, waiting for command. Captain James was on his way. The area commander, a dark-haired woman with small fierce eyes, strode toward me as I exited the car and strapped on my jacket. I was drenched in sweat. I pulled my gun and loaded it as she briefed me.

"We've been told to lock the place down and wait for further instruction. The south section will be in place in five."

"You've got the cordon, Chief," I said. "I'm going in for my partner."

"I can't offer you backup at this minute."

"I don't need it."

My face seemed to get the message across. She took a step back and let me through. I jogged up the long gravel driveway into the dark. The wind was picking up and I smelled fire. The one thing they tell you to remember when you're closing on a hostile area is to keep your breathing regular. Focus. In, out. I found a wire fence and followed it along, past a clearing filled with junk and rusting car bodies, a barbecue area, a group of vans. No one was around.

I glanced up at the sky, saw bats trailing over the trees in the fading light far away. In a group of vans beyond a small breakfast area I stumbled on a small wiry man stumbling down the foldout iron steps of an ancient Jayco, still zipping up his fly.

"Police! Hands up!"

Jackie just looked at me, his mouth hanging open. I rushed him and thumped his narrow shoulders into the door of the van. Put him on the ground like a doll.

This can't be it, I thought. *This can't be how it ends. Something's wrong.*

"Where's Eden?"

"Who?"

"Eden Archer." I gave him a few good punches to the back of the skull, glanced about for backup. "Eadie Lee, the blonde, you sick little fuck."

"What's happening? What?"

I lifted Rye and dropped his head on the bottom stair. Cuffed his limp body and moved on. The van was empty. In the dark behind the cluster, another fence.

Across the fields I spied a bonfire burning. Within seconds, a vehicle I hadn't even seen rolling through the dark of a paddock with its headlights off exploded, windows blazing orange squares hovering in the night.

I ran along the fence line toward it. A chopper crossed overhead, flooding the paddock with light.

Under the cover of an awning made from dying trees I spied a figure walking toward me in the dark. The figure's hands hung by its sides, lolling. It was tottering. I raised my gun.

"Police!"

The figure kept walking. I moved forward, my aim fixed.

"Stop where you are or I'll fire."

Eden was just moving her feet. When she stepped into the light of the moon I realized what she was draped in from neck to waist was not a lace shirt, as I'd first thought, but her own blood. She was crooked, her whole body slanted to the left and bowed forward. Her face was a mess, nose flattened, eyes black. I lowered the gun and rushed forward, skidded as a tall lean figure emerged from the dark behind her, a long arm wrapping around her neck.

"Hold up, copper," Nick Hart said, pulling Eden upright. There was a little steak knife in his hand. Probably grabbed from the breakfast area. I lifted the gun and sprayed spit with rage.

"Drop it, shithead!"

"Just when you thought it was safe to have a couple of beers by the light of a nice fire. The fuzz comes in and fucks it all up," Hart laughed. "Typical."

Eden reached into the pocket of her baggy, blood-stained pants, slid a long slender blade into the light. Hart grabbed her wrist, shook it. She was half gone. Her eyes lolled, found me behind the gun.

"Listen to me, Hart," I said. "That's a police officer

you've got in your hands there." I inched forward as he inched back, dragging my partner with him.

"I was just starting to think that myself."

"I'll shoot you dead right here, mate. I'll shoot you fucking dead."

Nick laughed, and there was genuine triumph in it. To get him, I'd have to shoot Eden. She knew it, too. Her eyes followed mine, rimmed in blood, her lips moving.

"It's okay," she said. "It's okay, Frank."

My hands were shaking. I didn't have the best aim even in the cool, sterile light of the shooting gallery. Frantic thoughts washed over me with unimaginable clarity, one after the other like deliberate calculations that had waited long enough to come to mind. I knew then, standing in the dark, that if I killed Eden Archer I'd be free of her. Of what she was. Of what she knew about me, and what I knew and wanted to forget about her.

This was the moment I'd been waiting for, my chance to put all the shattered pieces of my life back together. If I killed Eden now I'd be free of her devilish father and his landfill of horrors, of the memory of Martina that she carried with her everywhere like a perfume. She was the only piece that didn't fit in my recovery. The only thing stopping me from being whole again. Without Eden, maybe I could start over. If I killed her now, I could forget I'd ever known the monster that she really was.

Instead I dropped my gun. Nick laughed, shifted sideways, and as he did a bullet whipped past my ear, struck him in the jaw, and sent him sailing backward. I heard running footsteps behind me, saw a flashlight beam approach. I caught Eden as she fell.

"Oh no," I heard myself pleading. "No, no, no, please. Please God, don't do this. Eden? Eden? Eden!"

She was a dead weight in my arms. We slid to the ground as the officers swarmed around us. I wrapped my arms around her, lifted her, and ran through them, back toward the gates.

EPILOGUE

Hades sat at his table. He had been sitting there all day. The newspaper lay by his gnarled hand, untouched, the front page dominated by a picture of the young cop, Frank, carrying his daughter. He couldn't think about that now. He couldn't process what had happened to Eden, what it would mean for her, what they would have to do next. He needed to finish his time with Sunday. To finally say good-bye. Hades' coffee cup stood on the sink-top, upside down, dry. In his left hand, he held an ancient photograph of a little girl sitting upright on an old wooden stool, looking off somewhere, unfocused.

That was how she was, always. Unfocused. Distant. A wild creature. That's how she had seemed to Bear the day he found her on the beach as he crouched in the dunes picking plants for his lethal potions—a panting, panicked creature running toward him over the sand, her hair whipping in the wind and her arms out, reaching. A child of the earth, risen from a crack in the mantle somewhere, hot as fire as she slammed into his body, scrambled up his back like a possum, gripped onto his neck, her fingernails claws. The boys who had been chasing her up the beach came to a stop at the bottom of the dunes, one of them swinging the lump of wood by his side, weighing up their options against the huge man on the sand hill.

Bear had pulled the little girl off him with some difficulty. He found her barely conscious, racked by days on the streets. He held her there in the new sunlight, sat down, tried to figure where she'd come from, what the hell she was doing here. He called her Sunday. His runaway. One of a number of children he rescued over the years. Strays. Wild things. Children of the wind.

There was nowhere to visit Sunday, and that might have been the hardest thing for Hades, sitting there looking at his hands. Her body, buried deep beneath the well-kept and flower-laden headstone of Bonnie Melich, would be exhumed for DNA testing, then handed back to White and his family. Buried, probably, where her people had come from, miles from where the old man sat.

He had seen White on the news, railing at reporters about what he wanted done to retired Detective Tom Savet, what it had meant to his family, his mother, to have lost Sunday, the one piece of joy the old woman had ever experienced in her cold and loveless life. The Melich family had been there, too, stiff and noncommittal, still emerging from the lull they'd been enjoying for decades and into a new nightmare, a new uncertainty, for their lost child. Hades had switched it off after a time. It was all noise to him.

Now, as she always was, Sunday would be just beyond his reach. A moon drifting, following, teasingly close. Hades wondered what had happened to Bonnie

Melich, the girl in the pub doorway, whoever she had been. Hades wondered what had happened to all of Savet's case subjects, the little girls and boys, the old women, those lost souls he'd been too lazy to find. An inquiry would reveal it all, or kill Savet in the process. The young copper, Frank, told him that Savet was already locked down, extracted from his boutique retirement community in Woollahra and in custody at Silverwater. The young cop had made the call before he ever told Hades what he'd found. Smart. It would be harder to get at Savet now. Harder, but not impossible. Nothing was impossible for a man of Hades' history.

Hades closed his eyes, cracked his neck, and set the photograph down on the tabletop. When he opened his eyes, a man was walking down the short front hall toward him, his stride long, quiet, slow. Hades watched Mr. Grey as the light hit his smooth high cheekbones, as they seemed to lift impossibly higher with his stark white, devilish grin. The manicured cannibal took up the chair across from Hades, sat down, and hung an elbow over its back, the steel-colored jacket hanging open, revealing its salmon silk lining. A shard of light from the kitchen window, red from the setting sun, glinted in the hitman's eyes. For a moment he was a youthful Satan, come to collect a soul

"Greetings, old buddy," Mr. Grey said. "I hear all your little rain clouds have begun to clear away."

"Almost," Hades said. He took the Magnum from where it sat on his right thigh, lifted it, and shot Mr. Grey in the face. The cannibal's skull exploded down the dark hallway. The old man stood, stretched, felt the clicking of bones between his shoulder blades. The pinched muscle there that had been bothering him for weeks seemed to loosen. For a moment Hades felt young again.

Imogen stirred her coffee, careful not to hit the edges of the cup with her spoon, though she knew nothing would wake Frank now. He was flopped on his chest on the bed in the same position he'd fallen into the day before, barely stopping to get his bloodstained clothes off. He hadn't spoken to her, but Imogen knew from the papers what had happened at the farm and the hospital afterward.

They said that Eden Archer was stable, but that she'd sustained terrible injuries fighting with the killers of two young prostitutes. The farm had been searched. Several arrests, including that of two men for a series of rapes. No remains of the girls had been un-covered, but on the news police choppers kept circling a large shed, and there was some hysteria surrounding Rye Farm organic pork supplies to various Coles su-permarkets.

Imogen went to her desk, spread the paper out be-fore her, and read the articles again, from the cover to the extensive middle spread to the editorial. The front-page picture had been captured by a paramedic using his smartphone. Frank with Eden in his arms, running on a gravel road, his mouth open, shouting. Imogen examined the panic in his face. The vulnerability. It was strangely attractive to see him like that. In action. On the run.

Eden looked like a blood-drenched doll in his arms, her head fallen back, eyes closed and dreaming. She was naked to the waist, her small breasts cupped in a black push-up. The public would be eating up the grisly tale based on this picture alone. Imogen smoothed out the paper. She found the scissors and began to cut. As she clipped along the bottom of the photograph, she stopped. There was a rather unusual mark on Eden's ribs. A birthmark, almost electric pink in the image, shaped like a prancing pony. Imogen thought she might have heard people call that sort of mark a port stain. It was very pretty, crisply captured, distinct from the black blood that ran down her ribs. Just as Imogen noticed it, the mark seemed to dominate the entire picture. She put the scissors down. Felt strangely light-headed. She stared at the mark, and then, as though her world had been spinning and had suddenly righted, reached out groggily and pulled a folder from the middle of the stack on her desk.

The Tanner children case. Imogen flipped open the files, pushed them frantically over the desk. She found the worn news stock image of the slaughtered Dr. Tanner and his missing daughter, Morgan, at the beach. The respected scientist was stripped to the waist and hoisting a little dark-haired girl in a bikini into the sky. His big hands wrinkled the skin at her ribs but didn't go so high as the birthmark there, a pony, hooves reared, just under the child's armpit.

Imogen slowly put the two images side by side.

ACKNOWLEDGMENTS

I'll never be able to repay Gaby Naher and Bev Cousins for taking a chance on me, and for their ongoing commitment to my writerly dream. Thank you to Michaela Hamilton and the people of Kensington for all your hard work and dedication.

As a writer never content with the quiet monotony of a home office, I owe my thanks to bustling cafés who despite their traffic never disturbed me or hassled me for my table, regardless of how many coffees I didn't buy. It's difficult to find places with this kind of consideration, but Billy's at Maroubra Junction, The Upside Café on Broadway, and Marcelle on Macleay in Potts Point are a few. Thank you to a good number of online fans who never let me feel alone, or unworthy.

Finally, to my wonderful partner Tim. Thank you for getting it. All of it. Me, the books, the murderous tinge to otherwise everyday discussions. You're a good man, and I'm glad I found you.

Ready for more Archer and Bennett excitement?

Keep reading to enjoy a sample excerpt
from Candice Fox's next thriller . . .

FALL

Coming soon from Kensington Publishing Corp.

Before the blood, before the screaming, the only sound that reached the parking lot of the Black Mutt Inn was the murmur of the jukebox inside. It was set on autoplay, tumbling out the cheerful line-up of greatest hits, but there was none of the sing-alongs of usual pubs, no thrusting of glasses, no stomping of heels on the reeking carpet. The jukebox played in the stale emptiness of the building, and by the time it reached the car park it was no more than a ghoulish moan. It was windy out there, and the stars were gone.

The Black Mutt Inn attracted bad men and had been doing so for as long as anyone could remember. Nightly, a bone was broken on its shadowy back porch over some insult, or a promise was made beneath the moth-crowded lamps for some violence that would come on another night. Sometimes a plot was hatched; the corners of its undecorated interior were good for whispering, and the walls seemed to grow poisonous ideas like vines, spreading and creeping around minds and down necks and along legs to the rotting floor-boards.

On this night, Sunny Burke and Clara McKinnie entered the Black Mutt with their laptops and bags of chili jerky and bright, sun-tanned smiles. The man behind the counter said nothing, saw nothing—he just served the drinks.

Sunny and Clara walked to the counter and set up shop under the mirrors. Against the wall three men sat whispering. At the pool tables another two stood looking through the shadows at the two travelers fresh from Byron, stamped with its optimism and cheap weed stink. Clara ordered a champagne and orange juice and downed it quickly. Sunny sat nursing a James Squire and rubbing her legs.

Into the dim halo of light stepped a man from the pool tables.

"G'day, mate," the man said, thumping Sunny between the shoulder blades. The man was tall and square and roped with veins, and the two hands hanging from his extra-long arms looked all-encompassing. Sunny looked up, appreciated the density of the man's beard and smiled.

"Hey."

"Just down from Byron, are we?"

"We've been there a week," Clara said, beaming.

"I can see." The man brushed the backs of his fingers against the top of Clara's shoulder, a brief, brotherly pat. "Sun's had its way with you, beauty!"

"We're just on our way back to the big smoke," Sunny said.

"If you ask me, you've just come from the Big Smoke," the stranger jibed and nudged Sunny in the ribs, hard. "Tell me you've got some grass for sale. Please, tell me!"

Sunny laughed. "Sure, mate." He glanced at the other figure in the shadows, the man by the table leaning on his cue. "No problem."

The stranger threw out a hand and Sunny gripped it, felt its calluses against his palm. "No probs, no probs. How much are you after?"

"Aw, we'll do all that later. Hamish is the name, mate. Can I invite you to a game?"

"Yeah! Shit, yeah. This is Clara. I'm Sunny."

"Me mate over there's Braaaadley, but don't you worry 'bout him. He don't talk much. Plays a rubbish game of pool, too, don't you, Brad? Ay? Wake up, shithead!" the man squawked back toward the pool table but roused nothing in his partner. "Excuse me, miss, but me old Bradley's prone to leaning on that pool cue till he drifts off and no amount of slapping can get him back, if you know what I mean."

"Right," she laughed.

They racked the balls while Clara and the silent one watched, now and then letting their eyes drift to each other, the hairy man in the dark struggling beneath the weight of his frown, the young woman swinging her hips, holding onto the cue. She finished the champagne and wanted another, but the men were talking and laughing and making friends, and Sunny had always had trouble making friends, so she didn't interrupt.

"How about a little wager, just to make things interesting?" Hamish asked.

"Yeah, sure." Sunny puffed out his chest, ignored a warning look from Clara. "Where do you . . . ? I mean. What do you usually . . . ?"

"Five bucks?"

Sunny laughed. "Sure, mate, sounds great."

They played. Clara was the most excitable of them all, howling when she sunk the white ball, cheering when Sunny scored. There was plenty of kissing. Rubbing of backsides. The men in the booths watched them. The happy group at the table were cut off from the rest of the world by the cone of light that fell upon them.

"Very good, young sir," Hamish said, offering his big, hard hand again. "How about another?"

"Twenty bucks this time," Sunny said. "You can pay me in labor, if you like. The van needs a wash."

"Sunny!" Clara gasped.

"Listen to this guy, would you?" Hamish laughed, squeezed the young woman on the shoulder, and made Clara's face burn red. "What a cocky little shit. You're lucky you're so goddamn beautiful, Sunny me old mate. No one's gonna knock that gorgeous block off no matter whatcha say."

They laughed and played again. Hamish was hard on Bradley. The balls cracked and crashed and rolled in the pockets. Clara was good. Her daddy had taught her the game young, bent over the felt, his hips pinning her against the side of the table. But she knew when to sacrifice a shot so that she didn't lean over too far and give Bradley a view of her breasts, her arse. The man looked at her funny.

"One more?" Sunny said. The bar was empty now but for the bartender, who was motionless in the shadows. Sunny won, and won again.

"One more, little matey, and then it's off to bed with you. What's say you we make it interesting, uh? Everything you've won, you give me the chance to win it back. We go even. I lose, you take the notes right outta my hand, no hard feelings."

"Mate," Sunny drawled, "you win this and I'll give you double what you owe me."

"Sunny!"

"Oh ho! Just listen to this guy!" Hamish laughed.

"Sunny, no!"

"Cla," the boy drew her close, "they haven't won a game all night. It's fine. I'm just having a laugh."

"Sunny—"

"Just shut up, would you?" Sunny snapped. "I'm only having a bit of fucking fun."

Clara watched the men shake hands, rack the balls. Hamish leaned down, took aim, and began sinking balls.

The table was empty of Hamish's balls in less than two minutes. Then he sunk the black in a single shot. Sunny never got a turn.

"Mate," Hamish said when it was done, straightening and leaning on his cue, the smile and the charm and the humor forgotten. "Seems you owe me quite a bit of cash."

In the car park, Bradley walked behind them, keeping watch now and then toward the Black Mutt, although no such careful eye was needed. A hidden hole drilled straight to hell warmed the air as it breezed across the asphalt and ruffled Clara's thick, dark curls. Hamish's hand on the back of her neck was like a steel clamp. They approached the Kombi van, the only one in the lot, parked out in the middle of a huge barren wasteland so that the young couple would be safe from whatever might be lurking in the towering wall of dark woods around the bar when they returned. Clara put her hands out to stop Hamish slamming her into the side of the van and turned. Bradley had let a steel pipe slide down from where it was hidden high up inside his sleeve.

"Give me an inventory," Hamish said.

"There's the CD player, some cash, and Clara has some jewelry," Sunny was saying, fumbling with his keys. "There's the hash, too. You can take it. Please, please, I'm asking you now not to hurt us."

"You go ahead and ask whatever you like, you snotty-nosed little prick," Hamish said. "You bring out whatever you can from in there and we'll see if it's enough. If it's not, I'll decide if anyone gets hurt."

"Take 'em up to the ATM," Bradley grunted. Clara jolted at the sound of the silent man's voice. She turned and found him staring at her, eyes pinpoints of light in the dark.

"Sunny," Clara croaked, tried to ease words from her swollen throat. "Sunny. Sunny!"

"Shut up, and hurry," Hamish snarled.

"I'm going. Please. Please!" Sunny was pleading with anyone now. Clara heard the pleas continuing inside the van, heard the rattling of boxes and drawers. As soon as the boy was out of sight she felt the man with the concrete hands slip his fingers beneath her skirt. Hamish smiled at her with his big, cracked teeth and pressed her into the van.

"All this excitement getting you wet, is it, baby?"

"Sunny! God! Please!"

"Your pretty boyfriend better come up with something very special, very soon, babycakes, or I'm afraid you're footing the bill."

"How about this?" Sunny said as he emerged from

the van, hands full, thrusting the items at Hamish. "Will this do?"

The knife made Hamish stiffen, made his eyed widen as they dropped to the items in Sunny's hands, which all fell away and clattered to the ground, revealing the leather handle they concealed, the leather handle attached to the long hunting blade that was now buried deep in Hamish's belly. Sunny, as always, didn't give the man a chance to appreciate the surprise of the attack, but pulled the knife out of his stomach and plunged it in again, pushed it upward into the tenderness of Hamish's diaphragm and felt the familiar clench of shocked muscles.

Clara slid away as the young man went for a third blow, took her own knife, the one she kept flush against her body between her breasts, and went for Bradley. The hairy man backed away, but Clara's aim was immaculate. She set her feet, pulled back, breathed, swung, and let go. The knife embedded in Bradley's back with a thunk between the shoulder blades. The man fell and rolled like roadkill on the tarmac.

She went to the silent man and pulled out the knife, wiping it on the hem of her soft, white skirt. Bradley was still alive, and she was happy, because it would be a long time until she was finished with him. Clara liked to play, and though it wasn't Sunny's thing, she thought maybe because they were on holiday he would indulge her just once with some games. She turned. Bradley was still gurgling against the asphalt under his cheek.

"Baby." She turned on her sweet voice for her killer partner. "What if we took this one home and—"

A whistle, and a *shlunk*.

At first it seemed to Clara that Sunny had fallen, until she felt the wet spray of his blood on her face. She tried to process the noise she'd heard, but none of it made sense. She crawled, shaking, and with her hands tried to piece back together the split halves of her boyfriend's skull, grabbed at the bits of brain and meat sprayed across the asphalt around him. She knelt in the blood, both his and Hamish's, little whimpers coming out of her like coughs. Hamish was sitting up beside the van, his hands still gripping at the knife wounds in his belly.

A whistle, and a *shlunk*, and the top of his head came off. He slid to the ground.

Clara looked around at the tree line behind her, a hundred yards or so away, and then at the trees in front, the same distance, dark as ink and depthless. The silence rung. Under its terrifying weight she crawled, tried to get to her feet, heading toward the bar. Another whistle, another *shlunk*, and her foot was gone. Clara fell on her face and gripped at the stump of her leg. She didn't scream or cry out, because there was only terror in her, and terror made no sound.

Clara lay and breathed, breathed, and after some time began crawling again. She heard the sound of uneven footsteps, punctuated by a metallic *clop*, and looked up to see a figure coming toward her barely distinguishable against the dark of the trees. The sounds kept coming out of her, the shuddering breaths through her lips. The metallic clopping kept coming, and as the woman emerged into the light of the van, Clara could see she was leaning on an enormous rifle, using the gun like a crutch.

The woman stepped between the bodies of the men, and Clara lay in the blood and looked up at her. She thought, even as shock began to take her, about the woman's black hair, how it seemed to steal some blue out of the night and hold it, like the shimmer woven through the feather of a crow. The woman with the gun bent down, used the enormous weapon to lower herself into a crouch, and Clara wondered what wounds gave the other killer such trouble.

Eden looked at the trees, the bar, the girl on the ground.

"Just when you think you're deadliest fish in the water," Eden said to the girl.

Clara gasped. Her fingers fumbled at the wet stump where her foot had been. Eden sighed.

"I admire the game," Eden said. "I really do. It's clever. Two naïve travelers just waiting to be picked on. You flounder around like you're drowning in your own idiocy, and you see which predators come to investigate. Who could resist you? You're adorable. You lure them out into the deep, dark waters and then you surge up from below. Pull them down."

Clara fell back against the asphalt, her mouth sucking at the cold night air.

"If I were well, this would have been more personal," Eden said, her leather-gloved hand gripping the rifle tight. "But I haven't been at my best lately, so I'm afraid there's no time for play."

Clara couldn't force words up through the whimpers. They came out of her like hiccups. The woman with the long, dark hair rose up, pushing the rifle into the ground. When she'd risen fully she actioned the great thing with effort, hands once strong betraying her as the bullet slid into the chamber.

"I'm the only shark in this tank," Eden said.

The last gunshot could be heard inside the Black Mutt Inn. But no one listened to it.

Connect with U s

Visit us online at
KensingtonBooks.com
to read more from your favorite authors, see books
by series, view reading group guides, and more.

Join us on social media

for sneak peeks, chances to win books and prize packs,
and to share your thoughts with other readers.

facebook.com/kensingtonpublishing
twitter.com/kensingtonbooks

Tell us what you think!

To share your thoughts, submit a review,
or sign up for our eNewsletters, please visit:
KensingtonBooks.com/TellUs.